THE

BROWNSTONE

ON

E. 83RD

THE
BROWNSTONE
ON
E. 83RD

A HOUSES OF CRIME MYSTERY

JENNY DANDY

LEVEL
BEST BOOKS

To my family: first last and always

Praise for The Brownstone on E. 83rd

"At the heart of a book about a dedicated FBI agent father on a quest to find his missing daughter while working alongside the least expected partner to bring down a notorious scam artist is a story with provocative characters and their home-hitting struggles that will keep you turning pages and racing toward the Brownstone on E. 83rd."—Yasmine Angoe, Anthony-nominated author of the critically acclaimed *Her Name is Knight* of the Nena Knight series

"*The Brownstone on E. 83rd* is a book that kept me up at night—and then I couldn't wait to get back to it. Jenny Dandy's characters sizzle on the page and will stay with you long after you finish reading."—Benjamin Whitmer, critically acclaimed author of *Pike, Cry Father, Evasion,* and *Les Dynamiteurs*

"Ronnie Charles is a skilled thief whose attempt to escape the trappings of her past lands her in a precarious present; Frank Jankowski, an FBI agent who believes the failures of his past have thrown his only daughter into present-day crisis. Both the protagonists of *The Brownstone on E. 83rd* are backed up against fortress walls of their own creation; both, in the skillful, tender hands of Jenny Dandy, find ways through difficulty, around and over the worst versions of themselves, and, most importantly, towards greater understanding. Dandy accomplishes all this with seamless, spare prose, and builds The Brownstone on East 83rd with a level of narrative scaffolding that will satisfy any reader's itch for dramatic satisfaction. *The Brownstone on East 83rd* marks the debut of an auspicious new voice in American literature."—Jacinda Townsend, critically acclaimed author of *Saint Monkey* and *Mother Country*

"Who's conning whom? A vixen using her seductive powers to bilk New York City's wealthy elite, or the undercover FBI agent determined to bring her to justice while staying free of her spell. It's an intriguing tale of financial fraud, blackmail and deceit, and author Jenny Dandy's superb inner knowledge of Manhattan may just convince readers *The Brownstone on E. 83rd* is real."—Donnell Ann Bell, award-winning author of *Black Pearl* and *Until Dead*, a Cold Case Suspense series

"*The Brownstone on E. 83rd* is a twisty, propulsive mystery that moves from ultra-wealthy dinner parties to drug-infested flophouses with surprising agility, and leaves readers wondering which world is more dangerous. Special Agent Frank Jankowski and petty thief/master pickpocket Ronnie Charles are complex characters who become ever more compelling as the story unfolds. I'm looking forward to the next book from Jenny Dandy."—Tiffany Quay Tyson, author of *The Past is Never*, winner of the 2018 Willie Morris Award for Southern Fiction, the 2018 Janet Heidinger Kafka Prize, the 2019 Mississippi Institute of Arts and Letters Award for Fiction, and the Mississippi Library Association's Mississippi Author Award for Adult Fiction. Author of *Three Rivers*, a novel. Shorter work at McSweeney's Internet Tendency, The Rumpus Funny Women, The Belladonna Comedy, Slackjaw, Smokelong Quarterly, and more

"*The Brownstone on E. 83rd* grabbed my attention from the first page. Jenny Dandy's debut has all the hallmarks of a veteran writer: blistering pacing, rapid-fire dialogue, and characters that not only keep you guessing, but caring about what happens to them. Dandy is an author to watch."—Carter Wilson, *USA Today* bestselling author of *The Father She Went to Find*

"*The Brownstone on E. 83rd* is an amazing debut with sharp, hard-edged dialogue, lyrical and strong prose, and a fantastic setting in New York City. The story of FBI Special Agent Frank Jankowski and small-time thief Ronnie Charles will keep you guessing as well as rooting for these vivid and compelling characters. I hope to read more from Jenny Dandy!"—David

Heska Wanbli Weiden, award-winning author of *Winter Counts*

"Jenny Dandy's *The Brownstone on E. 83rd* hits the ground running and doesn't let up. Sharply drawn characters, evocative language, knockout pacing, and a strong sense of place make this one of the year's best crime novel debuts. It's ambitious, polished, and beautifully crafted. I can't recommend it enough."—William Boyle, author of *Shoot the Moonlight Out* and *Gravesend*

Prologue

Ronnie Charles slotted the dirty champagne flutes into the plastic racks as fast as she could, two at a time, her arms flashing between trays and crates. Her skin tightened, an overall prickling that never failed her. It meant danger, meant she had to be out of there quick. The bracelet lay heavy in the secret pocket of her trousers, bumping her thigh as she moved. Someone shifted behind her, too close, and she worked faster. She didn't have time to fight off one of those ass-grabbers who always seemed to work these big charity dos, creeping on anyone. Even when Ronnie dressed as a man like tonight, they would reach out and squeeze a handful. Ronnie swung her bangs out of her eyes, peeked over her shoulder.

"You'll give me back my bracelet, or I'll rip your balls off." The silky voice caressed her ear, the woman crowding her into the boxes before she could turn around.

The Feline. Ronnie didn't usually name her marks, but those two words had sprung into her head as she watched the way the calculating woman slinked through the room, eyed the crowd, pounced on her targets. Ronnie took a deep breath, got a whiff of expensive perfume, and then did the only thing she could in a situation like this. She made her voice higher than normal and said, "Ma'am, I don't have any balls."

The tall blonde stepped back. Ronnie whipped around and saw the guys lugging chairs and tables into the truck, the caterer with her clipboard, and the cleaning crew hard at work. She so needed to keep this job.

The Feline tilted her head, narrowed her eyes, examined her through mascaraed lashes. "Well, well."

She scanned Ronnie up and down, checked over the details of her slim hips in the black pants, her flat white shirt and bow tie, her short hair in a boy's cut. She studied the one thing Ronnie couldn't fake: her lack of an Adam's apple.

"It's not often I'm fooled." The Feline's voice was low, dark clouds in the distance. "We both know you have my bracelet. I let you take it because I wanted to see how good you are."

Ronnie sucked in a breath and watched the certainty come over her, her brown eyes shining. The Feline wasn't trying to hide her age with makeup the way a lot of women did. She proudly wore the fine lines around her eyes, the smile lines on her cheeks. She was as beautiful up close as she had been in the crowds. Ronnie had watched her, watchedthe men and women gather around her as if just being near her would save their lives.

"And you're good," The Feline continued, "but I'm better. I could've taken it back from you." Her eyes flickered to Ronnie's hand, which had moved all by itself to cover the secret pocket in her trousers. The Feline smiled, lines etching her skin. "I could have, but I was curious about someone almost as brazen as I am, working a crowd of this caliber."

Tiny beads of sweat gathered at Ronnie's hairline, and she crossed her arms to keep herself still. The first time she got caught by a mark and it was this willowy goddess. She didn't know why she'd taken it in the first place. Not like she needed it. "Look, lady." The caterer approached them. "You have to go. Here, I'm giving it back." She reached into her pocket and fumbled around, for some reason, not finding the opening. "I'll give it to you, and you can leave. I really need to keep this job."

The Feline ran her eyes over her once more then grabbed her upper arm and started walking Ronnie away from the crates. She smiled and nodded at Ronnie's boss. Under her breath, she said, "No, you don't."

Ronnie tried to pull away, but the woman tightened her grip and kept walking.

"I've decided you're going to come work for me." Her heels punctuated her words as they strode toward the exit. "You have skills I can use."

Ronnie caught a glance from another waitperson as they passed. Pure envy. Amazing the feelings this woman could pull out of people.

"I have a garden apartment you can live in while you work off the bracelet."

Isabelle cut her eyes to Ronnie, a lioness eyeing her prey. "Your androgyny will throw my marks off balance. I can teach you so many, many things." Her voice was hard, yet somehow soft at the same time. "I'm giving you an offer of a lifetime."

Ronnie stopped walking, planted her feet, and the woman's voluminous gown swirled around her legs as if to trap her.

The Feline stopped, too, but didn't let go of her arm. "Or I can call the cops."

No way. Ronnie could not go to jail again. She'd used up whatever goodwill the system had for her, and it would be prison for sure this time. She knew she could run, spin out of her grip, jump off the loading dock, and into the night. Down alleys and through back doors, up fire escapes and over rooftops, disappear into the grit and the cold and the peculiar community of the homeless of New York City. She sucked in her breath. Did she say "garden apartment?" The woman's earrings glittered at her. No more sleeping on the streets. No more dumpster diving. Okay, one night, that's it. She'd scope the place out, learn the alarm system and The Feline's habits. Tuck the information away for when she was desperate, and tonight, she could sleep in a soft bed. An offer of a lifetime.

"I have to get my backpack." Before Ronnie turned toward the setup tables where she'd stashed it, she caught the grin spreading over the woman's face, her eyes dancing.

Chapter One

Frank Jankowski burst through the emergency room doors, his sixteen-year-old daughter in his arms. He rushed to the front desk, pushed past people in line, yelled at the staff, tried to get someone to pay attention. Cathy moaned, her sweaty head lolling as if she had no neck. A rushing in his ears drowned out all other sounds, and his eyes darted from one person in scrubs to the next. When he opened his mouth to yell again, Cathy vomited on the floor. As if a director had yelled *Action*, everyone moved at once. A woman with a wheelchair waved aside the guy with the clipboard and yelled, *He can do that later!* They asked Frank for symptoms, for his daughter's name, then told the nurse at the desk to page the doctor. The curtain screeched as they yanked it back and deftly placed Cathy on the bed.

She looked like a rag doll. More nurses, stethoscopes, pulse-ox on her finger, someone in scrubs pulled him aside to quietly go over the symptoms with him, poking the iPad she cradled with each thing he said. The nurse turned him away as they inserted an IV in his daughter's arm and led him back to the waiting room to fill out the paperwork.

He got as far as "Catherine A. Jankowski" when his gut roiled, and he clutched the clipboard tighter, knuckles whitening, scalp tingling as he waited for it to pass. He breathed in through his nose, out through his mouth, counting breaths as images of his daughter surrounded by medical staff, machines, an IV hookup swam behind his eyes. *Not again.*

Damn. Susan. He called her, told her they were in the emergency room. "Everything's under control. Don't worry. I'll explain when you get here."

He didn't want her to think it was as bad as it had been a year and a half ago. "Really, it's okay. It'll be okay." Her worry would make her anxious, and her anxiety would make her yell at him. He pressed the button to end the call.

Whatever this was, and it certainly warranted the ER, it couldn't compare to the hit and run that took more than a year from Cathy's life. The long hospital stay, the painful rehab. But she was past all that, seeing friends, catching up on her schoolwork. So this was just—dehydration from whatever cold or flu had laid her low.

He gazed down at the clipboard as if it had just leapt into his hand. He wrote the address of Susan's apartment on the form. His old apartment. The apartment they had found when he was first transferred to the New York Field Office, the one he thought they would stay in forever, stretching for a two-bedroom because they planned on children. He had been glad she'd kept the walls white, hung cheerful photographs, so when he came home, put his keys in the dish on the table, trying to shed the thoughts of all the evil things people did to other people, the nastiness he worked hard to fight every day, he would pause and try to put himself in the photograph, try to hear the people in them laughing, feel the gentle breeze—

Someone sat down next to him and he shifted in the plastic chair, irritated that a stranger would invade his space like that.

"Frank."

Susan, his wife—ex-wife—pulled the clipboard away from him and began filling in the form, glancing up at him as if trying to determine what kind of stupid he was. The rhythmic scratching of pen on paper calmed him. She checked off that Cathy had had her immunizations, was current on tetanus, that there was no history of diabetes in their family. The pen hovered over *What brought you in today?* She raised an eyebrow at Frank. "Are you going to tell me?"

"I thought it was the flu." He stared straight ahead, not wanting to see the accusations firing from her eyes. "But then she started hallucinating…"

"The flu." Susan's pen scratched on the paper. "In August. You thought it was the flu."

"SuSu—" Frank turned toward her but quickly looked away when he

2

caught the flare of her nostrils and the flash of her blue eyes. He shouldn't have used his old name for her, but it had just slipped out. He watched the activity at the front desk for a beat, then said, his voice quiet, "You would have thought so, too."

"Not in August, Frank. I would never have thought that. Did she have a fever?"

"She didn't seem to. I felt her forehead because she was sweating so much, but—"

"No thermometer at your apartment? How can that be? All these years of Cathy over there, and you don't even have the rudiments of—the basics for—any way to take—"

Susan tripped over her words, sputtered in her anger, and Frank stayed still, waited for it to pass. A man a few rows ahead of them tapped on his phone, his three children around him squirming and kicking each other, whining at their father, who didn't respond.

"...her symptoms?" His ex-wife had taken on a neutral tone, perhaps deciding that the paperwork was more important than fighting Frank.

He listed the symptoms in the order they had occurred, the aches, the sweating, the vomiting. Her pen flew over the paper, her frown deepened as the list went on, ending with the hallucinations.

"Mr. and Mrs. Jankowski?"

Susan flinched, her lips thin, jaw tight.

"Could you come with me, please?" The nurse checked for them over her shoulder, an iPad in her hand, led them down the hall, opened a door. "Okay, Mr. and Mrs. Jankowski, let's go in here—"

"We're divorced." Susan forced the words through clenched teeth, sounding as if she wouldn't mind going through the proceedings all over again.

They followed the nurse into a small room crammed with desks. The young woman in her cartoon scrubs and bright clogs didn't ask them to sit. She shut the door and turned to face them. She held up her iPad as if it were a shield, aimed her question at the device, her tone mild as if merely confirming Cathy's age, "How long has your daughter been addicted to opioids?"

A shocked silence, both of them staring at her, Frank's ears clogged again, no sound getting through. Susan stood next to him, opened her mouth, closed it. The nurse looked back and forth at them, waited for an answer. Then all the noises crashed in, someone called down the hall outside the door, the nurse said their names, Susan shouted *what* and his work phone buzzed. The two women turned to stare at him as if he were suddenly naked.

He put his hand in his pocket and felt the buzz vibrate against his skin. Policy dictated that he answered his work phone unless he were dead, and he drew it out of his pocket on reflex. Susan yelled at him not to answer it, the nurse eyed him as if he held a knife. Nothing was more important than his daughter right now. But he always followed the rules, and this was the Bureau phone.

It was Pete. Maybe he finally had a break in the case. After all these months, the boss was ready to shut it down. His daughter, his work—his brain careened between them, his hand on the phone, thumb hovered as if it belonged to someone else. He reluctantly pressed the green symbol and raised the phone to his ear, his other hand on the knob to open the door.

As he stepped into the hall, Susan's words followed him, *he's FBI*, as if he had a disease. He closed the door, not needing to hear the rest. He already knew what she was thinking. The daggers her eyes had thrown at him said it all: *This is why we got divorced! I ended up married to the Bureau!*

* * *

"Pete." Outside, Frank held the phone tight against his ear, his back to the wall of the hospital. He glanced around to make sure no one was within earshot. "What's happening?"

Pete was surveilling today without him. "I'm thinking something's up, maybe you should check it out tonight."

"What kind of up?" A guy came down the street, peering into his phone. He wondered if the guy would crash into that garbage can.

"That guy you followed? Newsboy? He's coming in and out with bags and whatnot, a huge thing of flowers, practically the width of the whole sidewalk. I thought people this rich had shit like that delivered." Frank gave a grunt and Pete spoke faster. "It just seems like they've got something planned, y'know, a party or something. So I thought you might want to see for yourself tonight."

"I'll see what I can do." Frank disconnected the call and put the phone in his pocket. He needed to get back inside. He almost wished he were doing something boring like surveillance right now, talking trash with his partner while they watched and waited. Normally, he didn't tell people he was FBI unless he had to, but leave it to Susan to have that be the first thing she told the nurse. His gut clenched as he came in, the antiseptic smells and cheap flooring reminding him why he was here. *Addicted to opioids.* He had to return to that tiny room though he didn't want to. How he wished his daughter was merely dehydrated or something.

Susan and the pink nurse were still in the little room, and his ex-wife stopped mid-sentence when he entered. She turned away from him and spoke to the nurse, listing the medications Cathy had been on. He stood between them and tried but failed to get a look at the iPad.

"When was the last time she had the LorTab?"

"What makes you so sure our daughter is addicted? She stopped these drugs months ago." Frank looked at Susan for confirmation, but she wouldn't meet his eyes. "Let me see that." With one swift motion, Frank had the iPad and was scanning his daughter's chart—the long list of meds, the surgeries from the car accident. She'd scored twenty-six on the Clinical Opiate Withdrawal Scale. He stared at Nurse Cartoon. "What's a '26' mean?"

The young woman grabbed her iPad back, touched the screen. "It means her symptoms of withdrawal are moderately severe. I have what I need now. We'll administer Buprenorphine and then admit her for overnight observation."

"What is that? The buprenor—" Frank's voice came out sharp, and Susan whipped her head around.

"It relieves the symptoms of the withdrawal so she can continue fighting her addiction. I need to go get her started."

"You've explained what it'll do, but not what it is. How do you spell it?" He pulled his phone out and punched in the letters as she rushed through them.

"I need to get back," the young woman said, "I'll find you in the waiting room; we can go over the—"

"It's an opioid? You're giving her more opioids after you tell us she's addicted to them?" Frank followed her out the door, and grabbed her arm.

"Mr. Jankowski, please."

"Where's the doctor? I need to talk to the doctor about this. You're not giving her anything until I talk to him."

"Noooo! Make it stop! Stop!"

Frank raced toward the sound, his daughter's voice punching him in the gut. "What are you doing to her!"

Staff on either side of her bed held her wrists, her ankles as Cathy thrashed around, her hair plastered to her forehead, her eyes darting. The cartoon nurse got in front of him and herded him out of the room without touching him. He was nearly a foot taller than she was, but she'd somehow maneuvered him down the hallway toward the front room.

"She's in a lot of pain, Mr. Jankowski, more than you could ever imagine. She feels like her skin is on fire. The Buprenorphine is protocol in a case like this, and it will greatly reduce her pain and let her go through withdrawals."

He stopped craning his neck, looked down at her, the words settling into his brain.

"Please," she said, eyes on his. "Let us do our job and take care of your daughter."

* * *

Frank waited until dusk to leave Susan in her vigil over Cathy, and then he walked uptown to the brownstone. He might as well do something useful, instead of sitting next to his wife—ex-wife—in silence, each miserable in their feelings. He would take her place after he was done surveilling. His careful world had been knocked off kilter, and he needed the cadence of his footsteps to steady him, to give him a sense of normalcy. He focused on how Cathy was before today, laughing with her friends, spending too much time on her phone, sitting across from him at lunch. As if he could make it unhappen.

On the north side of 83rd, he walked up and down a few times, before he crossed to the south, leaned against the wall of the opposite building pretending to text, the brownstone in full view.

This had to be the most recalcitrant case he and Pete had worked. He tucked his hands into his pockets. The Bureau was sure the drug dealer was funneling money to a terrorist organization, but they couldn't get at him. He was that sewn up. After all the usual ruses including fire alarms and pizza deliveries, they had resorted to following the customers. Frank couldn't have been more surprised when the young man in the newsboy cap had taken him to this Upper East Side brownstone and disappeared into the garden apartment.

Good thing he had this case to focus on. This was something he knew, something he could control. Go after the criminals and the good guys win. They could get other people, or technology to watch the front door, but Frank liked the immediacy of doing his own surveillance. All the details and nuances he could only pick up in person.

Every light in the house was on, even on the top floors, so Pete was probably right, a party of some sort going on. He leaned against the wall, watched, waited. He could hear Pete's singsong voice saying, as he never tired of saying, *good things come to those who wait!* And sometimes they did. The trash pull the guys did yielded little other than a lot of takeout and the presence of a crosscut shredder. Pricey clothing tags, empty makeup containers, nothing alarming. Frank hadn't been expecting much anyway. Bills were all paid online these days, and the threat of identity theft made people more careful with their personal information.

A big silver car glided down the block, idled in front of the building a few seconds and then drove away. A Bentley? Christ, how did people afford something like that? Cathy's hit-and-run car had been big and silver, though there were thousands, maybe tens of thousands, in the city fitting that description. Since no one had seen the license plate, they didn't even know if it was registered in the city. The simmering frustration at not finding the guy, no justice for Cathy threatened to bubble up, and he focused on the brownstone.

The front door opened, and a couple came down the steps, the man with his phone to his ear. Frank took a quick picture of them. The woman was examining her phone, holding it tight, poking and poking at the screen, desperation in her movements. The Bentley came by again, idling. Must be picking someone up from the party.

The front door opened again, and Frank and the driver looked at the brownstone, the light spilling down the marble steps, the couple talking as they went. Frank looked at his phone, put it to his ear, sauntered off as he pretended to talk to the caller, the Gettysburg address standing in for conversation. He'd lingered on the street long enough, but he needed to observe who exited the premises, who the party guests were. So far, he'd counted four couples. A tall man, a slightly arrogant sneer on his face paused at the top of the steps, looked down the street. The silver car glided down and the guy descended, waited for the driver to hop out and open the door for him. His hair matched the car, his suit matched his hair, and the slight slouch made Frank think that the guy thought he owned everything around him and didn't care. A chill ran through him as the patrician dinner guest looked his way and seemingly looked right through him.

He hit the video on his phone and then, as if he were a tourist, he slowly panned the street, got the profile of the Silver Fox, paused the phone at the marble steps as one more couple came out. They conversed with each other then headed west. Frank paralleled them from across the street, followed for a bit, but he already knew who the guy was, and he could only assume the woman accompanying him was his wife.

He'd examine the phone footage later for confirmation, but he didn't really need it. Jeff Greenberg's face was routinely splashed across one page or another of the newspapers, usually pictured shaking hands with the Chief of Police while holding a large posterboard check.

He let out a silent whistle. Christmas just came early. A plan coalesced as he walked, the possible break in the case causing the usual frisson that ran down his back. He held up a hand at the corner, grinned to himself as a cab angled to the sidewalk. No feeling could compare to a case breaking his way.

Chapter Two

Ronnie took off her newsboy hat, removed the Oxycodone from the zippered compartment in the band, and hung it on the hook inside her closet door. She touched the fine, dark wool. She had never owned anything this nice. The suit Ms. "I need you looking sharp since you're working for me" bought for her hung on the rod, and she touched that too. Were these really hers? The Feline had totally nailed her size and had *given* them to her.

Two weeks since she'd landed here, and it had been nothing but training to get ready for tomorrow night. She'd only ever done tray service, and Isabelle Anderson, a.k.a. The Feline, spent a long time with her in the dining room, picking apart every move she made. "From the left! Serve from the left, take from the right!" "Don't breathe all over me! Stop hovering!"

The long con, she thought as she searched for a place to hide the Oxy, was so much work. Easier to find a wallet when she was desperate, disappear into the crowd. Isabelle's schemes made her head spin: Checkbooks, Objects of My Affection, Ambitious Parents. As near as Ronnie could make out, this meant stealing, sex for blackmail, and taking bribes to get their kids into a private school. The way her eyes sparkled when she said, *Objects of My Affection*, left no doubt about which was her favorite game. *One kiss. That's all, and he's mine. Follows me right on up the stairs.* She must've seen the skeptical look on Ronnie's face. *Truly, I just need that one kiss on the lips et voilà! You don't believe me? That's because you've never been kissed by the right person.* For a quick second Ronnie thought she meant to show her personally, so she took a step back and asked Isabelle about the dinner party.

10

The first time a boy had kissed her, she'd slugged him, and she didn't want to do the same to Isabelle.

Her boss told her that tomorrow night she needed to land her next Checkbook, someone who would donate huge amounts to her foundation, whatever that was. The Oxy was a favor to a few friends, Isabelle said, something to keep them happy and bring in a little extra cash. Carry-out, she called it, because she couldn't bear to say the name, admit she was dealing. Ronnie opened cupboards, found them full of stuff: vases, ugly ashtrays, lots of old magazines and hello—a box, all stained glass with a big metal turtle-looking thing where you opened it. The perfect size for the little bags of blue 30s, and Ronnie stuffed them all in there. Now, where to keep the box full of Oxy until she was ready to pass it to Isabelle's guests? Back in the cupboard, under her bed, top shelf of the closet, the freezer? No, right here on the coffee table. Hidden in plain sight.

"Veronica!" Isabelle's voice echoed down the stairs to Ronnie's apartment, making her startle and glance toward the apartment's front door. Her heart sped up, and she looked around for her backpack before she realized what she was doing. "Veronica! Upstairs now. Please."

Ronnie focused on her breathing, told herself that was her old habit, that it had nothing to do with her situation now. Growing up, if someone yelled her name like that, she would instantly run, knowing it was better to return when the person, usually her father, had calmed down. Or in his case, passed out.

She sucked in some air and headed for the stairs. Why had she told Isabelle her full name? No one ever called her that. It was as if that woman had some invisible power that made Ronnie share her secrets. She never told anyone her full name, especially since her brothers always teased her with it, claimed their mother had named her after a girl in a comic book.

"Coming, ma'am." She yelled up the stairs, not sure which floor Isabelle was on. These brownstones were narrow and tall, practically one room per floor, and Isabelle could be anywhere. Ronnie stopped short at the top of the stairs.

Isabelle stood with her arms folded across her chest, one finger tapping on her slender arm, her eyes narrowed, her eyebrows lowered.

"Do not shout in my house."

"Yes, ma'am."

"And do not call me 'ma'am.' I've told you that." She pivoted on her heel and marched to the kitchen. Ronnie glanced over her shoulder toward the front door, then trailed after Isabelle.

"What did you think this was?" Isabelle held up a small, square tablecloth, tags stapled to the corner, the pink plastic from the cleaners balled up on the counter like cotton candy. "Did you think I was hosting a doll's party? Honestly." Isabelle crumpled the offending cloth in her hands and thrust it toward Ronnie. "Take this. I don't care what you do with it. I have no use for it. But get one that will fit this time." Isabelle went to the cupboard and pulled out a coffee cup, a silly, delicate thing, paper-thin. Like it would break if she breathed on it. Her boss poured herself about an ounce of coffee and leaned against the counter to eye Ronnie over the rim of the flowered china. "I can throw together a very successful party with just about anything, but even that would look ridiculous." She set the cup down, a clink on the marble countertop. "Now that I have you, I can be more exacting. The dinner party tomorrow night is vital to my plans. Tonight is for practice."

Ronnie focused on refolding the material so she didn't have to look at Isabelle, wouldn't say to her what she was thinking: *you get what you get*. It hadn't been easy grabbing it off the van without getting caught.

"And here is a list of other things we need for tonight and tomorrow night. I'm sure that this time," she raised one eyebrow at Ronnie, "everything will be to my satisfaction." Her eyes flickered over Ronnie's face, then she went out of the kitchen, the cup on the counter waiting for Ronnie to wash it.

Ronnie wanted to give the back of her blonde head the finger, but didn't dare. That lady had eyes in the back of her head. She headed down to her apartment, conscious of her footfall on the carpeted stairs. Isabelle was probably counting each one, following her even as she was somewhere else in the house.

Shit, she's tough. Ronnie changed into her suit and shoved Isabelle's list in her pocket. And all this stupid training: how to open the door (*Before they ring the bell!*), hang up their coats, check the pockets for the money and trade it for the Oxy, how to serve (for the mark: *Wine glass full, water glass empty!*), how to set the table, decorate the dining room (*Candles everywhere!*), and what to say (*Nothing!*).

The day was way too warm to wear the newsboy cap, so she left it on the hook. She'd use one of Isabelle's shopping bags, complete the picture of the Upper East Side Butler running errands. People saw only what they wanted to see, never looking twice once their brain made a decision. A passing glance in the full-length mirror confirmed her look: flat chest, no hips, boy haircut, men's suit—definitely a guy. She thought there might be a florist on Madison, and even though keeping to the neighborhood wasn't the best policy for stealing (*don't crap in your own nest*, as her brothers would say), Isabelle had given her a long list and a short amount of time.

Ronnie took the steps up to the sidewalk, enjoying the movement. She walked less now that she was at Isabelle's, and it felt good to stretch her legs, though the Upper East Side was so not her territory. The sidewalks here were wider, cleaner, and there were flowers or smooth stones planted around trees, little wrought iron fences to protect them. Doormen swept the sidewalks, and the people were different—more dogs on leashes, baby strollers, children in school uniforms. But there were the same traffic noises, same sirens, same trash picked up and swirled by a breeze.

She still couldn't believe she had a place to live. She'd been all set to stay the one night, take an inventory and leave, but when Isabelle had shown her the downstairs apartment, made it clear it would be all hers, no chains, no locks, no pallet on the floor—nothing like she'd read in the papers about tortured household slaves—she'd ended up staying.

She was surprised at first when Isabelle said she wanted her to steal everything for her parties. Well, of course, she said it in some roundabout way like, "What do you think you can get." Never call a duck a duck—that was Isabelle. Ronnie figured she had this big house, she must be loaded, but as she cleaned, she saw where the carpet was thin, the upholstery stained, furniture and cushions arranged to hide them. Paint was chipped, floorboards creaked, curtains faded by the sun.

She decided a long time ago that she would never steal unless she absolutely had to, so she thought of this as Isabelle doing the thieving. A florist sat in the center of the block and increased her pace, made her arms wide as if she owned the sidewalk and, as she reached for the door handle, she expanded her chest, found the deeper register for her voice.

"That centerpiece done yet? We need it now!"

* * *

Ronnie poured the red wine she'd found on the back of a truck into Philippe's glass, turned the bottle as she stopped so it wouldn't drip. For the run-through dinner tonight Isabelle had invited Mr. Reynard so Ronnie would have someone else to practice on. Maybe with him there she wouldn't yell at her so much.

"Ronnie lucked into this, this afternoon." Isabelle gave her a smile like she was three and the plates before them had mud pies on them.

Philippe jabbed a fork into the pork dish courtesy of a high-end deli on Lexington. His fork traveled to his rather large mouth, his jaws ground away. Isabelle eyed him, as if to see what happened to him before she tried it. He took a sip of wine, dabbed the corners of his mouth, smoothed the napkin over his lap. He was a curious mixture of delicacy and muscle.

"Have you tried this?" Philippe threw Isabelle a look, turned his beefy back to scan Ronnie. "Did you taste this?" He eyed her.

"Well, I, I heated it up, and—"

"Get a plate! Sit down! This is tremendous! I've never had anything that tastes like this." He forked another heap into his mouth.

Ronnie eyed Isabelle. Isabelle looked between them, torn no doubt between pleasing him and training her.

"Come! Sit with us!" Philippe patted the tablecloth.

Ronnie stepped out of his line of sight and threw Isabelle a silent question. Isabelle moved her head a whisper to point to the empty spot opposite Philippe, so Ronnie went into the pantry and grabbed a setup, then the serving dishes too. Philippe might want seconds.

14

She slid into the chair without pulling it out so she wouldn't have that awkward scooching of her chair with herself in it. She eyed the big guy across from her, his head bent over his plate, his shoulders wider than the chair. He gestured at her with his fork and grinned.

"Cassoulet!" He waved his spoon. "So much better than all those silly restaurants that don't know how to feed a person."

Isabelle whipped a glance at him, no doubt wondering if that was a criticism of her choice of restaurants. He must know her well to get away with that.

"No, but my dear." Philippe patted Isabelle's hand. "I never feel I get enough to eat. All those fussy little things as if they think it should go straight into a museum and not provide sustenance for the stomach." He was too polite to pat his stomach, but Ronnie looked at it anyway, flat, muscular under his starched shirt.

Her hand still under Philippe's great big one, Isabelle eyed Ronnie. Ronnie could practically see the gears turning, as if she was sizing up this new competition. Isabelle smiled at Philippe. "Isn't she a gem?"

He suppressed a burp, settled in his chair, "So tell me, is it true, what Isabelle told me, that you stole her bracelet at that gala?"

"Yup." Ronnie scraped up the last bite on her plate. Leave it to the French to have a fancy name for pork and beans. "But she caught me. No one ever caught me before." Might as well toss her a bone. She still didn't know why she'd stolen it that night. Like Isabelle had cast a spell over her. Out of the corner of her eye she saw her boss relax, a satisfied smile traveling from her lips to her eyes.

"There I was," Isabelle swept up an arm as if raising the curtain on the scene, "charming a crowd of handsome, rich men, all drinking in my every word, and just as I'm sure I've hooked them, sure that I'll be taking at least one of them home with me—"

"You are so beguiling!" Philippe grabbed up his napkin, touched the corners of his mouth. "They turn to you because you are so striking, and then you capture them with your charm." His eyes twinkled at Isabelle. "You know just how to make a person feel like a god."

"So there I was," Isabelle started up again, her voice a little louder, "already knowing how wealthy this man was, knowing just what he needed to hear. And he was practically drooling, and what happens but—"

"Oh, I wish I had been there to see this!" Philippe turned to Ronnie. "You see, they can't help it. Like flies, they can't get free of her web. But then," he gave Isabelle a smile, "very few really want to. That's why she's so successful. I should know." He patted Isabelle's hand again. "I've never gotten free of you, have I?"

Ronnie didn't know what was more interesting in this conversation, the way Philippe kept interrupting, or the charms of Isabelle. She had seen for herself the way the woman pulled people in and held them there.

"You'll be here forever, darling." Isabelle gazed at Philippe, then removed her hand from under his. "But don't you want to hear my story? The man was completely in my sway—the whole group was—and then—" she gave Ronnie a toss of her head, "little Ronnie here takes my bracelet right off my arm."

Surprise and delight widened Philippe's eyes and Ronnie gave a little shrug, hoping to turn the attention back to Isabelle.

"It's true," Isabelle said, as if she wanted to pat Ronnie on the head. "You were good. The way you held up the tray, waited for everyone to laugh at what I'd said. And quick as lightning, too." She turned to Philippe, made sure his eyes were on her. "But I knew the second she had done it and I never let her out of my sight the rest of the evening."

"Until I was cleaning up."

"Then I found her and demanded she return it."

"You did? No need of my services?" Philippe's eyes crinkled at Isabelle.

"Oh, I channeled you, though," Isabelle said. "I needed to act tough. She was working my crowd, you see."

"What did you do?" Philippe's soft brown eyes didn't leave Isabelle.

"She said she'd rip my balls off if I didn't give it back."

Philippe looked back and forth between them, a low, rumbling growl turning into laughter that moved his chest but barely left his mouth.

Isabelle folded her napkin. Her bare shoulder gave a tiny shrug. "I didn't know. How was I supposed to know? She was in disguise."

Philippe's shoulders were moving up and down, little hee hees escaping his lips.

Isabelle slid her chair back. "Ronnie. We'll have our coffee in the living room," she said as she rose to her full height. "Come, Philippe, time for the children to do the dishes."

Huh. How many Ronnies did she think there were? Well, Cinderella couldn't stay at the ball forever. Ronnie slid the doors closed behind them, and the room seemed much smaller. The funny thing was, Isabelle had told her to keep the bracelet. "It'll be a reminder to me," she'd said, though of what Ronnie didn't have a clue. She stacked and cleared, loaded up the tray onto the dumb waiter. She did want to work it off, though. Fair was fair. Now, she thought as she scanned the dining room, what the hell was she going to serve tomorrow night.

* * *

The next night, Isabelle's mark was Harburger, the guy sitting on her right, so Ronnie made sure his wine glass was topped off and his water glass empty. More than once she'd seen him go for the water, find it empty, and pick up the wine instead. She'd almost laughed out loud. Isabelle worked him over the same way she had worked the crowds at that charity ball. She spoke softly so he had to lean way in to hear, touched his arm, twinkled her eyes at him, tossed her head, and laughed that laugh as if he were the funniest thing on earth and the only one in the room.

As Ronnie made a move for the wine decanter on the sideboard, Isabelle shook her head the tiniest bit. She looked the table over. Most of them had put their knife and fork across the top of their plate as Isabelle had said they would, so she began to clear. In the pantry, she stacked the china, silver, and crystal and put them in the dumb waiter thing to send them to the kitchen. She had just passed through to the dining room when Isabelle rose to announce coffee and dessert. Her voice was drowned out by the unmistakable crash of china and crystal. Ronnie's pulse quickened, and she swallowed hard, a glance at Isabelle. In the dead quiet that followed, in a split second while everyone else's head was turned toward the sound, Isabelle sent Ronnie a look that could've set her on fire.

Isabelle laughed a short laugh and said, "I just love a grand finale, don't you? Come, we'll all go back to the living room!"

She didn't look Ronnie's way, but Ronnie didn't think for one second she was safe. She'd seen the tightening around Isabelle's eyes, picked up on the fake laughter. Ronnie stood frozen and everyone filed out in silence.

She didn't like that look. Not one bit. She should run. Race down to her apartment and throw all her measly things in her backpack, put on the newsboy cap, grab some food from the kitchen, maybe go back down and take the pillow off her bed—oh—go back up to the kitchen, find a water bottle and make sure she had enough food for several days, find something she could sell, maybe several things, though not something Isabelle really cared about, then out the door...and back on the cold and dirty streets.

But how could Isabelle blame her for the dumb waiter breaking? She'd better finish out the evening and hope Isabelle saw reason. She searched the cupboards in the tiny pantry for a large tray. Why would she care—she had so much china, so many glasses...at least the silverware wasn't broken—you couldn't break a silver fork could you? The coffee service sat waiting on the narrow counter. She'd serve the dessert and coffee and do the absolute best job she could for the rest of the night. Isabelle would see that she needed her, see that she shouldn't kick her out. Maybe she would just yell at her, if that's what you could call that low, clipped voice that jabbed her like ice shards.

* * *

Everyone wanted coffee, and no one wanted the pastries she'd worked hard to grab, even though they were so nicely arranged on a fussy plate, with an even fussier doily underneath them. Ronnie hung around the living room, trying to disappear, catching bits of conversation. How did these people not fall asleep on each other?

"Okay, Isabelle," Bitsy commanded from deep in the down couch cushions. "You *must* tell us what your foundation is up to." She waved the brochure Isabelle had printed up yesterday. On the cover, a dirty little girl with big brown eyes hugged a violin like it was her baby sister, and scraggly palm trees waved behind her. Conversation around the room died out, and the heads turned toward Isabelle where she posed in front of the mirror over the fireplace. She turned to place her coffee cup and saucer on the mantle as if she didn't know all eyes were on her.

"Oh, it's nothing," she said to the room. "Just a little project to keep me out of trouble." At this she glanced down and turned the gold cuff on her wrist back and forth as if not used to speaking to a crowd, to talking about herself. Ronnie, coffee pot in midair, stopped to watch her. How had she done that? She seemed shy, almost embarrassed. That sure was something.

Predictably, a chorus of mostly female voices protested that they really wanted to hear and so, of course, they coaxed her to explain how music was so important and so out of reach for so many people. On and on, the details of the donations, volunteers, lessons on the instruments, the expressions on their faces when they held their very own flute, the tears of the parents at their first recitals, the joy brought to the hearts of the grandparents. And, thought Ronnie, the money they could get by selling them as soon as the volunteers left. She sucked in her breath as she left to clear what was left in the dining room. Isabelle almost had her believing it too.

* * *

In the foyer, after all the guests and Philippe had left, after Mr. Greenberg and Bitsy's husband Bucky had patted the pockets of their coats, checking no doubt for the treats Ronnie had left there, after Isabelle had tried and tried to get a check out of Mr. Harburger who said his wife took care of any donations and Ronnie thought maybe Isabelle wished she'd been nicer to that sour-faced witch, only then did Isabelle turn to Ronnie. Her glance swept over her slowly, and Ronnie felt like she had had too much coffee, a tingling, a narrowing of her vision. Her feet were glued to the black and white tiled floor.

"What was that all about?" Isabelle's eyes narrowed at her, and she spoke in the lowest, quietest voice possible.

It made Ronnie think of a snake. She almost wished Isabelle would hit her and get it over with, but she didn't seem to be the hitting type. And somehow, that was much worse. There she stood, seeming taller than she had earlier, looking down at Ronnie and just breathing. Ronnie didn't think she should answer.

"You. Just cost me. A major donation." She began pacing the entryway like a panther, and Ronnie backed against the wall to give her plenty of room. "How do you think I provide you with a place to live? Where do you think the money comes from? I needed that Checkbook!"

If Ronnie left now, she would have to go out the front door before Isabelle could grab her, and all she would have to her name was her butler uniform— no backpack for a pillow, no fancy wool hat, no cash, no knife, and she'd be leaving behind the picture, the only thing she had of her mother.

Isabelle stopped to point a long, painted nail at her. "You'll clean it all up tonight. I don't care how long it takes. I don't want to see one speck of anything in the morning. I'll assess the loss then and tell you what you owe me." She turned her back on Ronnie and headed for the stairs, then spun around so fast she was a big silky silver blur. "But if the Harburgers don't come through, you'll be working for me for a whole lot longer."

Chapter Three

"We had to, Susan, you know that." Frank watched his wife—ex-wife sniff, take a sip of water, not look up at him. She pulled a Kleenex from the depths of her straw bag and wiped her nose. "How did this even happen?" Susan's eyes went around the deli, the waiter rushing past their tiny table squashed against the wall. "The doctors prescribed those medications! We were just trying to keep her from all that pain. Oh God, if only that car hadn't hit her, if—"

"Shoulda woulda could—"

"Shut up, Frank. Christ." Her eyes were fiery, bulging.

Of course she would think this was somehow his fault. Well, the original hit and run was his fault, but he'd never admit that to Susan. He stuffed the guilty feelings down. "I only meant," Frank leaned in, his voice softened, "it doesn't help to wish it undone. We just need to go on from here, from where we are now, and putting Cathy in rchab was the only logical choice."

"Logical. Oh, logical. God forbid emotions should ever come into it for you. Mr. Black and White."

Frank sat back, gazed around, wondered how he had missed the couple coming in, sitting two tables over. No matter what was happening, he saw everything, alert to all activity and potential danger, but his senses had failed him today.

Susan was still talking. "But residential! Why couldn't it have been outpatient? The cost of it! She'll never go to college now." Her tears spilled down her cheeks, and she bent her head, her hair hiding her splotchy face and muffling her sobs.

"If we don't treat this addiction, she'll never—"

"God. Whatever Frank." Susan sniffed. "I don't see why we couldn't have handled it. She could've stayed in school. We wouldn't have had to explain and have that bitch Head of School looking at us like we were unfit parents. No one would've had to know—we could've grounded her, taken her to meetings, put a tracker on her phone, watched her like a hawk..."

Frank glanced around. That same couple was now on their phones, ignoring each other, thumbs working the screens. He felt Susan winding down, so he tuned in again.

"...you were always so hard on her, so restrictive, maybe she needed more freedom when she was growing up, then she wouldn't have rebelled like this..."

"Susan."

She stopped talking, mouth open, and Frank had no doubt there was a whole lot more she'd like to spill out.

"I don't think it's useful to blame each other right now. Remember what they said at the intake. It's better for Cathy if we're on the same page, working together so she knows we'll be there for her. A source of support."

Frank paused as the waiter slapped their plates down and rushed away. He picked his up and waited for his ex-wife to do the same. Sexism was alive and well among waitstaff, the guy giving Frank the tuna melt, his wife the salad. His ex-wife.

"I thought," Frank went on, stabbing at the romaine, rooting around to make sure the dressing coated most of the leaves, "a talk would be helpful. We could process it together, figure out—"

"We? Process?" Her voice was louder now, but not so loud that the phone couple tore themselves away from their screens. "There hasn't been a 'we' in a long time, Frank. You seem to think—"

"Tell me what I think. I'd like to know." He put his fork down and leaned back, arms folded. Because what he thought, if he truly admitted it to himself, was that if he had been the one overseeing Cathy's medications, talking to the doctors and nurses, figuring out how to alleviate her pain, then his daughter would not be addicted right now, they would not be depleting her college fund to pay for expensive rehab and the two of them would not be having this conversation. If she hadn't had the accident in the first place, if he hadn't—well, never mind about that.

* * *

"This the only way?" Frank's boss eyed him over the sheet of paper. "You've exhausted every other lead?"

Frank nodded and went over what he'd written up: how they'd staked out the dealer, bugged his apartment, put a guy in as a handyman and one as a customer, and, after all of that proved fruitless, just followed the buyers, Newsboy leading them to the stake-out of Isabelle Anderson's brownstone.

"How long's it been since you were undercover, Frank? No way you still got it." He tossed Frank's proposal aside. Picked up a folder and opened it.

"No, wait, hear me out." Frank laid out the persona he had thought up: Peter Franks, rube from Omaha, moving to New York City, wanting to introduce his wife to society, get his kid into Marshall Logan's since Isabelle was on the board. Now that he had sold his insurance business, he and his wife wanted to rub elbows with the fancy New Yorkers. Any mistakes he might make in front of Isabelle would be chalked up to his being from Omaha. He paused, and his boss looked up from the file he was reading. The guy insisted that he receive everything in hard copy, never mind the trees he was killing.

"You still here?"

"Sir, we haven't gotten to the dealer, and now we have a very good lead."

His boss frowned, eyes scanning the paper in front of him.

"And get this," Frank went on, "we spotted Jeff Greenberg and his wife leaving the brownstone after some sort of party. You could tell the Chief of Police that I, as Peter Franks, want to meet the Greenbergs—"

"Who're the Greenbergs?"

His first spark of interest. "Oh, you know the guy, the one in the photographs with the oversized check, the biggest donor to the NYPD Foundation?"

His boss scowled, then nodded uncertainly.

"So the Chief of Police thinks he's introducing Peter Franks to Jeff Greenberg." He paused to make sure he had his boss's attention. He wasn't usually this slow on the uptake. "And Peter Franks tells Jeff how his wife's heart is just set on getting little Johnny into the best school and my heart's set on keeping her happy and then—"

"You gonna get confused, using your partner's name with yours?" He put down the file and stared at Frank. "And what are you going to do for a wife? No way that's in the budget. All our female agents are busy on that other case."

"Easy. I'm here scoping everything out while she and Little Johnny are back home. He has school, after all. Gives me more freedom to hang around Ms. Anderson that way, too."

"I'm missing something. How does this Greenberg guy get you into the brownstone?" His boss started drumming his fingers, stared at Frank.

"Mrs. Anderson is on the Board of Marshall Logan."

The boss raised his eyebrows at him.

"The fancy private school? And I want little Johnny to get in, so naturally, Jeff will arrange an introduction because the Chief of Police introduced him to Peter Franks and then—"

"All right." His boss closed the folder and regarded him over his reading glasses. "You're damn lucky you figured this out. You've been on this case so long I was about to pull the plug."

Frank's heart beat a little faster, either from the excitement of the case or from the fear of his boss pulling the plug for the first time ever on a case of Frank's. Didn't matter. All that mattered was that he got the go-ahead.

"Okay." His boss picked up his pen, put a few marks on his proposal. "Not much in the way of expenses, so I don't have to go higher to get approval. It'll be covered by the original National Security Letter, so Tech can give you a few devices. And get on over to Wardrobe. See what they've got for you."

* * *

24

Coming out of the door onto Federal Plaza, Frank's chest expanded with the same feeling every time: an impressiveness, a reassurance. Across the park, the courthouses sat back from the street, demanding the long walk up the stairs. The comforting, blocky city offices offered up licenses or collected fines. City, county, state, federal: they were all here, humming along to take care of the citizens and carry out the laws that protected them. The heartbeat of an orderly society surrounded him, and every time he paused here, he knew why he had joined the Bureau. It made him stand a little taller, and he glanced upward, sure that his father looked down even now, bragged on him to everyone else in heaven, whether they wanted to hear it or not.

* * *

"Wardrobe" was the warehouse full of what they'd confiscated from criminals, and they made liberal use of it for undercover work. A lot of it, even Frank knew, was too much: layers of gold necklaces, Rolex watches as heavy as his gun, and men's fur coats. He held up a bespoke suit, no tags to indicate the size, nothing but the maker, Saville Row, clothiers to the Queen. Like she wore men's suits. The cut of it almost took his breath away, the double vent in the back, real buttonholes at the cuffs, the stitching fine and precise. He prayed it was his size because now no other suit would do. That fine maroon stripe in the weave, so tiny no one would notice, but mesmerizing, nonetheless.

He put on the jacket. Ran his hands down the front. The sleeves came right to his wrists, not too long, not too short. He moved his arms as if to give himself a hug. Plenty of room, like the suit had been made for him. The trousers had to fit. He looked down the aisle. No one around. Nope. He wouldn't risk it. He knew they'd fit him. This suit was his. Even without a mirror, he knew it showed off his broad shoulders to good effect. And made him feel rich. He raised his hand as if signaling his driver. Tipped an imaginary hat and gave a slight bow as if to a fine lady. He loved Peter Franks already.

He found a gold business card case with someone else's initials swirled and unreadable, a money clip, fancy cufflinks to go with a white dress shirt, and a gold watch so thin he wished he'd never have to take it off.

He gathered the rest of his guise, took it as a good omen that he even found shoes that fit, thin leather oxfords with no wear on the soles. And ties. Oh, some criminal had indulged himself with an amazing number from Hermès Collection, the patterns subtle and unmistakable. He selected seven, no eight, that were perfect, barely worn, no spots, no wrinkles. He would never keep any of this, of course, against the rules, but it was going to be fun wearing it.

* * *

Back at the office, time to do paperwork while he waited for the introduction to Jeff Greenberg. He fired up his computer and swiped his keycard, opened a blank 302. These were the backbone of every case, the bane of every agent's existence. Under Hoover, there had been a 10/90 rule: 90% of an agent's time should be spent in the field, with only 10% allocated to paperwork. Now, of course, what with all the CYAing they had to do to make charges stick, keep the lawyers happy, everyone grumbled it was a 90/10 rule. But you had to do the paperwork if you wanted to keep your job, keep moving up. Frank didn't get this far not doing the paperwork, and he wasn't going to get ahead by not doing it either. He knew the rules, and he believed in the system. Follow procedure, catch the criminals, make the world safer for everyone.

Well, that hadn't helped Cathy, had it? No criminals, just doctors and prescriptions, and then she's addicted. They had followed those rules, and look where they were now. That initial steely adrenaline rush from the race to the ER was now a Styrofoam squeak of general anxiety, a cloud hovering, threatening his usual optimism. No, no, things were going to work out. Cathy would be fine. After her recovery Susan had been worried about her. But he knew it was just a teenage phase, the ripped clothes, stringy black hair, black makeup that looked like it had been applied by a baby bear. All her friends looked like that, and he knew she'd grow out of it. Somehow, Susan was so focused on what was going on now, that she lost sight of their little girl.

Frank unclenched his jaw, worked it around as he saved the incomplete form. He logged out and immediately sprang up from his desk chair. He couldn't keep his mind on his work. He needed some air. His partner looked up from the other side of the partition.

"Lunch time?" Pete stood too.

"When is it not?" Frank didn't know where Pete put it all.

* * *

They sat on a bench in Thomas Paine Park, not far from the taco truck, surrounded by all the government office buildings. Their bench was shaded by trees but not protected from the traffic noise, the shouts, the backing up of garbage trucks, the sirens getting louder.

"Wouldya look at that guy? Right here, and the police headquarters just blocks away." Pete gestured with his massive burrito toward the middle of the park.

"Goddamn drug dealers." Frank put his cardboard box down, wiped his hands on the tissue paper napkin.

Pete took a bite, watched the guy as he palmed off the drugs, disguised as a handshake. "That's why we do what we do. Take the SOBs down."

Frank closed the lid on the lunch he was no longer hungry for, set it on the bench between them.

"Aren't you going to eat that?"

"That mini sleeping bag not enough for you?"

Pete put Frank's take-out container on his lap and stuffed the rest of his burrito in his mouth.

"Pete." Frank clasped his hands between his knees, stared at them. "You ever get impatient about how long it takes. Y'know. Ever think it'd be easier to just take them out yourself, one by one?"

"Ha! Sure I have." Pete drained his can of soda, then opened Frank's box.

"But that's not why you're in law enforcement, is it. You came, same as me. You believe in law and order and in the justice," he pointed to the courthouse steps made famous in the Dick Wolfe TV show, "that follows. Good guys. Bad guys." He got up and went to the trash can at the end of the bench, crammed the lunch detritus in. When he turned around the full trash can spit most of it back out. "And no vigilantism. That's what we believe, right, Frank?"

Chapter Four

Ronnie jumped in the shower before she had time to think about her dream. She closed her eyes and turned toward the spray, the warm water coating her in a cocoon of safety. Maybe it would wash away that feeling, the hangover from her dream, the dirt of the streets so real, Matt's voice still echoing in her head. She missed him. No way around that. She slammed the lever to cold, hoped to drive out all her thoughts, get rid of the dream, stop thinking about everything, stop feeling Matt beside her. They had done everything together. He'd been the nicest of her brothers, not ditching her when she tried to tag along, saving a piece of chocolate for her, switching beds with her that night—how had he known her father would come for her on that particular night? She could still hear Matt shouting when his father realized it was him, not her. *Run*, Matt yelled, *run!*

She stepped out of the shower, dried off, rubbed her skin extra hard to warm up. Maybe he'd just guessed, or maybe he had a second sense, but either way when he graduated high school and it was his turn to leave home like their brothers had, she grabbed her backpack and went with him. He didn't protest, even though she was only sixteen, even though it meant she'd never finish school.

* * *

"When you got it, you give it, dude."

The voice behind Ronnie made her skin crawl and she lengthened her stride, walked as fast as she could without breaking into a run. She knew

29

that voice, and it belonged to someone who could never find out where she was living.

"It's what we believe, man. Mutual aid."

Ronnie didn't dare look over her shoulder, give the girl a chance to confront her face to face. What was she doing way up here? Damn. Usually they stayed downtown, St. Mark's Place. She passed Isabelle's brownstone and kept heading east, hoping to shake this parasite, hoping the girl wouldn't want to go deeper into the Upper East Side. She could ruin everything.

"Dude! Wait up!"

Ronnie broke into a run, crossed against the light, the plastic bag with the cake in its pink box banging against her leg. She grabbed it up and held it with both hands, willed her legs to go faster, dared a glance over her shoulder, nearly running into a foreign couple consulting their phone. Tourists. Holding the cake in front of her, she doubled back down the street, but the dreadlocks and torn jeans kept up with her, waited for a break in the traffic to join her across the street. *Shit.*

Annie, "as in Anarchy," must've remembered her from when she and Matt would hang out with them, the crusties, as they called themselves. Proud of their stench and their begging community, living on the streets with their dogs and their backpacks, some of them going home to their parents when the adventure was over. Bitch must've followed her through the park.

At first, she and Matt thought they were friendly, the way they shared their food, offered their weed, played their guitars while sitting on their backpacks. How could they stand being around each other though—they smelled so bad. But Matt liked them, maybe liked this girl Annie, she with the circle A tattooed on her cheek, and he wanted to stay with them. It was something to do. A gang to feel a part of, safety in numbers and all that. But though Ronnie got somewhat used to the smell, she never got used to the philosophy and when Matt started in on the weed with Annie, she begged him to stop hanging with them.

"This isn't you! You know that." Ronnie had pleaded with him, reminded him of all the times Matt and their brothers had said never start, not even booze, look what happened to Dad. It wasn't until the incident with the police that he agreed to go somewhere else.

Here was this loose group of travelers and crusties, who talked about how free they were, no home jails with four walls and a roof, free to come and go and do what they liked (never mind they had to panhandle to buy food, at the mercy of those who felt guilty about their wealth), who believed in helping each other, sharing what they had. But when the cops came after them, scattering them, everyone grabbed their backpacks, dogs, sleeping bags and dope, ran through the park in different directions. Someone, two somebodies she guessed, tripped her and Matt so they went sprawling, *it's for the greater good* they said. The cops grabbed them and the crusties got away. As the cop pulled on her arm, Ronnie had seen Annie looking back at them over her shoulder with her wicked grin.

Ronnie headed now over to Park Avenue. No way this girl would want to follow her there, with the broad sidewalks and the doormen, the double lanes of traffic on the wide street, no place to hide, no one like her, all the awnings and fancy apartment buildings representing everything she was against. The slight uphill to Park grew more evident as she ran, the sweat gathering on her scalp, her T-shirt chafing. She may be flat chested, but she did have nipples, and they were being rubbed raw. Why couldn't she have been born a boy. Maybe this cake wasn't worth it. She threw a quick look over her shoulder. Damn if that girl wasn't still following her.

If Annie wasn't afraid of the Upper East Side, what would she do if she found out where Ronnie lived? She willed her legs to go faster, and she made it to the median between the four lanes of traffic right as the light changed. Annie would camp on her doorstep, find a way in. She was a leech. Ronnie's shirt stuck to her back, sweat poured down the sides of her face, and her lungs felt like they'd never recover. She dropped the cake to the ground and bent over, hands on her knees, breath coming fast. She wished she could go shirtless like her brothers, tear off her T-shirt and use it to dry off the rest of the sweat. Out of the corner of her eye, blonde dreadlocks danced on the sidewalk.

And it wouldn't only be Annie camping out. She'd bring everyone with her, all of them wanting to share in what Ronnie had, find a way into the house. Shit, shit, shit. Annie probably waited for a break in the traffic, ready to race across, claim the prize. Ronnie didn't want to give her the satisfaction of knowing she'd seen her, of seeing that Ronnie cared, so she straightened up with her back to her, looked for her own break in the traffic. She left the cake in its box on the median, the wispy bag flattening down with the whoosh of the cars. She sprinted, headed east, headed away from Annie. A taxi leaned on its horn, the driver put his head out the window to yell at her. She waved and kept running.

She knew of a bakery down on Second, a little ways uptown and if she could get there fast and luck was on her side, like someone leaving with a nice big box or several bags, and if she still had any breath and could run past them, making that box her own—then maybe, just maybe she would land at Isabelle's in time to run her head under the water, a washcloth over her skin, deodorant on her pits, jump into her butler uniform and serve the tea to all her ladidah guests. And pray her heartbeat returned to normal.

Chapter Five

To give himself time to pull on his new persona, Frank walked from his apartment to his new favorite brownstone. He texted Pete, *leaving to meet target,* and then mentally palpated himself, though he knew everything was in place: no Bureau phone and no gun, all the lovely bling from Wardrobe, his hair combed straight back with no part, the button mics in his right jacket pocket, microphone pen in the inside pocket. A full suit was too warm for this September day, but he thought it struck the right note, even if no one else would be wearing one. Or especially so. He wanted to appear wealthy and out of step with the New Yorkers around him, eager to learn from them, to join their coveted circles. If they thought he wasn't sophisticated, perhaps not as smart as they, then he would have the advantage.

He had hoped for more than just afternoon tea with Isabelle Anderson, but that's what Jeff Greenberg had offered, told him to meet outside her house and they'd go in together. Peter Franks, he decided, would be friendly, affable, folksy, neighborly.

Frank stretched out his legs as he strode along, avoided sandwich boards with menus, stepped on a spray-painted message asking Davey where he's at. Undercover made him feel productive, doing actual work in the field. And no wife to lie to, dissemble to rather, or to just not tell what he was up to. Not that the divorce was his idea; he thought everything was going great. He and Susan had been together since grad school, and he liked the life they had together. He didn't like lying though, so it came as a bit of a relief that he wouldn't wake anyone with his comings and goings, have someone asking questions, unsatisfied with the answers. He had assumed they would be married forever, a given he would never have to worry about, but Susan had had different expectations, so she'd felt short-changed, felt that he cut her out of his life too much of the time. And he missed all of the family milestones: the plays, the soccer games, the birthday parties.

Damn. Well, he hadn't missed this particular family milestone, the one he had never conceived of: *addicted teenage daughter.* Just when he thought he had Cathy all tucked away in the "Personal" compartment in his brain, too. The accident had been bad enough, the reel running over and over in his head: his daughter stepping off the curb, the car running the red light, the other pedestrians scattering. Over and over, he had tried to make it unhappen, put her on another street, in the apartment with no argument to send her running. In his head he would take the car away, slow it down, make the rest of the crowd go first. He had thought she was healed and that everything was fine, and now, bam! Addicted to opioids. Christ, Susan had been managing the meds, well now they both knew she had not been managing them.

All his careful scrutiny of his daughter as she hit the teen and preteen years—clamping down on her, calling parents to see if they would be home before he let her go over to a friend's apartment, monitoring her internet usage, her Facebook page, demanding to meet her friends, making them look him in the eye and shake his hand—all of that and he and Susan had been the ones to give her the drugs. Damn. Damn. Damn.

At the corner market, a bucket of chrysanthemums caught his eye, the shout of fall colors spilling out of their buckets. He pictured Peter Franks appearing at the brownstone with a cellophane cone of flowers and tossed that idea. Would it seem naive or charming to show up with a vase full of roses? He had bought Susan flowers only on special occasions—they were so expensive, a waste of money. But it wouldn't break his budget, especially since this case would be over in a New York minute, a checkmark in the win column.

He turned onto Madison and found a florist in the middle of the block. A girl startled off her stool behind the counter when the door chimed as he came in. Two dozen pale pink roses, big white ribbon on the tall vase. He could buy Cathy about ten lunches for what it cost, and he worked on keeping his face neutral. Peter Franks could afford it.

Jeff Greenberg waited for him in front of the brownstone on E. 83rd Street. He leaned against the wrought iron railing, stared at his phone, poking it occasionally. When Frank called his name, Greenberg glanced up with that dazed look as if his brain and eyes were still engaged with the screen. Like an addict.

"Sorry. Gotta take care of a few things before we go in there." He eyed the vase of roses. "Isabelle doesn't allow phones upstairs. Makes you put them in the closet. How're you doing?"

Darn it. The pen in his pocket better be enough without the backup of his phone. "Really?" He shifted the flowers so he could shake hands with Jeff. "I've never heard of that. No phones?"

"Nope. Digital-free social hour. I don't think she likes the interruption. Or the anticipation of one."

Frank agreed with the sentiment, but he hoped he could finesse it.

Newsboy saw them in, took his vase of flowers, held out a basket for their phones. Frank hesitated, mumbled something about an important call, but Newsboy continued to silently hold out the basket. Up close his features were almost feminine, his chin clean-shaven. Frank gave him points for that since most young men these days sported bristles as if they were on a three-day bender. He hoped he would get a chance to study him further. Frank glanced around as if admiring his surroundings, noted there was no panel for a smart house, no alarm in sight. The coat closet off the vestibule seemed full already, and Frank wondered just how many people Isabelle Anderson had invited to tea.

"Come in ! Welcome!" The lady of the house had descended the stairs without making a noise and Frank turned toward her, chastised himself for not being more alert. After Greenberg made the introductions, she turned with a swirl of royal blue silk, and they followed her up the stairs. A striking woman, she moved with a fluid grace, talking and laughing the entire time.

Once in the living room, she indicated where they should sit and, for some reason, put Jeff Greenberg, the biggest guy there by far, on a delicate chair next to the couch. Someone named Philippe, Philippe Reynard, occupied the couch. Frank took mental notes on him from his own chair next to Isabelle. The guy didn't speak, his eyes rarely leaving his hostess. His suit, clearly expensive, seemed too tight in the arms and across the chest. His silence seemed not due to reticence though. It put him in mind of a cougar waiting to strike. Or a cobra.

The door opened, and Isabelle announced Bucky and Bitsy Patterson. Bucky stooped a little at maybe six-feet-two and was dressed on the casual side—a bit of fraying at the collar, rumpled tie. She was shorter and athletic looking, her strong calves more suited to tennis shorts than a cocktail dress. Something about their casual bantering and lack of effort made Frank think they had been friends with Isabelle for long time.

The last guest sauntered in. The Silver Fox in the silver car from Frank's original surveillance. Frank mentally rubbed his hands together. Wouldn't it be great if he turned out to be involved in the drugs. The satisfaction Frank would get from putting cuffs on those chiseled wrists. The guy wore the same suit that matched his hair, a silk scarf stuffed into the pocket where a nicely pressed handkerchief should go. He slouched into an armchair and nodded to the Pattersons. When Isabelle introduced him as Ward McAllister, Bitsy turned to him.

"Ward? That's your name? I thought it was Mickey."

"It is. Mickey *Mc*Allister, you see." He waved a hand like he couldn't be bothered with any more conversation.

Frank rose from his chair to shake hands, but Mickey ignored him, said something to Bucky.

Newsboy came in carrying a large tray brimming with a silver teapot, stacks of cups and saucers, tiered affairs holding pastries and tiny sandwiches. He set it on the bar positioned under the largest mirror Frank had ever seen not in a public space. He carried over the pastry stands, setting one on each end of the coffee table. Newsboy dealt out cups and saucers, made a move to pour, but Isabelle waved him away, intent on serving the tea herself, all eyes on her. The butler backed away, not looking anyone in the eye, and hovered by the bar, eyes darting around as if he felt caged in.

Close up, the little cakes, cookies, and tarts appeared haphazard, broken around the edges, sandwiches flattened, and cucumbers escaping. A miniature eclair seemed intact, and he reached for it, but Philippe swiped it off the tray before he got there. The big guy's eyes never left Frank as he stuffed the whole thing in his mouth.

"Thank you, Ron." Isabelle nodded at Newsboy. And then as if something were amiss, she asked, "Would anyone care for a drink instead? Gin and Tonic to start your afternoon?"

The Silver Fox said with a teenager's petulance that he thought she'd never ask. Which made Frank's decision easy. He had to do what it took to fit in undercover, but there were also rules about how many drinks they could have (two) and he felt that it would better suit Peter Franks' personality to turn it down.

"No. Thank you, though. I didn't get to where I am today drinking in the afternoon." Frank let out a chuckle and wagged his head as if to say we don't do this in the Midwest. "But," he added, "don't let me hold you back." A magnanimous gesture of the hand to the rest of the group. The gold cuff link caught the light, and Isabelle's eyes darted to it as if to prey.

So now he had the Newsboy's first name, but he'd need a surname to run a check on him. The other guests would be researched as well, and if something pinged, he or Pete would dive further in. No doubt his best friend Google would find Bucky and Bitsy since he had their last names, since this was Upper East Side society, and someone probably mentioned them in a column somewhere.

Isabelle leaned in and asked him questions, invited him to tell the group, "Everything! We're just dying for new people around here!" She watched him intently as he talked, touched his arm, encouraged him with more questions. He could plainly see the group around him, but she made him feel as if he were the only one in the room, the only one worth listening to, as if she'd like nothing more than to spend the day hanging on his every word. He found it hard to keep to the aw-shucks attitude, to be the self-effacing, modest Midwesterner when she paid so much close attention, prodded him for more details about his life. He knew he shouldn't embellish, knew he should keep it simple, a little mysterious, so he settled for telling stories from his childhood, using a father not unlike his own, and amused the group with lessons learned ruefully as a rascally kid. He made everyone but the Silver Fox laugh several times and that kept him going. He never talked about himself for obvious reasons, but it seemed he could talk endlessly as Peter Franks.

"Well, I've said enough about me. Let's give someone else a chance." Frank glanced at Philippe Reynard who merely stretched his lips as if amused but didn't take the bait. "Well, let me ask you, does anyone have any kids? My wife just has her heart set on getting our son into Marshall Logan's. Does anyone know the best way to go about that?"

"Well Isabelle—" Bitsy began, but her host cut her off with a great throaty laugh as if Frank had made a joke.

"My," her eyes twinkled, "she certainly is aiming high. When do we get to meet your better half?"

"Ah, well, she's sent me on ahead to reconnoiter. She couldn't possibly leave our son when he's just started the school year. She wants everything in place before we move out here—well, except the decorating, of course. She wouldn't leave that to me." He gave Isabelle what he hoped was a self-deprecating smile.

"She does her *own* decorating?"

All eyes turned toward Peter Franks from Omaha. He had thought it clever to mention decorating, sophisticated even. But from Isabelle's inflection, the downward slide, and then the emphasis on "own," it was clear he'd made a faux pas. "She did want me to ask around for the best decorators." He glanced at everyone before settling on Isabelle. Damn. Who knew that merely decorating wasn't enough in this fancy crowd?

"That part is easy." Isabelle smoothed the royal blue silk on her thighs. "I can put together a short list for you. But Marshall Logan, you understand, is very particular. I don't think you could even get an interview without someone meeting the whole family." She stood up, and all the men stood as well, Jeff Greenberg's chair tipping a little as he got out of it. "Do you have a

38

card?" Isabelle held out a hand to Frank.

He made a show of patting his pockets, then pulled out the card holder he'd snagged at Wardrobe. Good thing the initials were so ornate they were indecipherable.

"Let me ask around. I'll call you." Her eyes tracked the gold card holder as it made its way back into his pocket. She waved his card at him. "And I'll text you the name of the only engraver left in the city." She patted his arm, eyes glittering.

Frank hung back to let the ladies go first and found he still held his napkin. He made to put it on the coffee table but managed to drop it. He looked around with an embarrassed grin at Philippe, who lingered as well. "Whoops. Butterfingers!" He bent over to retrieve it, jabbed the button mic onto the underside of the couch, and grabbed the napkin all in one motion.

"So, Philippe," Frank said as they went down the staircase. "I didn't get a chance to talk with you. What's your line of business?"

No answer. Behind him, Philippe had a hand on the railing as if herding Frank.

"Let me guess." Frank stopped to let Philippe catch up to him, but the man paused two steps above him. He seemed a lot taller from this angle. "I'm good at this. Something financial?"

Philippe studied him for a moment as if anticipating how to catch him if he ran. He cleared his throat with a growl. "I do not believe this staircase is wide enough for two men." Philippe's voice was low and firm. "You may go ahead."

"So," Frank said over his shoulder, "does everyone here have a butler?"

Philippe just growled, paused on the steps for him to keep going.

"I mean, should I hire one once we move here? Maybe I should ask him. Ron, is it?" They paused on the landing, and Philippe eyed him with eyebrows nearly meeting. Good, he'd annoyed him. Maybe he'd give him an answer just to get rid of him. "Do you know what agency I should call?"

"Ah, there you are!" Isabelle's voice floated up to them as Philippe jutted his chin at Frank. "Glad you make friends so easily, Mr. Franks!"

Frank could listen to Isabelle's lilt all day long. He'd have to figure out

39

another way to get a last name for Ron. Hoped he'd get another chance. He bestowed his best smile on Isabelle as he shook her hand—he was very grateful for anything she could do, this has been so enjoyable, he didn't know that New Yorkers would be so friendly, thank you very much for tea.

Isabelle laughed that seductive laugh and said, "Well, maybe not all of us are so nice."

Chapter Six

"Well, there you go." Isabelle watched Ronnie clean up the tea things.

"Ma'am?" Ronnie stacked the cups and saucers, piled the linen napkins, retrieved a half-eaten cookie from the table. She felt self-conscious, her every move followed like she was a baby bird and Isabelle a cat.

"Don't call me 'ma'am.' That's for school marms and matrons. As I was saying, I've been looking for the next Object of My Affection and poof! Jeff Greenberg just brings him over. What did you think of him?"

Ronnie paused, balanced the tray. What did Isabelle expect her to say? "I'm not very good at figuring out people. If it were up to me, I would've taken all their wallets at the door and left."

Isabelle gave out a surprised laugh. "It's a good thing I'm here to teach you new skills. Okay, listen and learn."

Ronnie put the tray down and sat on the arm of a wing chair as Isabelle listed what they knew about Peter Franks. Aside from his broad shoulders and good looks (though pity about the haircut), he'd recently sold his insurance company, a $200 million deal, so he had to have some cash. Had Ronnie noticed that watch? Of course she had, though she didn't get a chance to say so since Isabelle kept talking. The school would be her hook because she sat on the board at Marshall Logan, "and everyone wants their children to go to Marshall Logan!" So, Peter Franks would be a fine complement to her social circles.

"And so naïve! Did you see him staring around the room? His mouth was practically hanging open. He sure checked you out. It's like a breath of fresh air, that Midwestern lack of sophistication. So much better than the New Yorker cynicism. Oh, I think this will be just so amusing! Let's ask him to dinner, shall we?"

* * *

The next morning, Ronnie wandered the brownstone, picked up a brochure in the living room and put it back down. Everything was already dusted, vacuumed, and polished. No dinner parties to plan, no teas to steal for. Isabelle had no instructions for her this morning, and she didn't know what to do with herself. She grabbed a rag and went upstairs, running it along the banister as she went.

She was pretty sure Isabelle was out, probably at lunch with one of her pigeons, charming him into a shopping trip afterwards, making him buy her all that expensive crap. How did that get her money, though? Did she pawn it? Sell it? Ronnie went up another flight, the carpeting muffling her footsteps, the house eerily quiet. The weird thing though, Isabelle kept these guys around, these Objects of Her Affection. They kept coming for more, even after she'd blackmailed them. According to her.

She stopped to examine the pictures in the hallway, all hunting scenes. Dogs chased a fox with men on horseback, a guy aimed a gun, dogs with pheasants in their mouths, some big guy in a pith helmet stood over a lion, his rifle broken over his knee. She dusted the tops of some of the pictures. These must've belonged to her dead husband. Nothing like this anywhere else in the house. A door down the hall was open, so of course she went to it, cocked her head, listened for signs of life in any other part of the house, then moved in to snoop around.

She stopped just inside, not understanding what she was looking at. It was like this room was trying to swallow her up. Everything was black, or maybe a deep purple, carpet, walls, ceiling. Actually, the ceiling was mirrored, and the place smelled dank, smoky, waxy. No windows, or maybe they were blocked by that big wardrobe thing. Candles were everywhere, no bed, but weirdly, a saddle, an echo of the fox hunting picture, on a stand near one wall. She pulled the door open more to let in light from the hallway, went over to the wardrobe, opened both ornate doors, causing a jangle of belts, whips, masks, paddles, cuffs—Jesuschristalmighty. This whole long con thing took way too much equipment. Hanging on the left side were leather things with chains and loops and who knew what, dildos lying in a heap, and—

"See anything you like?"

Ronnie's body jumped before she could stop it. She kept her head in the cupboard so she didn't have to see Isabelle's expression, which she was sure would be triumphant. Every day, this woman lived up even more to the nickname she'd first given her: The Feline. She moved like a cat, silent, deadly, and she probably had nine lives, too.

"I don't see the camera." Ronnie immediately wished she hadn't said anything because Isabelle was all at once behind her, boxing her in, leaning over her, a cloud of perfume, wine, garlic coming with her.

"There it is, little one." Isabelle pointed to a hole high up in the back of the cupboard. "Infrared," she breathed on Ronnie.

"Nice." Ronnie backed up, ducked out from under her boss.

"Come, I'll show you." Isabelle put a hand on her shoulder and guided her to the room next door. It was tiny, one window taking up the whole wall, the other walls painted a normal color, not that swallowing purple-black next door. The camera sat on a shelf carved into the wall, a wire ran down to a computer, and a desk chair was pushed away as if someone had just left.

"That's where Philippe likes to sit." Isabelle raised an eyebrow. "Endlessly."

"What? He's in on this?"

Isabelle smiled, a glance at the chair as if he sat in it even now, as if she were humoring him. "Let's just say he helps out where he can."

"I thought he was just one of your marks."

"Was." Isabelle swirled around in the tiny room and paused at the door, seemingly bored with the conversation.

Ronnie touched the keyboard and a picture of herself looking into the cupboard, her nose big and round, sprang up on the screen. "What the fu—"

She threw Isabelle a look.

"Motion activated." Isabelle gave a shrug, left the room, her cinnamon perfume hanging in the air as if it would also watch Ronnie without her knowing.

* * *

After she had searched in every cupboard, corner, and on every shelf in her apartment to make sure there were no hidden, infrared, motion-activated cameras, she grabbed her newsboy cap. She needed to hit the streets, clear her head. This lady was no joke. Ronnie's hand was on the doorknob when her phone buzzed. She pulled it out, but who else would it be? Isabelle gave her the phone, Isabelle was the only one who called her.

"Come upstairs. I need you to do my hair."

Not in her job description. But then, what wasn't in her job description? She hung her hat back up, headed for the stairs. Damn, nearly got away, too.

Ronnie paused in the bedroom doorway. Isabelle perched at her vanity, three mirrors reflecting her face. Amazing how each mirror could show a different person. The left side of Isabelle looked thoughtful, the right a little devious, full on the perfection of a model in a magazine, and from the back—she held up her hair as if thinking about an updo, the mousy color underneath the blonde—just ordinary.

She spotted Ronnie in the mirror but didn't turn around. "There you are. At last. Come over here so I don't have to shout."

Ronnie picked her way through various outfits on the floor. One that seemed to have made the cut lay across a terrycloth-covered ottoman. Frills and flounces and a cloud of pink spilled over the cushion, ribbons and gauzy stuff making up the short skirt. She had never seen Isabelle wear anything that girly.

"Nice Mr. Can't-Keep-It-In is taking me shopping and then dinner and I need a hair style to go with that dress." She stopped holding up her hair and eyed Ronnie in the mirror. "He likes perky."

Seemed a lot of her victims couldn't keep it in. "Perky it is then." Ronnie

44

took the brush from Isabelle. Never in her life had she brushed someone's hair. Isabelle sat tall, a princess waited on by handmaidens. The bristles glided on the surface of the long blonde hair and Ronnie made another stab at it.

"What are you doing?" Her eyes blazed at Ronnie in the mirror. "Do you even know what you're doing? Didn't you have girlfriends growing up? Played dress up, had sleepovers?" Isabelle seemed to look right through her. "No, of course you didn't. Try again."

Ronnie began to get the hang of it. She found that the harder she brushed the more Isabelle seemed to like it. She traded the brush for the comb. At least she knew how to braid from that leather-working section in shop class. She moved around her boss's head, a loose weave that she curled all up in a bun, secured with nearly all the pins from the jar on the vanity.

Isabelle picked up a large hand mirror, swung slowly around in her seat, the back of her head popping up in all three mirrors. "Get those pink rosebuds—they're on pins—out of the right-hand drawer—second one down—and let's see what effect we get."

Ronnie poked and pinned, tucked and pulled until Isabelle was satisfied and then she cemented the whole thing with some horrible hair spray that no amount of perfume could cover up. Ronnie's eyes watered.

Isabelle rose from her seat and grabbed the outfit lying on the pink ottoman.

"Don't get me wrong. I mean, I'm happy to do this, but I'm just wondering." Ronnie tracked Isabelle as she went into the closet area, a step up, every door covered in mirrors, recessed lights glowing.

A *hmmmm* came from that staging area, so Ronnie went on. "Don't people usually have their hairdressers do their hair?"

Isabelle stood there in the pink fluffy dress, turned this way and that as if she were a ballerina in a jewelry box. "Don't talk to me about hairdressers!"

Ronnie went to the pile of rejected outfits, picked up a hanger.

Isabelle twirled, the skirt flaring almost straight out. "I'm glad I've got you in the meantime, because I have to find a new hairdresser."

"What happened?" Ronnie didn't really care, but she was glad for anything that made Isabelle stop scrutinizing her.

A strangled noise came from the closet. "Put it on my tab, Henry Norton said. The bills come to the office, he said. Mary will never know, he said." She sat down at the vanity again. "We need ribbons."

Ronnie put the outfits down and went back to Isabelle, threaded skinny pale pink ribbons in bobby pins while her boss watched.

"He didn't tell me that she goes there too."

Ronnie pulled out some of the satin rosebuds and jabbed little ribbons in their place.

"So, when I went to pay, a new girl was there, wasn't she. Started loudly asking questions. Well," she shook her head, making the ribbons dance, "I couldn't very well say," she swept a slender arm through the air, "'Put it on Mr. Henry Norton's account.'" She picked up a tiny brush, like a toothbrush for a cat, leaned closer to the mirror and flicked it over her eyebrows. "With his wife standing right there." She leaned back to admire her work. "And what do you think she says to me?"

Ronnie shook her head.

"*Oh,* she says, *we must get together! Henry would love to see you!*" Isabelle caught Ronnie's eyes in the mirror. Went back to her brushing. "Wouldn't that be a lovely threesome."

Ronnie scanned the room to get rid of that image. Isabelle rose and rummaged in the closet. She had seen her boss put on all kinds of outfits, become all kinds of different people, though usually slinky, a quiet elegance with that look in her eye—like she knew what you were thinking and didn't care, calculating how to use it to her advantage. But now, Isabelle seemed smaller, cuter, playful, and a little bit silly.

She twirled again in front of the mirrors. "This is perfect. He'll just die for this look, and I'll get him to buy me tons of things" She opened a mirrored door, slid clothes across the rod. "Let's see, I need to get something for Thursday night's dinner...he can take me to Bergdorf's..."

"Who's this guy? Doesn't Philippe care?"

Isabelle closed the doors and twirled around, then stopped to put on shoes, pink flats, a bow at the toe. "Philippe?" She laughed, long and musical.

46

"Philippe has nothing to do with this. Why would he?" She kicked a foot behind her and held it, turning her head to peer in the mirror. "This one is just an Object of My Affection. Too easy really, but he just keeps coming back, desperately calling, even after I told him I had it recorded for my own protection." She turned to Ronnie, fluttered her lashes, her voice high. "A girl's got to watch out for her reputation, after all."

Ronnie instantly pictured the whole scene: the coyness, the innocent little girl look, the helplessness, the man feeling protective rather than taken, so into Isabelle he couldn't let her go.

"So." Isabelle flicked something off her shoulder. "Every time he called, I suggested lunch, made sure he had a lot to drink, then hinted at going shopping. Now we just go straight to the shopping." She wiggled her hips, making the ruffles on the skirt and the ribbons on her head jiggle, and then she threw out a large throaty laugh, one not at all perky.

Chapter Seven

"So can you still breathe?"

"What d'ya mean?" Frank took a bite of his overloaded sandwich, chewed. He would never tire of this: cream cheese, slabs of pimento, sprouts, basil, Swiss, spinach, Russian dressing, on eight-grain bread. He eyed his partner.

"Spending all that time in the rarefied air of the Upper East Side."

He and Pete sat at their usual bench in the park, the air warm for fall, a few leaves blowing around.

"What have you come up with?"

Pete took a swig from his can of Coke and then burped, a large, wet sound. "Must be nice up there at all the parties while I'm at my desk drying out my eyeballs with the research."

"Boo-hoo. Just tell me you've found something."

"Okay." Pete turned his sandwich around, examined it from all sides. He started to take a bite then, thankfully stopped himself before he spoke. "I ran all those names and the only one that's interesting at all was the Philippe guy. Seems he went from Phillip Reynolds to Philippe Reynard when he was in his mid-twenties, then hung out a shingle and has been a money manager ever since." He pulled a piece of his bread crust off and threw it at a pigeon.

"Good grief, don't do that. Now they'll swarm us." The pigeon pecked at the bread for a minute, and others waddled over to see what he had. "Any reason for the name change?"

Pete shook his head, bit into his sandwich, then threw another piece out. "Nope. Nothing in any database." A shrug. "Maybe he just liked the sound of it."

They watched the pigeons for a beat, the padding and shuffling, the cooing and pecking.

"He pledges and gives to everyone: the Opera, the Ballet, The Met, MOMA, Lincoln Center—you name it, he's on their list, and I can't see where that money's coming from." Pete chewed.

"All charities for the rich."

"My kids like going to the museums. I'm not rich."

"Richer than he is." Frank pointed with his chin at the homeless man rolled up on the bench in the park across the street. "Anything on Ward, a.k.a. 'Mickey' McAllister?"

Pete shook his head. "A lot of traffic tickets, fender benders."

"Must be why he has a driver. And everyone else?"

"Just run-of-the-mill Upper East Side, clubs, sinecure jobs, Ladies Who Lunch."

"I suppose you think you're not being sexist."

"I'm not the one being sexist—they're the ones being sexist. None of the wives have jobs."

"What about Ron? Any luck on that?"

Pete balled up the bag from the deli and threw it toward the garbage can. In all the years he'd known him, his partner had never landed anything in a trashcan.

"I ran everything I could think of tied to that address. Ronald, Ronson, Ronford, Ronan. Even Oberon, but no luck. Nothing without a last name."

Frank half wished it would have turned out to be Oberon—the kid seemed like a mischievous sprite. As if they had agreed out loud, they stood up at the same time, headed as one to the sidewalk, a walk around before returning to the office. He would have to find another way into Newsboy.

"What about the house?" Pete jabbed the button to cross the street.

"What about it?"

"Can we hack it? That button mic didn't give us much."

"At least we know Peter Franks will be asked to dinner." They waited for the pedestrian symbol to turn white. "As I said in the report, it's not a smart house, no video doorbell, no panel, probably old-fashioned refrigerator too. Like she spends all her money on her clothes and jewelry instead of the house. No upgrades for a long time."

"I didn't find any construction permits since her husband bought it in '99." Pete kicked a paper cup into the gutter and kept walking, then stopped to watch as Frank turned around to retrieve it, holding it by the lid until he could find a trash can.

"What's a place like that worth?"

"Assessed this year at $12 mil, $20k a quarter in property taxes."

Frank let out a low whistle.

"I don't see how you can live in Manhattan. Stupid expensive."

"At least I don't have a long commute." Frank knew Pete spent at least an hour each way, stayed over if a case ran late, sometimes on Frank's couch. "So, is that why she buys the Oxy? To sell it? What do her bank records look like?"

Pete loved nothing better than to ferret around, especially in people's finances, and he hoped this would be interesting. "So, wouldn't you think," Pete shifted away as someone going the other way walked between them, "that a person at an address like that would have huge balances, lots of cash, lots of securities?"

Frank gave a shrug. "Sure."

They crossed with the crowd and Pete waited until they hit the sidewalk to continue. "Me too. Not much there." They went single file for a bit, the garbage bags waiting for pickup narrowing the sidewalk. "So, I went back five years to when her husband died, 2010, thinking maybe they had separate accounts or something, y'know." They paused as a delivery guy with a stack of insulated bags maneuvered his way across the sidewalk. "Funny thing is," Pete continued, "her cash balances barely changed after he died."

"Whaddya make of that?" They headed east, still some time before they needed to return to the office.

"Conrad Anderson must've been all hat and no cattle. He had the house, which he left her of course, and very little else. She had some securities, but she sold them steadily until they were gone."

"Anything on her personally?"

They waited for a garbage truck blocking the sidewalk to finish emptying a dumpster. The screech of the machinery drowned out Pete's words.

"—father unknown, mother in Greenwich, same address as Mark Matthews III—"

"Hold on." Frank stopped next to a store window, which was papered over like so many others, unable to compete with Amazon. He put a hand on Pete's arm. "You mean to tell me that our High Society Hostess is illegitimate? Boy howdy! Wonder if anyone else knows that."

"Besides her mother, you mean." Pete was in motion again. "Why would it matter?"

"To our case or to the Upper East Side?"

Pete shrugged next to him, then squared his shoulders and stared straight ahead, waiting for the guy poking his phone to run into him.

"Just might come in handy, that's all." Frank grinned as the guy stopped short of running into Pete, though he didn't apologize, just sidestepped and then returned the glazed look to his screen, poking, poking, poking.

Frank's own phone pinged, his personal ringtone set to just one note, and he pulled it out. "Susan," Frank said into the phone. She never called him.

Pete gave him a wave and headed down the street.

"Oh, Frank—It's—" Susan began crying and he turned toward the building as if he could give her privacy that way. It must be bad if she'd called him instead of a girlfriend.

"What is it? Can you talk? Where are you? I'll come there."

"I'm home," she whispered, and Frank was already walking, his other arm up for a cab. "I had to leave work, I just couldn't—" She started crying again.

"I'll be there in fifteen minutes. Hang on, okay?"

Her sobbing became louder and then it was muffled like she turned away from the phone. He gave up on finding a cab and ran to the subway entrance, dodged people on the sidewalks, wished he could fly, tried not to think what would cause her so much distress, and knew in his gut the only thing that would make her cry so hard.

51

"Do you want me to stay on the phone with you until I get there?" Frank hit the Canal Street station and raced down the stairs to the 4/5/6, swiped his Metro Card, and pushed the rotating arm the second it clicked.

"No…" Her voice sounded so far away, and Frank's first impulse was to take away the torment. But it would be his agony too, as soon as she told him what had happened.

"Are you sure? I can keep the phone to my ear. I'm on the subway. I'll be there in twenty minutes."

"Twenty? But you said—" Susan's voice cracked. Frank waited and she said, her voice fading at the end, "…call me when you get here…" A pocket of silence, then the line went dead.

The subway doors closed, and he leaned against them, automatically surveyed the car, noted the people, the exits, and wondered if he would ever stop doing that. The lunch crowd had thinned somewhat, though the car was still sprinkled with suits, newspapers, briefcases, but not the crush of bodies that made you wonder if you should stop ironing your shirts, stop getting your suits pressed.

What could've happened with Cathy that made Susan cry so hard? Wasn't she safely behind bars, as it were, the rehab place looking out for her? They hadn't let them visit at first, told them they needed to get her detoxed, get her started on therapy. At times, they had said, parents could cause a setback—as if this were their fault. Susan had flashed him a look as if she thought exactly that. His fault. She had no idea.

The train slowed and he looked through the windows opposite, his reflection thrown back at him, no station in sight. Keep going, please keep going. He couldn't get stuck in the tunnel. He would have to call Susan, she'd think he was making excuses, avoiding the whole situation. Well, he wished he could.

They stopped. Maybe it would be short. It would start up again. He looked at his watch. Nothing he could do about it, except wait. He went to the end of the car, through the doors, out onto the plates between the cars. He grabbed the bar grip and held on to the chain linking the cars, stuck his head out, looking down the tracks, as if he could get any indication of what was stopping them, when they'd start moving again. The damp air swaddled him, a dripping nearby, the rumble and screech of other trains filling the darkness. He could leap down, avoid the third rail, the rats and puddles, and walk to the next station. Just get his leg over the chain, take the step down, leap onto the neighboring tracks, hope the train didn't lurch …nuts, the train would move soon, he didn't need to put himself in that much danger.

* * *

By the time he stood at the door to Susan's apartment building, waiting for her to let him in, more than an hour had passed since her call. Susan buzzed him in the front door with an angry noise that she held longer than he needed. Great. He took the stairs, not because it was faster but because he needed to prepare himself mentally for whatever waited for him. He wouldn't be able to stand that crickety elevator, lurching through each floor, old cooking smells and moldy carpeting hitting him as the doors opened. The cement stairs had their own smells—dust, urine, a faint tinge of rot. Even in the nicer buildings you couldn't hide the dross of people's lives. Finally, he stood at the door to the apartment, out of breath, shoulders rising and lowering as his lungs filled and emptied. His old apartment to which he had no key.

* * *

He found it impossible to sit as she talked, the story coming in between tears and deep breaths, anguished cries of "Oh Frank!" and "What are we going to do?" He went to the window, twitched aside the old curtains, then paced the tiny living room, avoided Susan curled up on the couch, hit the kitchen for water for her, for him. He reached for his phone, the impulse strong to solve it immediately, but Susan protested. "You're not listening!" and he put it away.

She wound down and her sobs turned to snuffles, her eyes on Frank pleading. He sat down in the armchair, his elbows on his knees, his phone in his hand, the coffee table in front of him strewn with wadded Kleenex. It punched him in the gut. Cathy had run away from the rehab facility. He would process that later, but right now he had to act. "I have to start calling people." He made sure he had her attention. "We have to start now within this window before she can get too far."

"Who? Who will you call?" She stood up and took a step, paused, sat down. "I can't have the entire city knowing that our daughter—" She got up again and went into the kitchen and Frank heard water filling the kettle, the click of the stove, cupboards opening and closing. "No one even knew she was *in* rehab!" She shouted these last words at him, and Frank thought at least the neighbors would now know.

He waited for her to return to the couch, fighting the urge to crowd her in the kitchen, point out how unreasonable she was being. She needed his patience now, and he needed them to be a team. She brought two mugs, set one down in front of him among the balled up Kleenex.

He made his voice quiet, reasonable. "Have you called the hospitals yet?" She shook her head.

"Okay, we'll start with them. But otherwise, I have to call people." He paused to take a sip, take a measure of her over the rim of the mug, then placed it down. "Tell me how we find her otherwise. Susan, I'm in law enforcement. I have resources available to me. What good is my job to us—it split up our marriage, and now you don't think I should use it to find Cathy?"

"Oh, I don't know! How did this even happen? How can their security be so lax!"

They went on like this for a while, the dance they had perfected when they had been married, Frank logical, Susan sure he had no emotions. He made his case, wished he didn't have to spend the time, knew she had to get there thinking it was her idea. He nudged her along to the only conclusion available, she edged toward him with compromises ("What if we just alert the Staten Island police?", "Just the head of school, not teachers too!", "Only her friends, not the entire school. And no parents!"). She gave up where she could, he ceded ground, itched for his phone, knowing the longer it took, the harder it would be.

As soon as he made sure they were on the same side, he went through his contact list, called in favors, not caring who at the Bureau knew, told everyone the story, even people he didn't know well. They all said the same thing: they would help in any way they could, send them a recent picture, but you know the odds. A female teenage runaway in a city this size. Have you checked with her friends, her school? Anyone he could think of, he called, scaring her friends, sympathy-but-not-my-problem from her school. He had to get out, go. It had already been more than twelve hours, an unconscionable delay on the part of the rehab place, but he would deal with them later.

He called a friend to come sit with Susan, and he left, stopped to get Cathy's picture printed up, then worked his way south, hit homeless shelters, showed her picture. He got too many headshakes. He asked them where he should look, shrugs, an "LES" thrown over a shoulder as a volunteer rushed away. He was headed for the Lower East Side anyway, St. Marks Place, a favorite hangout for homeless, runaways, and kids with nothing else to do.

Evening came on, and the people he approached melted into the shadows. The ones who didn't were too stoned to make sense, but he left them Cathy's picture with his phone number on it anyway. He saw a few drug dealers as he made his way through the park., Too bad he wasn't the kind of guy who would take them out, one sharp hit in the right place…He hated them more than he ever had, and he imagined his fist contacting a jaw, the crunch of bone on bone before the guy went down.

He headed home. He believed in law and order, just like Pete had said, so no beating people up. He would scour the streets looking for Cathy, and the hard work would pay off. It had to. Tomorrow, he'd interview her friends one by one, grill them—at least he knew how to do that—pick them off, get them to point to the next person until he found whatever classmate it had been that she got high with. His stomach was in knots, but he ignored it. He knew he wouldn't be sleeping and so he would type up what he knew, what he had done so far, what he could do next. If he kept moving, kept trying, then he wouldn't have to take the idea of Cathy's running away to its logical conclusion, the final end of a long line of bad decisions, not all of them hers.

Chapter Eight

Ronnie's head was in the refrigerator when she heard Isabelle call her name. So much for not shouting in the house. She grabbed some grapes that had garnished a tray at the last party and chewed fast while she hit the stairs and wondered what Isabelle needed so urgently. She found her in her office, at her tiny desk, scowling. Ronnie wiped her hands on her pants.

"Ma'am?"

Isabelle threw some eye daggers at her and then peered at her computer like it had said something offensive to her. She clicked a couple of times then said, "We need more parties. More donations. This city is so greedy, I swear. And what do I get for all these taxes? Nothing. And the utility bills! Have you been turning on the heat?" Isabelle's eyes bulged at her over the laptop, the white glowing apple where her heart should be.

Ronnie shook her head. The leaves hadn't even started to change.

"These bills are going to be the death of me. Honestly. How fast can you throw a party together?"

"For tonight?"

Isabelle nodded, then clicked some more.

"It's already four o'clock. Can you ask people this late?"

Isabelle's eyes narrowed, brows down. "Of course I can! Who do you think I am? People are waiting in line for an invitation from me. Just you watch. You get the linens, flowers, food, candles, and I'll get the people. Can I ask people this late? Honestly."

The last bit was said more to herself than to Ronnie, and she paused to see if that was it. After no more words, just mutterings at the screen, Ronnie figured she'd been dismissed, and she ran down the stairs to grab shopping bags. Hunter-gatherers had it easier than she did.

* * *

"Linens for the table. A runner, this time, if you can get it. You know what that is, don't you?" The next morning, Isabelle raced through what she needed for yet another dinner that night, and Ronnie listened as fast as she could. "Napkins, of course," Isabelle continued, "hopefully matching the runner."

Ronnie wrote "runner" and "napkins" on a clean page in the small leather notebook Isabelle had given her for this very purpose.

"Check the candle supply. We need lots of votive candles so nobody can see, and speaking of that, if you can get a large flower arrangement, all the better. This is Peter Franks' first dinner party, and if he spends the evening stuck behind some greenery, he'll be relieved when I turn the charm on him." Isabelle stretched, the silk bathrobe fluttering around her. As her arms came down, she gazed at Ronnie, as if she knew Ronnie had been watching and wondered what she was thinking.

"Speaking of Peter Franks, set the table with the gold flatware." She arched an eyebrow. "You know what I mean, don't you? Here, come with me."

Ronnie trailed her up the stairs to the dining room where she opened the square door on the side table, pulled out a sturdy box with narrow drawers. She slid one open, lifted a brown cloth. Nestled together, each in their own slot sat spoon after gleaming spoon, all in gold. Ronnie surprised herself by gasping out loud. She reached toward one. "Are they real?"

Isabelle let the cloth drop before Ronnie's finger could touch one, and Ronnie pulled back as if she'd been stung.

"Of course they're real! Who do you think I am?" She lifted the cloth again as if to make sure they were still there and then, not taking her eyes off them, said, "Left to me by the great Mrs. Sandhurst Norris, thank God."

"Who's that?"

Her boss stared at the gleaming gold like it was pirate treasure. "What?" Isabelle dropped the cloth and closed the drawer. "She's famous. Everyone knows her."

Ronnie shook her head.

"Only the most renowned doyenne of Upper East Side society! Everyone was just dying for an invitation to her parties. She was like a mother to me when I first came to the city. I was her personal assistant. She couldn't do anything without me." She turned to go out of the dining room and then paused, scanning Ronnie up and down. "She loved me so much she gave me her Board seat at Marshall Logan." Isabelle went out the door, her voice louder as she walked away, "and I have her Rolodex!" She laughed like she had won something, and Ronnie followed that laughter back down the stairs.

In the kitchen, Ronnie continued her notetaking while Isabelle paced, as if the gold flatware had made her restless. "What kind of food should I look for?" She hoped Isabelle would decide this time to order it in, like she did for the two of them.

Isabelle stopped pacing. "What do you think you can get?"

Ronnie opened her mouth, then closed it. She was pretty sure Isabelle didn't mean dumpster diving. Isabelle eyed her. Ronnie smoothed down her hair, wondered if some of it stuck up at weird angles.

"You're a quick thinker," Isabelle said. "You'll figure something out. Steak or something. No. Find lobster. That'll impress them and be awkward enough to keep them on edge. But don't get enough for ten. I want them to drink too much wine. And check the cellar; I'm not sure what I have." She stopped talking, and Ronnie looked up from her notebook. "You know, don't you, that you only serve red wine with red meat? And with lobster we'll need white?"

Ronnie scribbled some words in her notebook. Way too complicated to have money. So many rules to remember, so many extra things like tablecloths and candles and flowers and two spoons and three forks and serve from the left. Or was it from the right?

Isabelle left the kitchen without saying anything else and Ronnie figured they were done, went down to her apartment to get shopping bags, tucked the list into her pocket. At least the Oxy supply was fine, no need to go to that weird supplier way over on York. So many street people she had to hit up before she was even allowed to ring the buzzer to his apartment. At least you could trust him, not like the dealers her brother would meet in the bathroom at the Central Park Zoo, who would disappear or dip into their own inventory and do stupid things to bring the cops. She hated drugs. But she guessed what she'd learned on the streets came in handy now that she worked for Isabelle.

Turns out a restaurant/fish market actually called The Lobster Place waited for Ronnie and her list over in Chelsea. She timed it for the lunch hour crush, and though it took her a subway and a bus and half an hour, it was totally worth it. Great piles of lobsters rested on cloudy ice, a glass wall between Ronnie and Isabelle's dinner menu. While the workers shouted at each other and raced to fill orders, she reached over and snagged several, stuffed them in the shopping bag, reached for more.

A woman behind her shouted, "Hey! You can't do that! I'm next in line!" The grating voice caught the attention of the guy behind the counter, so Ronnie sped up and disappeared into the crowd, Isabelle's tote bag banging against her leg, full of six lobsters, still alive. Guess she'd have to learn how to cook.

On the subway, she peeked into the bag and watched them as they waved their rubber-banded claws around, the protruding black eyeballs and little red antennas all in motion, and she felt kinda sorry for them. How long could they go, not in the water, away from their home, and stuck in the bottom of Isabelle's canvas tote? One of them tried to climb up the side, and she shut the bag on it, glanced around. Everyone minded their own business, paying attention to a book or magazine or a phone, headphones blocking out the world, eyes averted even if they had been watching her watch the lobsters. Only the crazies made eye contact or the muggers, something people learned real quick when they first came to the city.

Back at the brownstone, she shoved the poor things into one of the empty drawers in Isabelle's refrigerator. They crawled over each other in slow but determined movements. Time must move differently for them, one dominating the other in the time it would take her to run five cross-town blocks. Wouldn't that be great if your enemies chased you in lobster time, and you got to leave them behind in human time. She pulled out her phone and searched how to cook lobsters. Isabelle gave her like nanoseconds to throw a dinner party together.

Chapter Nine

Peter Franks found himself once more in Isabelle Anderson's living room, the lights low and the curtains drawn. Frank was glad to shut out the world outside, glad to focus on work. On the walk over, his thoughts were flooded with Cathy. He conjured images of her as a child, that cute way she would tilt her head at him when he said something silly, put her tiny hand, starfish straight, over his mouth. Two blocks from the brownstone he drew out Peter Franks, shot his cuffs, used the thin Piaget watch to remind himself of his role.

Tonight, Peter and the other guests milled around, Ron moving among them with a tray of drinks and hors d'oeuvres. Still no last name and no way to run a search on him. Frank played with the idea of getting a fingerprint, though how to do it without stealing one of Isabelle Anderson's heavy crystal cocktail glasses...

The same crowd he'd met at the tea were here, along with Jeff's wife Rachel, and an Amelia Harburger. He made a mental note to ask Pete to do a background check on them later. He entertained himself by attaching his own backgrounds to each couple, who belonged to the Colony Club, the Knickerbocker, or The Explorers; who had a house at Fishers Island or The Hamptons; which one had gone to Harvard, Smith, or Yale. The Silver Fox made his usual late appearance, stag, and Frank figured he was his date. Had to be Yale. Or maybe Trinity.

Jeff Greenberg greeted Mickey the Silver Fox, the conversation floating over to Frank. He heard Fishers Island mentioned, congratulated himself for guessing correctly. *I see you have a driver now* Jeff said, Mickey nodding, turning his back on Frank. *One close call enough*...Frank couldn't catch the rest as Ron the Butler cleared his throat and held up a tray for him.

He looked it over. Was this some sort of statement that he was missing, like one of those pieces of art that everyone understood but him? A plate full of carrot sticks crowded by mystery drinks sporting paper umbrellas. He shrugged and took a carrot, studied Ron as he did. Such feminine features, maybe transitioning, maybe they didn't even have the right name for him/her. Mental note to tell Pete.

"Don't mind if I do. So, Ron, is it? Didya grow up here?"

Ron gave a slight bow and said, "Sir." Then backed away to offer the tray to Philippe. Frank crunched down on the carrot. Philippe held on to his drink with the umbrella, brown puppy dog eyes glued to Isabelle. Why did he change his name? Something to hide? But no priors on Phillip Reynolds, no other departments local or federal looking into him.

Rachel Greenberg, petite, quivering, reminded Frank of a bird ready to fly off at the first startle, approached and said hello. He asked her about herself, listening while his agent radar tracked Philippe. He asked Rachel if she knew Philippe. Only slightly, she remarked. She told him that he was a money manager and a huge patron of the arts, someone their hostess seemed to be interested in, based on how often he was showing up at her dinner parties lately.

"She entertains a lot, does she?" Frank gestured around the room with his carrot stick. "Does everyone in New York have a butler?" Rachel giggled nervously at this and shook her head.

"He's new. I've only been seeing him the last couple of parties. Leave it to Isabelle to make a big statement with a butler!"

Frank told her he was looking to move here, wondered if he should have a butler, how you go about finding one.

"You'll have to ask Isabelle that one," Rachel turned to her husband who had just joined them. "Won't he, Jeff?"

He laughed loudly, heads in the living room turning briefly, and then he leaned toward Frank, his voice low. "Her husband must've left her more than I thought, for her to hire a butler."

"Well now." Frank flattened his vowels. "I wouldn't want to bother her, maybe I should ask—" he gestured toward Ron, hand stuttering as if he couldn't remember his name.

"Ron." Rachel nodded.

"Ron, uh…does he have a last name?"

"Why?" Rachel shook her head. "No one knows the help's last name. Just ask Isabelle which agency she used."

Isabelle announced dinner and led the way out of the living room and across the hall. Peter Franks, ever the gentleman, let everyone go first into the dining room, and Frank paused to scan the layout, note where the doors were, take in the scene. White tablecloth, delicate crystal champagne flutes and water goblets, gold flatware and a large gold plate at each setting.

For a second, he considered how much more straightforward going undercover on the streets with a meth dealer would be. This looked like major bullshit, all the small candles everywhere, how was a person supposed to see what they were eating, who they were talking to? A street dealer would be more honest. But, he reminded himself coming into the room, this is what Peter Franks needed—upper-crust New York City—to make his wife happy. Isabelle was already seated at the head, Cleopatra-like, untouchable, eyes that missed nothing. The only empty seat called to him on her right, and Frank edged his way around the table. How would she fit everyone in if she wanted dinner for ten? He watched the backs of the chairs, tried to avoid the shelves where the candles were. Last thing he needed was to set himself on fire.

"Isabelle," he said, "St. Patrick's Cathedral has nothing on you. All these nice candles!"

Someone, maybe Amelia Harburger said, sotto voce, "More like Midnight in the Garden of Good and Evil!"

If Isabelle heard, she ignored it, patted his arm as he sat down, and let her hand linger so that he had to take up his napkin with his other one. He reminded himself that Peter Franks, a married man in the big city on his own, would flirt without crossing the line. Flirtation seemed to be Isabelle's M.O. so far and he would have to figure out just where that line lay. He surveyed the array in front of him, glad there were only two forks and two spoons, a quantity he thought he could handle. He didn't know you could make a place setting out of gold. Even the champagne in the glass seemed tinged with gold and he took a sip, curious. Nothing cheap about that bubbly.

Ron placed bowls of something white in front of each guest, and the table resumed their conversations, a soft murmuring and words here and there reached Frank as he picked up a gold spoon.

Isabelle leaned over the corner between them, a musky perfume floating his way. "Peter, you must tell me all about the insurance business." The words came on her breath, her eyes intent as if it were the only thing she cared about right now. Like what he was about to say would be the key to everything. "Was it large-scale, or would you cover my house?" The softness of her tone, her emphasis on "cover," sent an image into his brain of wrapping a soft blanket around bare skin, the skin of a woman's body, in fact. What kind of magic did his hostess have command of?

He tasted his soup to ground himself and then put down his spoon. She would wait for his answer forever, it seemed. "Most people find insurance boring," he said. Which was why he picked it. In his experience no one ever asked for particulars if you said *insurance*. "Tell me," he gave her his best smile, "what do you spend your time doing when you're not hosting these enjoyable events?"

"Tell him about your foundation," Philippe said across from him. Frank thought he had cleared his throat after he spoke, but it sounded animal-like, a rumble deep down.

Peter Franks raised an eyebrow in question at his hostess, and Isabelle studied her untouched bowl of soup, her long lashes then fluttering up at him, shy, as if she weren't used to having the spotlight on her.

"A foundation? Charitable?" He could coax too.

She nodded. A small smile, eyes lit up.

"Tell me about it." Peter Franks smiled. "What or who does it benefit?"

He didn't have to fake his interest as she talked, etching into his brain all the details so he could research this later. She was quite persuasive on all the good things music did for children, painted a wondrous picture of lifting them out of their poverty, giving them hope—

"This is quite an amazing thing you're doing. What country is it?"

Philippe's deep guttural came across the table at him. "You should donate. I have. You should give her a check."

Frank turned to Isabelle whose eyes were shining at him like a true believer. "Do you have a brochure?" He shook his head. "I don't normally travel with a checkbook."

"Oh," she said, loud enough for the rest of the table, "you are a saint! Everyone, Peter is donating to my foundation! Isn't that wonderful?"

* * *

The rest of dinner played out in a cacophony of conversation and silver, or rather gold, on china, the volume increasing as the champagne kept coming. It seemed to Frank that his glass was constantly full, and by the time Ron had placed the top half of a lobster in front of him, he was at a loss as to how to deal with it politely. All he wanted was more to drink. He had no idea how to document how much he'd had for his report about tonight.

In the living room, he settled into the soft couch, watched everyone else as they stood around. He must've gotten more of the champagne than they had. This couch, so inviting, like it would curl itself around him, lull him while he listened to the murmuring in the room…he closed his eyes…His brain yelled at him, he struggled to sit up straight, the cushions swallowing him up as he pushed against them.

He was on a case, his brain said, the words floating away as he grabbed for them, tried to make them hold still. Oxy. He was supposed to be hunting for drugs here. He surveyed the room, decided it would be easier to look sideways than straight on, people blurring then coming back into focus. He struggled to sit up again, the couch cushions swamping him, and he felt like he moved through water. Water. He made it to his feet and wandered to the bar, leaned over it to ask Ron for a glass of water, held on to the edge while he waited, his eyes on Ron as he left the room.

The butler was taking an awfully long time. Frank opened the door to the hallway, but there he was, Frank's way blocked by a tray holding a single glass of water. He took the glass, drained it, nothing feeling so good as that water sliding down his throat, floating off to dilute his cells. He hiccupped.

"Oh, excuse me. Could I bother you for another one? And the bathroom?"

The butler, still in the hallway, gestured at a narrow door hiding in the paneling, and Frank aimed toward it, hoping he wasn't too big to get through it.

After all his ablutions, Frank felt better, though he didn't think the tiny towel he had to use to dry his face and hands was big enough. He perused himself in the mirror. You could never catch yourself looking somewhere else while you looked in the mirror. He took another pink Lilliputian towel out of the basket, ran it over his face, cleaned off the mirror, caught sight of his, rather Peter Frank's Piaget gold watch. He told himself he would use that as his reminder that he was undercover, that he would never again drink this much at Isabelle Anderson's, that he had a job to do.

He squared his shoulders and faced the door, reached for the clear glass knob. It turned, but the door wouldn't budge. Had he been locked in? He rattled the handle and pushed on the door. Pulled on the door. Why would someone lock him in here? He shook the knob, then remembered the lock underneath. He flipped it, heard the satisfying click of the old-fashioned weighty metal, swung the door open, stepped onto the carpet, and almost collided with Philippe.

Philippe let out a growl, and Frank took a step back. "Oh, sorry sport. Didn't see you there."

"Everyone is leaving." Philippe's gaze locked onto Frank.

"Well, then I must say goodbye to my lovely hostess as well." Frank made a move toward the staircase, but Philippe blocked him, his shoulders broader than Frank remembered. Frank shook his head to clear it. "Did you ever play football?" Frank made a show of looking him over. Frank was taller than he was, but Philippe was definitely wider. "Let me guess, defense?"

"College. Defensive Back." Philippe had to look up to meet his eyes. "How much should Isabelle put you down for?"

Frank cocked his head in a question, peered over the big guy's shoulder to calculate an escape route.

"Your pledge. At dinner Isabelle said you'd give $50,000."

"She did? Oh, well, I'm not usually in the habit of donating before I know more about it." Frank moved to one side. He would have to crab walk to get around the big guy. This defensive back who turned out to be more than just a dinner guest. But Peter Franks needed to make nice so he added, "I'll take a look at the brochure and I'm sure I'll probably be interested."

"Ah, there you are! Is this the after-party?" Isabelle's singsong made them both turn. Philippe stayed close to Frank. "Shall I tell Ron to stop cleaning up?" How had he not heard her approach?

"Philippe and I were just talking about you." Frank edged away from him.

"How interesting! Do tell."

Philippe cleared his throat, the growl even more pronounced than before. Isabelle had hold of Philippe's arm, and she gave it a little shake.

"Oh, come now," she said, eyes on Philippe's, "you'll scare our guest." It seemed to Frank that a secret message had passed between them, and he now knew for sure his case would be including Philippe as well. "Shall we have more libations? We'll chase Ron out of the living room, and we can—"

"I'd better take my leave." Frank gave her a slight bow. "It's been quite an evening, but it's getting late." He made a show of looking at his watch, and as he glanced back up, he caught Isabelle looking at it. He grinned at her. "I've had a really nice time tonight. Next time I hope you can tell me more about Marshall Logan's."

"Ah. Marshall Logan. Yes. We never did talk about that. Well, maybe lunch?" Her eyes sparkled at him as if they were the ones sharing a secret.

"And you'll bring your checkbook this time." Philippe raised an eyebrow at Frank, but Isabelle cut in before he could respond.

"Oh, Philippe, let's not talk about boring old business." Her musical laugh tugged Frank in.

Surely he could think of some amusing things so he could hear it again and again.

"Besides," Isabelle let go of Philippe and linked her arm in Frank's, "Peter is a gentleman," she said over her shoulder at Philippe, "and a gentleman always keeps his promises." She maneuvered them to the staircase, and she paused at the top. For a quick second Frank half wondered if she meant to throw him down it. Or kiss him. "Doesn't he." She released his arm and went ahead of him down the stairs, laughing that lovely laugh, not looking back at him, leaving him to follow and wonder what had just happened.

* * *

Back at his apartment he drank glass after glass of water, straight from the tap, the best water in the country. His apartment felt small, bare, a little seedy. From habit he went back over his evening as if writing up his report, naming everyone who had been there, mentally flagging the new guests for further research. The candles, the champagne, the way his suit moved with him as if made for him. The high-toned conversation about art exhibits and orchestras, Broadway openings and some famous chef's new restaurant. The gossip about marriages, affairs, divorces, summer houses, vacations. The way Isabelle made him feel that every word he spoke was all she wanted to listen to.

He put his glass in the sink and went to his bedroom. Well, Cinderella, time to take off these fine things, keep them safe, shake out the wrinkles so they're ready for the next time. He wasn't sleepy yet and went back to the living room, sat down on the couch.

The couch where Cathy had tried to detox herself, curled in a ball and screaming in pain, then hallucinating, thrashing, fighting him off. His stomach knotted, and he got up, went to the window. He peered down at the street, moved closer to the pane, angled his head to see if there was any activity on First. Everything just went on per usual, the city not caring his daughter was out there somewhere.

And it was his fault. That evening, before the accident, she'd been so mad at him because he didn't want her to go out dressed in the flimsy top—a slip, really, meant for wearing underneath. She'd changed, but she'd flung herself out of his apartment, her angry stomps echoing down the stairwell. If they hadn't had a fight, she would've been paying attention, his voice friendly in her ear, urging caution. But a big silver car had come out of nowhere, speeding, running the red light, hitting Cathy, and throwing her—he went to the kitchen and splashed his face with cold water. Nobody had seen a license plate. Could only report the size and color.

Too late to go out and distribute her picture, the city all rolled up, the street sweepers out, the garbage trucks making their rounds. He had kept his thoughts about Cathy, about the whole situation, at bay for the few hours he'd been at Isabelle's, and he half wished he could go back there, lose himself in the gold flatware and Isabelle's laughter. His gut clenched and he headed to the bedroom, wondering if the two or three hours of sleep he might get would be worth it, hoping he didn't dream.

Chapter Ten

Ronnie got up early the next morning. She needed to get the living room cleaned up before Isabelle saw it. She hadn't gotten enough sleep, but maybe a nap would be on her schedule today. As long as Isabelle didn't decide at the last minute she was hosting another damn tea.

Jeez. How could only eight people make such a mess? They were supposedly fancy, high society, but they left balled-up napkins, plates, glasses, coffee cups, half-eaten slices of cake all over the place. She surveyed the room, planned her line of attack. It seemed like forty people had been there. What had Isabelle done before Ronnie had come along? She'd bet her last nickel Philippe didn't do the work. It seemed Isabelle saved him for other things.

She started at the bar, put opened bottles of club soda, tonic, Diet Coke in the trash, hated the waste, but knew they were now flat, and Isabelle would never use them. She piled a bunch of stuff on the big silver tray, kept her nose away from the sticky glasses, used napkins, death by chocolate cake everyone seemed to have taken exactly one bite of. She nearly dropped it.

"I thought we'd discussed the rule of always cleaning up the night before, not the morning after."

Ronnie set the tray down, straightened up, turned toward the doorway to see Isabelle sail in, floor length white gauze trailing after her, reminding Ronnie of that scene in *The Titanic*, the wind blowing Kate Winslet around.

"And for Godsakes don't drop that. I don't think either of us can afford it."

* * *

After she'd carried the tray down the stairs, finding each carpeted step with her heel, making sure she was squarely on it before finding the next one, she'd run back up, partly for the release, partly to show Isabelle how hard she was working, but Isabelle was nowhere in sight.

She made several more careful trips and now had everything in the kitchen. She stood in the doorway of the living room, surveyed it one last time. The brochures lay on the side table, and she went over to gather them up, put them in their box. They were pretty slick-looking, and she studied one to try to figure out what Isabelle had done to make them convincing.

...transformative power of music...poverty denies artistry...Thank you, Isabelle Anderson Foundation! You changed my life! She had a long paragraph about how music helped with learning to read, along with results of music programs in poor countries. The pictures seemed real enough. The little girl Isabelle had put on the front wore ragged, dirty clothes that seemed too big for her, and her sweet smile made you want to do everything for her. Where did this child find food—did she have a mother to take care of her? Brothers and sisters? A roof over her head to give a little shelter from the weather? Her hair was curly and unnaturally red in places. Ronnie had heard somewhere that that was a sign of malnutrition, like the big bellies of those naked African children in old National Geographics. She wondered if Isabelle had lifted the photograph from that magazine.

She sat down in the chair by the window and stared at the pictures. All those years on the street, sometimes the hunger pangs got too strong to ignore, but mostly she managed to scrounge, worked odd jobs so she could buy something, and occasionally shoplifted when she had to. Usually she found food somewhere—in the dumpsters behind restaurants and bodegas, a McDonald's bag thrown in the trash at a corner. What was it like in these really poor countries, where no one had food, no possibility of food in the trash? She'd spent all her time on the street finding the next place to sleep, the next meal to eat, the next billfold to lift, the next day job to work. She never thought about people in other countries—children starving, dying of infections and disease. She had only thought about how poor she was, homeless, no family. But these kids. At least she'd had all her childhood shots, she'd learned to read and write. And now she didn't have to scrounge, but this little girl—

"Just put those brochures away. We may need them for someone else." Isabelle regarded herself in the mirror over the fireplace, adjusted an invisible strand of hair, her white gauzy outfit swirling like clouds around her. The way she sneaked around could give someone a heart attack.

Ronnie jumped up, still holding the pamphlet. "Where'd you get these pictures?"

"Oh, I just pulled them off the internet." She continued with her mirror work.

"Where is this? I mean, what country?"

"Who knows? Who cares?"

"How old do you think this little girl is?"

Isabelle turned from the mirror, eyes flicking over Ronnie. "What does it matter?"

Ronnie held on to the flyer and waited.

"Really." The sound was short, clipped. "Those pictures could have been taken years ago. That girl's probably dead by now."

* * *

In her apartment, Ronnie made her bed, wiped down the already clean counters in the tiny kitchen, folded and then refolded the Afghan on the couch in the living room area, aligned the box with the Oxy money square with the corner of the coffee table. Was that little girl really dead? Maybe she and Matt were having fun in heaven or wherever people go. She seemed like the kind of person Matt would take care of, play games with—

"How much money have you collected so far?"

"Jesus Christ!" Ronnie whipped around to see Isabelle standing at the bottom of the stairs, smiling at her like she'd won that point.

"Didn't mean to startle you." She looked around as she walked into the room.

Yes you did. Ronnie scanned Isabelle for a quick second. Maybe she could put a bell on her somewhere. She picked up the decorative box off the coffee table, handed it to her boss.

"Nice box." Isabelle took out the cash, handed the box to Ronnie and counted, a quick shishing of the notes against each other, her expert handling making Ronnie think of a bank teller. Or a bookie. "This is short." Her eyes narrowed at Ronnie. "Where's last night's take?" She gestured at her with the stack of money. "You didn't think you could keep a little for yourself, did you?" Her voice was low, deadly.

"No, I—I—"

"Thought I wouldn't notice? A little off the top, no one the wiser? What's a few dollars among family, hmmm?" Isabelle narrowed the space between them.

Ronnie took a step back, drew in a deep breath, expanding her chest, let it out slowly, carefully. "I would never do that." She stared hard at her boss. "I am not a thief."

Isabelle's eyes held hers, and then the woman's whole face crinkled up, and she threw back her head and laughed, a large, deep laugh that kept going until she had to sit down on the couch, one hand clutching the cash, the other on her chest as if to keep herself from splitting open. Real tears streamed down her face, and she was still making laughing sounds as Ronnie went to the closet, pulled out her butler pants, and retrieved the wad of cash from last night.

"Oh, that is rich. I didn't realize you were such a comedian." Isabelle counted the money Ronnie handed her, added it to the pile which now sat on the coffee table. "That was great. I haven't laughed like that in a long time." She dabbed at her eyes with the back of her wrist. They both stared at the money, the wrinkled notes lying one on top of another.

Isabelle grabbed it, fanned it out, waved it at Ronnie. "This may just be a side gig just for my old friends, but I always know how much is here, so don't ever think you can pull a fast one. We may be family, but this money is mine. Now." She peeled several hundreds away from the rest. "I want you to go visit your friend, replenish your supply, and also get some of the other stuff, the stuff that puts people in a partying mood." She handed the bills to

Ronnie. "You know. Makes them so happy."

Isabelle took the rest of the money with her, glided up the stairs, her laughter bubbling up.

Chapter Eleven

After Frank interviewed Cathy's classmates one by one, the picture that formed of his daughter clenched Frank's heart. She hadn't been popular, she was mostly by herself, she had been hanging out lately with a crowd from another school. He wondered if she had even been doing as well in her studies as he had thought. After many, many dead ends, he hit on a name from that other crowd, though it had taken him most of the morning. The same name was mentioned by several different girls.

Tomorrow he would start all over with that girl from another school, but right now he wanted to get to the Lower East Side, distribute more flyers, talk to more street kids. Even though he knew it would be slower, he decided to take the bus, try to clear his head up top rather than sink into the bowels of the city. Before he could call Susan, let her know what he had found out—not much, just a name—his Peter Franks phone buzzed in his other pocket. His brain switched everything else off, and he stood, pulled the cord to signal he wanted off the bus, answered his phone, made his way to the door.

The silky voice whispered in his ear. *I was thinking about you all morning.* Really?

Let's have lunch today. Le Domaine Perdu. One O'clock.

You got it, sweetheart. Actually, he simply said he looked forward to it. She hung up with that thrilling laughter and he half wanted to call her back just to hear it again.

He called Pete on his way to his apartment—luckily, a short sprint as it was already twelve o'clock. She must know people to get reservations at Le

Domaine Perdu on such short notice. He only knew it by reputation, but what a reputation.

"Pete, tell me some good news. I could use it."

"Okay. The stock market's up."

"Cute. I'm meeting the lovely hostess for lunch at one. Tell me about the brochure, the foundation. Anything I can use?"

Pete's research found that The Isabelle Anderson Foundation seemed legit. The 990-PFs were filed on time each year, showed contributions and expenses, grants and charitable activities. A lot of money going in and out right after it started in 2005; incorporated in Delaware, not unusual, Isabelle Anderson sole director, also not unusual. Activity seemed to have picked up in the last few years.

"But the brochure, that's where you want to concentrate." Pete sounded like he was eating lunch. "She's got this high school that supposedly helps out, but there's no high school in Sandusky, Ohio by that name, no NGO registered handing out instruments in Guatemala or anywhere else in Latin America." He stopped talking but didn't stop chewing.

Frank took the stairs to his apartment two at a time, cradled the phone while he let himself in. He pulled off his jacket, his holster, rid himself of everything Special Agent, pulled out his Peter Franks clothes. He put Pete on speaker so he could make the transformation unhampered.

"What are you thinking?" Frank wrestled on the cuff links, tied his Hermès tie, slid on the thin gold watch. "Any way this has anything to do with the drugs?"

"Dunno." More chewing, probably that slouching shrug of his.

Frank let out an exasperated gust of air, and Pete told him not to get his knickers in a twist, opined that the charity could be a conduit for the product, Ron the Butler acting as Isabelle's mule, carrying the drugs to the dealer from this Latin American country. Maybe one of her donors gave her use of his private jet, paid off customs officials.

"Okay. Document that I'm meeting our lovely target so gotta leave the Bureau phone here." Frank ended the call. He slipped into the suit jacket, shot his cuffs, and smiled at the Piaget. He mentally checked himself over, confirmed that he had on everything Peter Franks, nothing from Frank Jankowski. He felt the persona slide over him, cue the Midwestern charm. This time he would use his phone to record everything, and he had some ammunition now. The case would have to start breaking his way or the boss would pull it at his ninety-day review. He was due for some luck. And he was dressed for it, too.

* * *

He arrived at the snooty establishment ahead of Isabelle and he ducked in to check it out, noted the layout and exits. He didn't need to see the menu to know that it would be pricier than he thought. *Expensive* shouted out to him in the peach-colored walls and glittering crystal on the tables, in the individual lamps that shed a glow on the diners, and in the people themselves—the way they dressed, held themselves, contained but conscious of being on display. It seemed like everyone whispered, even the staff, and he shot back out to catch Isabelle before she went in. Maybe he could persuade her to go someplace else, protect his budget. Etiquette dictated that she'd invited, so she should treat, but Peter Franks would offer to pay, and even if they split the bill, it would be far too much.

She breezed up behind him, told him she was celebrating, handed him a thick square envelope, and went in ahead of him before he said more than hello. She consulted the maître d' and then slid into the banquette against the wall. Too late to suggest another place. Frank had to sit with his back to the door, not his favorite position.

But Peter Franks didn't need to sit with his back to the wall, and he certainly wouldn't think much about the prices, so when Isabelle hinted that a cold glass of Sauvignon Blanc would be nice, he said he'd have one too. She laughed and said, "Oh, but you should order a bottle, then!" Peter Franks graciously ordered one, but Frank Jankowski had never spent 100 bucks on a bottle of wine in his life, and her declaration made it clear that Peter Franks would be buying today. As he leaned his arm on the table, the impossibly thin Piaget watch glinted. He gave her a knowing smile. Just rich people together, having lunch.

He assessed her from across the narrow table. Isabelle's hair was pinned up, but somehow landed in curls around her face, eyeliner creating cat eyes, and to finish it off some fluffy pink sweater that gave him a further impression of a kitten. A kitten in makeup and pearls. She held forth about life in the city, educating Peter Franks on what to expect once his family lived here.

"I wanted to ask you," he gave her a serious look, held her eyes for a beat. "I heard Mickey has a driver. Does everyone have one? Should I get one?"

She laughed and shook her head. Windchimes in cool mountain air. "No, that's just Mickey. I believe he had a close call and decided to quit driving." She took a sip of wine, leaned forward. "They say it was a hit and run." Her eyes gleamed with that gossip bomb.

He sat back, picked up his wine glass to hide his reaction. She might as well have shouted it, the way it hit him. He didn't trust himself to speak. He lined his silverware up, meticulously matching the bottom edges as if he'd used a ruler.

Her chattering floated across the table to him, the pros and cons of having a car in the city, something like that. A breadbasket landed in the middle of the table and he grabbed something from it. He had hated Mickey the Silver Fox on sight and now...

"When was that?" He might've interrupted her.

"I'm sorry?" Her tone was polite, but her eyes flashed at him. "When was what?"

He didn't care. He had to know. "The hit and run? When he hit something or someone and fled the scene?"

She waved a hand as if she really couldn't be bothered. "Fled the scene? Oh, Peter, I think you've been watching too many Law and Order episodes!"

Damn. Get a grip. Pull on your Peter Franks persona. "Ah, well now." He emphasized the midwestern cadence, "I may have at that." He cleared his throat. "I'm just wonderin' if I gotta watch out for myself in the crosswalk." He made his eyes big and, he hoped, puppy-dog-like.

She placed her hand over his as if to comfort him. "Now don't you worry.

It was quite a while ago, and he's had a driver ever since. Opening night of Les Mis and he was late. Some girl ran right in front of him, they say." She waved a hand in the air as if to brush the conversation aside. "And it wasn't even on the Upper East Side." She patted him, and he stiffened, afraid Frank Jankowski might grab her hand and twist it behind her back. "Somewhere down in The Village, so we're all safe."

He had to get out of here. She filled the air between them with her conversation, but he could no longer hear her. He turned his hand over and placed his other one on top of hers, a warm, polite sandwich. He said he was awfully sorry, but he really had to excuse himself for a minute. "Please don't go anywhere, I'll be right back." He gave a little squeeze for emphasis, then a tiny bow as he got up from his chair. It was all he could do to keep himself from running for the door instead of gracefully angling himself between the tiny lamplit tables.

He burst through the bathroom door, startling the attendant who jumped up from his chair and slid his phone into his pocket. Not too many of those guys left. Frank went into the stall and leaned against the wall. How was he going to continue the charade, be nice and fun-loving when he now knew who had hit Cathy? He pulled out his phone, texted Pete, asked him what he'd found out on Ward McAllister, hit send, then deleted it. These people were a new kind of evil.

He flushed the toilet for appearance's sake and came out. The attendant stood on alert, but Frank ignored him, went to the sink, barely registering the black marble, the gold faucets. He ran the water and then stared at himself hard in the mirror. *Compartmentalize. Get a grip. You are Peter Franks from Omaha, wealthy, eager to learn from Isabelle Anderson. There is no Frank Jankowski. Go out there and be the charming Peter Franks. Now!*

Their lunch had come when he'd been in the gents, and he slid into his seat with apologies, examined his plate. Hardly worth eating. The price had been high enough that he was sure he was ordering a healthy hunk of the tenderloin, but here was one large plate sparsely populated with whiffs of filet mignon, decorated with dustings of something red, something green, a curl of an unknown vegetable off to the side. Very pretty.

Frank picked up his heavy fork, pausing it over the plate. It was like bringing a bulldozer to a fairy garden. He stabbed at a feathery thing he hoped was the beef.

"So." Isabelle leaned over the table, and Frank braced for more, a description of his daughter, the glee at getting away with it. "Tell me about your wife." She smiled her lovely smile, a pearl earring winking at him. "What's her name? Does she work outside the home? What charities is she interested in? And the Arts? What kind of music does she like?"

"Whoa now." Peter Franks gave her a twinkly smile. "Which question should I answer first?" She treated him to a laugh, the pearls glowing at him. Before she could respond he jumped in. "What kind of music do *you* like?" Get them talking about themselves. They'll forget you hadn't answered their questions. Peter Franks watched her every move, all attentive and absorbed, forcing Frank Jankowski into the back of his head where he could record everything for later.

As she went on, he assembled and reassembled his images of her, adding in her knowledge of her butler's drug activity, taking it out, wondering which picture was the more accurate: Society lady dealing drugs out of her brownstone, smuggler of drugs from Latin America to supply the dealer on the Upper East Side, or merely Upper East Side hostess who loved to entertain?

The Jankowski anger began to simmer, and he pressed his napkin to his mouth to ground himself. Isabelle shifted in her seat, recrossing her legs, and her foot brushed his shin, lingered. He dropped his napkin and watched her eyes as she continued talking. Had she done it on purpose? Did she realize that it was his leg her shoe moved up and down against? Peter Franks gave her a huge smile. The closer he got to her, the better his case. He needed to spend a lot of time at her house, and if he had to play footsie in order to do that, then that was what Peter Franks would do.

"Why don't you open that?" Isabelle gestured at her envelope which he had put on the table when they first sat down.

He cocked his head at her, hoping for a nice surprise. Bingo. Another invitation, this time to a cocktail party. To promote her foundation.

"I know you already said you'd give." Oddly, Isabelle seemed to read his thoughts. "You and Philippe will be there to encourage the others. It's such a worthy cause, don't you agree?"

Frank nodded, stabbed a mystery tendril with his fork, wondered if it was decoration or truly something he was supposed to eat. "Yes, your foundation. I've been giving a lot of thought to your cause." He held her gaze.

Her mouth opened in a wide smile, eyes glittering in the lamplight.

"Money," he continued, "is one thing. But what I'd really like is to help in a more meaningful way." He leaned forward over his plate, though he already had her full attention. Her hand landed on top of his. "What I'd like to do is go down there with you, help distribute the instruments."

Her eyes startled for a quick second, and then she bestowed upon him her throaty laugh. She paused to dab the corners of her mouth with her cloth napkin and then deposited it on the table. "Ah, Peter, you do think big, don't you? Must be that wide open Midwestern sky." She laughed once more, gathered her purse, slid out from the banquette, leaving most of her lunch on the plate. "Really, you are the first one to ever suggest a thing like that."

Frank stood, a reflexive courtesy, admiring the way her skirt came up as she slid along the seat, the pleats falling into place as she turned sideways to angle between the tables. He glanced around to see the waiter rushing their way.

"I'll meet you up front in a few minutes." She patted his arm on her way past him, headed to the back of the restaurant.

Well, Peter Franks, you sure know how to clear a room. This was interesting.

Out on the sidewalk, she tucked her hand in his arm and walked them toward Fifth. "These things," she said as if there hadn't been a break, "take time, you know. First, I have to raise the money, a lot of it, then I have to get the instruments, donated, hopefully. Which always takes time. Then I wait for the high school kids to get out of school—"

"Which high school was that?"

"Well," Isabelle gazed up at him, trusting him to negotiate the sidewalk while she talked. "I have been using that one in Ohio, but I might have to find a new one for this project." She pulled him in a little tighter to her, then almost whispered into his shoulder so he had to lean down to hear her. "So, you see, I need to raise the money first. And at the cocktail party, wouldn't it be lovely to showcase your $50,000 check." She pointed her chin toward his coat pocket where he'd stashed the invitation, "After all, these things spread like wildfire once people know others have given."

How had it come about that he was already committed to $50 thou? This case was supposed to be in and out, extremely low budget, all wrapped up in weeks. He needed to stall. "Is that how much Philippe is in for?"

"Ooooh, look!" Isabelle stopped them in front of a store window. "That suit would look just heavenly on you!" Her eyes were glued to the display in the Gucci window as if she were a tiger and the suit her prey. "Come!" She pulled him toward the door. "You must try it on! Won't this be so much fun!"

Isabelle had the clerks running and fawning, and Frank had the distinct impression they knew her. Funny how, on the sidewalk, she'd made it seem so spontaneous. They brought her a suit to inspect, and she stroked the dark blue sleeve as if she wished his arm were already in it. She stopped herself as if suddenly aware of her actions, then took the suit from the salesperson, thrust it at Frank. "Isn't this divine! And so you. You must try it on."

He had just gotten the pants zipped, was noting how nice the fit, how Isabelle knew his exact size, when the door flew open, and she came in. He watched her in the mirror as she chattered on, took the jacket off the hanger, and fit him into it as if they always spent time together in such a tiny space. She fussed and tugged, ran her hands down his chest and arms, the whole time exclaiming about how handsome he was, how no one in Omaha would recognize him, how he really looked like a New Yorker now. She took him by the shoulders and turned him toward the mirror, her grip on him firm. It was a nice suit, the fit perfect, the material fine and understated. How could he say no? Peter Franks was so wealthy and this would mean nothing to him. His aim was to move to New York, and so of course he'd want to fit in—he had to buy the suit. No way he would contradict her by pointing out that people in Omaha dressed like this, too. Or that Peter Franks had racks of this stuff at home.

She led him to store after store, and he let her. He bought the things she gushed over: scarves, earrings, keepsake boxes for Mrs. Franks. He bought two of everything, and every single time Isabelle looked surprised, then protested, then effused her thanks. At one precious boutique where the long-legged sales staff outnumbered the items on display, Isabelle oohed over a small purse, held it up, let it turn this way and that, spoke in a foreign language, it seemed, to the young ladies about the designer, the cut, the debut at Milan. Something that small couldn't possibly break his budget, and Peter magnanimously took it from her, handed it to the clerk along with his card. He signed without noting the total, distracted by the way Isabelle expressed her gratitude by practically wrapping herself around him.

It was instructive to observe her, she was kittenish yet sophisticated, shaking her curls when she flirted. And she flirted with everyone, cozying up to the salespeople, whether they were men or women. She drew them to her, leaned toward them, spoke quietly, breathily so they had to lean in too.

At the next store, a narrow, crowded space that Frank wouldn't have noticed if Isabelle hadn't stopped, he stood off to the side to stay out of the way, let her do what she did best. This store had just the one person working, and Isabelle engaged her in a discussion of a blouse. She stroked the sleeve, tweaked the collar point, laid it over her torso, evidently asked for an opinion. When Isabelle laughed and touched the young woman's forearm, Frank felt it on his own, a tingling feeling that recalled the intimacy he had felt at lunch. As if Isabelle knew what she had done, she threw her throaty laugh over to where he stood, her eyes sparkling. Peter Franks gave her a nod, an indulgent smile but Frank Jankowski thought he'd be safer staying in his corner. She still held the blouse up as if she couldn't decide, and just like that, her other hand flashed out, snagged a scarf off the display table, and whisked it into her handbag.

Frank startled as if electrified. The saleswoman slid hangers along the rack, chattering and finally selecting a skirt which she held next to the blouse. She handed Isabelle three more garments, the plastic hangers clacking together, and Isabelle nodded and laughed and touched her again.

"Peter! Darling, can I model these for you?"

Her words came at Frank muffled, through a fog, and he shook his head as if to clear it. "I'm sure if you like them, I'll like them." Frank didn't think he could move from his spot. His nerve endings were on fire, his breath came short, and his heart beat so fast he wondered if it would ever go back to normal. She said something like *have it your way* and disappeared at the back, the saleswoman following behind like an eager puppy.

He breathed. In through his nose, out through his mouth. He shook himself all over as if suddenly chilled. What was wrong with him? Undercover, he had seen far worse crimes than that sleight of hand. No, it had to be something else, something to do with the remarkable Isabelle, the connection she made with him, the way she stripped away everything around them, so it felt like just the two of them. And, as if she were Zeus, she had sent a lightning bolt through him.

He stood on the sidewalk with shoppers and tourists striding past him, and he could barely remember coming out here, leaving the store. He let the traffic noise wash over him, the horns honking, the squeak of the bus brakes, the sirens a few avenues over.

* * *

Back at his apartment, Frank hung up the Gucci suit that now belonged to the Bureau, put away the bling from Wardrobe, and pulled on his trusted khakis and everyday shoes. He put Mrs. Peter Franks' earrings, scarves, and silver trinkets aside to return, pulled out all the receipts from the afternoon. Not a tall pile, but when he mentally added them up his stomach dropped. That tiny, harmless little purse that Peter Franks so generously bought and gave to Isabelle took the biggest bite so far. One afternoon, and poof! a quarter of his budget gone. He'd better scramble on this case before his boss pulled the plug.

He went through every detail of the afternoon, mentally placed pluses next to his wins, asterisks next to things Isabelle had said or done that he should keep in mind, question marks for further contemplation or research.

85

His mind arrived at the little boutique where Isabelle had shoplifted. When she came out to join him on the sidewalk, she had no new shopping bags, and neither one of them mentioned whatever acquisitions nestled in her purse. He wasn't going to think about it any further.

There was no doubt she wanted him to witness her shoplifting, and he should've taken advantage of that. Instead, she had unnerved him, and he needed to figure out how so he could guard against it, keep her at a distance while Peter Franks got closer to her. He paced his tiny apartment. When he analyzed it, though, all he could come up with was that he had felt a thrill. A thrill at her daring, a thrill at her including him in her secret. He stopped in the kitchen for a glass of water, put it on the counter without drinking it. With that quick, illicit swipe, she had opened another world, one with just the two of them in it.

And all he wanted to do was dive back into it.

He went back to the bedroom where all the swag glittered still. When he was undercover, he could always separate, compartmentalize, be the UC and still retain the Frank Jankowski. But this Peter Franks. Maybe he shouldn't have used his first name for the UC last name. He matched receipts to purchases, gold earrings made ordinary as they lay on the flimsy paper. Somehow, he felt he *was* Peter Franks, he'd blended—become? No, Frank was still there, he'd merged the two people temporarily, enjoyed the moment where he wasn't worried about finding his teenage daughter or defending himself against her mother. Peter Franks had a much easier life, but that easy wouldn't come free. If he got too carried away in his pretense, he'd pay a price higher than the one Frank was paying. They would fire him, or worse, jail him, costing him his freedom and any chance of finding Cathy. And now that he recognized that, he could take care of it, keep the good guys on their side, the criminals over where they belonged.

He placed the trinkets and receipts in a bag and put it on the narrow console table next to the front door. He went to the windows and looked out on the street, the ordinary day of it, people returning from work, a bag of groceries, a briefcase banging against a leg. He had underestimated her, and that had to stop.

He went back to the kitchen and drained the glass of water. He opened his refrigerator. Some sad leftover salad, a jar of mustard. One beer. He closed the door and strode to the console, snatched up his keys, clattered down the stairs, and exited the building.

He headed east, aimed for the corner grocery store. Expensive, but cheaper than eating out. He lengthened his stride, his sturdy shoes solid on the sidewalk, his body avoiding people, his brain engaging in the calculations and moving him to one side or the other, slowing down, speeding up, reliably delivering him to his destination while he worked on the puzzle of the case.

At the corner store he looked over the vegetables, picked out tomatoes, onions, zucchini, mushrooms. Wait a minute. Why didn't he recognize it at the time? She thought they shared this. If he let her know that Peter Franks was thrilled by the danger of it, that he wasn't that different than she, then he could get closer to her, get to know more of her secrets, learn more of the criminal activity she was involved in. The shopkeeper came out, watched him, silently offered a basket to hold his selections. How could he have been so dense? He hoped he hadn't blown it. This was the best way in, and now he'd have to figure out how to bring it up again, let her know how much alike they were. He swiped his credit card, took the neatly tied bag of groceries. How much alike she and Peter Franks were, that is.

Back at his apartment, he heated oil in a frying pan, then chopped and sliced vegetables, smashed garlic with the flat of his knife. He knew now how he would play this. He would text her, tell her how much Peter Franks enjoyed watching her shop, could they do it again real soon?

He broke two eggs into a bowl, whipped them up with a fork. Everything he'd observed in that brownstone seemed legit on the surface, no indication of drugs, just Newsboy serving and clearing, taking their coats and phones. The drugs had to be somewhere, though. The surveillance revealed a lot of trips from that drug dealer, too many for just Newsboy's personal use. And Frank's close observation of him told him he wasn't using. The butler was certainly an enigma, although the way his eyes darted around indicated he'd lived on the streets at some point, maybe recently. With no drugs in sight and with the sketchiness of the Isabelle Anderson Foundation, there must be more going on in that brownstone, and what better way to find out than to become best friends with Ron? Or whatever Newsboy's name was. A two-pronged attack, no room for error. The case would be wrapped up in record time.

Chapter Twelve

The next day, Ronnie had nothing else to do, so she went up to Isabelle's tiny office to dust. She started with the shelves, took her time, examined silver framed pictures, wondered who the fancy people were, with a solo Isabelle, no husband. All the long gowns and tuxedos told her this photo must be some fancy party, no doubt a charity ball like the one she'd worked at when she'd taken Isabelle's bracelet. She looked closer and saw Isabelle had on that same bracelet in this picture, dangling from her wrist as she held her glass up as if in a toast. The photograph was washed out, like it was taken a long time ago, but Isabelle seemed pretty much the same, her blonde hair in an elaborate updo, her eyes glittering like she knew a secret about you that you didn't even know yourself.

"Ah, yes, the Princess Grace Foundation Gala! That's Princess Charlene with her arm around me."

Ronnie nearly dropped the picture. Jeez, by now, she should be used to Isabelle's sneaking around. Just like a cat.

"And that's Prince Rainier on my other side." Isabelle stood in the doorway in her stocking feet, holding a large bright red shopping bag, matching tissue paper spilling out.

"How was lunch?" Ronnie put the frame down and ran her duster over the tops of some books.

"Today or yesterday?" Isabelle plopped her shopping bag on her desk and sat down. She put her legs on the desk, crossed her ankles, curled her toes. Her long skirt fell away, revealing a well-toned thigh. Ronnie concentrated on dusting the shelves.

Ronnie shrugged at the knickknacks in front of her. "Either, I guess. Didn't you have lunch with Peter Franks yesterday?"

"Ah! My new Object of My Affection! Did everything just perfectly, bought me an absolute bouquet of lovely things."

Ronnie unfolded the stepladder and climbed up. So many books.

"You should have seen the look on his face when I came into the dressing room to help him try on a suit! And the heat of him. I just adore tall, broad-shouldered men."

"Huh. Guess you're glad you asked him to dinner." Seemed like these upper shelves had never been dusted.

"Of course I am! I'm never wrong." The tissue paper rustled, then the drawer to the little desk opened. Closed. "I have him right where I want him."

Had she even read any of these books? They looked so old and boring.

"But now I need to think about something." A pencil tapped.

"Ma'am?"

Isabelle took her feet off her delicate desk, opened her laptop, and frowned at the screen. She looked so serious that Ronnie paused. She had gone from playful sex kitten to businesswoman without even a wardrobe change.

"Omaha Pete may be a naïf when it comes to the city, but he said something at lunch no one else has." She clicked away on the keyboard. "I mean, these cynical New Yorkers, they make money hand over fist, and they feel so guilty they can't get rid of it fast enough. As long as they get their tax deductions, they never ask any questions." She got up, paced. "But Peter Franks," she came to the shelves and turned, arrived at the windows, "self-made millionaire from Omaha, asks questions and then genuinely wants to help." She turned from the window and threw Ronnie a look. "Do you know what he wants to do?"

Ronnie shook her head. Let out a breath she hadn't realized she was holding, glad the irritation was at Omaha Pete and not her.

Isabelle put her hands on her hips, her eyes darkening as if it were Ronnie's fault. "He wants to go down and help me hand out instruments to the raggedy children himself." She paced the tiny room again, moved from window to door to shelves to desk.

"What did you say to him?" Ronnie got down and concentrated on the next set of eye-level shelves.

"Oh, I deflected him." She flapped her hand as if a fly had gotten in. "I told him we had to do everything else first." She stopped to count off on her fingers. "Raise the money, get the instruments, make an arrangement with the high school students—"

"Won't that be enough to put him off?"

"Perhaps." Isabelle crossed her arms and began tapping a slender finger. Ronnie felt like she could see the gears and wheels turning in Isabelle's brain, everything shifting into place. "I'll have to bring him closer, close enough for one kiss."

Ronnie climbed up, away from her boss, the better to concentrate and get away from the pictures she was putting in her head. She straightened the books as she dusted, evened them up. What's a piece of paper doing here?

"Remember…"

Ronnie looked down at Isabelle.

She held up one finger. Wagged it back and forth. "That's all I need, just one kiss and then he'll think about so many things other than poor children in third world countries who don't even exist."

Ronnie turned back to the shelves and pulled the paper out, put the feather duster in her back pocket, climbed down.

"What is that?"

Ronnie opened the piece of paper. It was a couple of pieces, actually. Full of columns of numbers, names on one side, some of the numbers penciled in, some inked, a big X crossing out the numbers at the bottom of the columns. "Do you need to keep these?" She held the pages out to Isabelle.

"Let me see that." Her voice snapped, and Ronnie took a step back. But Isabelle stood with her hand held out like a teacher who had caught her passing notes, so Ronnie brought it to her. She felt guilty, and she didn't know why. Wasn't hers. As she folded up the ladder, she could hear Isabelle muttering to herself, *disaster* and *that prick* floating over to her. She had almost made it out the door when Isabelle spoke again.

91

"Why did you have this? Are you trying to undermine me? You produce this—" she shook the pages at Ronnie, "right when I'm about to reel in a new man? Why would you remind me of a—" Isabelle's eyes snapped like firecrackers. "—a *failure* when every other project has been such a success?"

This cushy gig was about to be over, and Ronnie didn't even know why. She leaned the stepladder against the door jamb and came back into the room, widened her stance, and drew herself up tall. "Isabelle."

"I thought we were a team." She balled up the pages and threw them toward her wastebasket as if she wanted to throw Ronnie away, too.

"Isabelle! Those are your pages, on your shelf that I was dusting for you. You asked me for them, and I handed them to you. I just found them. I have no idea what they even mean."

"Of course you don't." Isabelle pulled today's loot out of the bag, something lacy and silky, left the red tissue paper and shopping bag on the floor in a heap. She passed Ronnie on her way to the door, and Ronnie stepped aside, half thinking Isabelle might slug her. She certainly looked like she wanted to. Her voice was like a growling tiger, her words pinched. "You'd better be ready for four o'clock tea this afternoon."

* * *

Great. A punishment tea. Ronnie ran up the steps from her apartment, headed east, thought about all the stores she needed to avoid because she had hit them recently, calculated whether to go uptown or down, mentally ticked off the things she thought Isabelle might want her to pick up and have ready. In less than two hours. What had she even done to deserve that? She'd hit the dealer tomorrow. But fuck this, her stomach growled. Would she have time to grab something for herself?

Madison Avenue was mysteriously crowded for this time of day, and she stopped at the corner, edged off the curb, waited for a break in the traffic, a quick dart across the street, that bodega on the corner promising.

"Whoa there, young man," a voice right behind her said. "Maybe you shouldn't be jaywalking in this traffic." A hand grabbed her upper arm, and she whirled around, her own hand coming up in a fist. "Hey, hey, just trying to help." The man let go, hands up in a don't shoot gesture.

"Mr. Franks." Ronnie dropped her fist, mentally checked herself to see if she would still appear to be a boy to him. "I've got to run. I'm sorry, but Mrs. Anderson—"

"Ah, the lovely Isabelle." Peter Franks' eyes held hers for a moment, then shifted to over her shoulder. "The light's green. Where are you going? I'll keep you company. Carry your bags."

Shit. Ronnie crossed the street, lengthened her stride, turned uptown, threaded between two suits and one guy in scrubs, hoped Peter Franks wouldn't keep up. What was he doing here anyway? You never ran into people you knew, yet here he was, and she was going to be in big trouble if she didn't put this tea together for Isabelle. There went the bodega. Maybe a deli would pop up soon, but if Peter Franks was still here…she swung her bangs off her forehead, took a quick look out of the side of her eyes, and kept up her fast pace, but here was a corner, and another light, and his raincoat right beside her, so close he practically breathed on her shoulder.

"You sure are in a hurry. Faster than most New Yorkers," he said, though it didn't seem like a compliment. "I think you need a break. Let me buy you a sandwich, there, on the next corner."

Ronnie cut her eyes to him but couldn't read his expression. She had to be polite for Isabelle's sake, and which meant for her sake, too. But she had to get rid of him so she could lift her list. Her stomach growled, the traitor.

"Mr. Franks. Really, I work better on my own." Her eyes darted, streetlight, taxi, sidewalk, bookstore, people crowding them, waiting at the corner, spilling into the street. "Excuse me. I have to go." She ran. Across 86th, down the subway steps, past the white-tiled walls, up the other side, down the street past the brownstones, the garbage cans on the sidewalk, nearly collided with a stroller, almost tangling with the dog on a leash attached to the handle. She rounded the corner onto Third and ducked into a pizza place, pausing to breathe, her stomach responding to the yeasty heat, the smell of melted cheese, a tang of tomato sauce, and burnt crust.

"Shall we get a slice or a whole pizza?"

Yikes. Ronnie froze, all except her eyes, looking around, window, door, bathroom, kitchen. Peter Franks grabbed her upper arm and held on to it, steered her to the counter. He ordered a small pepperoni pizza, commented that she looked like she could use it, asked her what she wanted to drink. She tried to pull away, but he held fast and said, low in her ear, "I think you and I need to have a talk."

Ronnie went statue still, wished she could shrink her bicep so she could pull out of his grip. Wished she didn't have to be nice to him. She risked a peek at his face. He sure seemed a lot different from the gosh-and-golly-you-betcha man from Omaha at Isabelle's dining room table. The only back door had to be on the other end of the kitchen, the front door her best way out. She felt his grip tighten, and her stomach dropped. This guy could read her thoughts now? He gestured for her to grab the drinks while he carried the pizza with one hand, the other still on her. Her stomach almost flipped from the smell. She was getting soft, no doubt about it.

He aimed them for a booth and once she'd slid into her side, his big fat foot came up, blocking her in. He pulled some napkins out of the dispenser, tossed them toward her.

"Mr. Franks—"

"You eat, I'll talk."

Ronnie swung her bangs out her eyes and pulled off a slice, the cheese stretching, the pepperoni puddled with orange grease. Just the way she liked it. One piece then she was outta here.

"I just need a few moments, and then you can go."

She felt her eyes darting around the tiny restaurant, and he laughed. "You look like a feral cat. You used to live on the streets, didn't you?"

What the hell? She chewed faster, swallowed, put the slice down, grabbed another napkin to wipe her hands. She straightened up, summoned her butler voice, and said, "I'm sure I don't know what you mean—"

But he just laughed again. He reached into his back pocket and pulled out a cracked leather wallet, opened it, slid it over to her. A badge. An ID. Frank Jankowski. Special Agent Frank Jankowski. FBI.

The hairs on her arm rose, and she turned to run, but he had a grip on her, his arms across the table holding her in place. He couldn't be a cop; she would've known the first time she opened the door to him. But she hadn't known, her instincts failing her. He must be very, very good. She could feel her scalp pricking, her heart racing.

"Special Agent Frank Jankowski. How do you do?" His eyes held hers, drilled in. "Now, why don't you sit still and tell me about yourself."

Fuckfuckfuck. She had to get out of there. She didn't have to be nice to him anymore. He wasn't Peter Franks. What the fuck was he doing at Isabelle's? She pulled her feet onto the bench, felt his hand squeeze her arm harder. She was twisting out of his grip when she found him standing over her, both hands on her shoulders.

"Sit down. You're not in trouble. Yet. I just need to ask questions, and maybe it'll turn out that you can help me."

"What? Help? No way." She cut her eyes around, then said in fierce whisper, "I'm not a snitch!" Maybe she could slide under the booth, escape through the kitchen.

"Okay, then." The cop's voice was deep, calm. "We can go down to headquarters, talk about everything there, maybe cuff you to the table since you seem so eager to run." He held her eyes. "Then you can tell me all about that dealer over on 90th and York, and we'll hold on to you while we decide what else to charge you with."

She shook her head like a dog shaking off water, her adrenaline so high she thought she might throw up if she couldn't run.

"And you know how it is," he went on as if it was all so reasonable, "once we put those cuffs on, you become ours and we hate to let you just leave."

She gulped air, she couldn't see him, her vision blurring.

"But," he sat down, held both her wrists on the table, leaned toward her so that someone who saw them might think he was her father, holding her hands, soothing her, "I'd rather just talk to you here."

She couldn't. Catch. Her breath. She couldn't make. Her heart stop racing. She couldn't stop the sound rushing through her ears. She knew he watched her, but she looked everywhere except at him.

"Your pulse is pretty quick. Maybe you should have some of your drink."

The restaurant seemed to shrink around her, his words coming to her as if through water.

"Okay if I let go of one of your wrists so you can take a sip?" His voice seemed gentle, kind even. She nodded. As soon as he let go, she began to move, but just as quickly there he was, sliding into the booth beside her, arm across her shoulders, anyone would think he was just being nice to her. Cozy.

"I—I—I can't," Ronnie's chest heaved, "breathe..." The word came out on what felt like her last breath. The table loomed up at her, the walls closed in.

"Here now." FBI Frank sounded like Peter Franks again. "Have a sip." He held her drink up to her mouth and she managed a small one. "We'll get your breath back to normal." His voice sounded so understanding, kind almost, and she wanted to hold on to it like a life preserver. "Let's slowly count to ten. Each breath, a number. Can you do that?"

Ronnie felt drained, wrung out. All she wanted to do was put her head on the table and close her eyes. Somehow Agent Frank had gotten her calmed down enough so that he had returned to his side of the table, talked agreeably about the unseasonably warm weather, about the Pope's visit to the 9/11 memorial. The pizza sat to one side, cheese a solid white, pepperoni hard and lifeless.

"So, why don't we get to know each other," Agent Frank said, all Mr. Social. Out of the corner of her eye she saw him pull out a tiny notebook, slide out a pen, flip through the pages. "What's your full name?" He paused until she raised her head. "Your real full name?"

"Veronica Charles." A strangled sound escaped her, and Frank raised an eyebrow at her. "I never use it," Ronnie said. "I'm usually just Ronnie." She swallowed. "Or Ron, if I need it." She watched the pen scratch and then paused. "No middle name." It was as if someone else were talking, some wooden thing sitting here, letting loose as she watched. She could feel him look her over and she raised her head, tracked his eyes running over all the details of her face, her neck, her chest.

"Previous known address?"

Ronnie recited off her father's apartment, the address dredged from somewhere in the back of her brain. She watched him write that down. For some reason the wooden robot added, helpfully, "I haven't lived there in years."

"How long have you been living at Isabelle's?"

"A month, maybe two." Her mouth was dry. The paper cup that had held her drink had a few clear ice cubes stuck to the bottom in a pool of water, not moving when she shook the cup.

Frank pushed his drink toward her. "I haven't touched mine. Go on. No cooties."

She felt his eyes on her as she pulled off the lid, drank half the soda, wiped her mouth with the back of her hand.

"So, what happened between," he glanced at his notebook, "Garden City, New York and the Upper East Side, Manhattan?"

"I was on the streets. Actually," she took another sip, "in a penthouse on Park Avenue." He raised that eyebrow again, pen poised over the paper. "It was being renovated. I'd leave when the workmen came."

He held still as if he wanted her to say more. When she closed her mouth and stared at him, he asked, "How long were you homeless?"

She shrugged. "I don't really think about it."

"Well, let's think about it together. How old were you when you left home? I'm assuming the Garden City address was home."

"Fif—no sixteen." She shifted in her seat, her eyes darted around.

"And how old are you now?" His voice was so nice, warm even. Like he was helping her. "By the way, do you have ID?"

"I have to go."

"Just a few more questions."

"No, really. Shit!" She started to slide out. "The tea! I forgot all about it. What time is it? People are coming this afternoon and she needs me to—"

"All right, all right. I can help you out on your errands. We can walk and talk. But don't get pastries from the same place you got them for my first tea." He slid out of the booth but stood over her as she got out on her side. "No more running?"

She shook her head no.

"I can always find you, you know."

She shook her head again, stood, swayed away from him.

"Even on the streets." He moved aside to let her go ahead, a protective hand on her back. "But I have a feeling you've had enough of the streets now that you've found a nice soft bed at Isabelle Anderson's."

Who was this guy?

"The beds in jail are really just metal shelves." He sounded like he was reading from a Yelp review. "No pillows." They went out the door.

Once outside, she stopped at the corner, scanned for stores, Agent Frank right next to her, no deli, no bakery in sight. She felt better now that she was standing, moving, her lungs drawing in the air. "Look." This time she met his eyes. "I have to go now, get this stuff for Isabelle. I really need this job." And no way she was going to jail. She had too many priors. This would be the last arrest, federal prison for sure.

"Come over here, away from this busy corner and all this traffic noise." He herded her down a little way and stopped by some garbage cans. "All I want is to get to your drug dealer. I'm not after you." He must've seen the relief in her eyes because he added, "Unless you don't cooperate."

"I—I've got to—" Ronnie stopped.

He shook his head back and forth at her, like he was disappointed.

Her shoulders slumped. "I can't get you in."

"Can't? Or Won't?"

The stink from the garbage cans rose up at her and she breathed through her mouth. A car alarm went off up the street, and she shook her head, waited until it stopped. "It's not that easy." She looked side to side like someone might be listening. "I had to get four different people to vouch for me before he'd let me in. Please, I—"

"What if—"

"No." Ronnie backed up a little, trying to get upwind from the cans. "They won't stand up for you just on my say-so. They have to know you. You don't understand. This guy is scary." She stared Frank down. "I've got to find a bakery. I gotta go."

"I'll go with you while you tell me more." He moved with her, up the block.

"What else do you know about him?"

"That's all. I just gave him the money, and he gave me the Oxy." She headed uptown, lengthened her stride. The guy matched her, step for step.

"He never meets you anywhere but the apartment?"

She shook her head. "Never heard of that happening. I don't have time for you to tag along." She was starting to understand how her brothers had felt when they wanted to shake her off.

"Is there a code when you buzz his door?"

"And a camera." She turned the corner. So few stores around here. "Each customer has their own code." He was still next to her. "They give it to you once you're cleared. That's why it's so hard. Now—"

"Who gives it to you?"

The light on Park turned red, and she crossed to go uptown, to cross at the next block. "For fuck's sake."

"As I said, we don't have to do this here."

She stopped on the wide sidewalk, away from the doorman under the dark green awning. "Okay, I'll tell you this, and then you really have to let me go." She waited until he nodded. "The last person you meet with gives you the code." She lowered her voice even though no one else could possibly hear her. "They make you go from one guy to the next, meet in the Park, meet at the Starbucks. You tell them other people you know, they send you to the next one." She paused, but he nodded at her, eyes intent on hers. She looked away. "Then, maybe a week after you've started asking, the last guy takes your picture and gives you four numbers and the address."

"Why go to him if it's such a circus?"

Ronnie shifted from foot to foot. "He's the most trustworthy. Once you're in, you can count on him. It's just a business deal, not some sketchiness from an addict. He gives you what you need, and it is what he says it is. No one ODs because he's cut the shit with fentanyl. But, I mean, I don't get any heroin, just the Oxy. For Isabelle." She pulled out her phone to see the time. "Please, Mr. Fra—Agent Jank—Please, I've got to go. Isabelle will kill me."

Agent Frank scanned her face, but he seemed to be thinking rather than seeing her. As if he had come to a decision, he gave a short nod. "Okay, but

99

tell me this before I let you go: what does Isabelle do with the Oxycontin?"

Would this guy ever leave her alone? "She sells it as a favor to her dinner guests, friends. I dunno. They leave money in their coat pockets and I leave them the Oxy. Please—"

"Okay, one more thing." He reached into his pocket and she flinched. He held out a business card. "Memorize it, throw it away. And call me any time you think of something, or find out something I should know."

She didn't take it.

"It won't bite you. Just take it."

She shook her head, half turned away. "I've got to go." She felt something at her back pocket and whipped around, hand over her pocket.

He gave her a grin. "Go on now. You need to keep your job. For everyone's sake."

No shit she needed to keep her job. She got to the corner as the light went yellow.

"Hey!"

He stood where she'd left him, hands in his pants pockets, jacket open, the butt of his gun winking. He'd had a gun all this time she was talking to him.

"I don't need to tell you," his raised voice hit her, "not to say a word of this to your boss, right?"

She hesitated. It hadn't occurred to her to tell Isabelle.

Then just like that he was beside her, voice lowered. "Peter Franks is invited to the cocktail party next week and she better not know anything about today."

Ronnie took a step back and saluted him, then turned and ran. Every man for himself.

Chapter Thirteen

Frank paused on the sidewalk, grinning, watching Newsboy/Ron/Veronica/Ronnie run from him like a scared rabbit. No wonder those pastries at Isabelle's tea were so beat up.

He went to the subway entrance, the same one Ronnie tried to lose him in, and headed downtown. That meeting went pretty well. Her panic attack, if that's what it was, told him she had a lot at stake. So, Ron was just a girl dressing as a guy, gender fluid, they called it. As he had watched her run, her slim hips, the boy haircut with the bangs flopping over her forehead, he knew that when he had followed her that day, she had been striding along like a young man, shoulders back, chest up, taking up more sidewalk than necessary.

* * *

The express train slid into 23rd street, all brake-squealing, horn-honking, and he waited with the other passengers near the door, ready to spring out as soon as they opened. A guitarist serenaded them as they streamed past and Frank almost ignored him per usual, but then he swerved toward him, eliciting some swear words from the people behind him who couldn't have anticipated his sudden move. The guitarist appeared fairly clean, his case open in front of him with change and bills in it, a microphone and amplifier hooked up to better blast the crowd. Frank waited until the song, if that's what you'd call it, ended, pulled all of his change out of his pocket and sprinkled it in the case.

"Nice playing," he said.

The guy nodded, twisted some knobs on the guitar, adjusted the mic.

"Excuse me." Frank pulled out Cathy's picture, unfolded it. "Before you start again, can I ask you?" He held the photo up. "Have you seen this girl?"

The guitarist shook his head no, tested out a chord, made some more adjustments.

"Please, can you truly look at her? She's my daughter. She's run away."

Guitar guy took the picture, studied it, shook his head once more, and held the paper out to return it.

"Keep it? And watch for her, please. My number's on there." He had hoped the plea would be enough, but then he got out his wallet, dropped a twenty in the case, stared at the guy. Waited. The musician gave a shrug, placed Cathy's picture on his backpack, and returned to his strumming. As Frank walked up the stairs, up to the fresh air and busy streets, he knew it was a long shot, but he had to keep at it, distribute her picture everywhere. He could never predict when the case would break; he just had to trust that it would.

* * *

Susan had asked to meet after work sometime, and today he was available, so he headed uptown straight from the office to meet her in his old neighborhood, that bar near the corner where they would go, just the two of them. As he walked, he found himself bargaining with God, something he hadn't done since he was maybe in his early teens. First, the pleading, before he realized what he was doing, the words matched the rhythm of his steps over and over: pleasegodpleasegodpleasegod. When he had to stop for the light to change, he tried to break it, and that's when the bargaining started, as if he were a child: I'll be good, just please bring Cathy back. I'll do anything you ask, just bring her home to us. He hoped his father wasn't up there witnessing Cathy's—his heart dropped into his stomach. Christ if he had seen all this from whatever heavenly perch... He sped up as if he could leave his thoughts behind, images of his father's shocked expression, images of what Cathy was doing right now. Maybe she was already home, in the shower, waiting for her mom to come home, hoping all would be forgiven.

And Mickey McAllister. His feet pounded the sidewalk, his fists clenched. What he wanted to do to him. He didn't know whether he wanted to see him at Isabelle's next event or wanted never to see him again so he wouldn't be tempted to rearrange his perfect nose and smug smile. He circled the block. He couldn't steam into the restaurant like this. Susan would think the anger was aimed at her. The statute of limitations wasn't up yet on the hit and run, but there was no evidence, nothing he could use, unless he could get a confession out of him…

He found Susan in a booth in the back, a good spot because he could watch the rest of the restaurant, a bad one because it probably meant she wanted the privacy in order to yell at him. She had saved him the seat with his back to the kitchen, and he slid in, nodded hello, noted the half glass of white wine in front of her, the downturn of her mouth.

He glanced at his watch. "I didn't think I was late. Am I?"

She shook her head, took a sip of wine. "I would've ordered you a drink, but I didn't know what you'd want. Or if you'd want it. Are you working a case? Do we have time to talk or are you going to get a phone call and run out on me?"

He sat back, shoulders against the wooden booth, arms crossed, watched the emotions run over her face, her mouth working, her eyes flashing then subsiding, and now her face slack, her head down. She played with her wine glass.

"I'm sorry," she said into it. "You'd think I'd be over it by now." She had her thumb and two fingers on the stem, twisted the glass back and forth, back and forth, the cheap wine swirling. "Or used to it." She drained the glass, placed it near the edge of the table as if someone would magically appear with a refill. "What happened to us?"

He couldn't answer that.

"We were so in love, remember? So broke in grad school, but so sure of our future together…" Her eyes searched his, back and forth, as if there were actual words she could read. "Well, anyway, I just wanted to see what you've been up to. If you have any leads, any hope—"

A waiter appeared, took her glass, asked Frank if he could get him anything, rushed away. Frank bet himself it would be a full three minutes before he reappeared. He leaned his elbows on the table, glanced at his watch.

"I talked to that girl at the other school, followed the trail of each name, eventually got a phone number," he told her, "but it's for a burner phone. No answer. Who knows if it's still good."

Their drinks came, Frank losing his bet by forty-six seconds, Susan grabbed hers like she thought it would save her life, slugged a third of it down.

"I check in with everyone, but no one, the Locals, the Bureau, no one has any leads."

She drained her glass.

"Let's get some food." He held his hand up for the waiter.

By the time Susan had downed her third glass of wine, picked at a salad until Frank felt sorry for it, her eyes had filled and emptied several times, tears running silently down her cheeks, and she had used six napkins trying to stem the flow. It was his fault, of course. He shifted in his seat. It was his fault, but not in the way she thought.

"Why were you always so hard on her? Restricting her Facebook, grilling her about her friends, demanding to meet the parents." Susan sniffed, then took another sip of wine. "Like she was the criminal!"

Susan hit the nail on the head, and she didn't even know it. If Frank hadn't scrutinized what Cathy had been wearing that night, if he hadn't let her storm out...maybe she wouldn't have been in the Village, not paying attention as she and her friends crossed the street... Susan's voice quieted, and he tuned in.

"I guess I thought that she was so good as a child that maybe she'd go through adolescence unscathed." Her face was open, the skin sagged around her mouth, her eyes dark around the edges like they would never lose the hurt.

He toyed with his spoon which sat idle by his plate, stared at it a moment then ventured, almost to himself, "I never got in trouble when I was a teenager."

"Of course you didn't." Susan's voice was sandpaper dry.

"Did you?"

"Is the statute of limitations up?"

"Some things don't have a statute of limitations. Murder, treason, kidnapping—" He stopped mid-counting, one finger still on the ring finger of the other hand, because she had let out a snort.

"Christ, Frank. You take everything so seriously. That was supposed to be a joke." A pause while she studied him, then her face crumpled, and he almost wished she were angry instead. "Do you think we'll find her? Maybe she'll come home? Oh, Frank…"

* * *

They stood on the sidewalk, the night air still warm, the city a bit quieter in the gap between workers and restaurant-goers. Frank had promised to let her know what he found out, and Susan had started walking toward their—her apartment.

"Aren't you going this way, too?" She asked him.

He shook his head.

"Oh," she said. "Then where are you going? Oh, that's right," she turned around and headed up the block, still talking. "I can't ask. You can't tell me. Never mind." Her head hung down like the muscles in her neck couldn't be bothered, her rounded shoulders making her look small. She seemed oblivious to everything around her, and Frank followed her at a distance, eyes scanning the streets all the way to her apartment building, ready to race to her if someone approached.

* * *

Sauna hot, crowded, and noisy, Isabelle's living room created a perfect setting for Frank Jankowski. Peter Franks' invitation allowed him to attend the cocktail party from 6:30 to 7:30, so he figured it was one of those parties so big the guests had to be staggered. He had arrived at 6:00, found a harried Ronnie who merely thrust a hanger at him and went to open the door to the next group, not realizing he didn't have an overcoat. Nor that he still had his phone. She gave no sign that she thought of him as anything other than just another guest.

Earlier in the week he had found himself looking forward to returning to the brownstone, a vague positive feeling bubbling up whenever he pictured it. Maybe the decorating had caused it, the pale yellow of the living room, the pale pink of the powder room, the mirrors making the space seem larger. A rich, elegant escape from the mess his personal life was becoming. Or maybe it was his delectable hostess, the Svengali in her tugging him in. Whatever the reason, he was glad to be here, glad to be working.

In the living room doorway he paused, surveyed the scene. A silver tray with Philippe Reynard's check for $10,000 sat conspicuously on a sideboard, a crystal bell resting on a coaster next to it. Maybe Peter Franks should give $50,000. But the budget. Maybe he could write a check and have it bounce. Ha.

The same brochures covered nearly every other surface, proclaiming Instruments for Children! A group of men stood near the windows and he moved toward them. Children in third world countries might benefit more from something other than musical instruments. Evidently the denizens of the Upper East Side didn't agree with him, since the room was packed and he had to thread his way through expensive blazers and cocktail dresses, the conversation and perfume swirling around him.

Frank introduced himself to the group, memorized names, asked them how they knew Isabelle, did she give these kind of parties often.

"Oh," the guy with the buttons on his starched shirt undone too far gestured with his drink hand. "About four times a year she does one of these things. Figure it's an easy way to get a tax deduction and spend some time smelling her perfume. Have you seen her tonight? Never fails to disappoint."

A bell started to ring, a happy tinkling sound, getting louder as the crowd noise died down, everyone turning toward the jingling. Isabelle stood at the tray near the door, the crystal bell held high in her hand, the somewhat irritating sound fading. Her hair was twisted in an elaborate configuration tonight, and for a moment he wondered if he could take it all down merely by removing one of the chopsticks. The Asian theme continued in her dress, a cheongsam, he believed it was called: form fitting but buttoned tight at the throat; long but slit high up the thigh. It seemed to be molded to her body.

"I wanted to announce that my dear friend," she paused to look down at the tray, then quickly up at her guests, one of whom had snickered, "I just needed to see how much." She shot a look in the direction of the snicker. "Mickey McAllister, the lovely man, has donated $5,000 to this wonderful charity! I'm sure someone," and here she scanned the crowd, lingered on one person, then another, "would love to match or better him!" The murmuring started again, and one of the men she'd singled out reached inside his blazer. "And when you do, I'll ring the bell for you as well!" She let out a laugh, a silvery echo of the crystal bell, and someone else approached the table.

Frank hadn't seen the Silver Fox when he'd come in, but now he was all he could see. The man who had run his daughter over because he was late to the theater. And she had meant so little to him that he hadn't stopped. He'd made a calculation that her life wasn't worth the risk of the charges against him when the cops came. Frank shoved his fists into his pants pockets, focused on getting his breath back to normal.

"You should turn over your pledge." Philippe's deep voice came over his shoulder. He cleared his throat, releasing a growl at Frank. "Tonight. But when you do," he growled again, "she shouldn't ring the bell for you."

Frank stepped away from the big guy, gave him a grin as he patted himself down. "Forgot my checkbook." The Silver Fox moved to the door, Isabelle having finally released him from all the squeezing and patting. "In fact, I'll go back right now and get it. Excuse me."

He wove his way quickly through the crowded room. Isabelle still stood by the table, now surrounded by a group of men, her back to him, and her throaty laughter following him out the door. At least he wouldn't have to waste time saying goodbye to his hostess. He double-timed it down the stairs, waved at Ronnie as he burst out the door and down the white stone steps. He looked left, then right, a flash of silver going into the garage at the end of the block. Frank's feet moved before his brain instructed them, and he made it to the garage in time to see the Silver Fox heading up the ramp to the second floor.

"Hey, Mickey!" Frank hoofed it up the ramp, an engine starting up on a floor above. Either he hadn't heard him, or hadn't wanted to. At the top of the ramp, Frank looked around, the guy's fancy leather shoes tip-tapping on the cement. He sped toward the sound, caught him in the middle of the aisle. "Hey! Some party, huh? Good for you," he slugged Mickey's arm in an atta boy gesture, "for giving so generously."

The Silver Fox jumped back and eyed him.

"Peter Franks, you remember? From dinner the other night? Tea the week before?" He clapped his hand on his shoulder, just pals together. "Where are you parked? Is that your big silver car over in the corner, the Bentley?"

Mickey nodded. "I'm sorry, terrible hurry, gotta go." He quickened his pace.

Frank kept even with him. "Totally understand. You're usually in a hurry, aren't you? Late for Isabelle's, late for opening of night of Les Mis…"

Mickey whipped his head at him, a trace of fear in his eyes before he looked away. "Nice to see you, uh, Peter, I really need to—"

"Very fancy car. They say you have a driver these days." Frank bent over, ran his hand along the bumper. "So smooth."

Mickey's keys jangled, and Frank blocked him from the driver's side door. "Peter, I'm not sure what you—"

Frank looked to the corner, at the ceiling. No cameras. "You see, Mickey, about a year and a half ago, my daughter was hospitalized, had to have multiple surgeries, got hooked on the opioids they gave her for the intense pain."

Mickey took a step back, looked around like someone could rescue him. Or he could flee.

Frank grabbed his wrist. Squeezed. "I need you to hear me on this."

"I had nothing—"

"Big silver car, she said, her friends said. Fled the scene."

"Do you know how many—"

"But you hit someone, didn't you? Late to the theater, expensive tickets in your pocket, and you didn't care that my daughter lay there, all broken up, because you—"

"It wasn't my fault! The light was still yellow, she was jaywalking, wearing all black. I didn't even know until I saw the blood all over the hood!"

In one sudden motion, Frank twisted his wrist behind his back, bent his face over the hood. "Is this where my daughter's blood was? You just took off, didn't even bother to stop!"

"I'm so sorry. I didn't mean it. I thought everything was fine." His voice bounced off the metal. "By the time I saw my hood, it was too late. I couldn't very well turn myself in. But I have nightmares…it's awful."

Frank slammed his head into the car, lifted it, slammed harder, Mickey's nose giving way in a sickening, satisfying way, the sound of flesh denting metal echoing in the garage. He pulled him up, the blood gushing, splattering The Fox's silver suit. Frank spun him so they faced each other. Mickey's eyes no longer looked fearful. They were streaming from the pain of the broken nose, but he looked…relieved. Like Frank had given him what he wanted, what he felt he deserved.

Frank released him, took a step back, eyed him up and down. "Maybe you'll give Isabelle's invitations a miss for a while." He waited until the Silver Fox nodded, then spun on his heel, headed away, his hard shoes striking the cement, the sound like gun shots.

Chapter Fourteen

Ronnie had felt sick for the past few days. Not a cold, not a fever, but her stomach leaden, pain jabbing her every time she thought about FBI Frank. She couldn't eat, and if she managed to fall asleep, she woke up in a whoosh, sitting up suddenly, heart hammering, breath fast.

How long was she going to have this cop hangover? She avoided Isabelle as much as possible, worried that somehow Isabelle would read it in her face, know that she had talked to a cop. She wasn't a snitch, and in a weird way, that was one of the reasons she'd never tell Isabelle. Plus, Isabelle would blame her. Really blame her. Not just because everything was already Ronnie's fault, but because he'd followed her here, she'd brought him here, and if he found out she'd told Isabelle, he'd put her right in jail. She was not going to jail. But she didn't want to get kicked out of here either. What if Isabelle found out afterward that she'd known all along? But why was he still undercover if what he wanted was the drug dealer, and Ronnie had already told him he couldn't get to him?

Her thoughts spun. She visited the same questions over and over, and she didn't know what to do with herself. When she sat down, her legs jumped, and she got up and paced her apartment. She got to the front door, and then she was out of it, slamming it, taking the steps to the sidewalk two at a time, heading east, the horns, the people, the sirens. She tried to let all of it in, overwhelm her senses to drive out all thoughts, all feelings. Maybe if she walked long enough, she would be too exhausted to think.

* * *

110

Ronnie jolted awake. Jesus what was she thinking? You never fell asleep on the subway—those were the people she and Matt preyed on when they ran out of money. Matt. Would Matt have known what to do with an undercover cop? Hah. Matt would be surprised to see her working as a butler, serving like this, living where she was. She didn't know what stop was next, but she got ready to get off, held onto the pole even though it meant standing close to the guy in the suit. Her eyes ran down him without her thinking about it, looking for his wallet, a gaping jacket, a bulging pocket, the deft movement of her fingers hidden by the rocking of the train car. But she wasn't sure how soon the stop was coming, how much time before she could leave quick—she mentally shook herself. She didn't need to risk doing that anymore. The way things were going, this would be the time her number was up, and she'd get caught for sure. For the last time.

She headed up the stairs and hit the sidewalk before her brain wondered what she was doing. For some reason her legs decided to walk before going into the steamy tunnels again to return uptown. She couldn't take any more of the artificial light, the noise of the trains, the press of the people. Ronnie paused on the corner, glanced one way and then the other to learn which way was east, which way uptown, calculate how far down the island she had gone. Figure out exactly where she was. She turned left, hoped it was the right direction, searched for indicators, familiar street names. She must be way down near the end, the streets closer together, a few tall buildings, but mostly short ones, windows papered over at the street level, trash blowing around.

Her sense of direction hadn't failed her, and she picked up the pace, turned to head west, stuck close to Lexington for the subway when her legs tired. A prickling on her neck, and she looked around, lengthened her stride. Nothing seemed to be putting her in danger, so maybe it was just left over from FBI Frank. But then her stomach joined in on the warning signals, and she paused at the break in the sidewalk, peeking down the grimy alleyway. Dumpsters, garbage, large cardboard box no doubt doubling as a shelter at night for a homeless person. Her feet started into the alley, her mind yelled stop, her body ignored it. Puddles, damp air, cigarette smoke, urine, an odd silence, a lurching in her chest.

This was where it had happened. She searched around, as if he could still be here, even now. She stood still, her chest heaving, her eyes tightening around the edges. This was where she had woken up that morning, the day hot even in here, the grit in her mouth, eyeballs, between her fingers, car horns and loud engines a vague background as she turned to Matt. They had spent the last three nights in this alley, piling up cardboard for privacy and for a bit of a mattress. Matt had been leaning against the wall as if he'd fallen asleep that way, his head at an odd angle resting on his shoulder, and she moved to touch his arm, tell him she was hungry, going to find food. Her hand snapped back when she saw the needle still sticking out of his arm, the band still tight above his elbow. Her eyes glued to him as she backed away, the grey of his skin more pronounced, the stillness of him radiating, and she took another step away as if she could catch it from him.

Still his clothes, his hair, his face, mouth slack, bones knobbing through clothes. But it was an imitation of him, a prop they'd left for a movie set when Ronnie was asleep. She eased him down onto his sleeping bag, straightened him out, took everything from his pockets but his ID, paused a moment to study the picture of her mother, creased diagonally across, the white showing through where she held a child's hand. She left the needle in his arm and left him in the alley, grabbed anything useful from his backpack.

Even now she could feel the blast of the hot summer air that had slammed her as she hit the sidewalk, the sun promising the hottest day yet, the air humid, weighing heavy on her, her heart beating fast, and her legs breaking into a run.

* * *

Not ready to head home, Ronnie got off at Grand Central, wove her way through the crowds in the huge main concourse, sidestepping when a tourist suddenly stopped, pulled out her phone, turned slowly in a circle for a video record of her travels. Ronnie noted the backpack at her feet left unattended, calculated the quick swipe and a run through the crowd, then shrugged to herself, went up the escalator and out through the doors. Not her monkey, not her circus.

The library had been a nice refuge when she had lived on the streets, and she had doled it out, kept it as a treat, just in case the librarians got tired of seeing her, tried to usher her out. She went up the stone steps now, stupid tourists posing by the stone lions, the statues guarding and welcoming, their gaze out straight and steady as if to say, go ahead, everything is fine. More tourists just inside, in the cool, the dark, the warm wood paneling, the marble floors, few daring to go up even more stairs. Ronnie casually walked past them and up, as if she owned the place. She had quickly learned what so many people knew: if you acted as if you belonged, people didn't question your being there. Even the people who really did belong.

No one looked at her as she went into the huge room, row after row of wooden tables, each with the green shaded lamps and high stools, the books giving off a wise mustiness, a librarian behind a counter saying something low as she handed over a book to a patron. Ronnie found her favorite spot, in the corner in the back, the whole of the room spread out in front of her. Few people were there, maybe because it was the middle of the day, maybe because it was so nice outside.

She pulled out her phone, time to stop avoiding Matt. She typed in *where are homeless people buried in nyc?* Google immediately gave her Hart Island, and she pressed on that link, then dropped the phone, looking around as it clattered to the table. No one glanced up. The page that had come up said "Department of Correction." Eyeing the phone as if it might come after her, she slid off the stool. She let out a long breath, climbed back on the stool. Okay, this was silly. No way they could tell she was on their site. Plus, it was about a graveyard, not prison, but why was the Department of Correction involved in burying the homeless?

She picked up the phone by the edges, turned it over slowly as if it might let out an alarm, scream like a banshee at her. She refreshed the view. You could search for a person who might be buried there, and she carefully put in Matt's first and last name, hesitated over the button, not sure if she wanted the answer or not. She'd been dreaming about him so much, and then the alley today, it was like he was trying to tell her something. Not that she believed in ghosts or anything. She touched "search" and waited. And there it was. Matthew A. Charles. His skinny, drug-tortured body had been buried in the city plot, numbered, listed for the world to see. She went through the site to find out how she could go there and found her answer about the Department of Correction: they maintained the place, used prisoners, paid them fifty cents an hour. Ugh. Dammit. To visit she needed ID, to put in an application, show who you were. Jeez, why all these rules for dead people? These were only graves. Maybe they thought if a person was related to one of the prisoners who worked there, they'd bring a chisel and bury it for them or something.

She sucked in her breath. She had found him. Maybe they'd said something over him as they buried him. She was glad she had left his ID on him. Glad they could bury him with his name. She had some comfort in that. If she ever ran into one of her other brothers, she would tell them that. She shivered suddenly, then heard the downstairs neighbor's voice in her head, the little old lady who gave her cookies. "Someone must've walked over my grave." She shuddered, on purpose this time, then slid off the stool and slid her phone into her back pocket.

* * *

Two days later, Ronnie ran the vacuum, back and forth, back and forth over the thinning carpet, the nap so nonexistent that she barely made any marks, no sweep of dark to show where she'd already been. The living room didn't need it, but she did. She needed Isabelle to think she was being useful, and she needed some kind of activity to soothe her brain, try to get away from her dream from last night. Actually, she had the dream this morning—that time before you wake up when you're kind of aware of your dream, sort of watching it as you're going through it—this dream followed her around as she cleaned. It coated everything.

Of course, it was about Matt. Sort of about when he'd died, but somehow it wasn't horrible, not that shock of seeing him beside her on that hot, sticky early morning when the grit pressed into her skin and she knew it would be a day that just never left her alone.

No, this dream was different, and maybe that was why it stayed with her as she moved around the room, the quiet sunlight coming in the windows from the street. They were on a stoop together, talking, or just sitting, and then she remembered: *Hey,* she said, *aren't you dead? I mean, no offense, but didn't you die that time?*

He'd looked at her, his old self, the self she'd known forever before the Beast got to him, before he'd lost himself to the streets, and he smiled sweetly, like when she was seven and he would hold a piece of candy behind his back, teasing a little before he gave it to her.

Well, I did, and I didn't, he'd said in her dream, *I'm still kinda here, but not on the streets.* Then, in her dream, she thought about how she'd left him there. What kind of person leaves their dead brother in the alley?

She'd looked at him from under her bangs, wondering what he thought of that, afraid he might be mad at her, afraid she would never see him again. He slung his arm across her shoulders, pulling her closer to him, a sideways hug from the one brother who cared about her. She stole a glance at him to see if she could tell what he was thinking. He stared out into the street, but he had a smile on his face, that smile he had where it seemed like he thought the world was okay. And that okay feeling was what was coloring her morning as she went about her chores.

Ronnie put the vacuum away in the tiny closet and went to the kitchen for a glass of water, gazed out the window over the sink, wondered if Isabelle ever went out there. The okay feeling was from Matt, but her own guilt still nagged at her. Stumbling across the alley, and now this dream. She knew she had to go see his grave, as if somehow it would help, usher him into the next world or whatever BS people said. She didn't believe in all that woo-woo spirit stuff, but it made her feel a little better, knowing he'd been buried, thinking his mind was at rest, he was free from the drugs and the streets.

A glass of water was not going to cut it, so she went to her apartment, grabbed her jacket and left. She needed the motion to ease her mind, the people, the noise to help her think about something else. She'd head down to the Village. Something was always going on there. Maybe she'd slip into a theater, watch some weird independent film and lose herself. She was on autopilot as she walked, her arms swinging, her heels clicking, avoiding the guy buried in his phone, and the three girls taking up most of the sidewalk. Her brain must have made a decision before she realized it, because all of a sudden, she leaned against the wall of the building out of the sunlight, and pulled out her phone, punched on Frank's number. She listened, waited, got voicemail. She was not leaving him a message.

The bus came, slowly angled to the curb, spit people out, the ones waiting to get on barely gave them enough room to get off. New Yorkers. She'd heard that in Japan, everyone lined up, patiently waiting. But then she'd also heard there were special guards at the subway stations whose job it was to push the sardined people in so the doors could close.

No room of course, never were empty seats on the buses, though since people sat, there had to be sometimes. The bus moved slowly down Fifth. Ronnie hung from the strap, ducked to watch out the window as a crazy person stopped people on the sidewalk, tap-danced in front of them. Her phone in her hoodie pocket buzzed, making her jump. She looked at it, put it back. She'd forgotten that even if she didn't leave a message, he would still have her number. Great. Now, this phone tethered her to Isabelle and to FBI Frank. It buzzed again, a short one. He'd left a damn message. She sighed. She had called him, after all. She didn't want to talk on the phone—she didn't want to talk to him at all when you got right down to it, but she figured it was her best hope.

* * *

She waited for him on the bench at the south end of the Park, where all the tourists streamed in after pressing their noses to the lineup of famous stores on Fifth Avenue: Louis Vitton, FAO Schwartz, Tiffany. She'd watched them with Matt, groups of them jaywalking to The Plaza, taking pictures of the carriages parked in front, some of them getting in, a hundred-dollar ride through the park, something to post on social media for their friends to envy. The tourists were, of course, the easiest to borrow from, no radar, shopping bags hanging open, screeching at their friends to get closer to each other, the group crowding around the phone to see the picture, the fanny pack around the back just begging to be explored.

"Dude."

No. Not Annie, not now. Ronnie didn't answer, didn't even look at her. Maybe she'd go away.

She sat down next to her, a dog with a bandana around its neck on her lap. "Got something to share?" Annie half turned to face her, and Ronnie felt her checking her over as if she were hiding candy somewhere.

She crossed her arms and still didn't look at her.

"C'mon man, I know you're into something. Lookit your clothes. Luck came your way, and you should share it with an old friend."

"That tour group just got off the bus. Maybe they're feeling generous."

Annie sprinted with the dog to the corner, her hand out before she reached the group.

A man in a suit sat down, and Ronnie jumped up. So many people in this city.

"You called me, remember?"

Jesus. What was wrong with her. Agent Frank. "You got here fast. So many people around here."

"Like that girl with the dreads?"

"What the f—how long have you been watching me?"

"Long enough to think you two know each other."

"She's not my friend, whatever you and she might think."

He put his arm along the back of the bench. "So, what's up?"

Now Ronnie was sorry she'd called him. Practically the first thing she learned as a kid was that you never talked to cops. They weren't your friend. And if they were then you were the worst thing of all: a snitch. She stole a sideways look at him, all Mr. Nice Guy with his arm so casually thrown across the bench back like they were best buddies.

"No. Y'know what? This was a mistake. I didn't mean to call you." She got up to walk out of the park. "It was a butt dial," she said over her shoulder and lengthened her stride to full fast mode, calculating the route around the Japanese tourists bunched at the sidewalk.

"Are you sure?"

What the fuck? How fast could this guy move?

"Are you sure you don't have something for me?" Frank said, low and quiet, his eyes on the light as if waiting for it to change. She had to angle her head way over to see his face, the line of his chin, the reasonable expression he'd put on.

The light changed, but she didn't move. People flowed around them, someone bumping her. He took her arm, a gentle touch, said, "Let's go over here out of the crowd," and steered her to a bench against the grey brick wall in the shade, facing out onto the traffic on Fifth. He glanced at his watch and said he had plenty of time. It was one of those cheap black Casios, very different from the bling Peter Franks wore.

"You must know a lot of these kids who hang out here." Frank's tone was mild, a little curious even.

She shrugged, watched the traffic, the endless cars, taxis, buses.

"So why did you call me?"

She shifted in her seat, swallowed, then said, "I need something from you if I'm going to spy on my boss."

He raised an eyebrow at her. "My not arresting you isn't enough?"

"Forget it." She slid down on the bench, her chin on her chest, her legs stretched out on the bricks of the sidewalk. She traced the weeds growing in the cracks.

"Okay, okay. Tell me what you need, and I'll figure out if it's doable."

She rubbed her hands on her thighs and felt the bracelet in the right-hand pocket. She'd forgotten about it. She didn't know why she'd put it in her pocket today. A reminder of something? A good luck charm? "I lost my ID, and I need a new one."

He had leaned over to better hear her and when she stopped talking, he leaned away, his expression blank. He said to the traffic, "Why do you suddenly need an ID?" He cut his eyes to her. "Going somewhere?"

"No, I'm not—I don't have any money. Even if I wanted to, I couldn't go anywhere."

"Tell me why you want this. We both know," he paused while a taxi blew its horn. Frank waited for the traffic to start moving and the horn to stop blaring, then said, "You could get money if you wanted it."

"I told you I'm not going anywhere. I just need an ID. And I'm asking you because I don't have a birth certificate or anything else, and I don't want to have to answer a whole lot of questions." She blew out her breath. He had to do this for her.

"Besides mine, you mean."

"Okay. Besides yours."

He pulled out his little notebook, got down to business, asked her a bunch of things, what hospital, parents' full names, siblings. She surprised herself by remembering her mother's maiden name, not sure where she dragged that out of. This seemed a little too easy, and she wondered if she should have asked him for something bigger.

"Okay. I can take care of this. I need a picture of you, but the rest is no problem." Frank put his notebook away. "Now, do you have anything for me?"

"Once I have my ID."

Ronnie watched Frank's face. Mouth, eyebrows, lids—not a twitch. But he couldn't hide his eyes, blue as they were. He seemed to be weighing, assessing, calculating. He cleared his throat.

"You don't trust me."

"You're a cop."

"And we can get IDs, real IDs made, all the time. As I said, no problem. After I get your picture, you'll have yours in a week. But if you've got something important, something that might require action, I'd like to know it now."

She chewed on her lip, swung her bangs off her forehead. "I—" She stole a glance at him. "I actually don't have anything." He sent a sharp look her way. "No, really. I just thought that maybe something would come up during the week, so I could tell you something then."

"Delay tactic?" The eyebrow again. "Okay, I'll get you this ID, but I want you to find Isabelle's laptop. Know where it is, because next week I'm going to trade you the ID for a thumb drive, and then you're going to download the hard drive to it."

Ronnie's heart started racing and she sat up, eyes darting, sidewalk, street, trees, falafel vendor, bench. *Easy now*, she heard Frank's voice say through the rushing in her ears, and her mouth fell open. She edged away from him, wondering if her legs could hold her.

"Breathe." A hand patted her shoulder. She twisted out of his reach but didn't run. Why couldn't she have this panic attack in peace?

"Okay, don't worry about it."

She cut her eyes to him.

"Really. I mean it. Let's go find an empty side of a building to take your picture, and I'll text you when it's ready."

Ronnie put her head between her knees and waited for the buzzing to stop, her heart to slow down, the world to come back into focus. Just her luck. She lands a safe, easy gig, learning the long con, and it's already infiltrated by an FBI agent. No. Not already. He followed her. Damn. Well, she'd figure a way to stall him. She had to.

Chapter Fifteen

He used to be able to sleep, turn off the noise in his head, make his brain a clean slate, and get the rest he needed. But now, whenever he came home, put work aside per usual, Cathy came flooding in, and tonight, he didn't even feel like going to bed. He seesawed between hope that she would come home soon and despair that they would never find her. He thought he would feel better after confronting Mickey, but he didn't. Something in the way the guy seemed grateful that he'd broken his nose for him took the emotional pleasure away. He kept replaying it, and all he felt was a physical satisfaction, pleasure in the fight. He went through some of the motions of getting ready for bed, turning on the dishwasher, straightening the cushions on the couch, turning off the lights in the living room, and at the last minute he grabbed his coat and went out, a soft rain misting the air.

The city at night had a different personality, different people were out, the night people. Different from the ones you see on the subways commuting, the ones smashed into each other at 8:45 a.m., the ladies in their office clothes and scuffed flats, the men in ill-fitting suits, so many of them young-looking, waiting for their big break, unaware that the city would crush them. At night the uniform was a hoodie mostly, occasionally someone with their dog on a leash for a quick break, couples too in love to care where they were, a crowd of kids spilling out of a restaurant. Corner grocery stores were just closing, the light illuminating the raindrops, workers bringing in the buckets of unsold flowers, rolling security gates slammed down and locked, the shop owners hurrying home.

Frank found himself along the East River, far from his own apartment, and for some reason, he ducked into a bar. He didn't know he wanted a drink, but now it seemed like a great idea. No desire to talk to anyone, but he needed people nearby while he drank. He sat at the end of the bar, away from everyone else, with a view of the door, angled his stool so he could lean against the wall and not have anyone behind him. He nursed the whiskey and turned inward, aware of the other people but not interested in them. Cathy there, simmering below everything else, and though he didn't want to think of her, she came to him, nonetheless. How had it happened that he, Frank Jankowski, upright citizen, FBI agent, upholder of the law and pursuer of criminals, had a daughter so hooked on opioids she had to be in rehab? And now, his daughter, that sweet face, had run away. And where was she? Every time he thought of her out on the streets, a fist grabbed his heart and he wanted to move, run, shake it loose, smash the wall.

This bar was such a dive that he knew there was no chance he would run into anyone who would recognize him. So, when the bartender kept refilling his glass, he decided to stop counting the number of drinks. The smooth, thick liquid a shock to his tongue, the burning down his throat, the fire released in his stomach. When she was born, Frank had fervently wished his father had been alive to see her, hold her. She had been so perfect, so precious. Now he hoped his father was up there busy with something else, not seeing how far his granddaughter had fallen. Frank twisted in his seat, looked toward the back. People were going in and out, must be the bathroom. He might have to have another drink to get away from this abyss, but the thought of the bathroom made him aware of his bladder.

That last image he had of Cathy was when the staff led her away from them, the way she looked over her shoulder at them, her make-up so dark her eyes disappeared into something angry, like an alien from a sci-fi movie, as if she'd come from different parents, ones who hadn't loved her, cared for her, done everything they could to give her a happy childhood. Taught her to discern right from wrong, to study hard, to care about others, stay safe. This was not his daughter. He had to remember that: it was the drugs, like a monkey on her back, as the Director of the facility had said. When she made it through rehab, his daughter would return to him. To them. Now he had to find her, get her safe, and locate the sonofabitch who had supplied her the drugs.

He left three twenties on the bar and slid off his stool. The dark bathroom was tiny and inexplicably crowded. He just wanted to pee. He stood at the urinal, aware of the door opening and closing a few times. Somebody was in the stall, someone else pounding on the door, yelling at him to hurry up.

Frank zipped up, the bathroom seeming even smaller than when he came in. "Why don't you leave him alone?" He said to the guy as he turned to go.

"None of your fucking business." The door pounder was wiry, pale, soft, and, weirdly, wearing sunglasses.

"Probably not." Frank shrugged. "But why can't the guy take a shit in peace?"

He turned to the sink, the guy in the corner next to it, same one who had been there when he'd come in.

"He's not taking a shit! C'mon fuckwit, open up!" He started rattling the door this time.

"Maybe he's passed out," Frank said. "Maybe I can help."

"There's nothing here for you, old man." The words came from the corner near the sink, steady and low.

Frank looked from the stall to the sink and back.

"Go on. Leave." The guy next to the sink pointed to the door with his chin, just as someone opened it, came in, crowded Frank. He grabbed the edge of the door before it could swing shut, looked at the sink guy in time to catch the palm exchange, a flash of white, the hand sliding gracefully into the pocket, the money-green winking at him.

"Still here?" Sink guy straightened up, his lip curling into a sneer. "I said nothing for you."

Frank let go of the door.

"Old. Man."

Motion slowed as Frank came toward the guy, the background tattoo of the other guy pounding on the stall door muffled as air rushed in his ears. He knew the drug dealer scum must have a gun tucked into his pants at the small of his back, and before the guy had time to make a move, Frank open-handed him hard on the side of his head, his skin flattened, bone solid on Frank's palm, the guy's head smashing into the porcelain with a thwunk, a pause, then he slid down to the floor. All at once, sound and time sped up, and he ducked out the door, the dealer sprawled in the corner, the guy with the sunglasses standing and staring.

Frank felt nothing. He kept moving through the bar and out on to the street, the cold damp air slapping his face and making him hunch over, the echo of nothing here for you old man in a rhythm with his footsteps, over and over and over.

* * *

This time, Peter Franks and Isabelle skipped the lunch at the expensive restaurant and went straight to the stores. As far as he could tell, Isabelle never ate anyway, just sat across from him with her stockinged foot running up and down his shin, and encouraged him to order the most expensive bottle of wine and entrée. He was just as glad not to have her uneaten meal including dessert hit the budget.

This boutique was airy and light and held exactly one thing on each shelf, like a museum. At least the chairs were comfortable, the sparkling water welcome after all the walking. He had set his trap, Peter Franks texting her that he enjoyed watching her shop so much he hoped they could do it again real soon. And she had walked right into it, a return text dinging ten minutes later: *Meet me at BG old one same side as The Plaza 2:00* The lady certainly knew what she wanted. And he knew what he wanted, and it was for Peter Franks to pretend he had nothing better to do than indulge her in this luxury, to cater to her every whim so that Frank Jankowski could get all the evidence he needed to make an arrest.

She made quick work of Bergdorf's and they shopped their way south on Fifth, Frank mentally writing down each store to report back to Pete. This fancy perfumed store had pulled them in like a magnet, the traffic sounds muting as the doors closed behind them. Every store should have a seating area for the men, a salesperson who brought Perrier.

Isabelle came out of the dressing room in bare feet, and his stomach lurched at the sight. She wore the lingerie like it was a ball gown, a leopard print bodysuit complete with peep holes. The black lace outlined her curves, and as she twisted this way and then that, he reached for his glass of Perrier and held it over his lap like he was the most relaxed person in the world, like he watched lithe women model jungle underwear every single day. He breathed in through his nose, out through his mouth as surreptitiously as he could. He willed his face to stay cool, no blushing allowed.

She twirled. Came closer. "What do you think?" She leaned over, her cinnamon perfume surrounding him. She held out the tag for him to read: $1,225 handwritten in a delicate slant. "Don't you think Mrs. Franks would like one too?" She twirled away.

He closed his mouth. The shock of the price had made the Perrier in his lap no longer necessary, and he placed the glass carefully on the table at his elbow as if it were nitrogen. He cleared his throat.

"Well, I—"

She had disappeared back into the dressing room, the full-length door giving no hint to what she was up to. But he could guess. The door opened and he braced himself, but just her head and bare shoulders emerged. She told the salesperson she wanted to try on the Armani, and then the little gold number, and oh yes, the white cocktail dress that looked so divine. The woman raced through the store, handed stuff in, Isabelle handed stuff back, complained, chided, kept up a patter that had even Frank's head spinning. And he wasn't the one who had to keep track of all the things she was asking for. Finally, she emerged in the outfit she had come in wearing: loose black trousers and a loose chalk-blue linen blouse. She handed a pile of clothes and hangers to the clerk and said she'd get the panties and bra.

That was his cue. He fished out the American Express, half-wanting to kiss it for luck, wondered how high the balance could get before the Bureau cancelled it.

* * *

125

Out on the sidewalk, Isabelle announced she was famished, that she knew just the place, that they should get a cab because he looked a little peaked. He dutifully hailed a cab, held the door for her, and slid in next to her in time to hear her say, "The Russian Tea Room, please." Nice, expensive, touristy place. He hoped she didn't want him to get the caviar.

She took his arm, her eyes sparkling at him. "That was so much fun! Didn't you just love that leopard print teddy? I was afraid the black lace would give me away, but it lies perfectly flat under this blouse. Isn't that lucky?" She ran her hand from her shoulder to her waist, the linen smoothing and releasing.

He cleared his throat. "Lucky indeed." He squeezed her arm. Over $1,000 was a felony. He ran over the scene in his head. Had he played any part in it? No just carried the shopping bags while she carried herself and wore what had to be one of the more expensive pieces of lingerie in the city. So Frank hadn't crossed the line while undercover with criminals. The rules were clear: you did what you could to fit in undercover, but you didn't commit a crime unless it was an emergency. Life and death kind of emergency.

"Ooooh, but look what I found for you!" Isabelle rustled through the bags at their feet, and he shifted in his seat. She had not opened her wallet at any of these stores. Maybe when he left that one place before she had when he needed air, needed to get away from the perfumed and precious store?

Isabelle pulled out a closed hand, held it out to him, opened her fingers one by one, a Swiss Army Knife with all the blades out. Cozy in her palm, looking innocent and expensive, lay a pair of diamond cuff links.

"Oh no, darling, that's way too much for me." Frank grabbed the arm of the door as the driver hit the brakes, honking the horn at the same time. "I can't let you buy those for me. I insist you take those back, keep your money."

Isabelle laughed. It started low, a warm chuckle that moved up, expanded as it went, her eyes glittering, face crinkling until the laughter exploded, and she threw her head back, her lovely throat exposed, her blonde hair swaying. The taxi stopped, in the middle of the street, in front of the Russian Tea Room. Isabelle helped herself out of the car, left him to pay, to gather up

126

the shopping bags, to join her on the sidewalk where her laughter bounced off the windows.

"Oh, you are funny, Peter." She shook her head at him.

Or hysterical. If she stole those, and he carried the bags out, then he had committed a felony. She had committed it on his behalf, but the paperwork would be endless, the pause in his undercover activity unwelcomed.

She grabbed his wrist, and he put some of the shopping bags down. She stood close to him as she turned over his hand, his fingers relaxing open, a mind of their own. She gently placed the cufflinks in his palm like they were eggs in a nest, and she curled his fingers over them, giving him a little pat. "They're yours. You deserve them." Her words were a low hum. Their foreheads practically touched as they stood together, people flowing past them. "I can tell how exciting you find this. Now you can feel that excitement every time you look at these."

He slid them into his pocket so he could pick up the brightly colored bags, and he felt the cufflinks snuggle against his thigh, warm from her palm. She waited at the door to the restaurant, and he put the bags down again to open it for her. She swept in as if she were royalty.

Of course she ordered the full tea, complete with caviar and champagne, then made it seem like it was his idea. He sat along the banquet next to her, nodded and smiled while his brain, his second nature, observed and analyzed. Even the legendary Joe Pistone as Donnie Brasco had moved among the criminals and never committed a felony. This woman was far more dangerous than he had considered. Street smart, drawing room smart, city smart. She pushed things to an edge of her own choosing, not his.

"Wasn't that just so much fun!" Her laughter like glass breaking. Shattering.

He put the arm that wasn't next to her across the banquet and angled a little away from her. The better to study her. "Nothing like it." He gave her an indulgent smile. "Best thrill I can think of." He lowered his voice, leaned in. "Unless you've got something even more exciting going on I can be a part of."

She laughed. Other diners, tourists of course, turned to look. "Oh, Peter."

She rewarded him with a hand on his thigh, looked deeply into his eyes. "We've just begun and you want more?" She ticked her tongue like he was a wayward child. "Never satisfied, hmmmm?" She gave his thigh a squeeze, then reached for a scone off the tray, put it on the miniscule plate in front of her. It looked old, stale.

"Well?" He did his best imitation of an eager lapdog.

She drained her champagne glass. The laugh lines around her eyes crinkled again, though not as deeply. "Really, Peter. You are most extraordinary. And we are having fun. But I'm afraid I don't know you well enough to include you in quite everything. Yet."

The cinnamon, the muskiness of her perfume floated around them, as if her body had heated it up.

* * *

Frank and Pete met for their regular information dump on the undercover activities for the week. Pete should think about going undercover himself, since he was so good at changing his demeanor in this supervisory role. Gone was the banter, the friendship, the history together. They sat in the small conference room, once used for interrogation now the breakroom, Pete across from him with his notebook out, list of questions at the ready.

Frank went through his week, relating the initial shoplifting, the way she made sure he saw her, the conversation in the cab afterwards. "So that's why I decided that the way deeper in was through these shopping trips. Sent her a text, or rather Peter Franks sent her one saying how much he enjoyed the shopping and hoped they could do it again real soon."

Pete made a noise in his throat, but kept his head down, scribbled. Since he was left-handed and his handwriting was terrible, it was hard to read it upside down. "And the next shopping trip?"

"Bingo. The same afternoon I texted. We started at Bergdorf Goodman, made our way south." He listed every store, waited while Pete wrote them down, then pulled the purchases out of the bag and called them out with the prices. He returned them to the bag and pushed it across the table to

Pete. "I thought I'd return them all so they didn't hit the budget."

"I believe that's evidence for the moment. You're not spending anything otherwise, so let's hold off on that." Pete sat back, fiddled with his pen. "Let's talk for a moment about your making a tactical decision in the field when you had plenty of time to talk it over with your Supervisory Agent." He aimed a thumb at his own chest.

As if Frank didn't know who was supervising him while he was undercover.

"What made you think encouraging her felonious habits was the way to go?"

"Look, forget it. I'll tell her it scares me too much or something. Or Peter Franks will."

"Hold on, Frank. We'll overlook that oversight on your part. I truly want to know what it was that made it seem so right?"

"You know how it is…something in my gut." Let's just call it that for now. "She wanted me to see her snatch that scarf, and after, on the sidewalk, the way she snuggled up to me, to Peter Franks, like we shared a secret, a whole world opening up, we're in this together kind of thing."

Pete scribbled something down. "Okay. Makes sense. These are all the stores you went to? Then you went to the Russian Tea Room?"

"At that last one, the Chic Boutique, that was where she really went to town on the shoplifting."

Pete raised both eyebrows, pen poised. "Yes. And?"

"She walked out with $1,225 worth of underwear under her clothes."

"And you know this how?"

Frank caught a glint in his partner's eyes before he looked back to his notebook. He had a feeling this would be a main point that Pete would want to go over after the case, after they were done being official, and they could rehash all the delicious bits.

"She showed me the price tag in the store, then told me in the cab she had it on."

"So, now we have the lady committing a felony. Excellent. And the Russian Tea Room? How'd that go?"

"I tried to let her know I'd be interested in whatever else she had going but she deflected me. Said I was greedy. That she didn't know me well enough. Yet."

"Yet? That's what she said, 'Yet?' Boy howdy. I think you were right, Frank. This is the way to her very crooked heart. Okay, let's talk about what the next steps should be."

They spent the next half hour throwing out and rejecting ideas, analyzing possible outcomes from one line of action or another. Frank couldn't initiate anything because of an entrapment accusation. His text saying he liked watching her shop was harmless, and Pete encouraged him to send more along those lines. But really, what else could he do but spend as much time with her as possible, get as close to her as possible and get her to let Frank in on all her schemes. Once they knew the extent of her activities, they might have more ideas for what he could do.

"I'll get the AG to give you approval in case she ropes you in for more than just watching. Plus, I suppose someone could say you're abetting these shopping sprees." Pete put his notebook away. "Felony theft."

Felony theft, indeed. Frank pushed his chair away, stood.

"Poor thing."

"I don't feel sorry for her."

"I meant you. Having to spend all that time with that woman in her leopard print." Pete gave him a goofy grin and Frank had an urge to wipe it off his face. He was glad now he hadn't described the way she looked modeling it. Or his own reaction to it.

"Nice." Frank opened the door. "Actually," he waited for Pete, "she scares me a little. She's like a black widow spider, enticing you into her web, catching you before you know what's hit you."

In the elevator, on his way to lunch, Frank stood in the corner, nodded as people in suits from other floors, office staff got on, the elevator making its slow way down to the ground floor. His hands were in his pockets, his right one curling and uncurling around the gold cufflinks.

Chapter Sixteen

For the past two weeks, Isabelle's brownstone had been teeming with entertainment, dinner parties right and left, afternoon teas most days, the doorbell often chiming, the front steps rarely empty. Ronnie would rush to clear the living room after the tea ladies left, the last crumpled napkin in the wastebasket just before the dinner guests trooped in. Each morning, Ronnie stumbled up the stairs to the kitchen, feeling like she had just left it after loading the dishwasher and wiping down the counters, hanging up the pots and pans, throwing the linens in the washing machine. And Isabelle would already be waiting for her, perched on a stool at the island, looking like she had slept for ten hours, tapping her pencil, head bent over her list. Isabelle didn't wait to see if Ronnie had her notebook ready before calling out the things she needed. She had Ronnie running a marathon each day just to get the food and flowers for that day's party or parties. She should learn to cook. Or bake. Or grow flowers.

She never had time to dust, so she covered the tables with Isabelle's brochures, fanned them out, and blew on the rest of the surface, hoping no one would notice. The crystal bell stopped doing the trick, so Isabelle handed out envelopes addressed to her foundation so people could mail her their checks. She played her guests, a hand on an arm here, a breathy smile there. Pulled a woman in close as if telling her an important secret, weaving stories that made her guests wish they could be part of it all. Ronnie hadn't seen too many envelopes coming back in the mail.

Tonight she ran late, so after everyone in the living room had their drinks, she ducked into the dining room and went around the table with her tray of silverware, laid out all the dumb forks and spoons. She'd have so much stuff to wash later, never mind if anyone actually used it. The door behind her slid open and she turned her head to see what Isabelle wanted. She felt the tray wobble and grabbed it with her other hand.

"I got your ID for you."

"What the hell."

Frank held out an official photo ID card to her, all glossy, city seals and everything. "Have you found her laptop?"

"Jesus Christ." Ronnie set the tray down and held out her hand.

"Nope." Frank pulled it out of her reach. "I need that laptop first."

She grabbed for the card, but he stiff-armed her and she stopped. She heard the door start to slide. Frank heard it too, shoved the card in his trouser pocket as he turned toward the doorway. It was Philippe.

"Isabelle said to tell you—" He spotted Frank, and his eyes narrowed. "What are you doing in here?"

Ronnie moved closer to Frank. She could pickpocket him, but she would have to be so much closer, and Philippe was already looking back and forth between them.

"Oh, I was just getting hungry," said Frank, aw-shucks in his voice. "I was asking Ron here what was on the menu."

Philippe stood in the doorway, his eyes first taking in Ronnie, then settling on Frank. Ronnie grabbed up her tray and went to the place right behind Frank, turned her back to the men.

"You'll know soon enough. Return to the living room." Philippe sounded angry. Ronnie's heart raced, but she whipped around to face him and slid her hand into Frank's pocket before he moved, slid the card into her own pocket as she stepped away. Took her tray to the pantry and sucked in a huge breath.

"Hold it!"

Ronnie nearly jumped, peeked around the pantry door. Thank God Philippe hadn't meant her. Frank looked frozen in place. He didn't look at Philippe.

"What is your hotel? You leave Isabelle's check with the concierge for me.

Tomorrow."

Frank tossed him a grin over his shoulder. "I'm just changing hotels at the moment. I'll let you know." He reached the doorway, but Philippe put a big, meaty hand on him.

"We'll meet at The Plaza. Tomorrow at two. Have the check."

Frank shook off his hand and went through the door. "Not sure that'll work for me."

"What was he doing here?" Philippe's wide shoulders blocked the doorway to the pantry, and he cleared his throat with his usual growl.

"Jesus. Nothing. He just asked about dinner. Like he said." Ronnie stacked plates on the tray. "Why do you do that?" She made a move toward the door and Philippe, in what seemed like slow motion, turned to let her through.

"Do what?"

Ronnie set the heavy tray on the sideboard, her back to Philippe so he couldn't see her face, couldn't see her pulse jumping, her breath coming fast. "Y'know, that growl thing."

He cleared his throat again and Ronnie almost started laughing, the way she had wanted to, needed to when her father was really, really mad at her.

"Isabelle wants dinner served now." He strode to the doors, slid one side open. "I'll tell her to announce it."

"But I—"

The sliding doors met with a bang and Ronnie moved like the cops were after her, ran around the table practically frisbeeing plates. In the pantry she hauled out the starter and plated the weird beet salad she had scrounged, ran back in, the last plate in front of Isabelle's seat just as the doors opened once more. She took up the bottle of wine and poured as the guests leaned over the chairs, searched for their name cards.

Ronnie returned to the pantry and slid that door nearly shut. The place cards still sat on the narrow counter. Let Isabelle seat them this time. Serves her right. Maybe tomorrow night she'd wait for Ronnie to announce dinner. She thought Frank had shifted a little when she picked his pocket but couldn't be sure. Was she losing her touch? Isabelle rang the little bell, a baby sister to the one she had out for the checks, tinkling, tinkling, kept on ringing it like she was some grand duchesses in some grand estate. Downton Abbey in New York City.

Ronnie came through with the water pitcher, leaned over shoulders to fill glasses. She felt Isabelle staring at her and swiped a peek. Daggers. Ronnie straightened up, tracked Isabelle's eyes as they latched on to the candles on the table. The unlit candles. She put the pitcher on the sideboard and pulled the elegant silver lighter out of the drawer, then leaned over more shoulders to hit all the tea lights running up and down the table. As she reached over Frank, she heard a whispered *nice trick*.

The rest of the evening went kinda smoothly, though Ronnie could tell Isabelle was annoyed, even if no one else could see it through her laughter, her charm, her constant touching. Now that she knew about Frank, it was interesting to watch that charade. Here's Isabelle thinking she was playing him, no idea that he in fact had the upper hand. Of course she had shoplifted in front of him, and what did this LEO think of that?

Tonight he acted totally different from FBI Frank as he worked to get Isabelle to talk about the details of her foundation. Isabelle deflected him, and he kept coming back to it. Isabelle's eyes darted between his wine glass and Ronnie. As she took up the bottle and started at the other end, her boss gave her the tiniest head shake. Why she was protecting Frank, she had no idea. She didn't still need him. He needed her. But she didn't want him to haul her downtown, but why would he do that if she was only doing what her boss wanted and poured him some more wine, kept the water glass empty? Amelia Harburger put her hand over her wine glass and turned to Frank. Ronnie thought about pouring anyway, imagined the wine running through her fingers, onto the tablecloth.

"You should ask if you can come too," Frank said to Amelia, all helpful and nice. Why would anyone want to be nice to that bitch? She filled up his glass and bypassed Isabelle, rounded the corner to not fill Philippe's glass when Amelia screeched Isabelle's name, silencing the table.

"Isabelle!" she said again, sounding like an alley cat. "You didn't tell us we could go down and give out the instruments with you!"

All eyes turned to their hostess. How was Isabelle going to play this?

Philippe growled, his head turned toward Amelia. Maybe he thought he would leap over the table and cut off her windpipe if she spoke anymore. Her voice was so horrid Ronnie wouldn't blame him. Frank's eyes danced, and Ronnie wondered how much he knew.

Isabelle released her silvery laugh, a pretty, breathy sound that started high, cascaded down, reached everyone along the table, and stopped at Amelia. "Oh, my dear," Isabelle said to her as if she were the only one in the room. She smiled like Amelia was a small child who had said something silly but adorable. "What a lovely idea. Maybe we could all go on your plane!" Everyone turned to Amelia except Jeff Greenberg, who asked Anthony Harburger what kind of plane he had. Amelia's husband shook his head, a small frown on his lips. Point Isabelle.

Chapter Seventeen

Philippe called him on the Peter Franks phone, left a message: he would be waiting for him in The Plaza at 2:00 tomorrow afternoon. Be there with his pledge. He pulled out his exercise mat and lined up weights at the end. No way the Bureau could put together a check in Peter Frank's name that fast, and as soon as Isabelle tried to deposit it, her bank would tell her it was a fake. He hit the timer and began counting how many sit-ups he could do in a minute, aiming for forty-four. Philippe was boxing him in, no doubt about it. Nine, ten, eleven. Hold on. Fourteen, fifteen, of course, eighteen, nineteen, he would text him back, twenty-three, twenty-four, tell him the check was already in the mail. Thirty, thirty-one, no need to drop by, thirty-four, thirty-five, thirty-six—alarm.

Damn. A score of zero on the fitness test. He needed to concentrate. He had aced his training test back in the day, but he wasn't going to ace anything this way. Putting his keys in the inside pocket of his sweats, he went out for the mile and half run, forcing himself to think about his muscles, his breathing, the way his feet hit the pavement, the relaxation of his stride. Fall was full force in the city, no mistaking that. The East River path, covered in leaves, the air cool on his face, the dog walkers jacketed, the wind picking up.

He didn't want to admit it, but he was kind of impressed with the dexterity Ronnie had employed, removing her ID right in front of Philippe. She and Isabelle made quite the team. But he was also irritated with her, of course, for taking away that easy hold over her. Oh well, back to threatening prosecution. Of course, he did get back at her, when he dropped the thumb drive in her pocket while she served the table.

When he got back he used the Peter Franks phone to text Philippe, told him he had instructed his office to cut a check. That should hold him for a little while. After showering and dressing in something nondescript, he grabbed a stack of flyers and headed out. He promised himself he would do this every free day he had, for as long as it took. If he kept moving, he could keep all those dark images away, the stab in the gut of imagining where Cathy was, what she was doing. Why she had done this to them. To herself. He headed for the Lower East Side, or LES as everyone said these days, all the big parks and little, have you seen her, have you seen this girl, could you take this, call me if you do. He also had a big wad of ones, handing them out one at a time, several at time, please, she's my daughter, I just want to know she's safe.

"Why'd she run away, then?" A teenage girl, maybe even Cathy's age flicked her eyes over him. "Whaddya do to her?"

Frank handed the flyer to the kid next to her and turned to answer. What had he done? Nothing. Loved her, fed her, clothed her, tried to keep her safe. "It wasn't me," he said, his voice low and soft. "It was the Oxy."

"So, you find her. Then what." The girl scratched up each arm like she wanted to peel off her skin. She slit her eyes to her friend, said, "she runs away again. That's what." They both let out big whooping laughs, like they knew something they would never share with Frank.

"My number's on there." He gestured at the piece of paper. "We love her. We just want her home."

He went from park to park, Tompkins Square to Stuyvesant, Union Square, Washington Square and all the pocket parks in between, some people scattering away from him, some listening, waiting for the money. They asked him for cigarettes, for food, for more money. They studied the picture, eyes going from his face to hers, maybe wondering if it really was his daughter. They would scrutinize him, his jacket, his khakis, his shoes. "You a cop?" they'd ask, almost as if they didn't care, just wanting confirmation of their street sense. Sometimes he said it didn't matter, sometimes he said FBI but off duty, and sometimes he said he was just a father looking for his daughter.

The wind picked up, swirling trash, paper bags and plastic, napkins lifted into the air, dust and grit following them. Frank zipped up his windbreaker, stowing the last of the pictures of Cathy flat against his chest, sure the elastic at the bottom of his jacket would keep them there. He had been working his way west and found himself not too far from Benedict House. It had been on his list, of course it had. The largest homeless shelter, the first place he'd called after the hospitals. He went up the short flight of stone steps, the old doors opening onto a waiting area reminiscent of police stations: the acrylic glass protection for the check-in person, the linoleum, benches and chairs littered with people, some of whom were lying down, some asleep. A fluorescent light flickered overhead, and Frank thought it might give one of these people an epileptic fit. He waited for the person at the desk to be free and then slid Cathy's picture under the plastic barrier.

The guy shook his head at Frank and then looked over his shoulder to help the next person. Frank shifted to block his view. He leaned in to speak into the metal thing with holes, like a singer to a microphone. "I'm looking for my daughter. Have you seen her? Can you just look at her picture? Please. She's underage. She—"

"Please step away so I can help someone get a bed for the night."

Frank didn't move.

"Sir, I'll send out a caseworker you can talk to. Please. Curfew is soon and I need to check these people in."

* * *

The caseworker had been helpful, seemed helpful, but as Frank hit the sidewalk, the night air a relief from the peculiar mixture of commercial cleaner and homeless hygiene, he felt worse than when he'd gone in there. All the people he had called, talked to, talked to again. All the law enforcement resources he could tap into, and none of them coming up with anything. He must've held out more hope for Benedict House than he had realized. They sent people out to find the young girls, she'd said, to give them a safe place

138

for the night, but, she'd said, the city was big, and if the girls didn't want to be found...she looked at Frank then her eyes seemed to make a decision, and she added, or if someone else has gotten to them first.

Frank stopped under a streetlight and pulled out Cathy's picture, a little damp from being next to his body, a little wrinkled. Before she was born, he thought his life was complete: wonderful wife, terrific career, living in the best city in the world. And then when he first held her, so hard to believe she'd come out of his wife, an alien all red and wrinkled and so tiny—as the months went on, he fed her, changed her, bathed her, paced the apartment with her to soothe her—he realized that he hadn't been living up until then, that he had never truly loved another person. As if he had just been born, too. The way her head smelled when she fell asleep on his chest, the way her body snuggled into his, and he knew that nothing, absolutely nothing, could be more important to do than to lie there with her until she woke up. He had vowed to keep her safe, that the evil that he came across while doing his job would never ever touch her, she would only know rainbows and laughter and everything pink.

How in the hell had it come to this? Those prescriptions had been provided by professionals. But where, he thought as he studied at Cathy's picture one more time, where had she gotten the drugs once the prescriptions had run out?

His head was against the lamppost as if by protecting her picture, he was protecting her. He straightened up and automatically headed east. Goddamn drug dealers. That's where. He'd always hated them, but now a fury rose, infused his body, and his fists curled, crumpling her poster. He put her back inside his coat, against his shirt with the others.

It had felt so good to deck the Silver Fox. And then that guy at the bar. He had been selling drugs right in front of him. Frank never bought into the argument that they merely gave people what they wanted and resources should only go to helping the users. He knew these guys went out and actively got people hooked. Fucking cartels, too. Maybe that was what happened to Cathy—she'd gotten off the painkillers, and then one of these dealers came along and gave her something, and bam, instant lifelong customer. Going after them through the Bureau was slow going, but the absolute right thing to do, work within the law, work on the side of right. He flexed his right hand. Still a little sore.

He picked up the pace, hoped to dissipate some of his anger, put it to good use. Maybe someone in a doorway, a group of kids on the corner, a veteran who had staked out a bench, maybe, maybe he would hit on the right person, and someone would have seen his daughter.

A group of thinly dressed young women called to him from across the street, soliciting. He shook his head, stared at the sidewalk, kept moving, but then crossed over. He had to talk to everyone, he reminded himself, no matter what.

"I'm looking for my daughter," he said as he approached, holding out the flyer. He wondered how many times he'd said that, how many more times he would have to say it. Three of the girls came forward to take a look, two of them held back, disappeared into the darkness of a narrow alley.

"Sure you're not looking for a good time instead?"

"C'mon Carmine, knock it off. Look at the pic." She grabbed it, held it up, moved it away and then close in. She elbowed the young woman next to her and handed it off.

"Hey! Is that—"

The one called Carmine interrupted the other one, solicited him again, told him they needed to make some money tonight, her friends crowded him, the picture nowhere in sight.

He reached for his wallet, three pairs of eyes on him, then on the bills as he opened it, lacquered nails grabbed for the money, squeals from the others. He was faster than they were though, and he gestured with the bills in one hand, returned his wallet to his pocket with the other.

Frank eyed the one who had been interrupted. "Do you think you know her?" He folded the wad, mostly ones, he knew, but a twenty on the outside. He hoped they thought it was all twenties. "Did you recognize her?"

The woman pulled her short coat around her and sniffed, eyes darting, a flicker at the alley behind them, then held out her hand. Frank shouldered past her, peered into the darkness, felt the women close behind him, then a small shove on his back. He whipped around to face them, widened his stance, pocketed the money so he could have both hands to defend himself.

He kept an eye on them and aimed his voice behind him, into the darkness. "Cathy? Cathy? Are you back there?"

They all laughed, snippets of words hit him as he tried to face them and peer into the alley at the same time: "Cathy!" "—no Cathy here!" "C'mon big boy—" "—fun with that wad of cash!" They crowded him into the alley and he backed up. The last thing he needed was a fight. Drug dealers were one thing, but these scantily clad, underfed sex workers—they were victims, too. He held up both hands, as if to say he wasn't a threat, but also to say stop crowding him.

"Have you seen her? Do you know her?"

One of them, the one in the highest heels and shortest skirt, seemed to relent, her eyes softening. "She your daughter?" She reached for his wrist. "I can take you to her." She tugged him, hard, like he was just a heavy sack of laundry. Back on the sidewalk she squeezed his wrist tight. "But it won't be free, 'cause I'm missing the customers, doing you a favor."

He reclaimed his wrist, pulled the wad out of his pocket, and handed it to her.

She charged up the street, not looking to see if he was keeping up. She'd better not be running with his money. How could she move so fast in those shoes. He drew even with her at a boarded up building.

"She's in there. Go on."

The door, the windows, all had plywood nailed over them and the first step was gone. "Very funny." He pulled out the flyer to hand to her. "Look, if you see her, could you call—"

"What rock did you crawl out from? Don't you know anything? Just pull on the board, you'll get through." She traced an X over her chest. "Scouts honor."

The smell smacked him in the face as he fumbled for his phone, turned on the flashlight. Things skittered away as he shone the light around, and he put his arm to his nose. Several things had died in there, the mold and decay fighting with the vomit, urine, feces. In the room to the right of the door were several lumps, bodies, slumped over each other.

"Cathy? Cathy, are you there?" The building seemed to swallow up his words. He spoke louder this time. "It's me, Dad, honey. Cathy?" He went into the room, shone the light. A girl with long dark hair over her face. His heart quickened., That couldn't be her, so filthy, so strung out. He leaned over and moved the hair off her face, dropped his hand with a start. He felt like he'd been looking at a cadaver, the eerie pale skin, the sores, the stubs of teeth.

He straightened up and felt a jab at his back.

"Gimme your money." The voice was hoarse, broken. Whatever it was, a knife maybe, poked him again.

He couldn't move forward away from the knife, the junkies between him and the wall, and if he moved sideways and the guy jabbed him…he put his hands up. Probably a none-too-clean knife. He did not want to find out the diseases it would introduce to an open wound. "Okay if I reach into my pocket?" He gave a glance over his shoulder to see what he was dealing with, but the knife jabbed harder. "Okay, okay. I'll move slowly. Just one hand. I have a wad in my right pocket." He hadn't gotten his hand with the cash all the way up before it was snatched away, a deep scratching of his skin like he was dealing with a bobcat. He whipped around. A shadow through the doorway, thuds receding to the back of the building.

He gave the room a last look around, but he knew Cathy wasn't there. She would never be in a place like this. The hooker had set him up, probably getting a cut of his cash off the guy who robbed him. And he needed to leave before that zombie figured out just how little money he had given him.

He sprinted all the way to Eighth Avenue, pausing in the light of a noisy café to get a Lyft. The blood hammered in his ears, and he took deep breaths. It could've gone so much worse. The blood from the back of his hand had smeared on the front of his coat, and he looked at the jagged line opening up his skin. His tetanus better be up to date.

Chapter Eighteen

Ronnie was attempting to make crackers, something that had looked easy, butter, flour, cheese, a little salt. Anything to avoid having to steal every day for Isabelle's teas. Isabelle didn't have a rolling pin, so she had to use a wine bottle, thank you Google. Ever since her downstairs neighbor caught her when she was little, she'd promised herself she would only take things that weren't hers when she absolutely had to. Life or death. She didn't know why she'd taken the little glass dog. The neighbor had been so nice to her, stopping her on the stairs on her way up after school, feeding her cookies, milk, sandwiches. Something very satisfying about watching the dough level out, ease itself to the edges as she rolled. Mrs. Anaheim hadn't even yelled at her. Maybe that was why she never went back. The yelling she understood, the kindness, well, that was somehow much worse.

Isabelle came into the kitchen, still in her coat with the fur around the collar. Her boss had her phone to her ear.

"Philippe. Yes, I've just returned. It was awful." She tossed the phone onto the counter and watched it slide toward Ronnie. Isabelle eyed it as if it might come alive and she would have to defend herself from it.

"No luck?" Ronnie patted the dough. The tricky part was getting the whole thing the same thickness.

Isabelle paced, then wrestled herself out of her coat, throwing it on a stool where it settled, then slid to the floor. "That man. Scott I'm-all-that Hodge. How dare he." She went to a cupboard, stared through the glass door at the shelves, turned to pace again. "I ran the lunch just as I do every lunch! The expensive restaurant, the laughing, the flirting, crossing my legs, running my foot up and down his leg, paying him every attention like I could just die over every single silly utterance of his." She made the rounds of the kitchen and landed on a stool opposite Ronnie. "Oh, he was all for all that, yes he was, don't think he wasn't. The way his pupils dilated, the smile, the flushed cheeks, everything." She stopped speaking, and Ronnie glanced up, waiting for the rest of the story. Isabelle got up and opened a cupboard, and got a water glass.

"Can I get you a Perrier from the bar?" Ronnie put the rolling pin down, wiped her hands on a dishtowel.

"Don't be ridiculous." Isabelle filled the glass at the sink. "That's just for show. And guests, if they insist." She leaned against the sink, facing Ronnie. "Don't you know how much that costs?"

Nothing, when your butler finds an unguarded truck. "So, what happened?"

"What happened? I'll tell you what happened!" Isabelle drained the glass, then dropped it in the sink where it shattered, the glass an alarm against the cast iron. "He. Left." Isabelle bit off the words and Ronnie hazarded a look at her through her bangs. Her eyes bulged. "His face turned an ugly purple like it was one big bruise and he didn't say anything to me. Not a thing."

"He left? Before you even gave him the thumb drive? Really?" No one had ever walked on Isabelle before. They always just caved.

"He was there for all the fun and games, wasn't he?" Isabelle paced, the sound from her heels filling the kitchen.

Ronnie rolled over the dough, not pressing this time, just for something to do. She didn't want to look at her phone because Isabelle would think she wasn't paying attention, but she needed to read the next step in the recipe.

"I gave him the envelope. Of course I did." Her stilettos punched each word. "Said that he would know what it was worth just as I always do." Step. Step. "I looked at him through my eyelashes as if I could barely stand to ask. But also, in my matter-of-fact voice—" Isabelle stopped pacing, imitated herself: "Of course, a girl has her reputation blah blah blah." She threw her hands in the air and nailed Ronnie with her dagger-look.

Ronnie patted her dough to make sure it was even all over, and Isabelle moved around the kitchen again.

"Always works with the older guys, the idea of protecting me. Maybe I should have been hardnosed about it, threatened to tell the wife, put it on Facebook. Damn him." Isabelle plopped onto a barstool, got up, opened the refrigerator door, closed it. "That kind of money is nothing to him and everything to me. But what does he do? His face turns purple, his eyes stabbing me, he stands up so fast his chair falls over and he throws the napkin down and leaves the restaurant. It was mortifying. Everyone looking, the maître d' rushing up."

She stopped pacing and stopped talking, and Ronnie looked up to see where she'd landed. She stood staring out the window into the garden, looking deflated, all the air seeping out, nothing to hold her up.

"It's worked every other time. What is wrong with that man?"

The doorbell rang and Ronnie went to the sink to clean her hands, dried them on her pant legs and went around the island on the opposite side of Isabelle.

"And," she said as if Ronnie didn't need to answer the door on her behalf, "he left me with the bill. The bill! I had to pay!"

After she ushered Philippe in and he and Isabelle saw their own way up the stairs, Isabelle still fuming, her voice echoing up the stairwell, Ronnie returned to the cheese crackers. It would be funny if Isabelle weren't so mad. Maybe Philippe would calm her down.

The dinner with Scott Hodge had been rushed, Ronnie had thought at the time. Not the usual tea first, big dinner party second, getting to know you, softening him up until he melted. Bitsy had made the introduction, and Isabelle went straight to the dinner, like she was desperate. Philippe had been there for cocktails, but he made his excuses when Ronnie announced dinner, so she had to rush in and remove his place setting, noticing that Philippe took the stairs up, not down. So. Not leaving.

Isabelle had squished herself into a black sequined dress, her bra working overtime to push everything up and out, so when she leaned over to breathe all over him in that low voice, Ronnie thought her boobs might spill out onto his plate. By the time Isabelle was getting him to drink the champagne out of her glass, Ronnie was bored, ready to clear and call it a night. She was in the pantry stacking the china as silently as she could when she heard Isabelle ask him if he was ready for a little fun. That was her cue. She grabbed the special champagne flute sitting at the ready, poured the champagne over the powder, then went out and switched it for Isabelle's empty one. Isabelle's eyes flashed at her and Ronnie gave her the tiniest nod, then removed his glass so there could be no chance that he would drink from that instead.

All according to Isabelle's plan, the way it had worked for her every other time.

* * *

The next day the front doorbell rang and Ronnie flew up the stairs, dragging her fingers through her hair to try to tame it down, smoothing her hands down her T-shirt as she slid in her socks on the tile, stopping short of the door. She expanded her chest, moved her voice down a register.

"Good afternoon. Who may I say is calling?"

The guy took up most of the doorway, came into Isabelle's house like Ronnie wasn't standing there, like he owned it. He stopped in the entry hall, head angling over toward the kitchen, then eyed the stairs. Before Ronnie could say anything, he went up them, two at a time, threw over his shoulder: "Where is she?"

Ronnie pulled out her phone and hit the numbers as fast as she could, called up to him. "You can't just go up there! Wait! She'll be down in a minute. Isabelle, there's a guy—I couldn't stop him," she said into the phone, "he just came in—" Isabelle had hung up on her, and she hit redial, went up the stairs after him. She had to stop him somehow, but he must have at least a hundred pounds on her. Isabelle's phone went straight to voice mail.

"…now! Drop whatever it is! I need you here." Isabelle's anxiety zoomed down the stairs, but when Ronnie reached the second floor and saw her rounding the banister, she was tall, regal, angry, confronting the big guy in the cheap suit. She only had to tilt her head up slightly to look him in the eye.

"Our visitors are announced here." Her eyes blazed at him. "Now, would you like to tell me who you are?" Her hands were at her hips, and though her arms were slender, she filled most of the hallway and seemed to have stopped him. The guy's head was shaved, his neck as wide as his skull, ripples of skin sitting at the top of the collar of his suit jacket.

"Mr. Hodge sent me."

Isabelle looked him over, as if he'd brought her a present and was hiding it somewhere on his body.

"Well. Then we will go in here and sit. Ron will bring us drinks and we'll see what the divine Mr. Hodge is giving me." She turned her back on the ape and strode to the living room door. "What can Ron get for you? Coca-Cola? Something stronger?" She threw Ronnie a look that was hard to read but seemed to have some desperation in it.

The guy eyed Ronnie, scanned up and down as if assessing her threat. "Tonic water," he said, then added, "No ice," and followed Isabelle through the doors.

Ronnie sprang to the pantry off the dining room just a few steps away, grabbed a tray, two tall glasses, put ice in one. Everything else was at the bar in the living room and, she thought, as she threw a starched white napkin over her forearm, Isabelle would need her there anyway.

She came through the door as Isabelle said, "Are you sure he didn't tell you to give me something?" Isabelle's voice was sweet, a song as if she were trying to play this guy. "Mr.—uh—" she gestured at him as if to help him remember his own name. "A nice thick envelope, perhaps?"

His back to the door, he perched in the spindly chair next to the couch, tensed as if afraid to put all his weight on it. Isabelle had commandeered the armchair facing the couch, both arms resting as if it were her throne.

Ronnie cleared her throat and no name gorilla stood up to face her as if she had brought in a gun. He had to grab the chair to keep it from tipping over. She went behind the bar and worked quickly, the tonic opening with a hiss. She grabbed a cherry Coke Zero for Isabelle, poured it down the side to minimize the foam.

"Sir." She held the tray out to the guest, watched the bubbles in the glass rise and break. The tonic was warm.

She pivoted to Isabelle who took the glass and emptied it as if it would save her life. "Bring me the bottle, please." Her eyes flashed at Ronnie, sending her a signal but Ronnie had no idea what she coded to her. "And a napkin." The brown soda had left traces at her lip line and Ronnie gave a slight bow, a nod. She half wanted to wipe her mouth for her, give her back her confidence.

"Ma'am."

No one said a word as Ronnie got the twelve-ounce bottle and brought it back with the napkin. She returned to the bar and stood against the wall. Ape man still hadn't sat down again. He stared at Isabelle and then gestured his head toward Ronnie.

Isabelle leveled her eyes at him, held her stare as if he might bite her if she looked away. "Ron can hear whatever it is you have to say." She took up her glass, ice cubes clinking as she waved it in Ronnie's direction, and said, a little louder now, "But when Philippe arrives, show him straight up."

The big guy grunted. "Mr. Hodge wanted you to know that no one blackmails him. No one. Got that?" He moved closer to her chair, but she refused to look up at him, held her glass like it was a shield. "He said—"

"Do sit down. Have you no manners?"

He opened his mouth, closed it, inched toward her, got no response, and then lumbered to the couch and sat on the edge of it. "He said to tell you if you won't promise that you won't take it no further, that he will—"

Isabelle stood up in one swift motion, pointed her slender finger, the blood red nail polish coming to a point aimed at his heart. "No one threatens Isabelle Anderson!"

Ape guy stood as well. "Listen." His face darkened, eyebrows came together. "There's no threat if you just make the promise. Because he knows all the same people you know. He can make sure no one ever comes—"

"How dare you!" Isabelle had her hands on her hips and had somehow grown taller, leaning over him, a thundercloud about to burst. "You tell your Mr. Hodge that he's had it in this town. He should just go back to—" she waved her hand, a gesture toward another state far away "—to wherever it is he came from in the first place—" her voice grew louder, but not higher like most women's would and Ronnie was glad she had never made Isabelle this mad because she didn't think she could stand the blast.

She had made the guy even angrier though, and Ronnie watched as his fists clenched and he shook, making her think of a frustrated toddler. "You! Scott isn't going anywhere. If anyone goes, you will! He'll buy this house, and you'll be homeless, and then—"

Isabelle grabbed up her glass and threw the contents at him. The ice hit his face, the brown soda splashed him, the couch, the coffee table, the rug. He grabbed toward her throat, and she knocked his hands away, yelled at him as ice cubes clattered on the table. Before she knew it, Ronnie raced toward them, her only thought to protect her boss. She leapt onto the couch behind him, the bar towel in her hands, a sling to pull him back with, but it was too short, and he twisted around to grab her.

In a roar Philippe came through the doorway, aimed for the man, yelled for Isabelle to get out of the way. The big guy fell into the couch as Ronnie sprang back, his hands grasped at the air, his foot kicked the lamp off the side table, a crash of glass in the silence as everyone stopped moving.

Ronnie scrambled to her post behind the bar, and Isabelle stepped away from the men, stood near her as if she were ordering a drink. Philippe grabbed the ape guy by the front of his shirt and hauled him to a standing position. They stared each other down, one cheap suit, one expensive, both breathing hard, both with clenched fists, the bulkiness of them seeming to fill the room. So this was why she had Philippe, the broad back, the flexed muscles against his suit, his wide stance. She thought there was a bulge at the middle of his back and promised herself if he reached for it she was out of there, every man for himself.

"You don't barge in here," Philippe said between breaths, "you don't just come here and threaten Isabelle. In her own house." His voice was low, a rumble, scarier than if he yelled. Ronnie felt her pulse increase. She got busy pouring Isabelle another drink whether she wanted it or not. They both watched the bubbles burst, watched a drop of water edge its way down the outside.

"Threaten? I'll tell you threaten—" Ape man jabbed the air in Isabelle's direction. "She's the one who tried to blackmail my boss, she's the one with all the threats. And she's not gonna do it no more, is she?"

"The only thing I'm going to do," Isabelle's cool voice cut the air, "is send Scott a bill for the antique lamp and table." Everyone looked at the spot where the two items lay, the lampshade at an angle like a drunk at a New Year's Eve party. "And perhaps for cleaning the couch and carpet as well."

"What? You threw the drink at me. You should be paying for dry cleaning my suit."

Isabelle grabbed up the tall glass off the bar, and the big guy took a step back like he was afraid she was going to throw that too. "Not on your life." She swept out the door, head held high.

Ronnie made a quick exit, too, not waiting to see how Philippe got rid of the big guy. Though he seemed much smaller next to Philippe. In the kitchen, Isabelle sat on a stool at the counter, stared out the windows, her glass of Cherry Coke in front of her.

"Can I get you anything?"

Isabelle didn't answer, just drummed her fingers, or rather clicked her nails on the marble countertop. Ronnie was so hopped up after all the excitement she nearly grabbed her boss' hand to stop the clattering. Instead, she opened the refrigerator, examined each shelf while she let the air cool her.

Philippe rushed down the hallway and into the kitchen. "He's gone." He went straight to Isabelle's side. "Are you okay? Did he touch you?" In a minute he was going to start petting her hair.

Isabelle's eyes flickered over his face, his hair, his shoulders as if trying to put each piece together to form a whole picture. She went to stand at the window and it seemed to Ronnie that Philippe held his breath too. Isabelle whirled around and they both exhaled.

The color returned to her cheeks. "How dare he." She eyed each of them as if they had been the ones who dared. "He sends that big galoot in here to—to—as if he doesn't have the nerve himself, the coward." Her eyes settled on Philippe. "Of course he didn't touch me, that horrid man. I had complete control of the situation." She whipped around, opened a cupboard, pulled out a plate, examined it, put it back. "I am glad you came though, Philippe. If you hadn't," she moved to the sink and ran the water, raised her voice over the sound, "just think how many more expensive things he would've broken." She slammed off the faucet, leaned with her back against the counter, folded her arms across her chest.

"Oh, my dear, I will always be here for you."

Ronnie thought she might puke if he said anything more like that. She edged toward the door.

"Yes, Ronnie," Isabelle said, and Ronnie flinched in spite of herself. "Go clean that up. We're going to have a lot more parties around here, don't think we won't. More people, more brochures, more teas, more lunches, more cocktail parties." Her eyes flashed. "And Scott Hodge will not be invited to any of them! Let's just see how he likes that!"

Chapter Nineteen

He approached the dealer like he had all the others, pulling the sketchy knit hat down low, gathering his ratty old raincoat around him. He hunched over, itching and jittering, stumbling like the smooth sidewalk was uneven. *Man, dude,* he whispered, voice hoarse, *You got some for me?* The guy came out of the shadows, a sneer on his face as if he knew he was better than this junkie, about to tell him to get lost, sure he didn't have any money. Lightning quick, Frank jabbed him in the carotid artery, a sure punch to make him crumple. And he did. Frank sauntered down the long block, mentally dusting off his hands. Another scum drug dealer taken out. That one's for you, Cathy.

The unmistakable zing of a bullet whizzed past him, and he broke into a run, the report of the shot followed him as he hugged the buildings so he was out of the light. He pumped his legs faster than he knew he could, rounded the corner and ducked into the subway, raced across to the exit stairs, his lungs burning. His feet pounded up the steps into the dark, and he aimed west, out of the sketchier neighborhoods. He hit the sidewalk hard, the steps loud, bouncing off apartment buildings, a siren behind him, the gunshot called in.

On the subway uptown, he stood with his back to the door and worked on slowing his breathing. Frank swore over and over in his head, castigated himself for being so stupid, for missing the punch, for searching for dealers in the first place. He had never felt so naked without his gun. His legs started to tremble, and he leaned against the door, the subway shaking as it went along the tracks. He wasn't a stranger to gunfire, you don't take down meth labs in Omaha without a few bullets flying, but this was different, personal for some reason. That reason was Cathy. Because he was doing this for her, it felt like she had been with him on that sidewalk. He had brought her along into the danger.

The train approached the station, and he sat down as it slowed. People got off, got on. A couple sat across from him, both made up like David Bowie, and they started arguing quietly. Cathy was out there, somewhere. He just knew it. He needed to hand out more flyers, search more places, talk to more people. And he couldn't do it if he caught a bullet. The drug dealers were a distraction, and every night when he sought them out, he descended into their dark world. This was not who he was. Frank Jankowski was an FBI agent, upholder and follower of the law. He was the guy who put the drug dealers behind bars, not someone who left them unconscious on the sidewalk. No honor in that, no accolades for getting shot while not on duty.

And more to the point, that was not the principled way to approach it. He was stooping to their level, breathing in their fetid air, and he needed to rise above that. Christ, what would have happened if the city cops arrived sooner? The Bureau was a close-knit family, gathered around him in this crisis, but they would fire his ass over this. What if that bullet had found him? His reflection shimmered in the dark window opposite, the train winding its way through the tunnels, and he stared, trying to find his features in the amorphous head-shaped image.

Who had he become? He rubbed his face with both hands, kept his palms there as if he could hide. From himself. A vigilante, that's who. This went against everything he believed in, against every reason he had become an agent. He dropped his palms, the better to face himself.

He massaged his right hand. When he decked those drug dealers—it felt so right. He stopped criminal activity, protected their victims. Justice prevailed. Faster and more efficient than the system. A shadow Frank had emerged, a doppelganger, a nighttime Moriarty. His impulse was to push down, lock away this heinous side, the devil on his shoulder egging him on. But maybe that would make it worse, the dark side fermenting and then exploding at some point, much more damaging.

As his stop approached, he got up and took off the raincoat, put it over the guy stretched out across the seats opposite him, left the knit hat on his stomach. The cold air from the streets swirled around him as he went up the subway steps, and he walked quickly to his apartment, surprised by how much warmth that old raincoat had provided. Good for the guy on the subway; it would be useful to him.

Once in his apartment, he didn't bother turning on any lights. He moved straight to the armchair facing the window, sank into it, springs groaning, cushion flattening. If he couldn't sleep, he might as well do it here. He unlaced his shoes, eased them off, then slouched down and put his stockinged feet on the windowsill, a sliver of sky visible over the building across the street.

The night sky was always pink when there were clouds, the light reflected back. Office buildings were lit up, the Empire State Building, sporting red, white, and blue. His mood had been dark before he'd gone out tonight, and the aftermath of the adrenaline rush sank him deeper. Why he had kept those cufflinks, why hadn't he told Pete about them? Peter Franks would've kept them, he was pretty sure. But not Frank Jankowski. That guy was by the book, cross those T's, fill out the forms and move along with the slow pace of the bureaucracy to get the job done right.

He went into the kitchen for a glass of water, ran the water over the dirty dishes in the sink, waited for it to become very cold. Cathy's running away, her addiction had thrown him into a completely different world, turned everything upside down. He used to know what was right and what was wrong. There were good guys and bad guys, and he was a good guy, and he put the bad guys in prison. He had never lied, cheated, or stolen. He was the parent who worried at first that playing Santa Claus with Cathy was teaching her you didn't always have to tell the truth. That when she grew up, she would know they had deceived her.

He drank down the water, went into the living room, and straightened up couch cushions that didn't need it. Of course, every time he pretended to be Peter Franks, that was a lie. But it was like pretending to be Santa Claus. Harmless, for a good cause, the right kind of lie. And those cufflinks—

Peter Franks had to wear them, a signal to Isabelle that she could trust him, that they were alike, that she could bring him closer in. He went into his bedroom, opened the felt-lined box that still held his wedding ring, the dried-out boutonnière from his wedding day, a tie clip he would never wear. The diamond cufflinks sat in the center, the Peter Franks watch curled around them.

He shut the lid, wandered back to the living room. They would just go into evidence for this case. Plenty of time to turn them in. He stood in the middle of the room, turned, surveyed. The room had never felt this small, this stark.

Peter Franks had gotten an undeniable thrill watching Isabelle's daring. The hairs on his forearm bristled when he caught sight of the shoplifting. He thought of that physical reaction as his crime radar, his body telling him criminals were near, that he was on the right track to bringing them down. Several days' worth of mail lay in a jumble on the console by the door. He left everything there, went to the window to see how many people in the building across the street were up. He could use the company.

All this time, had his crime radar actually been an exhilaration, not a warning? He recalled the feeling, the way his skin tingled, the slight grab in his gut, a near buzzing in his ears, behind his eyes. Watching Isabelle, the way she seduced everyone she met—the warning sensation was almost sexual. Maybe that's what it was all about: still his crime radar he could count on, but Isabelle jamming the signal with her come-hither looks.

The next invitation to that brownstone better come soon. He had to get closer to Isabelle, needed her to need him around for more than just a check. He liked going there, liked the atmosphere, a world so very different and so very removed from the dark streets and homeless people, away from the stink of the garbage in the greasy alleyways, the hopelessness of a human being teetering on the edge.

He should be glad of this undercover assignment, safe, warm, and well-fed. He would push Isabelle more next time. Let her know how much alike they were. That he understood her, had done shady things himself. After all, how did she think Peter Franks had grown his insurance business, through honesty and generosity?

Chapter Twenty

The juice from her hamburger dripped, ran down the side of her arm. She put it down on the plate and found her napkin, ran it up her arm, and scrubbed her hands with it. The burger was good, and she was hungry, but maybe she'd give it a chance to rest. She looked over at Frank's plate. How could a big guy like that survive on just salad for lunch?

Frank smiled at her. "How's the burger?"

Ronnie nodded without speaking, mouth full.

"You sure can eat a lot for such a skinny kid. Where does it all go?"

She didn't think she was supposed to answer that, so she kept chewing.

"So, tell me. Why did you need the ID in such a hurry?" He settled against his chair, arms crossed, eyes on hers.

Ronnie put down the burger, grabbed her glass, drank, put it down, wiped her mouth with the back of her hand. What else could she do to avoid answering him? She twisted around as if to find the bathroom.

"Ronnie." His voice turned serious, his eyes held hers. "You think it's not my business? Of course it is. Everything about you and everything about that brownstone is my business. And, if you're going to run, we'll find—"

Ronnie shook her head and opened her mouth, a burp escaping. Jesus. She shook her head again. "No, no. I'm not running. It's just—I mean, I wanted to—I have to find my brother."

"Which one?"

Dammit. Why hadn't she thought of that before she gave him all that information? He'd run her name, the address, he knew all about her now.

She had spent all these years under the radar, and poof! One piece of information, one keystroke…her eyes darted, kitchen, bathroom, door to the sidewalk. She had to find Matt, his grave, but she'd just helped Frank build her own trap.

Frank leaned on the table, arms folded, his blue eyes darker, kinder. "Just tell me about it. We can find people."

She sat back, away from him, but found herself saying, "It's Matt." His eyebrows went up a little, a question. "I—I know he's dead. I meant I wanted to see his grave. Visit him, kind of."

Frank seemed so interested, like he really cared.

"He's on Hart Island, I know that, and I needed the ID to go there. To see him."

Frank nodded at her.

"That's where they bury people they don't know, a potter's field, or if they do know who it is, if no one claims the—the body. Y'know." She was not going to cry. She was not a baby. She clamped her mouth tight, and her eyes tried to tell him she couldn't speak.

"I see." He nodded, straightened his spoon, aligned his water glass. "Maybe I could help with that, too." His eyes searched hers, back and forth. "You have to apply, right? Do you want me to help you do that, fill out the paperwork?"

She nodded, her eyes filled. She whispered "bathroom," and practically ran to the back of the restaurant, made it into the stall just in time to lose her lunch. Why did he have to be so nice to her? She grabbed some toilet paper and wiped her mouth, flushed, watched it swirl down. She could handle the roughness. It was the kindness that really got to her.

When she came back out, he stood by their table, looked like he had all the time in the world just for her.

"I figured you were done." He gestured at her plate. "Unless you want it to go."

She couldn't look at it, just shook her head. Her stomach felt like a solid chunk of cement.

"We're all settled up; we're good to go." Frank waited for her to go first. Gentleman or cop? Why was he so nice to her, duh. Needed her to spy for him. But he didn't have to help her find Matt.

They went down the street, and she turned at the corner, stopped halfway down the block, and he did too, looked a question at her.

"I'm not so stupid that I think you're doing this just because you're a good guy. What do you want in return?"

"Smart girl." His kind, helpful face dropped, and an all-business face took over. "You got the thumb drive the other night?"

"I never felt you put it there. I thought it was Isabelle's somehow. Maybe you're in the wrong business."

Frank gave a grunt. "Plug that into Isabelle's laptop, let it run, you'll see the screen, know when it's done. Then text me right away and I'll get it from you."

"No. I can't. Isabelle—"

"Sure you can. That's why you're my CI."

Ronnie flinched, checked around, looked to see if anyone could have heard that. She never thought she'd hear Criminal Informant and herself in the same sentence. She ran. She didn't even know she was moving until she was at Fifth Avenue, at the stone wall in front of Central Park. She went into the park, sat down on a bench, elbows on her knees, head almost resting on her clutched hands. So that was what she was now. She looked past her hands, the squashed gum on the blacktop, the leaves, a button. She raced through images, through to when Frank had first approached her. Could she have made a different decision, not have become a snitch? A rat, a stool pigeon, a nark, a corpse. She sat up.

Frank sat down next to her. Of course he did. She'd never be free of him. "Does the 'C' mean 'confidential' or 'criminal?'" She didn't look at him. He didn't answer, and she risked a peek.

He gave her a little smile. "It stands for 'confidential.' Or you could be a Confidential Witness," his eyes scanned her face, "and testify. Which is better for the case in the long run."

"No way!" She got up from the bench, then looked right and then left down the path. "No one can know it was me—you don't understand—I can't—"

"Sit down," Frank said, then his voice softened, and he repeated it as if afraid she would run. "C'mon, sit back down a minute, let me think."

She sat on the edge, a little further away from him this time.

"If that's how you want to play this." His words fell out on an exhale. He sat up a little straighter. "Okay, I think this could work. Our UC will get the drug dealer, and you'll get us everything on Isabelle's laptop. And you can remain behind the scenes."

She squirmed. She couldn't figure out who she was more afraid of, Frank or Isabelle. Isabelle was terrifying, but after all the yelling, Ronnie still had a bed. But Frank. Frank was always threatening to exchange her soft bed for a prison bunk. But if she gave Frank what he wanted, then Isabelle didn't have to know it was her.

She stood, gave her new boss a nod, and walked away.

"Hold on. Come back."

She stopped. Turned. He patted the bench next to him. Smiled at her like they were friends. She rolled her eyes. She'd let him win this time.

"I need something more from you."

"More? Haven't I done enough?"

"I don't think you're in a position to protest."

A razor scooter wove in between the people on the pathway, the guy riding it way too big for it. Stolen, probably. Ronnie crossed her arms. Waited.

"We need to know the name of the first guy you approached and how to find him. We can take it from there."

"And no one will know it's me?"

"No one will know where we got the information."

She let out her breath in a long whoosh, felt her shoulders relax, eyed him. She had been afraid he was going to ask for something worse. "Pinkie swear?" Ronnie watched impatience and annoyance cross his face. She held up her little finger to him. His face broke into a smile as if he couldn't help it.

"I haven't been asked to pinkie swear since my daughter was six." He shook his head, but she kept her finger up, eyes on him. At last he put his up too and she curled hers around it. Wiggled them together.

160

She gave him the information about the homeless guy, where to find him, what he looked like. "But I only know his street name: Digger."

"Digger? Like dig a hole?"

She nodded. Shrugged. She hadn't named him that. "We done?" She left without waiting for confirmation. Tossed a look over her shoulder to see how he took that. He had pulled out his notebook. Made it official. Damn. She was probably official now, too.

"Hey."

"What now?" She picked up the pace. Headed to the park exit.

"I'll let you know when I hear about Hart Island. What's your email address?"

"Uh…I might have one from a long time ago. I don't use it. I don't even have a computer."

"You have a phone." His chin jutted at her. D-uh. His eyes twinkled at her. "Need another card for my email?" He pulled one out. Held it out to her as they walked. "Just shoot me an email then I'll have your address."

And you'll have another way to get to me. "Can't you just text me?"

"Suit yourself. See you tonight."

Damn. He was on the list for tonight. To be seated on Isabelle's right, place of honor. Place of intense attention by Isabelle, reserved for her favorites who would soon be relieved of a lot of their cash.

She hurried away, a goodbye hand up with her back turned. Probably FBI cash anyway, serves them right for spying on the brownstone. She watched as the runners and bikers on their special street went by, waited for a break, then crossed. How was she going to find another dealer for Isabelle's friends' purchases? She couldn't say to Isabelle, well you see, I told an FBI agent about him, so…sorry. Where did Isabelle get it before Ronnie showed up?

"One more thing."

"Jesuschristalmighty! Don't sneak up on me!"

"Sorry." Frank did not look at all sorry.

"I gotta go get ready for your dinner tonight." Ronnie shifted from one foot to the next.

"Just wait one second. Please." He looked up and down the sidewalk, moved them closer to the parked cars, away from the people. Swallowed. Cleared his throat. "I'm wondering if you could do me a favor."

Ronnie crossed her arms, stared at him.

"A different kind of favor."

What he was up to now? She shrugged one shoulder.

"You know the streets, right?"

"Is that a trick question? You know I do. Did."

"My daughter? The one I used to pinkie swear with?"

Ronnie nodded. Where was this going?

"I…I'm wondering," he paused, swallowed, went on, "if you could go with me, help me—" His voice was low and soft, nearly a whisper on the last words, "—help me find my daughter."

Holy shit. Ronnie took half a step back, shoved her hands into her pockets. She met his eyes, and he turned away, as if the traffic on Fifth was a criminal activity that needed his attention all of a sudden. She studied him. A person after all. Not just a cop. Someone who wanted her help. Someone who had a daughter who used to pinkie swear and is now on the streets.

"How old is she?" She said it low, a whisper, as if to not scare him away.

He turned to her, a grateful look and something else. Embarrassment. "Sixteen."

"Have you looked in the Port Authority yet, Union Square, St. Marks Place? How long has she—"

"Twenty-seven days. And eleven and a half hours." His voice was tight, the words pushed out as if they'd rather stay in his mouth.

"How come she—"

"Rehab." Frank's eyes looked miserable.

"That's okay. I don't really need to know, I guess. I mean, that's your business, but sometimes it helps, y'know?" Her phone buzzed in her pocket. They both looked toward the sound. "I better go." She reached a hand out to him, thought he needed a hug, or a pat, or something, but he straightened up, now towering over her, and her hand jerked into a salute. "Chief." Her phone buzzed again. "I never know if Isabelle is going to surprise me with a dinner party at the last minute, but maybe I'll be free tomorrow night." She started up the path, tossed over her shoulder, "I'll let you know." She turned her head to check on him in her peripheral vision, but he wasn't there.

Chapter Twenty-One

U mbrellas clogged the sidewalks as the rain punished the pedestrians, and the wait for Lyft was half an hour. Isabelle's demand came just as Frank had sat down to eat his salad. *Shopping! WFC today Meet me I'm on my way*

Even though the World Financial Center had been remade into a shopping mall called Brookfield Place, no one called it that. Just as no one ever called it "Avenue of the Americas." Frank made it to the subway without soaking his Peter Franks shoes too much and texted her back while he waited on the platform. *Hotel cars all spoken for. Be there as soon as darling*

Not that he felt very romantic. More like a wet canary, irritable and put-upon. Well, better shake it off because he signed up for this, and now it was showtime. He snagged his usual position with his back to the train doors, grabbed the bar, and saw the gold cufflinks. Good reminder as to who Peter Franks was and why he'd be eager to see Isabelle. He also gave Frank Jankowski a talking to since he should be just as eager to make progress on the case.

The lectures worked because Peter Franks had a warm smile for the inimitable Isabelle, and they exchanged air kisses in front of Bottega Veneta. Her eyes sparkled at him, and she linked her arm in his, steered him to a store called "Bonobos."

"You know about the Bonobo, don't you?" Isabelle snuggled into him, her voice melodious. "Only primate that has sex for pleasure!" Her laughter rang out as they entered the store, and three salespeople turned their way. One broke off and approached.

"Good afternoon, sir. Are you looking for something in particular?"

Frank surveyed the tiny store. "Well, I—Isabelle, this is all men's wear. I wanted to get something for you."

Again the laughter, not as throaty, but making him wish he could hear it again nonetheless.

"Oh, Peter, but it's your turn. Really." She looked at one of the associates, holding his gaze long enough that a flush started up his neck. "Are you a bonobo?" She dropped Peter's arm and closed the space between herself and this new victim.

"We're just looking, actually." Frank almost felt sorry for the blushing salesman. He couldn't be more than twenty and certainly had no defenses against someone like Isabelle.

Turns out the store was just a way to their catalog, there so customers could try the merchandise on, then order it. So, not much to lift. Thank goodness, although it seemed to put Isabelle in a bad mood. She sailed into other stores, Gucci, Zenga, Omega, Louis Vitton, came out with nothing. Frank saw the storm clouds gathering on her forehead, heard the strain of her muscles rearranging her face into a smile. Time to put her back into her good mood, ensure this adventure went well.

"Darlin'." Frank stopped walking and she whirled on him, eyes flashing before she crinkled them into a smile. Maybe he should stop calling her that.

"Yes, *dear heart?*" Her eyelashes fluttered, but the effort seemed more like she was trying to keep out the dust.

"I'm famished. Why don't we go over there to Sant Ambroeus, get an espresso and something sweet." To sweeten your mood.

They were led to the bar, the last possible seats left, and if he weren't taxed with figuring out how to cheer her up, he might find it funny how angry it made her. When he pulled out her stool for her, she nearly wrestled it away from him. Her skirt was so narrow she had trouble climbing on, and she finally dropped her large purse under the bar, hiked the fine wool up her thighs, and sat, sliding her skirt back into place once she was seated.

Frank hoped she'd have to use the bathroom so he could watch that

165

operation again. He thought about warning her about purse snatchers, but the bartender arrived, wiped down the gleaming wood in front of them. Frank hooked the purse handle with his foot, the least he could do.

"What'll it be, folks?"

Isabelle bristled. Like a cat.

"The lady and I will each have an espresso—"

"—martini! I'll have an espresso martini, and he'll have—" Isabelle looked his way, then flapped a hand. "Whatever it is he's having." Like it was poison.

Frank nodded at the guy. "Just espresso for me. And we'll each have a Principessa." For the princess.

"I can certainly order for myself, thank you."

But the guy was at the other end of the bar putting in their orders, and Isabelle clicked her nails on the wood as if her martini couldn't get there fast enough.

"Isabelle, darlin', I'm just trying to be nice. I thought it would sweeten your mood, make up for our lack of progress today."

"Look, Peter." She swiveled to face him, her knees banging into his. "I'm doing all the work here, and it seems you're getting all the rewards." She gave a meaningful look at the gold cufflinks at his wrist. "It's time you stepped up, did your part. Have some fun, take some risks."

"Well now." He took her hand in both of his and he thought for a second she was going to take it back. Or claw him. "You are feisty, aren't you?"

She cocked her head at him.

"And I think I might like it." He gave the hand a pat, dropped it, but not before he took in her dilated pupils, the small smile playing with her mouth.

Their drinks arrived, and she saluted him with the martini as if she weighed the idea of tossing it in his face. She drained it. The glass hit the counter with a clink, and she crunched on the coffee beans. "I don't know why you wanted to come here." She waggled her glass at the bartender who seemed not to see her. "So touristy and such bad service as well." Her voice was a little softer like she decided not to fight.

Frank sipped his espresso. He hoped he didn't pay for it tonight, so jumped up on caffeine he couldn't sleep. He watched Isabelle in the mirror behind the bar. She really did remind him of a cat, her fingernails like claws, bristling all over like she was about to spit, but now softening, like he could reach out and pet her and she'd lean into his hand, tail raised.

The bartender whisked her glass away and they both watched as he made her another. Now that Frank thought back, he knew he hadn't seen her drink anything stronger than champagne before this. Maybe things weren't going so well for her, and this would be the perfect time to get closer. The bartender moved down the bar to take care of someone else and as soon as Isabelle had the glass at her lips, Frank leaned over to murmur in her ear. "I think it's time you played to my strengths."

She put the glass down without taking a sip, the motion comically slow as if keeping herself from smashing it. She probably wanted to be the one who called the shots.

Frank looked at her in the mirror in front of them. "Don't we make a lovely couple?"

She raised an eyebrow at him. No attempt to smile and flirt.

"Look, darlin', I'm no good at all at this sleight of hand." He leaned over, her blonde hair tickling his nose. "No, I'm much better at deskwork, y'know, all those papers, moving them around, filling them out, confusing people so they don't even read them."

He leaned back to watch her in the mirror. Both eyebrows were raised now, and she tensed, a lioness waiting for her prey.

"After all," Frank leaned toward her again, whispering now, "how do you think I managed to grow my insurance business so big in such a short time?"

* * *

After lunch, when he came into his apartment and saw Cathy's couch where she had hallucinated that horrific afternoon, for once his stomach didn't lurch. It was her couch, the only place for her to sleep when it was his weekend, and he imagined her on it now, earbuds in, swaying to music. He put his keys in the bowl on the tiny console table, placed the stack of mail next to it, and went to the windows. He missed her. She was out there somewhere, maybe staying with a friend from school, maybe on her way home even now, tired of the cold and dirt, the bunk beds in the shelters, the cops, tired of living on the streets and doing—well he wasn't going to think about what she was doing. He pulled up the binds so he could look down the block, see what the miniature people were getting up to on his street.

The afternoon with Isabelle ended well after the unfortunate beginning. She deflected him, of course, about his working with her more closely, but he would've been suspicious if she hadn't. He saw the gears turning as she considered the possibilities and even the wily Isabelle couldn't hide the smile etching around her mouth. The rain had let up, a mist turning to diamonds in her hair. Of course, she made him spring for a town car, and they waited together under his umbrella. They were cozy, a world apart from the rest of the city, his arm protectively around her. For a minute he thought she was moving in for a kiss, her height such that she needed only to lift her chin, but at the last second, she turned away and wondered aloud if that was their car.

He surprised himself by the disappointment he felt when she turned away, a feeling that he'd missed his only chance. His heart rate had increased, his breath came short, and he was thrown back to his very first teenage kiss, the oddness of seeing the girl that close, the once-in-a-lifetime feel of those first lips on his, the softness, the melting into, the smell of another he could never forget. Something about Isabelle made it all seem new again, unique, as if nothing would ever be the same.

He let the venetians clatter closed again. His agent self couldn't brush off the disappointment as purely professional. That the chance he missed was just in furthering the case. He could still smell her musky, cinnamony perfume, as if she'd sprayed it on him when he hadn't been looking. But of course he'd been looking, he couldn't stop looking. She was unlike any woman he knew. Certainly Susan's opposite. Susan was comfortable, known, like his everyday khakis and button-down shirts, built to last and see him through whatever came his way. But Isabelle. She was the diamond cufflinks, exotic and expensive, the style unmistakable and out of his league, the winking facets myriad and ephemeral.

* * *

Two days later, as he dressed to meet Isabelle at the Met, buttoning his cuffs and eyeing the Piaget, pulling Peter Franks over him, ridding himself of all things Agent, his phone dinged, the Peter Franks phone. A text from Philippe, reminding him to bring the new check today. He hoped Philippe would not be there. He had suggested the museum as an afternoon date precisely to exclude the big, growling man. He looked himself over in the mirror above his dresser. He could pretend he hadn't seen the text. He could say a secretary in Omaha had cut a new one. He could ask him what was wrong with the New York City Post Office.

Isabelle hadn't yet responded to his proposition, but she was quick with the text to his invitation, shooting back *2nd floor 2:00!* He would wave off the donation check as chicken feed compared to what he could do for her. The museum would give him a chance for long conversations, eliciting from her how she could use his skills in her schemes. He texted Pete to let him know of the subject meet.

* * *

He made his way over to Fifth, the cool air perfect for the crosstown walk, the leaves on the trees that lined the upper east side streets turning. He looked forward to seeing the lovely Isabelle, to hearing her mellifluous voice, making her laugh that lovely laugh that made you feel like a million bucks. Agent Frank let Peter Franks indulge in the images, the feelings. All part of the persona. But he needed to be very careful around this minx. She had a way of getting under your skin, of sneaking in and grabbing a person by the—he turned the corner right into a Great Dane who commanded most of the sidewalk. The black head came nearly to Frank's shoulder, where he would normally wear his gun. At least he was on a leash, the thin leather taut, held by a woman who had to weigh half what the dog did. Frank held himself very still, and he and the animal eyed each other, his liquid brown eyes intent. The leash strained further, and Frank planned his escape route without breaking eye contact. He felt like he was in some alternate universe in which only the dogs had suddenly been blown up to three times their normal size.

"Manheim. *Sitz!*" The leash-holder barked.

This alternate universe also gave tiny women large voices.

Manheim lowered his hindquarters, but his eyes never left Frank.

"*Platz!*"

Damned if Manheim didn't lie all the way down on the sidewalk. The woman gave Frank a look that said, *What are you waiting for?* Frank darted across the street. No way was he going to walk past Manheim. Though he wasn't sure which one of them, the giant dog or the tiny owner with the fierce voice, made him more nervous.

At the next corner he waited for the light, he shook himself a little, as if he could physically get rid of the emotional hangover from the encounter with Manheim. He had no doubt that if that dog were on his hind feet, he would be taller than Frank, a murderous Scooby-Doo with his paws on his shoulders and jaws around his head. Well, if he found Peter Franks getting too hot under the collar around Isabelle, he could just conjure that scene on the sidewalk. He crossed the street, headed north, ducked under scaffolding, the sidewalk like a cave. In fact, the main reason he asked to meet her in the middle of the day, on neutral, public territory, was an uneasy sense of the strong pull of the brownstone, a silk lasso thrown by the lovely owner, drawing, tugging, seducing him.

The Isabelle Anderson Foundation was definitely shaky, but legal, the 990-PFs filed every year. Took in nearly a quarter of a million in donations, spent all of it, claimed 75% went to charitable activities, 25% for overhead. He doubted that. His gut, his infamous gut told him there was more: drugs coming back in the airplanes that supposedly delivered the instruments, suspicious donations, suspicious contributors, suspicious expenditures. He had reported all that, without mentioning his gut, to the boss to keep the case open. The boss tasked Pete with doing what he did best: comb through all the financials available to them without a warrant, sleuth down each donor, follow all the rabbit trails and see what popped out.

* * *

No sign of Isabelle on the second floor, and Frank checked his watch. Well, he couldn't call her truly late, but there weren't many places up here to wait for someone. He poked his head in the galleries leading off the staircase, the store, the restaurant. Plenty of people, but no tall blonde woman with flashing eyes.

He texted her, waited, no response. He went down a hall, room after room opening off it, skylit, muted walls, paintings and drawings perfectly hung, tagged, cordoned off. Someone sat with an easel, art student no doubt, copying one of the masters. Rooms opened on to other rooms, shotgun style and he went quickly through, wishing he could spend the time to peruse, appreciate, absorb all these great works.

He squared his shoulders to remind himself he was working. He pulled out his phone and turned on the recording feature. Today, after all this time on the case, would be the day that he would get something meaty, something to show the criminal activity he knew was going on at the brownstone. Peter Franks—with his offer of help, his boast that his expertise could make all the donations seem like pennies—would finally get her to tell him what she does and how she does it.

He continued through room after room, a dead end at the western tip, a guard watching him, a gaggle of school children in front of a very large oil, "Washington Crossing the Delaware." All this stimulus threatened his sense of direction, and he paused as if he could ascertain the sun from the room light. You could spend a lifetime on this floor alone. He'd go back to the staircase, reorient himself, make sure she wasn't waiting for him. He poked his head in a side room he hadn't yet checked, and there, in the middle of the room, stood the lithe and winsome Isabelle Anderson, her back to him, her arms crossed, a pleated white skirt swishing below her knees. At least she was covered up today.

As if she were thoroughly absorbed in the painting in front of her, she didn't turn as he came in. When he was nearly abreast of her, she said, as if continuing a conversation, "Of course you know the myth. So many painters through the centuries captured it: da Vinci, Reubens, Boucher, Correggio. Often many times. But this, I think, is my favorite."

He looked from her to the painting. It wasn't large, maybe two feet high, and he went closer to read the label. Lossow, Heinrich (1843-1897).

Her voice floated to him. "They could use the Greek Myths to depict the female body in a way that was at once erotic and acceptable."

"What is it about Leda and the Swan that you like? Hello, by the way."

"Lossow has caught the very act of the rape. Zeus, disguised as a swan, ravishes Leda, wife of King Tyndareus, daughter of King Thestius." Isabelle stepped up to the painting. "See there, her feet are still in the water. The swan leapt out and surprised her. But look at her face. She likes it." She looked closely at Frank. "I'm partial to this depiction because you can picture yourself as either being."

Frank swallowed. Pete's gonna love listening to this.

"Leda's beauty," Isabelle continued in her professorial voice, "attracted Zeus and one of the results of this union was Helen, whose beauty destroyed Troy."

"Lethal."

Frank sat down on the bench conveniently placed in front of the painting. Only bench in the room.

Isabelle sat down beside him, her chaste pleated skirt falling away, a secret slit in it revealing nearly the entire length of her thigh. She gestured at the painting. "Look at how he treats her skin, the light and the shadow, the smoothness of her body, her arm, her thigh, her breast, the way her back is arched. Ecstasy."

Frank's collar was already unbuttoned, and he imagined unbuttoning the whole shirt so he could cool off.

"Now, other artists have chosen to depict the moment just before, or the moment after, but Lussow chose the during, the pene—"

Frank cleared his throat. "So you're saying she had a child from this? According to the myth?"

"I thought you were well educated. Actually, she had four, because she slept with her husband this same day, and then conceived two sets of twins:

CHAPTER TWENTY-ONE

Castor and Pollux, Helen and Clytemnestra."

Frank got up from the bench, looked at other paintings in the room, but they were all scenes of seduction, of naked women and dressed men, nothing to cool him down. He shoved his hands in his pockets to affect a casual air, his fingers finding the diamond cufflinks. He cradled them. "This is quite the exhibit you've chosen, Isabelle. Listen, I wanted to talk to you about—"

"It's my absolute favorite. Sex Through the Ages. Didn't you see the sign when you came in?"

"I was dodging crowds of children." He scanned the tiny room as if they might be here but he hadn't noticed. A couple moved from painting to painting, heading toward him, and he returned to Isabelle and the bench. Her legs were crossed now, both stockinged thighs exposed, one shoe hanging off her heel, swinging back and forth. Like a pendulum, like a watch on a chain, back and forth, back and forth. "Isabelle, really, I wanted to meet with you so we could talk about what I can do for you."

Her hand, warm, nearly weightless, rested on his forearm. "Oh, I knew you were a naughty boy." She breathed the words out and they hung in the space between them, so soft and low no one but Frank could hear them.

"Please, Isabelle." Why was he whispering? It made her lean into him and her enchanting perfume caressed his cheek, clung to him. He squared his shoulders. "Why don't we go get a cup of coffee or something?" He leaned away but her hand remained on his arm. "I'd really like to talk with you about how I can be of use."

She threw back her head and laughed, a large, throaty laugh that made everyone in the gallery turn and look. Frown at them. A guard stepped forward as if Isabelle had broken the rules, and Frank grabbed her by the wrist and pulled her to standing, pulled her out of the room and into the main hallway, apologizing as they went.

She was still laughing, her eyes wild, a little crazy. Like she had seduced herself. She put a hand on his chest as if she needed the support in order to stay upright. "Oh, Peter! I would love to use you!" Again, the laughter.

Frank Jankowski wanted to strangle her, shut her up somehow. But Peter Franks gave her a confused grin as if he didn't know what exactly was going on, but he thought maybe it was a good thing. He put an arm around her and steered her into the café. She calmed down as they waited for a table, wiping at the corners of her eyes with her slender fingers, breaking into a smile when she caught his eye. His Peter Franks' grin was like a Guy Fawkes mask, and he was relieved when Isabelle excused herself to use the ladies once the waitperson showed them to their table.

He glanced around the little café, testing himself to make sure he hadn't missed any details in the cloud of Isabelle's perfume. Door to the kitchen, every table occupied, couples, families, lone person on a laptop. He took a sip of his water and then drained the glass. He had clocked it all, and now that Isabelle wasn't with him, he felt he could think more clearly. Four waitstaff, cashier, line at the door. Shopping bags on the floor, stroller in the corner, one service dog looking bored. Yep. Good. Back to work. Take control of the conversation and get Isabelle to tell him what she does for a living. He pulled his phone out, checked that it was still recording.

"Surely I'm much more interesting than Solitaire!" Isabelle, silent as a cat, evaded his radar once again.

He rose to pull out her chair for her, and unlike most modern women, she didn't protest, make him sit back down. Like royalty. And damned if that perfume didn't get to him again, just as his head was starting to clear.

She ordered tea, looked him up and down, and told the young man to bring Peter a few things from the bakery display. "You look like you could use it. A little pale." When the waiter pressed her for details, she waved her hand as if to say she couldn't be bothered and *why are you still here.* "Whatever you think. You look like a smart young man." But she wasn't looking at him, she was leaning on her elbows across the table at Frank like she wanted to devour him. "Gives a person an appetite, doesn't it? An exhibit like that."

The waiter still hovered, and Frank looked his way. "Coffee, black. And don't worry about the pastries."

"Oh, Peter, really. You should see yourself. Bring him a slice of chocolate cake and two puits d'amour."

Frank sat back in his seat, away from the perfume, away from the sparkling eyes. "Now Isabelle, I asked to meet with you because I'm so interested in how I can help you. Philippe texted me asking for my donation—"

Her eyebrows went up, and she leaned closer. Obviously money was just as alluring to her as sex.

"—and I think what I can offer you makes $5,000 seem like chicken feed. I think we'd make a good team, Isabelle. You pull them in with your charm, and I—"

The server arrived and they each leaned back as he placed a mug, a silver tea pot, a basket of tea bags in front of Isabelle. A mug of coffee, cream and sugar nestled together on a miniature tray, a slice of chocolate cake, and a plate holding two tarts in front of Frank. He looked down at them. They were piled up with some sort of creamy mixture, an areola of sugar burnt on top.

Isabelle smiled a wicked smile at him, her foot finding his leg under the table.

"Don't those look delicious." Frank moved the plate to the center of the table. "I'll save them for after." The foot moved up and down his leg. "Maybe you would like one." He pushed the plate an inch in her direction. The foot was at his knee, sliding past it. He grabbed it. "I give a mean foot massage, but maybe someplace more private." He took up her foot and carefully lowered it. It felt soft. Her toes, curling into his palm, sent electrical pulses up his arm. He dropped it and grabbed his water with the same hand, the cool glass grounding him. Steady now. "Maybe just tell me what sorts of things you're already into, and I can tell you where I can help out."

She pushed her lips into a pout that looked like she wanted to give him a kiss. He wiped his forehead with his napkin. She picked up the tart and licked at the top, her tongue running around the burnt sugar, her eyes watching his. He swallowed.

* * *

"That's it? She never answered you?" Pete took his headphones off and swiveled to face Frank.

"Well, you heard the part where she said I should give her the check, and she and Philippe would discuss it."

Pete put his headphones back on, used his mouse, nodded. "There was so much traffic noise at that point I was going to leave it to the tech guys to parse. What did you say?"

"I deflected. Told her I was sure it had been sent from Omaha. I'd look into it."

"Well, at least we have Philippe. That he's more than hired muscle."

"I kinda figured. Didn't you?"

"But now we have it on tape." Pete rubbed his hands together. Like *oh boy*. "I can't wait to get in there and root around. Even without a warrant, I know I can find more on Philippe Reynard nèe Phillip Reynolds." He turned back to his screen. "Got you now!"

Frank had an image of a prairie dog scampering into his hole. He sat down at his desk, swiped his ID card, opened a 302. Too bad Pete couldn't fill this out for him. Right up his alley.

Pete's chair slid on the plastic floor mat. "But Frank, we gotta talk about this."

"It's all on the tape." Frank pecked away without looking at his partner.

"I need to stretch my legs. How 'bout you?"

This wasn't an idle offer. It was his UC supervisor asking for more, outside, while they were walking, where Frank would feel like opening up, where Pete could ask some hard questions. Frank let out a long breath.

* * *

The sharp air reminded Frank that winter was just around the corner. He shoved his hands in his overcoat pockets, picked up the pace.

"Just describe it to me, Frank."

Frank buried his nose in his scarf and kept walking. He got to the corner and stepped into the crosswalk, but Pete stopped him with a hand on his arm.

"Let's go get some coffee or something. Too cold to walk."

Plus, Pete and food were never long apart. Frank followed him into a precious wood-paneled coffee shop and settled in at a narrow booth in the back. Sure as shootin', Pete came back bristling with containers of coffee and several biscotti.

He dunked the biscotti, took a bite, eyes on Frank. "Okay, look. If you just listen to the tape, it seems like you don't know how to handle your subject. She deflects you every time, and you're practically stuttering." He dunked again, chewed, sipped. "And you're a seasoned agent, so I know there's something more. Extenuating circumstances."

"As it were." Frank sipped. Lukewarm, bitter. He put it down. He cleared his throat. "Well, you heard how she started out, talking about the painting." He pulled out his phone, poked at it, then showed the screen to Pete.

Pete wiped his hands and took the phone, used two fingers to enlarge the image. His eyes widened, and he handed Frank the phone. "They allow those paintings in public?"

"An entire exhibit of them." Frank described to Pete the way she looked, the peekaboo skirt, the length of her thighs on the bench, the way her perfume lingered on him.

Pete stared at him, mouth open, hand holding the biscotti paused over his coffee cup.

"And that perfume. It's like there's a drug in it. I tried to get away, clear my head, stop smelling it, but I couldn't. Hooked me at first whiff." He described her stockinged foot on his leg, the electricity up his arm.

Pete didn't move.

Frank pulled out the phone again, found the picture, and aimed the screen at Pete.

"And then she ordered these, ostensibly for me, but she picked one up, ran her tongue around the top, and I swear, I could feel her tongue on me."

Pete's biscotti broke off, the dunked half in the coffee, the nub in his hand. They both looked at his cup. Pete took up a spoon and fished around in his coffee. "Frank. This is worse than I thought. No one could withstand that."

"I think that even if I were gay and not the least bit interested in women, she would still unnerve me."

Pete dusted off his hands. "You should find out what her perfume is. The bureau could use a weapon like that. Enhanced interrogation."

Chapter Twenty-Two

Finally a break in all the entertaining and Ronnie had a chance to clean the living room. She backed through the door loaded down with the vacuum cleaner and dust rags.

"There you are!"

"Ma'am?" Ronnie put everything down.

Isabelle paced the living room as if no room was big enough to hold her feelings. She stopped in front of Ronnie. "I've been thinking."

Ronnie stiffened. Willed herself to relax.

"Peter Franks hasn't given me his check. But he acts as if nothing's wrong. He says he's sent it."

Ronnie picked up a rag, moved to the table with the brochures. Said nothing.

"Maybe he has sent it. You bring me the mail. Maybe you saw it and thought you would save a little something for yourself. Cashed it."

Maybe pigs can fly. "I would never do that. I wouldn't know even know how." She would not beg that Isabelle had to believe her, but her heart beat faster and she kept her back to her boss, fanned out the brochures oh so carefully.

"So you've thought about it." She paced. Stopped, pointed at Ronnie. "Philippe said he caught you two all cozy together in my dining room the other night. What was that all about?"

Damn Frank. She closed the fan of brochures, picked them up, dusted the table. "That wasn't *about* anything. He wanted to know what was on the menu. I told him. Then Philippe came charging in and yelling."

"But that same night, you were pouring water for him when I clearly wanted you to keep him drinking wine." Isabelle's hands were on her hips. "Like you were protecting him. Why is that?"

Ronnie ran the dust rag over the coffee table. "Isabelle." She straightened up and looked her boss in the eye. "I don't know what you mean. I work for you, and I try to do everything you ask. I'm sure I make a mistake or two. Who wouldn't with these long hours and hard work? We've been having back-to-back parties, and maybe I gave someone water when I should've been giving them wine." She ran the rag around the base of a lamp.

Isabelle's face darkened. "Long hours? You dare complain to me?" She pointed a long, silver-polished fingernail at her. "Just what do you think I've been doing? You think you do all the work around here? It's nothing compared to what I do."

"That's not what I meant." Ronnie went to the windows, shook out the heavy drapes. Dust motes filled the shaft of sunlight like fairies dancing.

"Look at me." Isabelle pulled Ronnie's shoulder and turned her to face her. "I work hard to bring in these checks so you have a place to live." Isabelle's musky cinnamon perfume hung in the air between them. "And how do you reward me? By going behind my back with my mark. Maybe he's not the only one. Maybe there are other checks I'm missing. Maybe—"

"Isabelle." She felt her scalp start to tingle. She couldn't start sweating in front of her.

"Do you know, little girl, what happens to people who go behind my back? Double-cross me?"

"I haven't—" Ronnie ducked away from her boss, went to the bar, ran the rag on the gleaming surface.

"I'll make your life miserable. You thought living on the streets was uncomfortable? Ha!"

A bar cloth lay in a crumpled heap, and Ronnie picked it up.

"You would never work in this city again! Especially after Philippe was done with you. You probably wouldn't even be able to hold a cup or sip through a straw. Why, after he—"

"Isabelle!" Ronnie had the bar cloth twisted in each hand like her body decided to use it to defend herself against the switchblade fingernail. Or to strangle her boss. She wished her ears would stop roaring.

"What." If ice shards could speak, that's what they would sound like.

"You don't know me at all." Ronnie stared at her, refused to look away. "If you did, you would understand how loyal I am."

Isabelle made a noise, a protest. "I just know there's something between you. I can feel it." She crossed her arms in front of her. Glared.

"No. I'm a one-man dog, loyal only to you, following at your heels, hearing only your commands." And spying on you for Frank. Ronnie released the bar cloth and moved to the couch, fluffed pillows. "And I'm really hurt that you would even think anything like that. After all this time."

Isabelle said nothing, and Ronnie sneaked a peek at her. She seemed to be considering what she'd said. "Besides, didn't Philippe ask him for it? Maybe he has the check."

Isabelle's eyes flashed at her. Maybe she'd gone too far, pointing the finger at Philippe. She plugged in the vacuum. She turned her back on Isabelle like she didn't consider her a threat, but her hand was so sweaty the vacuum might just slip out and run around the room without her.

After a few minutes, Ronnie turned the vacuum cleaner around and saw the room was empty. She let out a long breath, left the machine running so Isabelle wouldn't know she'd stopped working, and collapsed onto the couch. Her legs trembled like she was getting tased. Isabelle had left just in time. One minute more, and she would've seen Ronnie in a heap on the floor.

She sucked in a long breath, blew it out. Damn. Damn. This was getting way too complicated. She pressed on her thighs, willed her legs to stop shaking. Frank talking to her in the dining room when he was supposed to be Peter Franks was like that play she and Matt sneaked into once, when the actors left the stage and came into the audience. She had squirmed then, wanted to leave. Those actors belonged on the stage, and they should've stayed there, not mixed in with the audience. And Frank should stay Peter Franks when he was at Isabelle's. If Isabelle turned into razor wire because of Ronnie filling his water glass, what would it be like if she saw them together outside of the brownstone? Or found her downloading her computer onto Frank's thumb drive?

She launched herself off the couch and grabbed the vacuum cleaner. She needed to move, needed the motion and the noise to drown her thoughts. She ran over the carpet for real this time, bumping into chair legs and almost toppling an end table. She slowed it down. Last thing she needed was Isabelle coming back in to see why she was making so much noise.

* * *

Back in her apartment, her heart had finally calmed down, thank God. But Isabelle—it was more than serving water instead of wine. She accused her of double-crossing her, of stealing the checks as they came in. Ronnie didn't know if she was mad about being so misunderstood or scared of Isabelle firing her. Or Philippe coming after her. Shit, would he actually—it was probably all because Philippe saw them together in the dining room. Damn Frank.

She grabbed up her phone and tapped out *WTF Iz is so mad! Why did you...* She stopped and looked around, as if typing her name could make her appear. She held her thumb on the backspace and erased everything, threw her phone on her bed as if it might bite her. The woman knew her way around spy cameras. Maybe she'd put new ones in after Ronnie had checked that time. Plus, she had given her the phone, maybe she somehow knew what she texted, maybe she—Ronnie sat down on the rug next to her bed, rested her back against the side. She thought she might throw up.

Think. Think. Think. It wasn't just a matter of a place to stay anymore. If Isabelle suspected—if she threw her out—then she wasn't useful to Frank—then she would go to jail, and the Feds and not Isabelle would be giving her a place to stay. She found she was pulling at the fluffy rug, a silly pink thing that felt good on her bare feet first thing out of bed. She didn't even like pink.

* * *

The next couple of days, Ronnie tried to avoid Isabelle, and she left her phone in the drawer of her bedside table. She did have to speak with her boss to find out her marching orders for the day—two teas and one dinner party— notably without Frank, or rather Peter Franks. Amelia Harburger seemed to be taking over for him though, peppering Isabelle with questions about the charity. At first, Isabelle tried to deflect her, patted her arm, and changed the subject by asking about her children and whether she still wanted to get them into Marshall Logan. *I am the only person who can guarantee your children a spot. We should have lunch tomorrow!* That would be something to see, the moment when the tightfisted, poison-mouthed Amelia realized the only way to get her children into the most prestigious school in the city was to fork over a ton of money to Isabelle.

That night, after all the dishes had been washed, the dishwasher run twice, all the counters wiped down, all the cushions in the living room fluffed, and balled-up napkins tossed, Ronnie was soaking her feet in the bathtub when she heard her phone ring. What could Isabelle possibly want now? She dried her feet and padded into her bedroom, the carpet cool and soft.

"Hello."

"I've been trying to reach you."

Ronnie pulled the phone from her ear and looked at it, almost dropped it. Frank's voice sounded far away, tired.

"I…I, uh, I've been really, really busy," Ronnie whispered, eyed the door to her bedroom.

"I thought you were going to let me know when you were free."

"Frank, listen, I can't talk." Ronnie went into the closet, pulled the door closed. "What if she knows it's you calling me?" She sat down next to her work shoes, nicest ones she'd ever had, from Isabelle of course. "You got me in so much trouble the other night. Why did you do that? It's like she knows."

"Slow down, tiger. How could she know?"

"Philippe told her he saw us together in the dining room." She put her head between her knees to muffle her voice even more. "Plus, she gave me this phone. She pays for it. Can't you tell, y'know, from the bill or something?"

"There's no need to worry. This isn't the Peter Franks phone. She wouldn't know this number." Frank sounded a little less tired, more awake. "As for the other night, I thought Peter Franks was just asking about dinner. Didn't that satisfy Philippe?"

"Isabelle has some spidey sense that we know each other." She let out a long breath. "She was so mad at me. She thought I was double-crossing her, taking your check. Why haven't you given her the check yet? It's making her suspicious."

"I'm hoping to finesse that. Fifty thou is a lot of money, in case you hadn't noticed."

She almost asked him what "finesse" meant but decided to wait and see if what he said next would explain it.

"About the phone," he said, "didn't you have friends before you met her?"

Ronnie nodded, then said yes out loud.

"Then maybe I'm one of those friends?" She shrugged her shoulders, and he went on as if she had spoken. "If it makes you feel any better, I'll get the Bureau to link this number to a fake friend of yours, just tell me the name."

Ronnie thought about it. "Um...I can't think right now."

"Who's your favorite cartoon character?"

"Linus." It just popped out. She didn't know why.

"Okay. Linus. Pick a last name."

"My brain has stopped working. I'm so tired. We had a dinner party tonight and—"

"Dinner without Peter Franks? What do you make of that?"

"Dunno. It was a weird night. Maybe she's mad at you. Who knows how Isabelle thinks? You should have seen Amelia tonight though, she—"

"Time for Peter to call her, ask to meet."

"She likes going to lunch." Ronnie wrapped the towel around her legs a little tighter. "She told Amelia they'd talk about Marshall Logan over lunch. Maybe that's your in."

Frank grunted. "I'm pretty sure we're past Marshall Logan by now." He cleared his throat, and his voice became softer. "I was just wondering if you would have some time maybe, maybe tomorrow? Maybe see your friends in Central Park, ask around some more?"

The way his voice faded at the end made Ronnie feel a little sorry for him. He must really, really love his daughter. What would that be like, someone this determined to find Ronnie? 'Course, she wouldn't know they were looking. But still.

"Well," she started to say, just as he said, "How 'bout it?"

"Um, I guess. If you're sure your number'll be safe. I'll text you as soon as I know what her plans are for tomorrow. We'll hit up the crusties, who will probably be useless, and then we can try some more places."

"That's great, thanks for that."

"Frank," Ronnie paused, made sure he was still there, then continued, "think about finding her dealer."

"They're the scum of the earth."

"But if it's the only way—"

"Nope. We don't need them. We'll find her ourselves."

Chapter Twenty-Three

"Isabelle said you think your donation is chicken feed." Philippe delivered the statement in a growl.

They were seated in the middle of the room, not Frank's ideal situation. When he proposed lunch to discuss how they could work together as a team, Isabelle had blown off his invitation, telling him instead to meet them at Philippe's club. Also, not ideal. Especially since Philippe took charge, no small talk, no chance to flirt with the divine blonde seated between them. He imagined each of her stockinged feet on each of their legs and then decided that image would not help him right now. He looked across the table at Philippe to ground himself. Isabelle still took up his peripheral vision, her sparkling eyes mischievous.

"Well now." Peter Franks selected a piece of bread from the basket, placed it on the tiny plate next to his water glass. "It's a lot of money—whether it's the five thousand I was prepared to donate," he glanced at Isabelle, "or the fifty thousand you seem to have me down for." A nod to the gorilla. He retrieved a pat of butter from the silver bowl nestled in ice. "Why don't you tell me what you already have going, and I can tell you what I can do with what she's already got?" The butter was rock hard. He left it and the bread on his plate. Gave Philippe a benign smile.

"Why don't you give Isabelle your chicken feed donation and I'll do something with it?" Philippe's eyebrows lowered. If looks could kill. "You've been playing cat and mouse long enough with this money you pledged."

"Ah. Philippe. Truly. If this were a game of cat and mouse, then I would be the dog. You have no idea how much I could make for Isabelle. I turned my insurance company from a little mom and pop outfit to something that sold for $200 mil." He put his hand on Isabelle's arm, turned the Peter Franks charm on her. "Now, wouldn't you like to see that kind of money sitting in your bank account?"

Her eyes widened, and she breathed in through her mouth as if bracing for something big. Money and sex seemed to be on equal footing in her world. He inhaled her musky perfume and finally tore his eyes away to regard Philippe. The touching didn't seem to bother him. Maybe he really was just the muscle in this relationship.

The waiter had only taken drink orders, not given them menus, and he deposited their drinks in front of them now. Did that mean they weren't eating? Or a prix fixe menu? Or Philippe had ordered for them? Frank lined up his silverware, the salad fork even with the dinner fork along the bottom, the tines ready like soldiers. He looked around the room as if for the waiter, noted the exits, the door to the kitchen, the white tableclothed tables full of mostly men in jackets and ties, a few women in business attire, a hush over the wood-paneled room.

"Oh, Philippe." Isabelle's hand landed on his arm, pale against the dark suit. "What I could do with that kind of money!" Her voice was low, the words on her breath like she didn't want to startle him.

Frank hoped his phone recorder could pick that up. More exhale than actual words.

Philippe covered her hand on his arm with his, like he owned her and leaned toward Frank. "You are not the dog. I am the dog. Isabelle is the alpha dog. I guard her and keep people like you from preying on her."

Well, woof, woof. "I see her more as a princess, a queen in command of everyone around her. I don't think she really needs that kind of protection."

Philippe cleared his throat with a growl, and Frank wanted to laugh, but he needed to keep them talking. "Tell me, Philippe, besides barking, what else do you do for Isabelle?" Isabelle looked from one man to the other, retrieved her hand and sat back in her chair like this was a competition she didn't want to miss.

"You don't need to know my business."

The waiter arrived with bowls of soup and the table was silent until he left. Cream of mushroom soup, perhaps. He hated cream of mushroom. Philippe grabbed his soup spoon and went after it like he hadn't eaten in weeks. Isabelle twinkled her eyes at Frank, like they were his parents and they both agreed how adorable Philippe's behavior was. She sipped her white wine and left her own soup untouched.

"Well, Philippe, actually, I do need to know. I thought this little get-together was to seal our partnership, and if we're going to work together, I need to know how you fit in, what you do for Isabelle, and what sorts of things you're into so I can tell you just how you can make—" he leaned forward and looked at the tables around them, then said in a whisper, "hundreds of millions."

Isabelle clapped her hands and laughed her windchime laugh, bells ringing. Several heads turned at the sound, several pairs of eyes lingered on the alluring Isabelle.

Philippe seemed unmoved by her charms. He dropped his soup spoon in the empty bowl, the heavy silver clanging with a dissonant counterpart to Isabelle's laugh. Frank wanted to make her laugh again. Philippe threw him a skeptical look. "Just how do you propose to do this, this magic trick?"

"No magic." Frank held up his hands, wiggled his fingers. "Fastest keyboarding this side of the Rockies."

And Frank got his wish. Isabelle laughed, a delighted, victorious laugh, her head back, the length of her throat exposed, her perfume in the air between them. "Oh, how fun!" Her eyes were dark now as she looked back and forth between them. "Philippe, can you just imagine?"

A busperson came to clear the soup course, another two servers set up a tray on a stand. Others rushed in with a variety of bowls, plates, and implements. Isabelle watched with a wide smile on her face, Philippe glowered at Frank, and Peter Franks aimed an affable we're-all-on-the-same-side expression at him.

Philippe looked like he had swallowed something that tasted terrible, and Isabelle looked delighted with the activity at their tableside. The guy who had first handed them their menus was chopping up raw meat, the cleaver lethal, light glinting off the blade ever so often. Frank did not see any heat source.

"So, Philippe, tell me," Frank paused, made sure he had Philippe's attention, "what is it exactly that you do?"

Philippe scowled, turned his head to the food-making activity.

"I mean, your day job, the main thing that keeps you busy. Something financial, is it?"

"Financial planner." Philippe barely opened his mouth, the information a grunt.

"Ah. I see." Frank lined up his knife, spoon, other spoon. "How are you liking the markets right now?" Out of the corner of his eye, Frank saw an egg being cracked into a bowl, a splash of Worcestershire sauce from the iconic paper-covered bottle. Raw steak and egg. Just what the Board of Health ordered. Isabelle's smile was still wide as she watched the tableside show. Seemed like she might like to mince the meat up herself. With her teeth.

Philippe regarded Frank for a long minute. "You know what the market is doing right now." His hand roller-coastered the air in front of him. "You don't need to remind me." He bit the last sentence off as if he thought it was all Frank's doing.

"Well, what about bonds, government securities? What's safe these days?"

A cadre of waitstaff dealt out the plates, then decamped. Frank looked down at his. A mound of raw meat decorated with a bouquet of chives lay in the center. Arranged around it was what Frank supposed would be called a deconstructed salad: tiny bits of lettuce, three minuscule tomatoes cut in half, a sprinkle of purple onions, and some green-grey things he didn't recognize. Now, how was he going to eat this?

Isabelle took up her fork and sliced into the mound of meat. Philippe watched her, indulgent, expectant, as if he waited for the aria at an opera. Her eyes rolled upward, then she closed them, her smile so naked, so blissful, Frank had to turn away. A waiter rushed up to the table, and Philippe held up a *stop* hand, eyes not leaving Isabelle. She dropped her head, opened her eyes, awe and wonder, almost disbelief painted her expression. She sat back as if drained. Philippe lowered his hand.

"Everything all right, sir? Is there something—"

"Young man, it couldn't be more perfect."

Frank sipped his water, not ready to speak quite yet. He mushed around the stuff on his plate, then he wiped his mouth with his napkin and dropped it over the whole thing.

"Philippe, this really is a fine lunch. I'm hoping—" Frank glanced at his thin gold watch. "—before I have to go, that we could nail this down." He threw an apologetic look at Isabelle. "Sorry to rush since you're enjoying this so much, but I do have an appointment I can't miss, and I want to work with you. So, if you could just tell me—"

A growl floated over to him from across the table. Philippe's plate was scraped clean. "You ask too many questions. You tell us what you can do, and I will tell you whether we want you on our team or not."

Frank, or rather Peter Franks, touched Isabelle, gave her a pleading look. "I thought we were already working together? That this was a meeting to go over details, firm everything up." He leaned in. "Help you make millions." He held his hand up, palm down as if to show her how high the stack of money would be. He whispered, "*Hundreds* of millions."

Isabelle swayed in her chair. He had her. He knew he had her. He gave her the slightest nod, like a shared secret, a smile between them.

"I thought you had to go." The low rumble sounded like a threat.

Frank and Isabelle still held each other's eyes. "I have enough time for a list of your activities, so I can tell you how I would maximize your results, with just the tiniest percentage for my expertise." He pinched the air as if he required almost nothing.

"A percentage?" Philippe rumbled.

"You wouldn't trust me if I worked for nothing, now would you?"

"I didn't trust you when I first met you, and I trust you even less now."

Frank broke eye contact with Isabelle to give Philippe a quizzical, hurt look, a puppy cocking his head.

"You have not been honest with us."

Uh-oh. No way. He'd been too careful. They couldn't possibly know.

"You pledge but don't make good on it. Isabelle, this man should not come to your house again." He aimed a stubby finger at Frank. "You'll be crossed off her list."

"Oh, well now. I don't think—"

Philippe shoved back his chair, stood. He waved away the servers who had rushed over, threw his napkin down. *Apoplectic* sprang into Frank's mind. With a final look at Isabelle, Philippe left.

Frank watched him go, the broad back striding past diners, the thick neck holding the large head perfectly straight. Philippe stopped to talk with the maître d', hopefully to say to put their lunch on his bill, not leave it to Frank and the Bureau to pay. This may be the last time he would see the big guy. Or have lunch with the wily Isabelle.

The staff cleared the table, carefully stacking plates on the temporary station that had recently held their steak tartare. How had this meeting gone so wrong? Didn't trust him? Why ever not? He had the face of an Eagle Scout. He had been nice, friendly, as comfortable to be around as the family pet. He could see Isabelle in his peripheral vision. She seemed completely unfazed by Philippe's tantrum. He felt weighed down, a dark mood engulfing him. The case was over, the first time in his career he hadn't been successful. He twisted the stem of his water glass back and forth. Back and forth. He would have to put Peter Franks away. Turn in the impossibly thin gold watch, the bespoke suit, the diamond cufflinks. No more candlelit dinners at the brownstone, no more spending the evening forgetting the outside world, listening to the cascading laugh of the lovely Isabelle.

"Penny for your thoughts." Isabelle's hand on his arm.

He looked at the hand. Those long, lovely fingers, the nails polished in mirrored silver, filed to nearly a point as if they doubled as weapons. No more Isabelle, no more getting lost in her perfume, no more shopping trips with the adrenaline rush of wondering if they would get caught when she swiped something.

"I'm not sure how I angered him." He kept his eyes down, worried that too much emotion would show in them.

"Philippe? Who cares about him?" She waved her hand, part maestro, part shooing a fly. "Excuse me," she flagged a waitperson. "Could you bring us coffee and the dessert menu?"

He might as well have dessert even though he wasn't hungry, draw out his last minutes with her. Enjoy the teasing seduction, the way she made him feel that he was the most important person in her world and always would be. The heat of her hand came through his jacket sleeve. He had never met anyone like her. She exuded sexuality with every gesture, every touch. Her mind brilliant and her laugh infectious. Her perfume was intoxicating, sometimes literally so. She drew people to her, and the thrill of danger he got from just being next to her, unmistakable.

Isabelle removed her hand to peruse the dessert menu. She threw him a glance, then ordered for them both, flambé something, chocolate something. He took a sip of water. He missed her hand already. The case couldn't be over. So much left to do. He wasn't ready to give up.

"Now, Peter." Isabelle's voice was low, intimate, something just for the two of them. "You really must tell me what's going on with you. I've never seen you like this."

Frank let out a long breath. How could he possibly explain this? "Crossed off your list? Never come to the brownstone again?" He shook his head back and forth. "I can't imagine New York without you."

She laughed. She threw her head back and laughed, startled the server with the coffee pot. Her long, pale throat offered up, her blonde hair swinging. "Oh, Peter, you are so droll." She patted him, watched the servers put a slab of chocolate cake between them. The flambé they lit with a flourish at the side table, shook the pan around until the flames died, plated it, and presented it. What a lot of nonsense.

"Now listen." All trace of mirth was gone from her voice. She picked up her fork, waved it at him. "What makes you think Philippe, or anyone else, could possibly tell me who can and cannot come to *my* house?" Her fork sliced into the cake like a guillotine. "*I* make the rules, *I* say what's what. No man has ever told me what to do." She held her fork up to Peter's lips, which seemed to open of their own accord. She slipped the cake in. "I am not some helpless damsel in need of rescuing." She waved the fork. "Now.

CHAPTER TWENTY-THREE

Isn't that just so delicious?"

Frank nodded. Cut the sweetness with a sip of coffee. Cleared his throat. "I wasn't trying to imply—you two seem to be a team—he sounded so definitive."

"Don't you worry about him. He'll get over it. The important thing is that I trust you and I want to keep you around. Now, try this Peach Flambé. It's to die for!"

* * *

The air in Frank's apartment was stale, the heat from the radiators stifling. Frank cracked open the window, plopped into the chair in front of it. Breathed. Night would slam down soon, but Frank didn't want to get up to turn a light on. He was still in his alter ego's clothes from lunch. He should hang them up, keep them from wrinkling too much. He breathed again. He couldn't shake that feeling of intense disappointment he'd felt when he thought the case over. He shifted in the chair. Old and lumpy, a compromise from their divorce. If Frank got the standing lamp, he had to take the musty armchair. And, he had to be honest with himself: the disappointment at the prospect of not seeing Isabelle had been far stronger than the specter of a failed case.

Frank got up and closed the blinds. He took off the blazer and shook it out, took it to the bedroom, and hung it on the wooden hanger that would eventually be returned to the Bureau. When had he become the kind of person who wanted to spend time with the criminals? At what point had the line between Peter Franks and Frank Jankowski blurred? When had the bad cop overtaken the good one? He slid the diamond cufflinks out of the French cuffs, nestled them in the velvet lined box, added the Piaget watch, and closed the lid.

He went down the hall to the bathroom, turned on the shower. The water hit him full in the face. One of the best things about this apartment, the water pressure. He would sort things out on his own, maybe tell Pete when it was over, laugh about the magnetism of the charming UES hostess at the brownstone on E. 83rd.

* * *

"Hey Frank!" Pete's voice sailed over the partition, and Frank rolled his chair back to look at his partner. Anything was better than staring at his computer. "So, y'know I've been looking into every donor—I'll have to say this, she is thorough on her tax reports—and get this, a lot of them died of unnatural causes."

"Really? Is she some kind of black widow spider?"

"Hanged, jumped off a building, slit their wrists, mariticide. Over a period of three years. Four dead donors."

"Matricide?"

"No, mariticide, like husband-cide."

"Damn. Have you researched them?"

"Just starting."

"Lemme know, will ya? Not that I'm feeling suicidal, but I would feel better knowing if there's a connection."

Chapter Twenty-Four

Ronnie got off the train first, led Frank up the stairs then up another set, waves of people crisscrossing, fans of humanity coming and going from all sides. The Port Authority was the busiest terminal in the world. She'd looked it up. Eight thousand buses and 225,000 people every single day came through here. Some were commuters, some came from airports, some were tourists meeting their sightseeing buses so they could then stare out at the jungle from the safety of their seats. It was like a small city down here, store after store lined up, and so many open when so many were papered over up top.

She waited while Frank went over to two officers standing side by side, doing nothing but scanning the crowd. They examined Cathy's picture, shook their heads, said something, nodded, looked over his shoulder at the crowd. She let him talk to the kids hanging outside of Dunkin' Donuts, sitting on the ground where the retail ended, but she knew where she had to take him to search for his daughter, and it was down. Down, down to the darkest places, the furthest away from all these people.

Across platforms, down flights. It seemed like miles, dodging the people who walked purposefully, past tourists clumped around maps and speaking to each other so rapidly it made Ronnie wonder what English sounded like to them. Frank stopped her on the level with the gates for the buses.

"I've already been here," Frank told her, and she shook her head, kept walking. This time of night it wasn't as busy, though certainly busy enough, plenty of dazed people getting off buses. You could pick out the runaways as if they had an arrow over their head, the too-full backpack, the scared eyes but the face set as if to feel braver, lips in a firm line. Frank started to approach a skinny guy coming out of the gate, but Ronnie touched his arm.

"He's just arrived here. He wouldn't know."

"But maybe he'll see her, maybe—"

Ronnie figured it would make him feel better, so she waited, then headed for the last staircase, the air getting danker as they went down it. She leaned over the tracks, looked down the platform, the dark tunnel damp and no doubt crawling with rats, the worst of the worst. She thought she saw a person move and started walking, then grabbed some flyers from Frank.

"Let me go first. You might scare them."

Frank took a step and then stopped, opened his mouth, closed it.

At the very end of the platform, where normal people would think the station ended, she edged on, hugged the last pillar, and flattened against the wall. She placed one foot down and then the other, tightrope-walking her way on the ledge, and let her eyes adjust, her cheek nearly brushing the tile. When the wall ended, there was more room for her feet, and she faced the tunnel, the dim yellow from a light next to a utility door nearly lost in the darkness. She heard the voices and walked toward them, called out so they knew she was one of them, harmless.

The first time Ronnie came down into the tunnels with Matt, she begged him not to go in there. He had given her a quick touch and a smile, his way of assuring her he knew what he was doing, and then he led the way. She had held on to his jacket in the dark, tugged on him to slow down. A bit of light came from the station, but then petered out, leaving them in the darkness, the air damp like she was breathing the earth, a smell of brakes and the sound of skitters from something small and nasty, the crunch of maybe glass, as they crept along. An overhead pipe dripped, and by the smell of the tunnels it could've been from the sewer. Tonight, she knew what to expect, and it was easier, though the sounds and smells and darkness hadn't changed.

She turned at a break in the wall, a tunnel you wouldn't notice unless you already knew it was here. Not much of a crowd this time, backs against the dirt and rock of the wall, knees up, some passed out, some sleeping. She spoke softly to them, gave them Cathy's picture, told them she needed to find her friend. One girl, looking about the right age, clearly strung out, leaned on a guy's shoulder, and she stopped in front of them.

"What's her name?" She asked the guy, though he looked like at any minute he might pass out too, eyes rolling up, brain shutting down. She'd seen Matt do that so often. She shook the shoulder that didn't have the girl on it and waited for him to see her. "I'm looking for someone. What's your friend's name?" He shoved the poor girl and her head lolled, then in slow motion, she fell onto his lap. Ronnie couldn't tell if he thought he was waking her or if he wanted to remove himself from her. She realized now she should have brought something to give out, food, clean needles, condoms. When she and Matt had been down here that time, that was what the people who came to help did, and she'd watched them talking to the kids, handing out resource information, some of the kids even keeping the pieces of paper.

Ronnie backed out of the tunnel to get a little more light, tapped on her phone, and sent a text to Frank: *go get food meet you back down here* Anticipating his question, she typed: *anything* She peered into the tunnel. These two weren't going anywhere, so she sidled out into the light of the station and felt the air as it pushed through the tunnel, blowing her bangs up away from her eyes, a train clacking and screeching in. A few people got off, a sleeping homeless man in a rumpled raincoat stretched out on a seat, immune to the bright lights of the subway car. She stayed near the end of the platform, just in case some of those runaways decided to leave, decided to try their luck in the pockets of the unwary on the platform.

Several more trains came through, each one seeming to carry fewer people, and in the pause between the stops, she watched a rat wrestle with a hot dog, dragged it, stopped to get a better hold, moving pretty fast along the wall. She thought that for humans that might be like dragging a couch or something. She put her hand in her pocket. Maybe she should text Frank. How long could it take to get food this time of night? Maybe he had gotten lost. She'd just decided to wait until two more trains came through or until the rat disappeared with his catch, whichever came first, when she spied Frank clutching several boxes with the distinctive orange and pink lettering popping out at her. Exactly what she hoped he'd find.

"We have to go carefully here," she said over her shoulder, hoping his tall frame could flatten around the pillars. Once they had more room, she took a box from him and opened it, donut holes piled up, sticky, cinnamony, the chocolate ones lost in the darkness. They went from person to person, offered the food, showed them the picture, Frank silently watching them, holding out the box, studying their faces. They came to the tunnel where the girl had been, and Ronnie felt a buzz in her stomach. Maybe she would turn out to be Frank's daughter. Next to her she felt Frank move, saw him get out his phone, but she stopped him, a hand on his arm. "Don't use the flashlight, they'll think you're a cop." She thought she may have seen one corner of his mouth move as he put it back in his pocket, a silent "d-uh," and then a nod to her expertise.

Deeper into the tunnel she led him, though it was more of a cave, and Ronnie was sure the boy and girl hadn't been this far in, a dripping sound, the scuffling of rats, the dampness and a toilet smell buffeting her face as she went. She breathed through her mouth to avoid the smell, but she couldn't avoid the feeling that those kids were no longer here. If they didn't want to be found, no amount of donut holes was going to bring them out. She stopped and felt Frank next to her.

"They're not here," she whispered.

"You sure? Maybe you got the wrong tunnel."

"I wanted you to see her. She was about the right age. I thought if you talked to her—even if it wasn't Cathy, maybe she'd seen her."

He pulled his phone out and shined the flashlight on the dirt walls bulging around them, a digging out of the earth with no need to smooth it down. The light flicked on a tiny hand and Ronnie and Frank sucked in their breath at the same time. They moved forward, and the raccoon turned and ran, a striped tail the last thing they saw.

* * *

They had gone through the Port Authority again, every floor, giving out the last of the donut holes, almost all of the flyers, the runaways scared, defiant, sleepy, none of them any help, though some took the flyer, saying *I hope you find her, man.* Now Ronnie and Frank sat at a round table in an open area filled with tables and some late-night people, suitcases, backpacks, bulging bags of belongings.

Ronnie, though exhausted, felt keyed up, her leg starting to jump, and she pressed down on it with her hands. "Maybe it's time to find her dealer." She watched Frank for his reaction. His eyes were dark, skin sagging like he'd aged fifteen years since she last looked at him.

Frank blew out a long breath. "How do you even know she's using?" He stared at the floor. "Those parasites. They should be locked up or dead." He shook his head. Then met her eyes and asked, "What about the crusties? That girl you were talking to at the Park?"

"We can try them again, but I think her dealer is the way to go."

"I'm in law enforcement." He cleared his throat. "Better to just take them all downtown, put them in cages, interrogate them, find the one selling to my daughter—"

"Frank." Ronnie started to put her arms on the table and then saw the shimmer of something spilled, crumbs, a straw wrapper. She put her hands in her lap. "Think about it."

He shook his head, like he was saying "no way," then got up and paced near their table.

"How many of them do you think are out there?" Her eyes followed him as he walked a square, like he was the one in a cage. "And so, you bring them in and what happens? You can only keep them so long, but meanwhile, someone else starts selling to her."

He stopped and turned his face to her, but she didn't think he was seeing her, the wheels in his head churning.

"So they go back on the streets," Ronnie went on, "and you keep rounding up dealers. You spend months interrogating them, and it's not even for a case. How does that even work?"

Frank sat down, the chair squeaking against the floor under his weight. He shoved his hands in his coat pocket and stared at the table, his mouth a thin line, a muscle in his jaw jumping.

"Let me get this straight." His eyes found hers, held them. "You're trying to tell me that the only way for me to find Cathy is to work with criminals?"

She nodded. Held his gaze.

"Not arresting them because they're engaging in criminal activity, not alerting the local police to them, but working with them, letting them continue to—" He got up so quickly his chair fell over, the clatter of metal echoing in the empty space. He didn't look at it. He didn't look at Ronnie. He just left, his shoes hammer taps on the floor, seeming to get louder even though he was moving away from her.

"Frank!" She went after him. "Frank!"

He kept going, not looking back, but something in the tilt of his head told her he had heard her. She caught up to him by a nail salon, the security gate down, the windows dark, one light at the rear of the store showing chair after chair in shadow. She grabbed his arm, and he spun around, his face hard, a solid mask.

She held her ground. "Frank," she said a little softer this time.

He shook his head at her, at the security gate, at the Port Authority around them. Hell, at the whole world for all she knew. "No way."

"Do you even want to find her?"

"What in God's name kind of question is that?"

"At least you haven't lost it completely. Look, Frank, you know I'm right. You know this is the only thing that makes any sense."

"I am not working with criminals."

She let out a long breath, then stared at him. "What the fuck do you think you're doing when you go undercover?"

* * *

Frank had asked couldn't they talk to the crusties first, before he started working with drug dealers, so on Ronnie's next free night she brought Annie. She didn't want to bring Annie. In fact, it was so hard to convince Annie to come that she finally had to promise her a hot meal afterwards. She figured

Frank was getting off easy.

They waited by the Eighth Avenue door of the Port Authority, watched the cars and buses go by, someone on roller skates dodging bumpers, a cruiser slowing making Annie press into the shadows of the building.

"Hello, you must be Annie." Frank held out his hand for a shake and then dropped it.

"You didn't tell me he was a cop!"

"Annie, c'mon. He's a father, and he loves his daughter. You said you'd help look for her."

"Annie," Frank said, "I'm here as a civilian, same as you." He pulled out his flyer, a more recent picture Ronnie was glad to note. He'd finally taken her advice on that, the previous picture too young, too cute. "This is Cathy, my daughter. I can't tell you how grateful I am that you'll help me search for her."

"Yeah?" Annie didn't bother to look at the picture. "How grateful?" She examined Frank as if she could see through his pockets, add up his cash.

"Annie, I already told you." Ronnie cut her eyes to Frank then said to Annie, trying to keep the pleading out of her voice, "He's buying you a hot meal after we look."

"What else you got in that bag?"

Frank opened the bag to show her. "Just a tape gun."

"How far y'gonna get with that this time of night?" She grabbed the bag and headed toward Times Square. Ronnie and Frank exchanged a look and then followed her.

She stopped at every person young, old, in between, even the really crazy-looking ones. Most people took a flyer, some even gave it a glance then shook their head. Frank and Ronnie followed her further away from Times Square. They left behind the lights, the crowds of tourists, the barkers dressed as characters trying to lure people to the show. They hit the dirtier streets, streetlights out, people asleep on stoops, a few boarded up buildings, a greasiness, a cold that hit Ronnie's core.

"This seems a little skanky." Frank pulled his coat tighter around him.

Ronnie realized there weren't even cars coming down the street. All warehouses now, the loading docks about four feet up, other buildings with metal doors on the sidewalk for hand-loading down steps into the basement.

"Annie! I don't think—" Ronnie called to her down the street. She said to Frank, "I would never have gone here." She stopped walking and he turned around, closed the space between them. "It's too empty. We would never be on this street. What is this?"

"It's the Garment District. Busy in the daytime."

Ronnie shivered. Annie came closer, plastic bag swinging from her wrist.

"What's in the bag?" The guy moved out of the shadows, a knife glinting in his hand. Annie whirled to face him, suddenly statue still. The guy pointed with his knife at Frank's shopping bag, then pushed it through the air at her, back and forth, like all he wanted to do was sink it into Annie's stomach. Ronnie's breath came quickly, her vision narrowed as time slowed almost to a stop. The damp, empty air cool around her, traffic sounds behind her, an animal smell of fear rising up between the four of them, and then it registered in her brain before her body that the guy with the knife was just as scared as they were.

"Run!" Ronnie shouted.

"Run!" Frank shouted at the same time.

Annie was way ahead of them, having dropped the bag, her white hair bobbing, feet pounding. Frank grabbed Ronnie's arm, pulled her with him, their footsteps echoing off the empty street, the two of them in a race, eating up the sidewalk, the empty warehouses looming and then disappearing, the corner in sight, cars, taxis, trucks filling the cross street. They were going so fast Ronnie had to grab the traffic light post to swing the corner, make the turn, the bright colors of Times Square up ahead, the crowds ready to swallow them up.

* * *

They went into a diner on a corner out of the main part of Times Square, full of tourists even still, but not so crowded they couldn't get a booth. Ronnie slid in and picked up her menu, her breathing almost normal. Annie slid in next to her, cramming her against the wall. Frank took off his coat, tossed it onto the seat, and slid in after it. Ronnie's mouth hung open.

"What're you hungry for? My treat."

"Yippee!" Annie leaned over Ronnie to look at her menu. Ronnie gave it to her, edged into the wall away from the smell of her.

"Frank."

Frank raised an eyebrow at Ronnie over his plastic menu.

"You had a gun all this time?"

"Yeah. So?" he said, eyes on his menu.

"But you ran."

"You're the one who said 'run.' I just did what you said." He eyed her over his menu, then put it down. "That's what it's there for. So I can run. I'm getting the cheeseburger. What'll you have?"

"I'm gettin' a double cheeseburger, onion rings, milkshake, fries, and pie!"

Ronnie ignored Annie. "What do you mean 'so you can run?' That doesn't make any sense."

Frank glanced at Annie. "Are you sure that's all?"

"Yeah, you're right. A BLT, too."

"What would you like, Ronnie?"

She didn't answer. She couldn't believe it. How could they think about food right now.

"Look," Frank said, "I've never shot anyone, and I've rarely had to unholster it. It's better to run and live." He took a sip of water. "Besides, it's too much paperwork. Everything stops, I mean everything." He held up a hand for their waitperson. Hand still in the air, eyes on Ronnie, he went on, "—when the Bureau investigates a discharged firearm. Besides," he grinned, "he only had a knife."

Chapter Twenty-Five

"Oh. Frank."

He turned from the store window to face the familiar voice. "Susan."

"I was just thinking that Christmas would be here soon, and I stopped to look and found myself reminiscing, and here you are, too." She shivered beside him, and his first instinct was to put an arm around her. Old habits died hard.

"Do you have someplace you have to be? Want to go get a coffee?" He gestured with his head, down the street, thinking maybe there was a Starbucks, or something cheaper.

"Oh! Well, I—" Susan glanced down the street, then at him, then away. So familiar, even still. The small orange flecks in her irises, the sprinkle of freckles faded on her cheekbones.

"It's okay. We don't have to. It's just that you look cold." He shoved his hands in his coat pocket, turned to the display window decorated for Christmas.

"No, I just—well, that would be nice, if you have the time."

He checked his watch. Nodded at her, and they both headed south, out of the swirl of shoppers, turned at the same time down the street and away from the busyness as if they had already agreed.

A tiny table in the window was free and they threaded their way to it, Frank waiting for her to be seated before he sat down. He could barely squeeze by without butting the woman in the table next to them, but he managed. He surveyed the restaurant automatically, noting the nanny with the stroller on her phone, not caring she was taking up the aisle, not caring that the child had slumped so far down in his seat he was about to slide out. He was kicking the table and the nanny looked up to tell him to stop, then went straight back to her phone.

"Have you..." Susan let the question hang, turned to look out the window. The waiter came up and they ordered, "just coffee," then Frank asked if she wanted to split a pastry and she looked over at the counter display, a slight frown.

"Oh, why not," she said.

Frank guessed she had been trying to calculate the calories but abandoned the effort.

"The fruit tart, please," she said to the waiter. "Two forks." Frank settled against his chair, a slight smile on his lips as he watched her.

"What? Isn't that what you wanted?"

"Exactly what I wanted." She knew him so well. A flash of color coming down the sidewalk caught his eye, and he watched it as it came nearer, the shape formulating into a tall blonde woman in a bright red coat with a fur collar, a distinguished-looking man at her side, the flirting palpable even at this distance.

"Excuse me. Bathroom." Frank didn't wait for a response, bumping the woman next to him as he hightailed it toward the back of the restaurant. The stroller completely blocked the aisle, and he grabbed the phone and put it on the table. The nanny looked up at him dazed, frowning.

"Could you move the stroller, please?"

"Why did you take my phone? I was in the middle—"

"Aren't you getting paid to watch this little boy?"

"Mind your own business."

"I'm trying to get by to use the bathroom, which is my business, and you're blocking the way with the stroller. Which is illegal." Frank threw a look over his shoulder. Too late.

"Peter!" Isabelle paused at the door, her slender arm Statue of Liberty high as she smiled at the few heads that turned toward her. Susan was thankfully gazing out the window, slumped a bit over the table as if the world was too much. He hurried to the front door.

"Well, fancy seeing you here." He turned to her companion and held out a hand to shake. "Peter Franks."

"Henry Norton."

"I was actually about to leave—" Frank checked his watch.

But Isabelle had angled her way away from the door, toward the table at the window.

"This must be your lovely wife that you've been hiding all this time from us!"

Susan looked up, startled, a frown beginning.

But Isabelle barreled on as Frank threaded through the tables toward them. "Oh, aren't you just darling!" Isabelle thrust out a gloved hand, "Mrs. Franks, I'm Isabelle Anderson. I've been so looking forward to meeting you!"

"I—Frank?"

Frank couldn't get around Isabelle in the crowded deli and remained standing. "No, Isabelle, sorry, this is Susan Jankowski, my head of HR."

"Oh dear, I do beg your pardon." She turned to Frank, and he could smell her trademark perfume, see the fur on her coat collar fluffing. "When I saw you two in the window, you just seemed like a comfortable married couple, I was sure you were Peter's wife!"

"Peter?" Susan seemed too slow on the uptake, and Frank stared at her, willing with his eyes for her to play along. "Oh!" Susan sat up straighter. "Peter, yes."

"Head of Human Resources?" Isabelle searched Frank's face. "I thought you had sold your company."

"Well, you know, loose ends and all that." Frank gestured to the table. "We were just finishing up." Susan gave him a quick look, but he went on, "Would you like our table?"

"Oh no, no, really." Isabelle gave a laugh that didn't make it all the way to her eyes. She patted Susan's hand as if they were old friends. "Henry and I would have never even come in here if I hadn't seen you in the window." She turned to leave and Frank let go an inward exhale of relief, then his head snapped up as she turned back. "Really, Peter, I thought I'd shown you so many other nicer places to stop for coffee and—" she eyed the fruit tart on the middle of the table, nose wrinkling, "a pastry." She drew out the word making it into three distasteful syllables.

Frank sat down and Susan leaned toward him, a question on her lips, in her eyes. Isabelle's words sailed back to them: "Sooooo lovely meeting you, Ms. Jankowski! Peter, you must bring her with you for dinner tonight!" And then they passed the window, Isabelle snuggling into Henry Norton. She gave a little royal wave at them, then turned to say something into the man's ear.

Frank and Susan looked at each other across the table. Frank shrugged as if to say, what can you do? And then to his surprise, Susan burst out laughing, the familiar laugh that said the world was so ridiculous and she was glad she was there to see it.

* * *

He hunched into his coat as he walked back to his apartment, ducked his head against the wind whistling up the street. That was a close one. What an idiot for sitting in the window. It could've been much worse. He could've been with Ronnie. What was wrong with him? But seeing Susan and Isabelle together. He mentally shook his head. Surreal. The meeting of his personal and professional world, the meeting of Peter Franks and Frank Jankowski. Like he had time traveled and his past self encountered his future self. It was unsettling. Isabelle was still her usual manipulating self, but next to Susan her charm seemed overly calculating, her gushing brittle. Susan was genuine, like she didn't need to wear the makeup Isabelle did. Not that either woman overdid it with the makeup. Susan had depth whereas Isabelle was all surface. But he could still smell the cinnamon and musk that had somehow got on him in the crowded restaurant. If only he could leave that on Peter Franks' skin, wash it off Frank Jankowski's.

* * *

In the office the next day, Pete showed him the videos, pointing to the screen, clicking to the next one. "This is what strings all these guys together."

Pete had spent the better part of the week combing the internet, diving deep into Isabelle's donors, who had ended up dead. And he had found old, anonymous social media posts of several of these dead donors in compromising positions. Whips, chains, handcuffs, underage girls and boys.

Frank turned away from the screen. Viewing sexual exploits like this didn't used to bother him to such an extent. He could compartmentalize, leave the personal at home, bring the professional to work. But now with Cathy on the streets, doing godknowswhat... He shook himself as if he could rid himself of the images. He gave Pete a glance. "Anything other than Isabelle Anderson that ties them together?"

Pete shook his head. "They belong to a lot of the same clubs, but all of Isabelle's dinner guests belong to those clubs. I've looked at it from every angle you could think of, and some you wouldn't, and I'm afraid Isabelle is the only common thread."

Frank let out a long, low whistle. "So, they donate to Isabelle's foundation, anonymous videos pop up on social media, and then they kill themselves."

"Or their wives do it for them."

"Can you trace who posted them?"

Pete shook his head. "Tech guys are on it. Whoever did it, knew how to hide their tracks. Plus they know their way around the digital software. The photos with the children? They're photoshopped. Really well done. I almost missed it."

Frank got up and went to the window. "The police reports?"

"Some of them had lost their jobs, their wives reported they'd been drinking heavily, shunning their friends." Pete made some clicks behind him. "These were all good people. Sure they associated with Isabelle Anderson, but they gave heavily to good, honest charities. One of them had a kid with Cerebral Palsy, and now that kid doesn't have a father, and his wife is left to take care of her alone. Terrible disease."

Frank shook his head. "And Isabelle?"

"Police never made that connection."

Frank let out a long breath.

"Frank? What're you looking at out the window? It's all clouds out there."

Chapter Twenty-Six

Ronnie and Frank met again at the Port Authority, at that place with all the tables and few people, a holding area waiting for someone to put in a restaurant.

"I couldn't find Annie tonight," Ronnie told him.

"Just as well." Frank scanned the tables around them. "She might be more trouble than she's worth. Almost got us knifed last time."

"Ready to go?" Ronnie jumped off the table she was sitting on. "Where do you wanna start?"

Frank nodded but didn't make a move. "You really think we have to approach the dealers?"

Ronnie shook her head. "No 'we' this time. You look like a cop."

"I could disguise myself."

She smiled at that. "It's a long way from Peter Franks of Omaha to junkie looking for a fix."

"You'd be surprised what I'm capable of."

"Evidently."

"Okay, watch this." Frank pulled off his coat, untucked half his shirt, loosened his belt and undid the button of his pants, messed his hair with one hand as if rubbing a cat the wrong way. He shuffled around, twitching, slumping while he went, bobbing his head to his own music. His pants were slipping down as he moved around, and Ronnie started laughing. She couldn't help it.

"Rub some dirt on your face and get older clothes, grease them up, maybe you'll have it!" He shambled up to a table of tourists and said something

210

to them, and she watched as they turned toward each other in an effort to shut him out. He began doing an odd dance for them, and they grabbed their suitcases and rolled away from him as fast as they could. He stayed in character as he made his way to her, wandering in circles and then landing in his chair.

"Okay, okay, you're in. You can ask too." Ronnie stood up, zipped up her jacket. "We need to get your clothes dirty, though." She looked him over. "And that raincoat, it looks too new."

He gave a shrug.

"I know. Come with me." And she left, not looking back, not waiting the way her brothers never waited, her little legs running to keep up. She took him down to the subway level, saw the guy stretched out along the bench. "Give me your coat."

Frank glanced at the guy, then said, "But, wait. This is a good coat! It's served me well all these years."

Ronnie waited, her head cocked slightly. When he still hesitated, she said, "Gotta pay to play bro." She watched as he shrugged out of it, then she sped over to the guy who completely reeked, saw that she didn't have to even wake him since his own coat was his blanket. She pulled it off him and fanned Frank's over him before he snored the next snore.

"This thing stinks."

"Yeah, I know, that's why I'm walking ahead of you."

They hit the streets, and Ronnie told Frank to hang back the first couple of times, let him get the feel of how to approach these guys. She walked up to a runner, gave him a flyer, then one to the dealer in his car, told him how they were looking for this runaway who liked opiates, and they weren't ruling out heroin at this point. She looked back at Frank after she said this, the dealer looking at him too.

"I don't know if he understands that yet," Ronnie said. "But that's his number there. She doesn't have to see him if she doesn't want to, but if she's your customer, at least he could get messages to her." The dealer stared out his windshield, drummed the steering wheel. "And give her money if she needs it." The guy nodded to her, took the flyer, then looked around her at his runner. "Thanks, dude." She went over to Frank.

She told him everything she said, except the part about his not under-standing the heroin yet. He flinched the tiniest bit at the mention of heroin, and she interrupted herself. "Dude. You're a cop. You should know this. Opiates are opiates, and Oxy is too expensive. Heroin is so much cheaper."

He nodded at her, said, "I know, I know, but it's Cathy…" He still looked miserable.

They turned down the block, the sidewalk nearly empty, their steps matching so that it sounded like one person echoing off the buildings. "Maybe she's not shooting it." Ronnie didn't add the "yet" she was thinking. "Maybe she's smoking it. Or snorting it." As if that would somehow make it better.

"And you told him she doesn't have to see me? Why would you say that?"

"Frank. Dude." Ronnie touched his arm. "The guy might not even call you otherwise." She stopped at the corner, looked both ways, wondered if downtown or uptown would be a better bet. "The dealer doesn't know why she ran away. But he wants to keep her as a customer, so it just seems that he would be more likely to call you if he's not thinking that you'll take her away from him." Frank nodded, but she didn't think he was convinced.

Ronnie watched as she sent Frank over to talk to the next guy. She saw the dealer look to the side, motion for Frank to go away. Either Frank didn't get it, or he didn't care. He shook the flyer at him, moved even closer. Ronnie's heart sped up, and she tensed, ready to run toward them. The dealer got up in his face and still Frank didn't back down, his voice louder, more insistent. A car went by, the bass all the way up and booming. A group of kids on the sidewalk crossed in the middle of the block, their laughter dying down as they kept looking back at Frank and the dealer. All of a sudden two guys came out of the shadows, walked toward Frank in a steady, purposeful approach as if Frank were their prey and they knew they would land him. Ronnie raced over, grabbed Frank's arm.

"Yo man, it's okay, he didn't mean anything. He's just worried about his daughter." She backed them both up, still facing the dealer, Ronnie calculating whether all three were going to make a move for their guns. She called out, "She's just sixteen, too young, y'know?" Step by backwards step, but not far enough away for a bullet. "She doesn't have to see him. He just wants to know she's safe. If she needs money." She pulled Frank down the street as fast as she could without running, no need to send signals of fear to those wild animals.

"Jesus, what did you say to him? Frank, you can't act like a cop with these guys."

"Technically, I'm not a cop."

They were both breathing hard, not from running, Ronnie thought, but from the adrenaline. They had rounded the corner and leaned against the building. "Then stop acting like one. You're a worried father searching for his daughter, not an FBI Agent trying to take down drug dealers."

"They're lower than the lowest form of animal."

"So? You need them."

Frank shook his head back and forth, not so much in a "no" as in a "what the fuck?"

* * *

The next morning Ronnie slept late, a restless sleep in which she could swear she knew every time she rolled over. She had just put the extra pillow over her head, thinking if only she could get a few more minutes, when her phone started buzzing. She rolled over. It began again with such a weird insistence she thought it might vibrate off the bedside table.

"Where are you?"

"Isabelle?" It came out scratchy like her voice box was protesting.

"Get up here. I'm not paying you to sleep. This is a big day, and we have to be ready!"

News to her. Ronnie splashed cold water on her face, clawed at her hair, went upstairs to see what was up.

"Oh, honestly." Isabelle scanned her up and down then went back to the newspaper open in front of her on the counter. "Go away and return when you're properly dressed."

Ronnie went down and took a proper shower, dried herself properly with the big fluffy towel, got into proper clothes, not the ones from the streets the night before, and combed her hair twice, very properly before heading up. She hoped she had time for a proper breakfast.

The coffee at the bottom of the pot had evaporated and burned up, and Ronnie set about making more, ignoring Isabelle, who still sat at the counter in a green brocade dressing gown, the tie at her waist coming loose, the top gaping open.

"Leave that. I've had enough coffee. Do you have your notebook? Good. Now everything tonight must be absolutely perfect. No need to ask whose glass to keep filling up, because it will be dinner for two. Now," Isabelle went on and on, one impossible demand after another, the flowers specific, the amount of starch in the tablecloth exact, a champagne she required which was not in the wine rack.

"And finger food for dinner."

"Fried chicken?"

Isabelle raised an eyebrow at her just as Ronnie's stomach growled. Isabelle's eyes narrowed at her. "I forgot to eat dinner last night," Ronnie told her.

"First you oversleep and now you have to waste my time eating? Honestly. I need you ready to work, not lounging around and rummaging in my cupboards!"

Ronnie didn't say anything. She didn't have to, her stomach said it again for her.

Isabelle waved a shooing hand and said, "I suppose you'll concentrate better if you eat. I need you completely at the ready tonight."

* * *

The day was grey, cold, the clouds pressing down on the city. Ronnie had Isabelle, or rather her Oxy money, spring for a lot of cab rides as she made her way around the city, trying to hit new places where the chances of someone recognizing her were low. She was dragging, no doubt about it.

Maybe she did better at night, maybe she wasn't meant to be out even on gloomy days. She wondered when Frank would give up on looking for his daughter. He sure was determined. He must truly love her to put all this time in, all the energy, risk all the sketchy situations just to find her.

She hoped Isabelle wouldn't remember that she had asked for raw oysters, because besides being gross, there was no place in the city this time of year where she could lift them. And she didn't dare risk buying them from the Oyster Bars sprinkled all over the city. Way too expensive.

No one in her family would try to find her like that. Except maybe Matt, and he was dead. She grabbed some flowers out of the bucket at the corner market, her body hiding them as she kept going. She'd trim them way down, have them floating around the table next to the votive candles, make it seem like there were more flowers that way. Frank's search made Ronnie think of the Marines, going back for their dead, risking their lives for that one guy. Would she do that for a child? Jesus. She couldn't ever imagine even having children.

* * *

Ronnie had barely put the comb down after running it through her wet hair when the doorbell chimed. She wondered who the pigeon was tonight and then decided she didn't care. She ran up, mentally checking herself, male butler not woman in her twenties, check. She took in a deep breath and swung open the door to the new mark—

Her eyes widened. "Fra—Mr. Franks, good evening." She held the door, eyes on the floor. Hoped Isabelle hadn't heard her slip.

"Good evening, Ron." He angled himself out of his coat, holding it out to her. "Awfully quiet—am I the first one here?"

"First, last, only." She turned her back on him to wrestle the giant shearling onto a hanger. Should she tell him—what, to be careful, to watch out for Isabelle—but he was a big boy, he could handle himself.

"That's what I like to hear!" His grin was wide as if she were about to hand him a big box of chocolates. Whatever floats your boat.

"There you are, you naughty boy!" They both turned to see Isabelle where she had paused on the stairs, her dress shimmering around her, the bodice so tight and low-cut. Ronnie couldn't imagine how she'd managed to zip it up herself. "Give Ron your phone so we can get this party started!" And then she turned on the stairs and started up, her dress trailing behind her, her entire back exposed.

Ronnie and Frank looked at each other, Frank hesitating, Ronnie holding out the basket.

"Don't keep a lady waiting!"

As soon as they were out of sight, Ronnie sped off to the kitchen, grabbed the shrimp cocktail platter, and raced up the back stairs to the pantry off the dining room. Shrimp cocktail would have to do instead of oysters for her boss. She grabbed up some cocktail napkins and then saw the champagne flute at the ready, the Molly crushed and waiting at the bottom of the glass. Ronnie reached for it, then stopped. She had to get this tray into the living room, start pouring and pouring drinks. She'd figure out later what to do about the Molly. Besides, she thought as she left the pantry, he was a cop undercover, he must know how to handle himself, had training for something like this.

As she came in, she decided Frank didn't need her pity. The two of them were sitting side by side on the couch, Isabelle practically draping herself over him like a silk scarf. She wondered if she should interrupt them to take drink orders or if she should just decide for them. Isabelle was easy: a vodka tonic with a lime wedge, no vodka. A drink that looked like a drink but wasn't. She knew whatever she made for Frank Isabelle would want her to double, so she poured him a beer. The least she could do.

The absolute least. She went to the pantry not even sure they knew she'd been in there, though Frank had to have been. He had eyes in the back of his head. Well, so did Isabelle. Aware and ignoring her. He seemed really happy to be here, not just an act like she imagined an undercover guy would put on. If he was so into it, he would get what he would get, and who was she to interfere? His case. His undercover activities. His look-out.

* * *

After dinner, after Isabelle led him back to the living room, after the Molly, Ronnie went down to her apartment. She would clean up later. With the dining room on the second floor and the kitchen on the first, she would no doubt witness some of the things Isabelle had in mind for him, and there was no way she wanted to see or hear that. She felt sorry for him again. Maybe he didn't deserve this. All in the name of a case. Maybe she felt a little guilty, too. She supposed she could have risked her job by dumping out the Molly. Risked her job, then risked her freedom because without her job, Frank had no use for her.

Okay, okay, think. She paced her apartment, tried to shut out the laughter that came through the living room door and down the stairs. If she got Frank what he kept pestering her for, then she could keep her job, keep Frank happy, and, if she was honest, maybe get back at Isabelle for targeting Frank. She ran a bath. More to shut out the upstairs than because she really wanted it. Tonight, after everyone was asleep, she'd find the laptop, plug Frank's silly thumb drive in.

Chapter Twenty-Seven

Frank found he was slouched so low on the couch that he was nearly horizontal. Too much to drink at dinner. How had he ended up here, his feet across the coffee table and the floating feeling taking over? Not how he usually felt after a couple of drinks. The table on his legs too hard. His shoes on the couch, the cushions cradling them. It would feel much better on his skin. He peered down the length of his body and it seemed to grow longer as he looked, his shoes moving further and further away. An arm, his arm, reaching for it, but his shoe in his hand, the laces a delightful knot. He started to laugh, unable to untie his shoes–if they were his shoes. It was all too funny, and he wanted to hug the world. His arms stretched out wide, the light from the lamp streaked across the room. He was still at Isabelle's, and her smile lit up the room. She reached for him, the touch on his arm sprouting flowers, and he stared at it, hoped she would touch him again. He followed her; he could follow her forever. The softness of the carpet licking, tickling, absorbing her green leather heels as they went up, up, up, and he reached out a hand to touch it, wanting to feel the smoothness, feel where the heel met the carpet at the stair edge, every texture beckoning him. The heel left his sight, and he moved up to touch it. The magic of it made his heart burst open, and he pulled off his tie, the silky smoothness of it, the sweat of his hands darkening, dancing on that blue, that electric blue. She called his name, a siren, he laughed, not a siren outside but a siren on an island calling to him and he asked his hand to please move up the stairs, his feet unable to move with it, the shoes, the hard shoe against a soft sock. He loved his shoe. His knee stopped, the siren called, singing to him, and he remembered something upstairs he wanted to see. The sweat streamed down his head. He pushed his hand through his hair, cupping the back of his head, a pulsing. The perfect fit, the palm, and his scalp, his skull tingling. He had lost track of who he was, now face down on a carpet, an electronic beat throbbed his body his brain exploded with colors, his nose in the carpet a warm, furry enclosure his nose trusted. His cheek would like that too, loud in his ear a crack, and he laughed. Giddyup. His brain grinned, traced the sound from the top of his head, watched it move down his spine, tingling as it went, another snap following it, settling in the soles of his feet, the soul in his body, and he laughed again. He was so happy to see Isabelle. His best friend. The warmth radiated from his heart, and he wanted to hug her to show how happy he was to be with her. But his hand wouldn't move, the wrist snuggled to the other wrist, wrapped around the hard metal. The dark carpet fibers curled around him, against his skin, his cheek. Isabelle's lovely green leather shoe sailed over him, a wondrous pierce on his back. The feeling of every pore. The sound tickled his ear. Her hair swept his back. Again, please. Do it again. So beautiful, so beautiful.

* * *

Frank slowly surfaced to the day and wished he hadn't. His tongue, thick and dry, took up his whole mouth, and his face smashed against the mattress. It smelled as if something had died nearby, and for some reason, his pillow lay on top of his head. He inched the pillow off, unleashing fireworks. He decided it wouldn't be wise to move his head anymore since a shipping crate of bricks had been placed on it at some point during the night. His jaw was clenched as if it would never release, and he reached up to see what was going on. He was thirstier than he could ever remember being, but he felt so depressed he didn't want to get out of bed. This had to be the flu. He felt so sick. He mentally palpated his body, his head exploding, his jaw sore, his skin crawling, his stomach heaving, legs trembling. He moved his hand along his skin, tried to detect a fever, then up to his throat, not sore, no congestion, only his jaw aching as if he had clenched it tight for hours.

A kaleidoscope of images from last night crowded in all at once, more than he could deal with, and he put the pillow over his head, the something dead smell returning. All the noise out the window—the traffic, the horns, the sirens pressed down on him, something about sirens, he couldn't remember, and his brain felt black. He wanted to cry because he couldn't remember about the sirens. Frank didn't get depressed, but if this was depression, no wonder people killed themselves.

But this wasn't Frank. He had to be sick. He rolled out of bed, his need for water too great to keep him there, but he landed on all fours on his pile of clothes, his face inches from the sweat- and vomit-stained heap. He traced with his eyes, picked out the tie, the shirt, the jacket, and he felt so sad he didn't want to stand. But the smell engulfed him, and he knew he had to make it to the toilet fast.

He sat on the old white tile, crammed between bathtub and toilet, his arm resting along the edge of the tub, his fiery head against the tank of the toilet. What had happened to make him feel like this. This wasn't sadness, this was full blown depression. He still felt thirsty, and he still felt unable to move. He reached for the sink, but it was too far away, and his arm came down, draping itself across the seat of the toilet. He had to get up, but everything felt so heavy, so dark.

He found himself in his kitchen, the water running in the sink, splashing on his face, drinking drinking drinking from the stream, wondering if he were crying too. He tried to remember the night before, the crushing weight of it, the stairs. He had been so happy, going up the stairs, following Isabelle's green stilettos. Had he been naked on the floor? He could feel the carpet on his skin, and he wished for that feeling again, sure that if he couldn't get it again, his world would fall apart, he would spiral down, lost in the darkness that kept closing in on him.

He was back in bed when his phone pinged. He must've slept and he felt only slightly better, but he couldn't make himself care about a text. He turned over so his back was to his dresser where the phones lay, all lined up waiting for him. He had his personal phone, but that one made a different ping. He put the pillow over his head. The Bureau phone, but that buzzed.

He opened one eye, his head pounding. He really didn't think he had had this much to drink. Champagne never did this to him. The ping had to have come from the Peter Franks phone, and there were only two people who knew it. Maybe he could get a hint as to what had happened last night. He rolled onto his stomach. What would knowing about it tell him? He couldn't ignore the phone though. Against the rules. Every contact, including text had to go into the 502s; and since it was their phone, they would know. He couldn't tell them he was too hungover to deal with it. Another ping. He had never been this hungover in his life. But then he had never met someone like Isabelle before either.

Lunch it said, *BG Restaurant* her favorite, 12:30 reservations an hour and a half from now. He felt like he was moving through a black ooze, everything in slow motion, not even worth the effort. If he lay still, maybe the ooze would swallow him up, and he wouldn't have to do anything more. Maybe those donors killed themselves because the Isabelle hangover was such torture.

He examined himself in the bathroom mirror. The cold water he'd splashed on his face dripped down, his eyelids sagged, cheeks grey and stubbly, a tic starting up in the soft spot under his left eye. He watched the skin jump and it made him want to cry. What was wrong with him? He never got depressed. Not even when his father died. Not even when Cathy ran away. He tried to make himself stand up straight, pull in all his training, square his shoulders, call on his core to tighten and hold everything, everything including this darkness engulfing him, and hold it inside just long enough to get dressed. He grabbed the Peter Frank's phone, thin and glassy, the screen black, waiting for him to dive in. He took a deep breath, held it while he tapped, *looking forward to it* and then he let out the breath in a rush, tossed the phone on the bed.

His Peter Franks clothes were trashed. A bad sign. One last white shirt, still in the box from the cleaners gave him hope and he shook out the tie, wondered if his blazer would cover up the worst of the wrinkles. And stains. He had other ties from Wardrobe.

He stared at himself in the mirror. Get a grip. You're on a case. You can do this. You've been undercover with much worse, seedy criminals with meth labs. He grabbed his overcoat and keys.

BG, the start of it all, where they met to shop together in earnest, the day that ended with a pair of diamond cuff links in his trouser pocket. Was this a signal of some kind, did she want to repeat that day? But they'd moved beyond the shoplifting, hadn't they? She'd invited just him for dinner last night, and he had been sure that was a sign that they would be working together much more closely. He was having a hard time putting his thoughts together. When had the stairs to the subway gotten so long? He descended into hell, the heat and steam from the cars, the grime the urine the rotting garbage. A screech of metal on metal, amplified music from a hustler so loud it banged his ear drums. He wanted to turn around, but there were so many stairs up, easier to keep going, get on the subway. He closed his eyes and hoped he would remember to get off at 59th street. He thought about how this was also the Pelham Express, and briefly entertained the idea of Robert Shaw or John Travolta arriving to end his troubles.

* * *

He went in Bergdorf's on the 57th Street side, the honks from the traffic all at once muted, the grit of the sidewalk left behind, a hush wrapping around him as he stopped to get his bearings. Dealing with Isabelle right now seemed like an impossibly strenuous activity, like he'd used up all his reserves just getting to the elevator. Everything was bathed in a sea green, offset by Art Deco silvered shapes. He eyed the escalator. It was steep and narrow and would treat him to seven floors of the same nauseating green. He could wait.

A susurration from the restaurant hit him as the elevator doors opened on the seventh floor, the conversations wafting down the hallway. Not quite ready to face Isabelle, Frank examined the 8 x 10 magazine covers and old ads lining the walls and emphasizing the Art Deco theme. All those curves and geometric shapes, clean lines in an old-fashioned effort to be modern, the last hurrah before the Great Depression.

As before, BG teemed with Pete's Ladies Who Lunch, tables jammed together filled with poufy-haired women trying to defeat time. What could the total expenditure on Botox and plastic surgery amount to in this room? The waste and the desperation did nothing to alleviate his dark mood. The restaurant oozed with more pastels, blue walls, green leather chairs, the white tablecloths offsetting it, but it seemed the colors all had a grey tinge, no cheering baby blue here. And the mirrors reflecting back on each other made the restaurant seem endless, as if it could swallow Frank up.

The maître d' led him to the windows with a view of Central Park, gestured to a tiny table flanked by bizarre gold leather chairs with half dome tops. "The Whisper Chair, sir." Isabelle swiveled toward him, and for a split second, he thought he must be at the wrong table. She appeared to be nearly twenty years younger, a college girl in a white blouse and blue blazer. Evidently, she did not share his hangover. Her hair hung straight down, held in place by a ribbon headband matching the golden brown of her eyes. Those eyes held him a quick second, too short for him to read her. Or it was too much effort to decipher.

He limboed himself into his seat and said hello.

"Good afternoon, Peter. You're looking a little worse for the wear. Have fun last night?" She gestured with her chin at the plate in front of him.

"What's this?" Frank tried a Peter Franks grin, but he was sure that what was meant to be sly and self-deprecating came off as just sad. He picked up the thick envelope lying there, *Peter Franks* on the front, written in fountain pen with a flourish. "Another invitation?"

"Oh, you naughty boy." She picked up the menu, lowered her eyes to scan it. "Wasn't last night invitation enough?" She breathed the question at her menu, and he had to lean forward to catch it, his head so close he could almost feel the exhale of the last word.

He let the Whisper Chair engulf him and felt the envelope. A small lump in the right-hand corner. This could only be—

"I don't think you need to open it here, do you?"

He folded the thick envelope in half and slid it into his inside jacket pocket. He couldn't help but glance side to side as he did so. Like in a second-rate

223

spy movie. The vixen had recorded it. Whatever it was. His turn to see what caused those donors to suicide, the doctored clips destined for social media. He wiped his forehead with his napkin. His career would be dead, too. Christ, how would Pete view him then, and if Susan saw this—or godforbid his daughter…

"Wh-what happened last night?" The words choked out, and Frank wished he hadn't shown his confusion, had acted more confidently. "You gave me something, didn't you?" And if she had, he had broken the rules by not getting himself tested, not documenting it. Not realizing in time. He thought it was just a hangover.

"Of course I did." She gave him a look of wonder and pity. "You just put it in your pocket." She raised a champagne flute at him. "I hope you don't mind that I started without you." She took a sip, her eyes not leaving his. "I just had to have the Veuve Clicquot." No bottle, no ice bucket, no flute at his place.

"I could use a little hair of the dog today." He squinted around the impossible chair for a waiter.

"Ooooh, I'm in the mood for lobster!"

Jeez that was loud.

"And none of this silly lobster salad. Honestly, none of these women know how to enjoy themselves." She waved her menu at the rest of the room.

"I like a girl who knows how to have a good time." Frank picked up the menu. His words sounded flat, perfunctory. He needed to shake this off and become Peter Franks. The menu listed the Veuve Clicquot at $25 a glass, and the non-salad lobster sported truffles at $41. He caught her eye, held it, and patted the pocket with the envelope and thumb drive. Gave her a smile.

"Oh Mr. Franks, I think you were the one having the good time." She lowered her eyes and looked at him through her lashes.

"And I'm paying for it today."

"You did consume quite a lot of champagne. Ron said it was an entire bottle. At least."

"I don't usually feel like this after champagne. Are you sure that was all I had?" He set his menu down. The word "morose" sprung up, pasted itself on his forehead.

"Well, Peter, I certainly wondered the same thing." Her eyes hit his jacket as if she could see through it to the envelope. "You were quite insistent."

He leaned forward. "Was I now." Uh-oh.

"But you know," and here she blushed and gestured at his jacket, "A girl in this town has to protect her reputation, don't you agree?" Damned if she didn't widen her eyes in innocence as she spoke. Frank sat back, his sore jaw slack. Had she just hinted that they—Damn. He couldn't remember the last time he'd had sex, and now he'd had sex and couldn't remember it. He watched her every movement, feeling sadder with each reach of the butter knife, each blink of her long lashes, each swing of her long hair. He had a leftover feeling of trust, as if she had been his best friend. He studied her, tried to make sense of it.

But he was an agent, and so he startled a little, sitting up straighter and pulling out his phone as if he had gotten a call or text. "I'll just mute this." He hit the record button. If his career was sunk, they might as well get an arrest warrant out of it. Too bad he couldn't take a movie as well, because she had transformed, all blushes and stammers and artlessness. She would be great undercover.

"I mean," she continued, her voice high and breathy, "a society hostess, a board member of Marshall Logan, running an important foundation that does so many good works—how could I keep all that up with something like this" she gestured with the butter knife, "hanging over me?"

She was good. Oh, she was good. Cue Peter Franks: "Well now. You have me at a disadvantage here." He took a sip of his water, then drained the glass. He gave her a minute, imagined her thinking, *Of course I do! That's the whole point!* "I have to confess," his turn to lower his voice, "I have no idea what happened last night." He looked regretful, shook his head, wiped his mouth with his napkin, and picked up his menu. Hoped he wouldn't start sweating again.

"No idea?"

"None at all." If he wasn't mistaken, he had scored the first point. No harm in adding "unfortunately."

Isabelle pounced on that last word. "That," Isabelle raised her crystal flute, "is exactly what I'm talking about. You'll see for yourself when you play that."

Frank watched her for a moment wondering what he could do to make her lose her cool entirely. "Now I'm really confused." He checked out the tables on either side of them, then behind them to make sure no waiters were in sight, even though it made his head hurt. "Did you just give me something," he patted his jacket, "that would be compromising to *you*?"

Her eyes darkened, matching her blazer now. He watched her flounder, then right herself. For the briefest of moments, he saw her eyebrows arch, her teeth flash—sharp little teeth, the kind carnivores need to rip the flesh from bones. But she morphed back so quickly to the innocent schoolgirl, the victim, that he wondered if he had seen it at all.

"I don't think your wife would be happy to find that in her inbox." Her eyes drilled into him. "Blackout or not." She raised an eyebrow and then seemed to remember that she didn't want to play this one mean. As her features softened, Frank had to admire her malleability. He thought about all the outfits and personas he'd seen her inhabit—sleek and classy befitting a society hostess, demure and sweet like today, a businesswoman, a siren, a jezebel, a chanteuse, the girl next door. But here at this table, he thought maybe her true self was a harpy. Or Medusa. He seemed to remember green leather high heels last night, a lizard or a snake crawling up her ankle.

"You wouldn't want her to see you begging," Isabelle said, "pleading, demanding the most amazing things. Quite the imagination, Peter."

The repartee exhausted Frank, and he let it go, let her talk, watched her order the most expensive dishes on the menu. The game playing took more energy than he had right now, and he hoped he could figure this out later, when he didn't have a hangover, when he crawled back out of whatever black cave he found himself in. Or she had put him in. What if he couldn't find his way out again? This dark feeling weighing on him forever. He slumped into the horrible chair, fiddled with his silverware, eyes moving to Isabelle with a huge effort. Let her do all the work today. Her show, her routine. Let her think he felt defeated.

He did feel defeated. And betrayed. Peter Franks had been so close to her. He remembered a feeling of elation as they went up the stairs. She finally trusted him, would let him into the inner sanctum, they would work together, and he could listen to her laughter and breathe in her perfume all he wanted. And now she had treated him like he was just another one of her victims, nobody special, no one worth bringing aboard.

Out on the sidewalk, Isabelle murmured, patting the envelope through his jacket, "I'm confident that you'll figure out just what my reputation is worth, you darling thing." She smiled up at him as if he were her hero. She searched his eyes for a beat, dropped the smile, leaned in even closer. "But Peter," her eyes dark storm clouds, "if you don't come through right away, if you draw it out as you have your pledge, then," she patted him again, "with my reputation at stake, I'll be forced to release it, and the world will know what you did."

So that was it. If he didn't pay, the footage would go out on social media. His career ruined, no hope of another job in the field, and the FBI family would kick him out. No wonder all those men committed suicide.

He didn't have to fake his alarm, nor Peter Franks' feeling of dejection. "Isabelle, what happened? I thought we were friends. I thought we were going to be working together." He dropped to a whisper. "I thought we were more than friends."

Isabelle patted him. "We are friends! Everyone is my friend. They protect my reputation, they take me shopping, we have lovely lunches and dinners together. Some of them even become my bodyguard." She winked at him. "And you, Peter." She planted a perfumy kiss on his cheek. Put her hands on his shoulders. "As soon as you show me how *much* of a friend you are, we can spend a lot more time together!"

He stood on the sidewalk as she walked away from him, headed uptown, her school-girl skirt swaying under her short fur jacket in a most unschool-girl way. Maybe now he could go back to bed.

* * *

It took him until the next afternoon to face the thumb drive she'd given him in the thick envelope, "Peter Franks" in a curly swirl written on the front. She must've had so much fun writing it. As an agent, he had to learn what was on the tape, but as an ordinary citizen, it was the last thing he wanted to see. He held the tiny thing in his palm, nearly the size of a dime, no extra plastic on it, "ScanDisk" in red on the black cap. How much damage could something so small wreak?

Frank was used to examining footage from infrared cameras, those funny green-grey images, but he wasn't used to seeing himself in them, and he wasn't used to seeing himself naked. His entire body all at once. He almost turned it off, but that would merely delay the inevitable. He mentally shook himself, squared his shoulders, took a deep breath, straightened his spine.

Interesting how adept Isabelle was at staying out of the frame, a stiletto here, a crack of whip there, her curtain of blonde hair sweeping over his backside. But it was mostly of him, begging, lying face down, his hands held behind him with what looked like police cuffs. He couldn't believe what he was asking for.

There was not much here to compromise her yet, except one section, her hand holding a short silver straw, her voice encouraging him to snort some white powder, telling him how great it would make him feel. And he lapped it up, rolling his eyes when the drug hit him, saying how amazing it was, begging her for more. Jesus Christ. What had she given him? This was not Frank. He didn't think the Bureau would come to that conclusion, however, which was why he previewed it on his home computer now, breaking the rules yet again. He had to subject himself to the whole thing, see if there was something that identified her. And there it was, near the end, her face next to his, a brief flash before her hair fell and hid it, her voice coaxing him, telling him it was time to wake up, time to go, but he'd had fun, hadn't he?

His stomach was made of lead, and his forehead tightened, a headache sure to follow. He couldn't use this against her, use it as part of the proof of her blackmailing. His Bureau phone dinged as if he were being watched. Pete. Because he hadn't checked in with him. Rules said he should talk with him every day, report on his activities. He would fudge it, make up

228

some excuse. He had broken protocol so many times already. He hadn't gotten tested right away to see what she'd given him, hadn't reported before he met with Isabelle for lunch, nor reported after, nor checked in with his supervisory agent for any of this. And now that he'd seen this footage, he knew there was no way anyone in the Bureau would be hearing about this, much less seeing it. He'd be suspended while he waited for the disciplinary hearing—even undercover he'd crossed the line. A line the Bureau would never bend. And then the blackmail. They'd all want to swoop in and arrest her, take his case away from him. And they would be right in doing so. There went his career. His friends. His family. His life.

His phone dinged. Pete must've left a message. Could not be good news. He ignored it.

If several people committed suicide because she'd drugged, blackmailed them, and then altered the tape and posted it on social media...He had to stop her before she did it to someone else. The kid with CP left behind, the worthwhile charities without their generous donors, wives without good husbands. Isabelle blindsided them, issuing an invitation to dinner, which turned out to be a dinner party for two. The champagne, spiked, the tape altered...false imprisonment, assault, blackmail, slander and defamation, manslaughter. She was evil, pure evil. She deserved to be behind bars.

He got up to pace his apartment. He had to get her on everything: the drugs, the financial shenanigans of her foundation, the blackmail, and subsequent suicides. But if he took too long, then she would put this footage out there, maybe alter it like she had the others. He would not only lose everything, he would be arrested for pedophilia.

He made it to the bathroom in time to lose his lunch in the toilet and not on the floor.

He had wanted to be an agent for as long as he could remember. The Bureau reinforced his comforting view of the world: Bad Guys. Good Guys. Right. Wrong. And the look on his father's face at induction, the beaming, the pride. That look always spurred him on to do well. He guessed that his standards of personal conduct were even stricter than the Bureau's.

He grabbed his coat, his keys, a hat. He needed air, needed to walk, to think, and to figure things out. He clattered down the stairs and out the front door, the cold dampness hitting him like a slap. Which he deserved. That footage showed him sweaty and delirious, obviously high, snorting more drugs, and, of course, he was naked. Everyone knew you disregarded a few rules so you could play the part undercover, but you always reported the illegal activity right away so the AUSA could issue you a dispensation. She had caught him, and she didn't even realize the true depth of the potential consequences. She thought it was merely a wife she was holding over his head.

As long as he was miserable, he might as well see what Pete had to say. He pulled his coat around him and listened to the voicemail. Pete's voice was tight, and Frank thought about cutting off the message, knowing it was going to be bad news. He eyed the traffic, waiting to cross, and heard his partner out. He had dived further into the police reports on the four donors.

"Frank." His voice rose. "You gotta watch out. The manner of death on two of these guys was 'undetermined.' Not the cause of death mind you. For one, it was asphyxiation, the other—' he paused, the rustle of papers "—subdural hematoma."

Frank crossed the street, the back of his brain looking out for a big silver car, but he mentally shook his head at himself. Mickey McAllister was probably staying home these days. Taking care of his broken nose. He tuned back into Pete's message.

"But the coroner couldn't determine the manner of death—whether it was an accident, suicide, or homicide."

Frank stopped in the middle of the sidewalk. Something hit the back of his calf and he spun around, gripped his phone tighter. A very old woman, hunched over like she would never look up again, made her way past him, her granny cart rolling in front of her. He called Pete.

"Frank! Glad to hear from you. Did you—"

"Just listened to it."

"This changes everything. You haven't given her the donation check yet, right?"

Frank told him no, and Pete allowed as how maybe he was safe for now.

"But Frank, I don't know how much longer you can stay undercover there. These donors, the doctored tape, the suicides, or worse…You still there?"

Frank nodded, then grunted.

"Okay, because I really don't feel like getting assigned another partner."

Frank pulled the phone away to end the call, and Pete's voice came, far away but distinct: "I may pull you anyway."

Chapter Twenty-Eight

Frank always picked a different place for their weekly meetings. How he found these dives was beyond Ronnie. Never a chain, no Starbucks, Panera, or Mickey D's. These holes in the wall seemed like nothing had changed since they opened fifty years ago. Same uneven floors, knife-graffitied tables, sticky menus.

"I thought you'd be happy." Ronnie gestured with her chin at the thumb drive between them on the scarred table. "I did what you asked, downloaded her laptop." She nudged it closer to Frank.

Frank grunted, picked up the tiny thing between thumb and forefinger like it smelled, like it might bite. "Took you long enough." His voice was gruff, eyes narrowed at her, and she looked away. "If this has on it what I think it does, then we'll be getting a warrant soon."

Ronnie's leg started jumping, and she pressed down on it. Her chair creaked and she hoped it stayed in one piece until she got out of there.

"Don't worry. We won't be coming for you." He pulled a plastic bag out of his pocket and put the thumb drive in it.

Warrant. Arrest. Maybe she should run now. Bathrooms, kitchen, front door.

"Hey, hey." Frank put his hand on her arm. "Look at me. You're safe." He lowered his voice. "You're my CI, and your information," he waggled the plastic bag and put it in his pocket, "will most likely lead to an arrest or arrests."

She moved her chair back.

"Not yours. Easy now. How many times do I have to say it? You're safe."

"Okay. Okay. Way to give a girl a heart attack. Who besides Isabelle is getting arrested?"

"Possibly Philippe. We'll know better once we go over the flash drive from her computer. Which, by the way, I wish I'd had before that special dinner the other night." He lined up his knife and spoon, centered his water glass over them. "Speaking of which, as my man on the inside, I would've expected you to warn me ahead of time." He seemed more sad than angry, eyes drooping as they met hers.

Ronnie hoped she didn't look as guilty as she felt. "I didn't know it was going to be you that night."

"You knew she was going to drug me. What was it?"

She sipped her warm Coke. "Don't you get training for things like that? What to do when you're undercover and someone slips you a roofie?"

"Rohypnol? I don't think that's what it was."

She looked away. She didn't want to imagine him in that room, all the equipment, Isabelle enjoying standing over him, Philippe watching from the room next door.

"And you knew about the blackmail."

Ronnie started to shake her head, as if wishing it weren't true, wishing she hadn't known, and saying so would make it so. He held her eyes. She nodded then.

"I need to know you'll always tell me the truth. Otherwise, you're nearly useless to me."

She didn't say anything. She couldn't. It was like her teeth were glued together. If he didn't need her, then...

"Okay? I have a truth for you." He cleared his throat. "I can still bring you downtown, make this official. A Confidential Witness rather than just Informant. You can testify against her and Philippe. In court."

Well, there went that friendship. She slumped down in her seat. She felt like kicking the table.

"With me now? Ready to tell me the truth?"

"Yeah, okay."

He put his hand to his ear, cupped around it like he hadn't heard her.

"I said, Okay!" She kind of hated him right now.

"Okay." He smoothed out his paper napkin. He glanced around them like he had just realized where they were. "The truth is, I don't want to take you downtown, so don't make me. I think we're a good team. You help me, I help you. Right?" He eyed Ronnie, waiting for confirmation.

Ronnie wasn't feeling like he was helping her so much right now.

"So," he went on, "tell me how this whole thing works. How often she does it. Who her victims are. Everything."

Ronnie told him. Everything she knew. The Molly in the champagne glass, the sex room, Philippe taping it, the blackmail lunch after. She stared at the table, traced the scratches in the wood with her eyes.

"And?"

She gave a small smile, hoping it'd loosen him up, "And here's the weird thing. All these guys she blackmails? They still call her up, ask to see her, invite her to lunch, take her shopping. Like she has a spell on them."

"Is that a fact?"

"Well, except for one guy. I guess her magic failed on him."

Frank stopped tracking someone behind her and locked his eyes on her. "Tell me about him."

She told him about Scott Hodge, that Isabelle had run it the way she'd always done, and he'd stormed out of the restaurant, leaving her to pay the bill. "Then he sends over some thug to threaten Isabelle and he and Philippe got into a fight. Broke a lamp."

"Scott Hodge? Is he on the thumb drive?"

Not like she expected a medal from him, but he could be a little happier about the information she was giving him. "I didn't look at it, did I? I just risked my neck to get it for you in the middle of the night."

"Which night was that? Last night?"

"No, the other night. The night you were there. After you were gone, and Isabelle was asleep."

Frank's face became hard, his jaw worked away like he was chewing nails. "And you're just giving me this now?"

"It's our weekly meeting. I thought since it had taken me this long to get it, another two days wouldn't matter." She wished she'd ordered something to eat just to give herself something to do so she didn't have to look at him. But no way she could eat anything right now.

"Are you sure you didn't look at it? Didn't tell me you had it so you had time to erase something? Maybe to protect your boss. Or yourself."

"I wouldn't." Ronnie shook her head. "Not to protect me or my boss."

He still stared at her. His eyes like blue rocks.

She shook her head "no" again. She didn't want to say anything because she was so angry and frustrated right now, she might burst into tears.

"What are you not telling me?"

"Nothing!" She hadn't meant to shout. She dropped her head, spoke to the table. "I'm just so tired of not being believed, of not being trusted." She raised her head, gave him a level stare. "I'm loyal. Probably to a fault. And right now, you're testing that loyalty."

Frank sat back, crossed his arms. "Loyalty to—"

"You! And you're testing it because you don't trust me. Because you're accusing me of going against you when all I did was get you what you asked for, and now that I'm handing it to you, you're mad at me."

Frank took a sip of coffee. Shook himself a little bit like it tasted bad. "Okay." Like he was talking to himself. "Okay." A little louder like it was meant for her. "You didn't access the information on the thumb drive."

She nodded.

"And your loyalty lies with me, with the Bureau, and not Isabelle."

She nodded.

"Okay." He patted the pocket the plastic bag had gone in. "And we have one guy that she couldn't con." He cleared his throat. "So, what if the information is in code?" His voice more conversational, less forceful.

Ronnie shrugged. "Probably is. She can never call anything what it is. Like the oxy is 'Carry Out.' And her marks are 'Objects of my Affection,' or 'Checkbooks,' or 'Mr. Can't-Keep-It-In.'"

"What does she call me?"

"Omaha Pete."

"Nice. I don't suppose you know what's in store for Peter Franks next, do you?"

"I don't really know what happens. I think everyone but Scott Hodge pays up and is still her friend. Like Philippe."

Frank raised an eyebrow. "Philippe was one of her marks?"

Ronnie nodded, finished off her Coke, put her glass down. Wiped her mouth with her sleeve.

"Will wonders never cease. The power of that woman." Frank tipped his coffee mug to look into it before setting it upright again. "Speaking of which, is she working on someone new?"

"Yep. I'd better go. She's got someone scheduled for tonight." She scraped her chair away from the table.

"Well." He stood up. "I don't have much time, I don't think, before she broadcasts it all over social media. I'm guessing her next move will be to send Philippe." He mumbled behind her, as if to himself, "Meanwhile, we'll see just how much the Bureau likes this footage."

They went out the door not quite together, Ronnie turned uptown, Frank down, like they always did after one of these meetings, pretending they didn't know each other. At the corner, she stopped and sneaked a peek at him. He looked smaller, hunched over. She almost wanted to run after him, pat his back, tell him it would be okay. Just then, without turning around, he held up his hand as if greeting someone. There was no one in front of him, and his head was down, so it was like he was signaling to her. Well, she guessed they were friends again.

* * *

The next night Ronnie went with Frank to look for Cathy again. They started way downtown in Battery Park, visited the gun ports where some of the homeless slept, and always, always passed out Cathy's picture, asked if they'd seen this sixteen-year-old. Ronnie cut a look at Frank, the two of them walking side by side, her stride matching his. He hadn't said anything about Isabelle, or the night she drugged him. Like there was an agent Frank and a father Frank. She still couldn't believe a father would spend all this

236

time searching, never giving up. Of course, no one at Castle Clinton, or anywhere else in Battery Park had seen her. Frank said they should take the subway uptown, maybe start in Tribeca, keep heading up.

Standing at the edge of the platform, she watched the rats scurry around the tracks while she waited for the subway. All that life down there, a whole world that humans mostly ignored, coming in contact when the rats got bold, when the people dropped food, or tried to get rid of them. But they were a permanent part of the city, maybe in some ways they were the city, humans only borrowing it from them. One day these rodents would exterminate them, take over everything.

Once they were on the train, Frank's phone buzzed, and his face lit up while he listened, his eyes on hers. His mouth moved around like it was trying not to smile.

"Benedict House." He put his phone in his pocket. "There's a girl the right age who checked in for the night."

Ronnie nodded, said nothing.

"I know it's a long shot." Frank found a different place for his hand on the pole between them. "But I've got to check it out." He looked at the subway doors, and Ronnie did too, the reflection in the window throwing them back to themselves, a tall man, a shorter person next to him, hands near each other on the pole. "After all the flyers we've given out, maybe this is the break we've been working so hard toward." The train jostled them along, lights and stations whooshed by, the lights in the car went off and then came right back on. "They said she called herself Amber, no last name."

Ronnie raised her eyebrows at him.

"She always said she wished we'd named her that."

* * *

At the intake desk, the woman who had called Frank watched their approach, and Ronnie tried to picture them in her eyes, the man in the puffy down jacket looking vaguely cop-like, with the younger person, hard to tell if a man or a woman, not quite looking homeless, but you never knew.

"I'm Frank Jankowski. Someone here called me about a girl calling herself Amber?"

After she checked both their IDs and wrote down their names, she led them to the women's section, the lights dark except for exit signs glowing red, a streetlight peeping through the slatted blinds.

Rows and rows of bunk beds, the funk of unwashed bodies, coughs and murmurs, the restless turning over, snores, breathing, and open eyes that caught the light as they passed by. Ronnie paused, stiffening because she was back with Matt, dirty, hungry, scrambling, but afraid of places like this, so institutional they seemed like one step away from jail.

The front desk person pointed to the bunk, a top one. A tiny mound like a pile of rumpled blankets, hair tangled, mousy from dirt or nature, a whimpering.

"Cathy," Frank whispered, his face level with the back of the girl's head. "Cathy." His voice stronger this time, his hand on her shoulder.

"Please don't touch her," said the Benedict House employee.

Frank dropped his hand and said her name a third time. Ronnie almost jumped when a voice came from the bottom bunk, "Leave her alone. Her name is Amber."

Frank didn't move, just stared at the girl in the top bunk. Ronnie squatted down to find herself face to face with an older woman, eyes wide in the dark.

"Do you know her? We're trying to find his daughter, and he thinks she may be going by another name."

"Then she doesn't want him to find her." She said it as if she'd shut the door on Ronnie, and she started to roll over, face away from her.

"Wait, wait." Ronnie still whispered. "Do you know her? His daughter ran away from rehab. Opioids. She was 16. How old is Amber?"

"Dunno."

"How'd you meet her?"

"She was cold and hungry. Didn't want her to be trafficked. They prey on girls like that." Her voice was gruff, muffled.

Frank shifted behind Ronnie, a strangled sound coming from his throat.

"I know," Ronnie said. "That's great you did that. Where was she? Did she tell you anything about her situation?"

"Nope. Just brought her here." The large woman rolled over completely. It would be useless to ask any more questions. She knew this woman from the streets, maybe not this particular woman but others like her. She'd probably been on the streets for a long time, never talked to anyone, but shared food, gave out a sweater, or a warning to run.

Ronnie straightened up and glanced at Frank, who shifted from one foot to another. "Maybe we should come back in the morning. Talk to her then."

"Cathy, c'mon, sweetie, time to wake up." Frank stared intently at the pile of blankets on the top bunk.

Ronnie imagined it was the same voice he would use to wake her on a school day. His voice was soft and singsong, as if bringing her back to a world that was safe, pretty.

"Frank..." They should go. Ronnie took a step away as if that would give Frank the idea.

"I told you to leave her alone!" A hand shot out from the lower bunk, grabbed Frank's leg. Ronnie could see her nails digging in, the material scrunching.

"Ow!" Frank yelled, tried to jump away, but the woman's grip was tight, her arm bulging. People around them woke up, yelled at them to be quiet, a sad whiny voice asked what was happening.

The woman from the desk rushed over, whispered fiercely at Frank, then bent down to the woman, cajoled, pled with her to let go. She finally released Frank, and the employee shoved the air in front of her like she could herd them out that way, her eyes flashing. Frank paused, stared down at her. His hand moved to his back pocket, then stopped, thumb hooked in it as his eyes went from the top bunk to the employee, and back. Maybe he was going to pull out his credentials, pull rank, get in her face. But he gave a glance to the bottom bunk, then a shrug.

"I don't think it's her anyway," he said to Ronnie.

* * *

They came out of the building and turned as if they'd agreed out loud that the evening was over, time to get on the subway. Ronnie shoved her hands into her jacket pockets, wrapped the black leather around her more tightly, the wind off the Hudson buffeting both of them.

"You should go back in the morning before that girl leaves."

"That wasn't her." Frank picked up the pace, head down, shoulders hunched. "Maybe she's stopped using. Maybe she's staying at a girlfriend's. Maybe she's just mad at us for putting her in rehab. Maybe she's—"

He walked even faster away from her, words fading as he juddered down the subway steps, his head disappearing in jolts, and she ran to catch up, just behind him as he swiped his card, followed him to the S train platform, glad they were going the same way. The train was leaving the station, a few people scattered on the platform. Weird how you only knew the time of day down here by how many people were coming and going, if there were a lot of suits, or small children with nannies, or groups of young people, an older couple all dressed up sitting close to each other on the bench headed to a play or the opera.

"You on the East Side?" Ronnie asked, neutral territory as they stood on the platform.

Frank nodded, stared at the tracks.

"Do you really want my help?"

He broke his stare, his eyes so full of torment she watched the tunnel for the train instead. "You really think that someone that looked like that, so dirty, so—so broken, could be my daughter?"

The blast of warm, damp air announcing the next train hit Ronnie in the face, and she turned her head away for a second, peered down the tunnel the other way, the tracks disappearing into the dark, and she thought of all the places a runaway girl could go. Their train screeched into the station, they found seats together, and the train rumbled on its way like it was any other day.

"The streets," Ronnie said low, just to Frank, "they change you. And the drugs." He winced. "Frank. C'mon, you know she has to still be using, otherwise she would've come home, right? She wouldn't be at a girlfriend's all this time. If she was clean, she would've called you to come get her. Come straight home. Where she would be safe."

Frank hunched forward, rested his elbows on his knees. He looked terrible in this light, the fluorescents crevicing his face, his eyes in shadow. "We gave her everything." He spoke to his hands clasped in front of him. "We love her so much. She's everything to us." He sat up, rested against the seat, turned to Ronnie. "She was so smart, good grades. Never rebellious, lots of friends, did her homework. Christ, she was in so much pain, I couldn't stand to see her in all that pain." He looked away, down the length of the car, and Ronnie waited. "Why the hell did they prescribe those drugs if they're so addictive? How were we supposed to know? They're the professionals. We did what they said. We thought she was all right, she'd gone back to school, she was off the painkillers." He let out a long breath, and his shoulders slumped.

They rode in silence to Grand Central, then switched to the 4/5/6. Frank got off at 59th street, Ronnie at 86th. No matter how many times she came out of this station, she was always turned around, coming up top on a corner she hadn't expected, turning this way and that to orient herself, not sure which side the East River was on because it was so dark. She spotted the bodega that should've been on her side of the street, the light spilling onto the sidewalk, and she crossed over, sure now of which way to go.

What she hadn't said to Frank was something he had to know but probably couldn't face: all the things his daughter might be doing to get money for the drugs. The addiction was so hideous, the streets a horrible place, especially for addicts—there was nothing she could say to him that would help. She'd never seen someone who loved someone as much as Frank loved his daughter. She wondered what her own father thought when he realized the apartment was empty, she and Matt the last ones to go. Probably good riddance. The place all to himself, no one to try to stop him from drinking an entire bottle every night, no one to get in his way so he had to hit them. Maybe he was dead by now.

She let herself into her apartment, turned on a lamp. What was it like to be loved like that? She shrugged, removed her jacket, hung it up, shrugged again, and went to run the tub. What was it like to lose someone you loved that much? She sank into the water, the temperature perfect, just shy of hot. She would soak off the memories of her homeless years, get rid of the dirt and the grime and the exhaustion from tonight. She hoped for Frank's sake that he could find his daughter. And, she promised herself as she held her breath and went completely under, she would never love anyone so much that she couldn't stand to lose them.

Chapter Twenty-Nine

The thumb drive Ronnie had given him still sat on the table next to Frank's laptop. He hadn't taken it out of the bag, just laid it on the table. But he hadn't brought it to Pete yet. Hadn't written up his report on the meeting with Ronnie. He knew he couldn't stall, Isabelle's new victim probably about to be drugged, filmed, blackmailed. He went into the bedroom, so he didn't have to look at the drive, got busy making his bed.

Philippe's text gave an angry buzz on the Peter Franks phone.

I'm coming over to see you right now

No can do Frank texted, then erased it. He was so close, he needed to keep them all happy for a little longer. *I'm sorry, I'm in the middle of something right now. Can I meet you in two hours?*

I'll come to your room. What's the number?

Hmmm…No problem, Frank typed out, *I'll meet you in the lobby at 3* Then he turned off the phone. He could imagine Philippe growling and huffing, a cross between a bobcat and a bull, pawing the ground. He called The Plaza and made a reservation for tea at the Palm Court at 2:45, easy enough to get off-season. Too bad he couldn't show up as Special Agent Frank Jankowski. The big guy deserved it, but he would get Philippe in due time, and the look on his face would be worth it.

Even though he had a couple of hours before he had to meet Philippe, he began the process of becoming Peter Franks. A ritual that helped him separate the two worlds, compartmentalize Frank, and transform into Peter. As he undressed, he put his normal world away, and as he got dressed, he reminded himself of all that was Peter Franks. Omaha, a little shady, flirtatious, wife and son back in Nebraska, nothing to do in New York but be entertained by the wily Isabelle Anderson. He opened the little leather box that Cathy had given him—

Damn. Cathy. She was always there, hovering, waiting to break into his thoughts. Before, whenever he thought of her, no matter what age she was at the time, all the other ages came flooding in, all the pink tutus and sticky hands, awkward limbs, and soccer goals. But now he had to add her angry face from the fight they'd had before her accident, the hospital bed after emergency surgery, the tubing crawling up her arms like vines. And the last sight of her at the rehab facility, her makeup smudged, anger, defiance, in her eyes like her parents had betrayed her.

He shook himself as if he could make the thoughts of Cathy fly out and leave him. Chances were Philippe, the big thug, protecting Isabelle and chasing down slow checks was the one who helped the donors complete suicide. He slid on the Piaget, the metal warming on his skin. He slotted the diamond cufflinks into the French cuffs, went into the bathroom to tie the Hermès tie in front of the mirror. The diamond cufflinks winked at him. He dropped his hands. He stared at himself hard in the mirror.

That was it. It was one thing to hold back some silly jewelry, pretending that Peter Franks had to wear it in front of Isabelle to play her game. He leaned closer to the mirror, his eyes hard. Quite another to hold back the evidence that his CI had downloaded from the subject's computer. This was the line. This was far enough.

Frank pulled the fancy tie off, removed the cufflinks, and unbuttoned his shirt on his way back to his bedroom. He would turn them in with the watch when the case was done, but he wouldn't wear them again. He pulled on a blue button-down that belonged to him, not the Bureau, which didn't require cufflinks. He wouldn't wear anything else he hadn't gotten out of Wardrobe.

He went back to the mirror to work on his tie. Isabelle was pure evil, a criminal who belonged in jail. Peter Franks could flirt all he wanted, but Frank Jankowski would not be seduced. He was done with that. He had lost touch with himself to the point that he was on the brink of destroying evidence in order to save his career. Because of course the Peter Franks footage was on that thumb drive. He didn't need to look at it to know since Ronnie had downloaded it after Isabelle had betrayed him. Scratch that. She had drugged Peter Franks, no need for Frank to feel betrayed, because Frank shouldn't enter into the equation. She had seduced him all right, seduced both of them, and he had lost himself in her world, flattered himself that she was attracted to him when all he was to her was a blackmail victim. One of many, nothing special.

He tightened the knot. Too much. Loosened it. He needed to redraw his line, the line putting the criminals on one side, himself on the other, erase the grey that—oh good grief. He made a face at himself in the mirror. Wasn't that how he'd gotten in trouble in the first place, not recognizing, not being aware of all the grey areas, and in ignoring them, empowering them. If he wanted to be in control, he had to acknowledge that grey areas existed so he could deal with them.

In the living room, he went to close his laptop, noticed a new email. Ronnie's paperwork to visit her brother's grave at Hart Island had come through. He pulled out his phone and texted her the link. If that was his final act as an agent, then at least he'd done some good. He picked up the evidence bag with the thumb drive. He couldn't risk having it in his pocket for this meet, so he went back to his bedroom and placed it next to the cufflinks in the leather box. He mentally checked himself over, made sure his guise was complete. He was doing the right thing. He wouldn't tamper with evidence, would turn in the flash drive intact, though it meant the end of his career. But that would mean he could face himself every morning in the mirror after this. He texted Pete that he was meeting Subject B and would report when it was over. He'd turn over the thumb drive Monday and most likely be either fired or put on probation as soon as Pete wrote up the report.

* * *

He arrived at the Palm Court a good three minutes before his reservation and hopefully a full eighteen minutes before Philippe got there. He surveyed the space, the stained-glass ceiling, the palm trees circling the tables, the pink tablecloths, and Pete's Ladies Who Lunch. He wondered if Isabelle's friends ever came there but didn't see anyone in the crowd he recognized. Maybe too touristy for that group.

As he sat at the tiny table next to a wall, facing the entrance, he wished he had taken Cathy here at some point. He picked out which table they would've been sitting at, the tower of tea cakes—Christ, what was he thinking, way too expensive. He lined up the knife and spoon in front of him, made sure the edges were exactly even, then did the same for the two small forks. He hadn't yet put his napkin in his lap, thinking he would wait for Philippe. He stared at it now, folded elaborately into a swan, the pink tail fanned out on his plate. Another thing he hoped his father had missed: his granddaughter, whom he had never met, on drugs, in rehab, now on the streets.

His phone rang, and he pulled it out, noting the time. Philippe was early. "Peter Franks."

"You're late. You're not in the lobby. I'm coming upstairs."

"Hiya, Philip. How's it going?"

Philippe grunted, and Frank cheerfully went on before he could say anything.

"I'm actually down here. I managed to get a table in the Palm Court for us. C'mon in, you'll see me." He ended the call, hit the record button, and then grinned at the entrance, anticipating Philippe's reaction. He was not disappointed.

Philippe's face was puffed and red as he stood between the planters that marked off the entrance to the Palm Court, a fern brushing at him. His wool coat was black and long, the bulk of his body seeming even larger next to the small tables and pale pink cloths. He spotted Frank and his face darkened more. Good. If Philippe was angry, Frank would have the upper hand. He gave him a grin, a friendly wave.

The maître d' rushed over just as Philippe arrived at the table. "May I take your coat, sir?"

246

Philippe growled and wrapped the large overcoat around him tighter, wedging into the tiny seat and refusing to acknowledge the guy. He stared at Frank while he said, or rather snarled, "I'm not staying."

The maître d' turned to Frank and told him the tea would be right out, glanced at Philippe again but seemed to think better of whatever he was going to say and left.

Frank and Philippe eyed each other for a moment. Frank, still cheerful, said, "Are you sure you're not staying? I've ordered us tea. Maybe you'd like coffee instead. I just love all the little sandwiches and tiny cakes, don't you? Just like at Isabelle's." He smiled as if they shared a secret, as if Philippe wasn't a big black lump taking up too much space across from him.

"Isabelle is why I'm here."

"How is my favorite hostess? I'm afraid I must've missed a few dinner parties. I've been so busy, you know." He gestured with an open palm at Philippe as if they were in this together, businessmen who knew all about being busy.

"The invitations will start again after you've given her what she's asked for." He shifted on the spindly chair and cleared his throat, the small growl giving weight to his words.

A waiter brought the stand of tea cakes, a ridiculous three-tiered affair, all held together with circles of metal making it look like a Ferris wheel and taking up a good part of the table.

"I don't remember her asking me for something." Frank took up the little silver tongs and placed two minuscule sandwiches, a purple macaron and a fussy petit-four, on a plate, then placed it in front of Philippe. "Go on," he gestured at it with the tongs, "you look like you could use it. You're looking a little peckish." Frank filled his own plate up, Philippe watching his every move.

Philippe moved the plate in front of him aside as if it were poisoned, and his voice rumbled. "You know what she wants. I'm here to get it."

Frank popped a sandwich in his mouth, took a sip of tea, placed the paper-thin cup in the saucer, and hoped the restaurant wasn't too noisy for his phone recording of the conversation.

Philippe reached across the table and took Frank's plate, plunking it down on top of his own. "Enough!" Conversation around them paused, then the gentle buzzing in the room started up again, porcelain clinking, a laugh from the table near the entrance.

"Easy, fella." Frank glanced around. "The place is mostly tourists, you know. They pay more attention than your average New Yorker. And they always seem to be recording stuff on their phones. Maybe you should lower your voice and tell me more calmly exactly what it is you, or rather Isabelle, is wanting from me."

"She already told you." Philippe looked at him like he was an idiot.

"Let's say that one passed me by." Frank ran his hand through the air over his head, an airplane making a near miss. "Can you please just spell it out? Make it Peter Rabbit simple?"

Philippe let out an exasperated breath. "She recorded you. She will post it for everyone, including your wife, to see. You don't want that. You will pay her what it's worth to you, so that doesn't happen." His bushy eyebrows almost met as he gave Frank a hard look, pausing as if to let his words sink in. "And then," he gave what he probably thought was a smile, but seemed more like a grimace as if his stomach hurt, "and then, poof! Invitations, you can play with Isabelle, continue to meet all the nice people in the city so your wife will have the introduction she craves to the upper echelon of New York City."

"Let me make sure I understand you," Frank reached over and retrieved his plate, a chocolate petit-four with a green icing bow glimmering at him. He popped it in his mouth. Chewed longer than the little confection warranted. Made a show of swallowing and then sipping his now cold tea. "Isabelle wants me to pay blackmail money so that my reputation won't be ruined? My wife won't find out?"

Philippe growled. Low and long. "We don't use that word. Isabelle is protecting *her* reputation. You took advantage of her, and she thinks you know what it's worth."

Frank held out both hands as if to show they were empty. "Honestly, you got me. I have no idea what you're talking about here."

Philippe shifted in his seat, and the china clinked. Frank grabbed the tea stand, afraid it was going to go over. Philippe shoved his hands into his pockets and said, "You know why I wouldn't give up my coat?"

Frank shook his head, one hand still on the stand.

"Because I have a gun in my pocket. And now I'm pointing it at you, under the table."

He studied Philippe, his body hunched over the table, his hands hidden, his eyes intent on Frank, his mouth a straight line. Could have a gun. But why would he risk it in this crowded place?

"No you don't!" Frank laughed out the words and leaned over the side of the table, lifting the cloth and seeing only bulky dark wool. He straightened up. "Nope. Can't see a thing." He plucked a tiny sandwich, all the crusts cut off, a thin layer of something green painted between the slices of white bread. He eyed it from all sides, bit off a corner, gestured at Philippe with it. "Have you tried this kind? I'm trying to figure out what's in it."

Philippe growled again, long and slow, eyes not leaving Frank. His arms moved around under the table and then his left one came up, a flash of dull grey next to the baby pink tablecloth. A Beretta Nano, nothing sticking out to get caught in your holster or pocket.

"That's what you city slickers call a gun? Tell me something." He paused, a teacher making sure he had the pupil's attention. "How can you make it look like suicide if you shoot me?"

Philippe's eyes turned hard, and his face red. He grabbed up his gun and lunged across the table at Frank, knocking the cake stand to the floor, scattering silverware and plates, the crash of it bringing several waitstaff in the ensuing silence. Frank stood up, made sure a waiter stood between him and the big guy. Philippe was having a hard time extricating himself from his chair, and he shoved the table at the waiters and stood.

"I'm sorry," Frank said to the phalanx of staff, "my companion here has had a rough day. He's naturally clumsy, you know, and today has been one of the worst ones." He cut his eyes to Philippe, who looked ready to charge at him again. "I'm sure he'd be happy to help clean it up, pay for the breakage. Maybe even agree not to ever come back here." Frank turned to the server next to him and said in a stage whisper, "His name is Philippe Reynard, if you want to alert the doormen."

Still facing Philippe, Frank took several steps away, then turned and slipped through the back, the kitchen busy, too intent on their jobs to care if a tall broad-shouldered man sped through and then out the door, the stink of the dumpster hitting him in the cold. Even the fancy tea cakes eventually rotted.

* * *

"Jeez, Frank, cheer up. Nothing's that bad."

Frank stared at his partner until his goofy grin fell, and he started talking again, "Oh man, I'm sorry. Did you hear something—find Cath—"

Frank cut him off with a shake of his head. "No."

"Then," continued Pete, "that must be one helluva hangover."

Sometimes Frank hated his partner.

"Okay, this should make you happy." Pete turned to his computer, tapped on a few keys, and then swiveled back to Frank. "I just sent you the report."

Frank studied Pete for a moment.

"Yup. Lightning fast on this report." Pete looked like he was waiting for Frank to put a gold star on his forehead.

So, this was it. Pete was happy, and Frank was doomed. He knew this was coming, but he had fooled himself that he would have more time to get used to the idea of getting fired. Conduct unbecoming, the Integrity part of Fidelity Bravery Integrity expunged from his record. His pulse increased as he clicked his keyboard, looked for the report. His mouse hovered.

"You won't believe all the movies she had in there, naked men, writhing, begging—the soundtrack alone—boy howdy, you could post this and make millions—"

He broke off when Frank looked up at him.

"C'mon Frank, you know I would never do that. It was just a way of saying how steamy it is. You used to like my humor."

Frank didn't know if that was entirely true.

250

"All I'm saying," Pete went on, "with the spreadsheet she hid on there, I know we have probable cause. We can seize her computer, run some accounting forensics, get the testimony of Scott Hodge, and nail that woman."

"What's on the spreadsheet?"

"Here, I'll show you." Pete leaned over his shoulder and grabbed the mouse, clicking a few times. "Names, dates, amounts. She was raking it in, I tell ya."

"Is Peter Franks on there?" He tried to make his voice even, the question logical.

"It's mostly initials and nicknames. 'HN,' 'CKII' 1, 2, 3, and so on. You think that's like junior, senior, and third? Several generations she was fucking over? No 'PF,' just an 'OP,' but it was blank." Pete sat down on his desk chair, rolling around on it like he was a kid. "Hey! Didn't we hear on your button mics that she called you 'Omaha Pete?'"

Frank nodded. "OP was blank?"

"Yep. I think you were next for the bullwhip."

Frank studied his partner. He may act like an idiot, but he was plenty smart.

"Man, you get all the lucky assignments." Pete rolled back to his desk, disappearing behind the carpeted wall that separated them.

No video of Peter Franks, no spreadsheet entry of the date of their meeting which he hadn't reported. How was that possible? "Were there dates on the video, the last time the spreadsheet was updated?"

"Yup yup. Look here." Pete came back, eager, helpful. Frank's questions were right up his alley.

His partner tapped his screen and stepped back. Frank leaned forward like he couldn't read it unless he was up close. He didn't want Pete to see his reaction. The last date was just before his session in Isabelle's handcuffs. Frank let out a long breath. How was this possible? He couldn't get his head around it. He'd been all set for his career to be over, and now... God bless Ronnie. But somehow, he felt he'd cheated. He couldn't atone for breaking the rules, for lying by omission, not reporting the drugging and the taping and the blackmail lunch. He had been rewarded for it. He had gotten away with it.

"Isn't it great?" Pete practically wiggled where he stood.

Frank didn't trust himself to show his face to Pete yet. He pretended to look through the report.

Pete rubbed his hands together. "Dontcha just love it when a case comes together?"

* * *

The warrant seemed to be taking an extra long time. Frank sipped his single malt. Neither Frank nor Peter Franks had any extra time. Isabelle's patience would run out, the footage all over the internet, and Frank…he'd have to leave town, move to someplace in the middle of nowhere, change his appearance. Like he was a fugitive. He couldn't stay here, but then who would be searching for Cathy? He tipped his empty glass at the bartender, who chose that moment to help someone else. And that would probably compromise the case. Isabelle Anderson would continue her blackmail, her heinous broadcasts of upstanding citizens whose only crime was to fall for the irresistible society hostess. And if Philippe was killing them, making it look like suicide, would he be next?

He moved his glass to the edge of the bar, and the bartender came over, took the glass, leaned over like she wanted to tell him a secret. *I think you're done.* He should've been counting. Was she really cutting him off?

The fierce wind off the East River sliced through him as he came out of the bar. He turned his collar up, hunched into his coat. When the warrant came through, maybe he would stop drinking for a while. But if she doctored that file, put it out there…

Back in his apartment, he slumped into the armchair without taking off his coat or turning on any lights. He pulled out his phone. Where had Isabelle's contact info gone? He had to text her, tell her the money was coming, and she would be happy with the amount. But she wasn't in here. The chair held onto him when he tried to get up, and he fought against it, ending up face down on a rug in need of vacuuming, tangled in his coat.

CHAPTER TWENTY-NINE

Maybe he'd stay here until it was all over.

When he woke up the next morning, he wished he hadn't. His Peter Franks phone lay in bed with him, and he snatched it up. That's why he couldn't find her in his phone last night. He'd been trying to text her on the Frank Jankowski phone. Oh God, had he texted her last night? He couldn't turn it on. It was dead. He was probably dead.

* * *

Three days later, he still wasn't dead. Turned out a drunk Peter Franks had texted Isabelle, and she evidently liked what he'd said, despite the typos, because the damning video wasn't on social media and Philippe hadn't killed him. Someone was sure looking out for him.

When the warrant finally came through, Pete had given Frank permission to go ahead of the team for the sake of his CI. Ronnie's eyes widened when she opened the door to him. Under her breath, she asked, "How come you don't look like Peter Franks?"

He turned to show her the back of his windbreaker which had "FBI" in big yellow letters, and whispered, "Peter Franks is gone."

"Philippe, darling! I'm upstairs."

They both looked up the staircase, but Isabelle hadn't come down. Must be yelling down from the second floor.

"I'm taking her in today. The rest of the team will be here soon, and I came ahead to be triple sure that you understood we're not coming for you."

Ronnie took a step away from him.

"I really need to get Isabelle. We okay?" He put a hand out, wanting to comfort her or something, but she moved out of his reach. She was nodding, like she understood, but her eyes darted around. "You're okay, really. Trust me?"

She nodded.

"Is she dressed?"

Shrug.

"Do you want to come up?"

253

She shook her head, vigorously. "She'll think I'm in on it!"

"I'll tell her I asked you to come with me. Demanded it."

Isabelle sat at her vanity, a triptych of mirrors giving him three different views. She was surrounded by clouds. Some frothy white outfit billowing around her. He almost laughed. She was no angel, no matter how she dressed.

"Hello, Isabelle."

She didn't turn, just found him in one of her mirrors. "Peter." She spun to face him. "Whatever are you doing in my bedroom? And what are you wearing?"

Frank leaned against the door jamb, hands in his khaki pockets, badge and holster showing. Ronnie hovered in the hallway behind him.

"Is it career day at school? Dressing up as a cop?"

"Technically, I'm not a cop." He retrieved his ID, held it out to her. "Special Agent Frank Jankowski. FBI."

She didn't move to look at it. In fact, she returned to her mirrors and treated him to her large, throaty laugh. "Oh, that is rich." More laughter. "FBI!" She shook her head, picked up her brush, and ran it through her long blonde hair. She put the brush down and picked up something else, began applying it to her eyes. "You know, I've dressed up as many, many different people, but it never occurred to me to pretend to be law enforcement." She finished with her eyes and began dusting something on her cheeks. "But you might think about using a different last name. Quite a mouthful." She pursed her lips at her image, picked up a tube of lipstick. "Are you here because you've brought me what I'm due so we can continue to be friends?"

"I'm here because I'm Frank Jankowski, and I'm going to arrest you. I thought I'd give you a chance to choose your wardrobe before the rest of the team gets here and pulls apart your house." He turned to Ronnie and motioned her to come into the room. "I've asked Ronnie up so she can help you choose your booking outfit."

"Booking? Nice imagination, Peter. I did think you enjoyed those handcuffs the other night. Maybe we could playact your little story in the other room. Though I might put *you* in the handcuffs again." She fluttered her eyelashes at him, then looked past him at Ronnie. "I have no need of you. Philippe is coming and your job is to open the door to him."

"She stays." Frank guided her all the way into the room. "Seriously, Isabelle. Jankowski is my real last name. I'm really an FBI Special Agent, and I really am here to arrest you. And I will. I just thought as a courtesy, I'd give you a warning, so you don't go to jail in—" he gestured at her "—whatever that is you have on." They both looked at her outfit. "It wouldn't go with those plastic shower shoes they make you wear."

She shuddered the tiniest bit, but returned to her mirrors, perhaps thinking she'd covered it up. "You don't get to order my butler around. And please leave while I dress. I'm not dressing for you. Philippe is taking me out to lunch."

Ronnie stood between them, looked back and forth.

"Sorry, I can't leave. But you don't have much time, so I suggest you change."

She rose from her vanity and came toward him, forcing Ronnie to sidestep out of her way. She got right next to him, her voice low. "Maybe later we can get together. Once you have a nice fat envelope for me, Peter." She moved in, chin raised, eyes on his. "We never did get a chance to kiss, you know. Don't you want to find out what happens to a man when I kiss him?"

For the briefest second, a heartbeat or two, he smelled her perfume, and he felt a powerful desire to keep smelling it, to keep her close, to feel his skin on fire as she—he stepped back and pulled out his handcuffs. Held them up.

"Once I have these on you, you'll have to wear that downtown. And when you're released—whenever that might be—you don't want the press running your picture wearing that. You'll look bedraggled enough after your time in the jail cell."

"Press? Jail?" Her eyes narrowed. "You're not kidding, are you?"

He shook his head, jangled the cuffs.

"I'm not going with you." Her voice rose. "I'm not some common criminal you're going to drag out to the street." She shouted now. "Out of my way." She lurched toward the door, but he blocked her way. "Who do you think you are?" Isabelle's eyes were daggers, her hands claws, like she was ready to use them on him. "How dare you. Get. Out. Of. My. Room." She turned her back on him and Ronnie leapt out of her way. "All of you. Out!" She picked up her hairbrush and Frank tensed, ready to dodge when she threw it.

Ronnie looked like she was ready to run as well, and Frank shook his head at her. He took two steps toward Isabelle, cuffs in front of him. "I'm not leaving without you Isabelle, and if you want to go downtown in that, so be it."

Isabelle froze, back still to him. Just as well that he couldn't see her face in her vanity mirrors, because the fury he'd seen on it before she turned away was an image he wouldn't soon forget. Like a demon.

"Okay. Ready to be reasonable?"

Isabelle didn't say anything, but she also stayed where she was.

"Ronnie, please find her a suitable outfit." He gestured with his chin to what must be Isabelle's closet.

Ronnie took the step up into it. Lined with drawers, shelves, and mirrored doors, it was basically a small room, the size of a jail cell. No one said anything while Ronnie opened and closed things, slid hangers along the rods, several skinny kid reflections coming back to Frank. And presumably to Isabelle, though maybe her eyes were on fire, and she wasn't seeing anything. Finally, Ronnie brought Isabelle an outfit for approval, a cream-colored blouse, dark trousers with the legs over her arm like a ventriloquist's dummy.

Ronnie looked around Isabelle at Frank. "Do you mind turning away? There's no door."

He made a half turn with his body as if that would give Isabelle privacy. No way would he leave the doorway. He looked over her room, tried not to see the undressing and dressing going on in his peripheral vision. Finally, Isabelle emerged, looking smaller and more subdued than she had in her poofy white thing which now took up most of the floor of her ballerina box closet.

In two strides, he had the cuffs on her right wrist and was reaching for her left when Ronnie stopped him.

"Wait a sec." She pulled something glittery out of her trouser pocket, placed it over Isabelle's wrist, fastened it. "That's for when you get out." Her voice was a whisper and Frank nearly didn't catch the words.

He secured her wrists behind her with a satisfying click and the diamond bracelet Ronnie had put on slid against the heavy silver cuffs. Must be a metaphor in there somewhere. Frank grabbed Isabelle's upper arm, aimed for the door. He stopped them short because there was Philippe, blocking their way, filling up most of the doorway.

"What is going on?" Philippe looked like a bull pawing the ground, ready to charge. "Isabelle! Are you—why is Peter—what are you doing in Isabelle's bedroom?"

"Frank Jankowski, FBI." Frank went to reach for his ID, and just like that, Philippe whipped out his gun. Frank didn't like staring down the barrel of any gun, much less one in the hands of someone that angry. He should've taken it from him at the Palm Court. "Easy now. Please put down the gun. I was just retrieving my ID, so you know I am who I say I am." Frank's pulse increased. Good. He would need the extra strength from the adrenaline for whatever came next.

The gun stayed trained on Frank. His grip was firm, the gun steady, a tool his hand was used to holding.

"Okay. How about if you put down your gun and Ronnie gets my ID. Brings it to you."

"Don't move. Neither of you." He waved the gun back and forth between them. "I knew you two were in something together. You're her father, aren't you?"

"Easy, easy. You might hit Isabelle by mistake." He still held Isabelle's arm, and it felt like holding a live wire, the air electrified around them.

"Isabelle, come here, next to me. Peter, or whoever you are, you let her go."

Frank thought he was in a better position having Isabelle next to him, his guarantee that Philippe wouldn't fire his weapon. On the other hand, you usually obeyed if the person giving the orders also had a gun aimed at your heart. He shouldn't have left his vest in his car.

257

Isabelle yanked her arm free and went to Philippe. A look of triumph painted her face when she turned to face Frank. Even though his human shield was gone, Frank mostly felt relief, the air no longer humming next to him.

He put both hands up. "Philippe, you don't want to do this. Truly. Let Ronnie show you that I really am FBI, and then you'll also realize that there are more of us coming."

"Of course. And I have an army behind me as well. Ronnie," he aimed the gun at her, "get me his gun."

Ronnie looked as if her heart was beating like a trapped rabbit. Her eyes darted and Frank could smell the waves of fear coming off her.

"Go on, Ronnie." Philippe's eyes and gun went back to Frank.

Ronnie didn't move. Frank didn't know if she could.

The gun went back and forth between them. "I will shoot you. Get his gun and his ID."

Ronnie found her feet and her voice, as unsteady as it was. "I'm not touching any gun. I hate guns." She moved closer to Frank. "But I'll get his ID for you."

"All you have to do is pull the handle. There's no snap on the holster." Frank stared at her, hard. "Don't worry, the safety's on." Frank hoped she got his message.

Philippe must've gotten the message too, realized Ronnie would then be holding the gun by the grip, not the barrel. "No, wait." His gun wavered like it was linked directly to his brain, and he was having a hard time thinking. "Never mind. Just bring me the key to the cuffs. I will shoot him before he can draw."

Frank told her where to find the key and she brought it to Philippe, stood directly in front of him so she was between the big guy and Frank. Philippe reached for the key, and Ronnie kicked him hard in the groin, a near scream escaping from him. He collapsed on the floor, writhing and moaning. Ronnie ran out the door, but she couldn't have gone far because there was no sound of footsteps thudding down the stairs.

Frank leapt at Philippe and kicked the gun away from him. It skidded and tumbled on the thick carpet, stopped far enough away, just out of reach. Though right this minute it was very much an extra precaution since Philippe was in a fetal position, moaning. He would be incapacitated for a while now.

Frank took Isabelle by the arm, poked his head into the hallway. Ronnie stood to one side, a mixture of defiance, fear, relief painting her face. "Please get Isabelle's cuffs. I only brought the one pair."

Isabelle bristled beside him while he waited for Ronnie's return. She opened her mouth a few times but closed it again. She never looked at Philippe.

Just as he suspected, her cuffs were police-grade, and he told Ronnie to watch Isabelle while he cuffed the still writhing Philippe. Ronnie had aimed well. Note to self: always have the street kid on your side. He retrieved Philippe's gun, tucked it into his own waistband, and then grabbed up Isabelle's arm again, led her down the stairs. Their progress was slower than it needed to be, but Isabelle's helpless victim ploy didn't sway him one bit. She must've realized this because she changed tactics, went back to bristling.

"This is how you repay my generosity? I invited you to all those dinner parties." Isabelle looked up at him but he concentrated on their progress. "Fed you, gave you delicious drinks, expensive wine, introduced you to the crème de la crème of New York." They turned at the landing, the hallway with the hunting scenes on the wall ahead of them, both doors open, a familiar dank, waxy smell buffeting Frank before they started down the next flight.

"Why couldn't it have just kept going? All the champagne, the lovely things." She stopped in the middle of the narrow staircase, and Frank looked down at her. "And this is how you treat me."

"Tell me, Isabelle, why did you do it?"

"Why? Why does anyone entertain? Because it's fun." The way her voice fell at the end though, made it sound like it was anything but.

"You know what I mean." His voice was quiet, reasonable.

"Don't be so naïve, Frank." Isabelle resumed her awkward descent. "How do you think I paid for the champagne, for the caviar?"

"You never served me caviar."

* * *

Frank had Isabelle on the sidewalk by the time the team arrived. Cars and vans idled on 83rd, and dark blue windbreakers swarmed up the steps. Frank filled Pete in on the situation, handed him Philippe's gun, briefly ran through the layout of the house. Ronnie came out with a coat in her hands, gestured with it toward Isabelle. Frank gave her a nod, and she put it around her shoulders like a cape. It wasn't until Frank put Isabelle in the backseat of his car that she realized Ronnie wasn't going with them.

"What? What is this?" Her eyes were wild, her hair staticky in the winter air. "She's not coming? Why ever not?"

Ronnie hugged her arms around herself in the cold.

Frank slammed the door on her protests, on the looks she gave Ronnie, the confusion, anger, frustration. She swiveled around in the back seat to watch Frank as he went to the driver's side.

He opened the driver-side door. "Don't be so naïve, Isabelle."

Chapter Thirty

Of course it would be raining today, great big sheets letting loose on the day Ronnie was going to Hart Island. She and Matt hated it when it rained, nowhere to go to get away from it, trudging over to Grand Central, hoping they wouldn't get kicked out. Ronnie thought the rain would wash away everything, but it made the streets greasy, the subway steps slippery. Always big huge puddles, people ballet leaping, holding their umbrellas up so they didn't jab someone's eye.

When Frank sent her the link, she'd been surprised. She'd thought he'd forgotten about it. Too busy getting ready for the arrests and raid. She'd figured she'd never get to see Matt's grave, or she'd have to find another way, and it would be years before she did.

The city had a free ferry for Hart Island once a month, and her day came right before Frank said they were done at the brownstone, that she'd have to be out soon. A subway, a bus to City Island, checkpoints at the pier on Fordham Street, then the City Ferry. It was like she was trying to leave East Germany. She stood at the railing, watched the grey sky, the churning oily water, the white of the boat's wake. He appeared out of nowhere, an apparition in the mist.

"Jesus. I told you not to sneak up on me."

"Thought you could use the company."

"I can never use the company."

Frank smiled at that, turned to stare out at the water with her. Maybe he knew her better than she knew herself, because all of a sudden, she was a little glad not to be doing this alone. She had been nervous this morning, couldn't even eat breakfast, checked herself in the mirror twice, as if Matt would actually be seeing her.

If she wanted to analyze it, which she didn't, she was probably nervous because she didn't know how she would react, how she would feel when she saw the white post marking Matt's spot, marking a mass grave of hundreds of other people, all poor, some unknown, none with family to claim them. With Frank there, it would be easier to pretend it didn't bother her.

As they approached the dock to the island, two small angel statues, white in the grey of the day, grey of the island, waited on either side while the ferry docked. The ride was so short, it was as if they got on one side of the boat and off on the other. A white sign painted on a brick building, "PRISON KEEP OFF" made her heart race, made her wonder for a second if they would let her back on the ferry, wonder if Frank was back to being an agent and cooked this up to nab her. She cut her eyes to him but there was nothing to read on his face, the lines around his eyes and mouth spiderweb thin.

After all the bureaucratic waiting, they were led to a white post, in the middle of a field of white posts, and Ronnie looked around, the darker brown of disturbed dirt, the crumbling buildings, a smokestack, the water between the islands, the great buildings of the city poking up, the grey clouds breaking over Manhattan, a finger of sunlight filtering down as if an omen that things would get better. What was it like for Matt, a plain pine box, stacked in threes, crammed in with how many other pine boxes.

The silence of the place was what got to her, the ache in her throat like she'd swallowed something too big, knew that if she opened her mouth, she might start wailing trying to rid herself of the agony. She clamped her hand over her mouth, and the tears spilled over, streamed down, and animal sounds, pants, snuffles, and muffled howling came through her fingers until her whole body shook. Then everything went black around her. She must have fallen. Frank picked her up, held her up with an arm around her shoulders. Her knees were wobbly, her palms covered in dirt, the brown of everything around her closing in.

* * *

They sat side by side on the subway, not talking. As the train pulled away from the station that came before Ronnie's stop, Frank cleared his throat. His voice was low, and Ronnie leaned closer, missed parts of what he said.

"...forensics...computers...no Peter Franks footage."

The train slowed, the brakes squealed, and the white walls went by, the station seemingly endless. Ronnie got up, and Frank raised his head, studied her a minute, his eyebrows a question. Other passengers moved toward the door to go on with their lives, and the train came to a stop.

She gave him a grin. Punched his arm. "You're welcome."

Then she went out the door, stepped onto the platform, moved as quickly as she could toward the exit, climbed the stairs with everyone else, walked up, up, up until the air in the street wafted down, a little cleaner after the rain.

Chapter Thirty-One

Frank supposed that if anyone watched him and Susan as they sat together at this table in the corner, and if the person watching them was at all curious about them, they might look like an old married couple, together for so long they didn't need to talk, happy enough to sit and enjoy each other's company in silence, knowing each other so well that their thoughts ran the same way, at the same time, and if they didn't always agree, they did know what the other was thinking.

But of course, they weren't. They weren't married, they weren't content, and they were silent because they didn't know what to say to each other. They were each in their own head, but they didn't know what the other was thinking, wouldn't want to hazard a guess.

"How's work?" Frank hoped to steer them toward safe territory.

"The usual." Susan took a sip of wine, set the glass down, eyed Frank. "How's your work going?"

"We're wrapping up this case, so that's good. Bad guys arrested or about to be, the world back to spinning right." He wished he hadn't added those last words. "Or nearly so."

"Any word?" Susan said this almost in a whisper, as if afraid to ask, as if the words had escaped before she could stop them. She fiddled with her place setting, turning the knife on its side, laying it flat, turning it over and on its side again.

Frank shook his head. Susan glanced at him and then down at her knife as if she had expected the answer. "That girl from the other school one of her friends said she hung out with?"

"A bust. More gossip rather than truth."

The waiter brought their orders, and for a minute they each stared at their plates as if confused by what they'd received. Susan picked up her fork first, stabbed around in the pasta, then stopped, fork still upright in the middle of the plate. She looked at Frank. He wondered if his eyes mirrored the misery that he saw in hers, and he hoped he wouldn't see them fill with tears because he was feeling so raw his might too.

"I go out every night I can," he said softly, "looking everywhere I can think of. I've even been down in the subway tunnels, under the Port Authority, where a lot of runaways sleep." He cleared his throat, picked up his fork, sliced into the halibut, white flesh gleaming, so perfectly cooked it was firm but fell away easily. He moved it around in the sauce and then rested his fork on the edge of the plate. "I got a call from Benedict House, but it wasn't Cathy. I thought it might be because she was calling herself Amber."

Susan's glance was quick, an intake of breath and Frank knew she was hearing Cathy's child voice, wanting to know why they hadn't named her Amber.

"We—I might start trying to find her dealer, try to find her that way."

"We did everything for her." A statement from Susan, no hint of bitterness, no questioning to belie the words. "Everything we possibly could," she added. "That's all any parent does. The best they possibly can." She touched the corners of her mouth with her napkin, though Frank thought it might be reflexive, not sure he saw her actually eat anything.

He used his napkin, wiping his whole mouth, then dropped it in his lap.

"I'm seeing a therapist," Susan said. "She's helping me work through this, understand some things—"

Frank studied her, wondered how anyone could possibly make sense of this.

"—more about myself than the situation. You can't possibly make sense of the situation, just accept it and try to find a way to be sane through it."

"Good for you," Frank said, and meant it.

"It's not easy. How do you remain sane? Our little girl out there somewhere—"

"It's eating away at me."

Susan's glance was sharp, but then her mouth opened in an "o," and her eyes softened. "You never would have said that in the old days. Is this new? I mean, is the feeling new, or is the telling of it new?"

"What do you think?"

"I always thought things didn't get to you the way they got to me. I thought you were a rock." She took a sip of wine and set the glass down. Frank watched the light hitting the Chenin Blanc, the little swirls as it settled down. "That's one of the reasons I loved you, you were a rock I could count on when I felt unmoored." His eyes found hers, and she returned his gaze steadily. "But," she took up her fork again, wrapped the pasta around it, "that was also what drove me nuts about you." She took a bite.

Frank waited while she chewed. Some things don't change.

"It wasn't your fault. I knew that was the way you were when I married you. I was looking to you to solve the problems I couldn't face in myself. As if," she lifted her glass, gestured to him with it, "as if you could wave a magic wand and poof! I'd be all better."

"I wanted to. Make everything better. Protect you, protect Cathy from the nastiness of the world." He sat back against his chair, shoulders sagging, stared at, but didn't see, his plate. "And look how well I did that."

"Frank, listen to me." Susan leaned forward, waited until his eyes found hers. "This isn't your fault. That's one thing I've learned, been trying to learn and really know, really feel. It's not your fault, and it's not my fault. It does no good to run through the "what if's" as if we could relive those years and do it differently. It stinks. But this is what is happening right now." Her eyes were intent, searching his as if trying to make sure he was listening, truly hearing her. "We did everything right, and she got sucked into the opioids, and when we tried to fix that, she chose," she pushed her wine glass away from her, off to the side, away from Frank too, "she chose to run away."

Frank couldn't say anything and he couldn't look at her, finding instead the table, the salt and pepper, the bread plate with the untouched roll still on it.

266

"All we can do," Susan said, "is what we are doing. Look for her. Be here for her when she comes back." Quieter now, her voice soft, she said, "I've been volunteering at Benedict House."

"You have? Since when?"

She shrugged. "For a while now. I had to do something, and I thought maybe Cathy would come in there, and if she didn't, maybe I could help runaways like her, maybe I could make some sort of difference." She paused to nod at the waiter who wondered if she were finished, Frank observing neither one of them had eaten much, wished he could give it to the street kids. "And for something to do so I don't go crazy." Her smile was rueful like she knew it was nearly useless, this attempt to fend off the craziness.

"We all have to do something, anything," Frank said. "It's what keeps us going. Gets us up in the morning." He pulled out his wallet, extracted a credit card as he looked around for their waiter. "But you're not doing just 'anything,' you're actually helping people, and that is certainly something." He saw her reach for her purse and said to her, "Let me get this. At least I can do something too."

She shook her head at him, even as she put her purse back. "You're doing so much already, Frank. But I think I know what you mean: it's never enough. It never feels as if it's enough."

Out on the sidewalk, they paused before going their separate ways, and she touched his arm, "You're a good man, Frank. Don't ever forget that."

Frank gave her shoulder a squeeze, hoped she would know what he meant, because he sure didn't trust himself to say anything. He patted the shoulder for good measure and then turned to walk downtown, listening to the sounds of the city, the distant sirens, the whoosh of the bus stopping, the conversations passing him, his shoes striking the sidewalk. Rain misted down, settling over everything, making the lights blur and the streets wink.

Chapter Thirty-Two

Ronnie opened the drawer to her dresser, grabbed all of her underwear, and shoved them into the bottom of her backpack. Frank told her he had convinced them to let her keep her stuff, that she had been important to the case, but she had to leave everything of Isabelle's there. She had come to Isabelle's with everything she owned in her backpack and thought she could leave the same way. She opened the next drawer. Lying there, the whole drawer to themselves, were the PJs Isabelle had given her or rather made one of her "Objects of My Affection" buy. A cool, baby blue cotton, piped in a darker blue along almost every edge, still creased from the folds from the store. Who even knew if they were her size? She placed them on the bed. Of course they were. Isabelle always knew her size, knew what would fit her just right. The weirdo.

She'd see later if she had room for them. The rest of the dresser held the T-shirts she'd come with, some shirts and blouses Isabelle had bought— acquired—for her, trousers, and jeans…how could she own this much stuff?

She went into the living room area, glanced around. Would she miss this place? The agents had left her apartment a mess, that was for sure, but, she thought, as she opened the narrow closet next to her front door, she didn't care if Isabelle had blackmailed the men to get them for her. They were hers now. The closet was stuffed full—suits, coats, the newsboy hat. She had been wearing that when Frank followed her here.

She shook herself. She couldn't waste time going over all this stuff. She would take what would fit in her backpack, wear the hat even though it was a little warm for it. But these suits. Expensive, beautiful to wear, the fabric gliding over her. She couldn't leave them. She'd need them for catering gigs, well, the pants anyway, especially these dark ones. And the shoes. They were in her closet. She took everything into the bedroom, pulled out the flats and brogues, the dancing pumps Isabelle insisted she wear. How does a person know what shoes will fit someone else, like a glove, the leather fine. These will last forever. She would definitely take these.

But how? She couldn't carry all this around with her, all day, every day. Christ, how was it that she owned so much stuff? She'd violated her own rule: never have more than what will fit in a backpack so you can run anytime. Run from street crazies, run from Annie, run from the cops.

She sat back on her heels, studied the small bedroom: dresser, door, bedside table, bed, closet. The pillows on the bed were so soft, fluffy, the comforter puffing over the bed, the covers still pushed back from when she got up this morning, the pillow indented where her head had been. As if waiting for her to get back in bed, as if she had nothing more to do than spend the rest of the day in it. She could crawl in, pull the covers over her head, block out the sunlight, the day, the city, the sidewalk.

Bullshit.

This was it, time to get going. She used to love to be on the move and now she was weighted down, this house pulling at her.

On the floor of the closet, lying where the agents must've tossed it, was a duffle bag, a ridiculous thing for Isabelle to have. Probably why it was stashed in this apartment. Of course, it wasn't just some flimsy thing you take to the gym, it was a dark green canvas, leather straps wrapping around it, a heavy brass zipper. Of course it was. Shoes on the bottom, socks, and underwear stuffed inside, suits rolled up, shirts too. She would sling it over her shoulder. It would make a better pillow than her backpack. She didn't know why, but she laid the PJs on top, the flat pearly buttons winking at her. A promise, maybe.

She went into the living room area, surveyed the mess. Where was the little box with the turtle clasp? Probably a waste of time searching for it, the agents had turned everything upside down. She moved aside a cushion, bent down to peer under the couch. She got all the way flat, her head squished on the rug, saw a magazine in the dark. She reached under and pulled it aside, and there was the box, just out of reach.

Not out of her reach, though. No sense in letting the FBI have this money. She needed it more than they did. Kinda earned it. The house creaked overhead, loud in the emptiness, and Ronnie startled. As if the brownstone knew she had betrayed Isabelle.

That was ridiculous. She headed up the stairs, found herself going quietly as if Isabelle were still in it, as if not to disturb her. In the kitchen the copper pots and pans reflected a little light, the bottoms not as shiny as when she'd first arrived. She was probably the only one who had ever used them. After her tour of the house, she'd make a sandwich, grab some water.

The entryway, with the mirrors, the closet floor a riot of all of Isabelle's coats and hats, wooden hangers, scarves and lifeless boas. How many coats had she hung up here, how many phones placed in the basket, how many dollars swapped for Oxy. No phones left in the basket she could sell.

Up the stairs, hand sliding on the banister as she went, never going to have to dust these posts again. Thank god. She would not miss the housework, that was for sure. The living room, silent, wastebaskets full of stuff from the last party tipped over and pawed through. The curtains were still drawn shut, a shaft of light cut through the gap, dust motes danced as if they owned the place.

She went through room after room, up the stairs, silently stepping as if she had never lived here, opened doors and closed them with a click, left cupboards and drawers hanging open. Let someone else clean it up. Philippe would never sit in that tiny room again, watching, watching. What a creep. Isabelle never again putting a silvered stiletto on her victim's bare back in the room next door. What was that phrase one of her dinner guests had used? All hat and no cattle. All stilettos and no sex. She could hear her laughter echoing, that laugh where she threw her head back, eyes shut, mouth full open, letting loose as if she knew she had won.

Ronnie aimed a salute up the stairs. She wouldn't go into Isabelle's bedroom, not remember the last time she'd been in there, dressing her boss as if for an execution. Maybe she shouldn't have given her back the bracelet. She could use the money. But then, there was Isabelle getting out of jail, the Feds having confiscated everything, including her house. *Proceeds from criminal activity* Frank had said. No, Ronnie was much better at making do with nothing. Isabelle wouldn't last a minute on the streets.

She sat on the top step, looked side to side as if to check if the house watched her, then she straightened her legs out, inched to the edge, and slid down as if she were in a toboggan, bumped gently on each riser, gathered speed until she ran out of stairs, ended at the landing, her butt warm.

Down in her apartment, she slung her backpack and duffle over her shoulders, grabbed the hat and put her hand on the doorknob. She glanced over her shoulder as if maybe her apartment were disappearing behind her. Idiot.

She hit the steps to the sidewalk, turned west, toward the park, the sun hitting the top of her head, promising a nice day.

"Where are you headed?"

The car had come down the street so quietly she hadn't even heard it. As if he had killed the engine and glided toward her. But no, the engine was running on the big fat American car. If she was going back on the streets, she'd have to be more aware than that. She bent over to look him in the eye, the duffle bag trying to pull her down to the sidewalk. Someone, must be his partner, next to Frank, bobbing his head, a goofy grin on his face.

"You tailing me?"

"You're not answering your phone."

Ronnie straightened up and pulled it out of her pocket, glanced at the screen. She shrugged, put it in her pocket. It was Isabelle's account, and, like everything else about her life right now, it was shut down.

"You offering me a ride?"

"Get in." Frank leaned over and opened the back door on his side. Wasn't the back seat where criminals sat? She stepped back onto the sidewalk, hefted the duffle. Damn. No way she could run with all this stuff, but if she had to, she would somehow. So Frank was finally coming for her.

"C'mon." Frank stuck his head out the window. "The cars are piling up. I have a job you might be interested in."

Ronnie turned to study the brownstone, the white steps up to the front door, the windows dull, shadowed. It looked just like so many others in the city, the bars on the basement windows, the trash cans battered, leaning against each other. Nothing at all to say it once belonged to Isabelle Anderson, hostess of the Upper East Side.

"What kind of job?"

Acknowledgements

There are so many people without whom this would not be a book. I am eternally grateful for my family and their unwavering support and constant encouragement through all the years it took to get this book to publication. Lighthouse Writers Workshop was invaluable with their dedicated instructors, the fabulous craft classes, and lively workshops. I am grateful they believed in my writing enough to accept me into the Book Project. I would still be wallowing around with the wrong antagonist and way too much exposition if it hadn't been for my mentor and first reader, Ben Whitmer.

My trusted critique partners, whose names should probably go on the cover because of all their brilliant suggestions and searing ability to pinpoint exactly what a scene or a chapter needed: Alex Baron, James Shade, Brooke Terpening. To the many beta readers who slogged through the early iterations of this story, I am indebted to you for the time you spent, for your encouragement, and for your key observations. I hope you'll read this again to see how the story has morphed since then.

Thank you to my New York friends for helping me get things right: Helen and Russell Pennoyer, Susan Sylvan, and Janet Rassweiler. And for the apartment Margaret Pennoyer gave up so I could have my personal writing retreat. For all things FBI-related, thank you, Stephen Chapman, for giving me permission to insert a flux capacitor once in a while. All mistakes are mine, having nothing to do with Mr. Chapman's excellent advice. Thank you, Sisters In Crime, for providing a forum for experts to answer questions large and small. And to my son Robert for his myriad knowledge base, which I trust completely but am afraid to ask from whence it came. His expertise is a wonderful resource for a writer, but a little scary for a mom.

I still have some PTSD from the querying process, but as soon as I spoke to Gwyn Jordan, I understood why agents insist they have to fall in love with the manuscript in order to offer representation. She gets it. And she understood just what the story needed. You would not be holding this in your hands right now if it weren't for Shawn Simmons and the team at Level Best Books. I am so grateful to them for their insight, expertise, and beautiful cover. Everyone who has touched this book has made it so much better in ways I could not have anticipated, nor done on my own. Thank you, thank you, thank you!

About the Author

Jenny Dandy is a graduate of Smith College and of Lighthouse Writers Workshop Book Project. Though she has lived and worked from Beijing to Baltimore, from Northampton to Atlanta, it was New York that held onto a piece of her heart. She now lives and writes in the Rocky Mountains, where she would never lift a wallet or scam her dinner guests.

SOCIAL MEDIA HANDLES:
　　https://www.facebook.com/jennydandyauthor/
　　https://www.threads.net/@jennydandyauthor
　　https://x.com/JenniferDandy?t=13GKj4XYqSNHyWHW0p7lfA&s=03
　　https://www.instagram.com/jennydandyauthor/
　　Twitter handle: @JenniferDandy
　　Instagram handle: @jennydandyauthor
　　Facebook: Jenny Dandy

AUTHOR WEBSITE:
　　jennydandy.com

9 781685 126353